RECLAIMED

KERRIGAN BYRNE

D0813969

Reclaimed © 2013 Kerrigan Byrne
Released © 2013 Kerrigan Byrne
Redeemed © 2013 Kerrigan Byrne
Reluctant © 2013 Kerrigan Byrne
All rights reserved

ISBN-13: 978-0615840789

ISBN-10: 0615840787

This book is licensed for your personal enjoyment only. This book may not be re-sold or given away to other people. If you would like to share this book with another person, please purchase an additional copy for each recipient. If you're reading this book and did not purchase it, or it was not purchased for your use only, then please purchase your own copy. The book contained herein constitutes a copyrighted work and may not be reproduced, transmitted, down-loaded, or stored in or introduced into an information storage and retrieval system in any form or by any means, whether electronic or mechanical, now known or hereinafter invented, without the express written permission of the copyright owner, except in the case of brief quotation embodied in critical articles and reviews. Thank you for respecting the hard work of this author.

This book is a work of fiction. The names, characters, places, and incidents are products of the writer's imagination or have been used fictitiously and are not to be construed as real. Any resemblance to persons, living or dead, actual events, locales or organizations is entirely coincidental.

Cover Art © 2013 Kelli Ann Morgan / Inspire Creative Services
Interior book design by Bob Houston eBook Formatting

Other *Heroes of the Highlands* Novellas
by Kerrigan Byrne

Unspoken

Unwilling

Unwanted

Unleashed – The First Highland Historical
Trilogy

Released

Redeemed

Reluctant

And now:

Reclaimed – The Second Highland Historical
Trilogy

KERRIGAN BYRNE

Danger and redemption
lurk in the Highlands...

RECLAIMED

A Highland Historical Trilogy

RECLAIMED

A HIGHLAND HISTORICAL TRILOGY

KERRIGAN BYRNE

Dedication

To Darlene Ainge
Your open heart and generosity have touched more people then
you will ever know.
You are my hero.

Acknowledgements

As always I want to thank Tiffinie Helmer, Cynthia St. Aubin, and Cindy Stark. You ladies are my true and lovely friends and colleagues. Also, the extent of my weekday social life. Thank you for your tireless encouragement and support.

To the Writers of Imminent Death; Heather Wallace, Heidi Turner, Mikki Kells, Tiffinie Helmer, and Cyndi Olsen. Thank you for being the best part of my work week. We're going to go far together.

I want to give A LOT of love to *Kerrigan's Celts*. Every morning I look forward to spending time with you. You all are the reason I do what I do and I can't imagine being able to repay what you've done for me. I want to especially give warm and genuine gratitude to Dawn Sullivan, Amy Byrd, Amanda Pizzo, Janet Juengling-Snell, Tracie Runge, Dannielle Scheuer, Brandy Thornton, Suzanne Goldberg, Sunshine Kath, Kylee Moss, Jennie Nunn, Nicole Garcia, Lori Decker Fenn, Suzi Behar, Robin Fletcher, and Karen Wells. You all keep me in such good company and plenty of laughter.

To Paul Furner and Jessica Menasian – I've hardly known truer or more wonderful friends. I cherish each moment we spend together and each thing I learn from the both of you. It's so rare to find so much inspiration under one roof! Thank you for sharing each of your incredible gifts and talents with me.

To Lynne Harter—I watch you take each day with grace and poise and humor. You motivate me to always strive to be better. I can't tell you how much I appreciate you!

And forever to my Husband—Thank you for your endless encouragement, support, friendship, and love. No matter what I aspire to, I have already achieved the one thing in life that is most important.

Table of Contents

Released   10

Redeemed   110

Reluctant   248

About the Author   332

A Highland Historical Novella
by the Bestselling Author of *Unleashed*

KERRIGAN BYRNE

Death is only their beginning...

RELEASED

released

a highland historical novella

Chapter One

If she could muster the courage, she'd burn him alive.

Katriona MacKay floated across one of Dun Keep's bedchamber floors. She'd waited this long, she could wait until he awoke to kill him.

For untold months she had haunted the ashes of the washhouse with her sisters, keeping soft and helpless vigil at their mother's side as her burns blistered, bled, infected, healed, and then turned to painful scars. As they kept watch, their anger and despair became hotter than the flames in which they'd met their death.

Katriona's lips twisted at the sight of Rory MacKay, youngest of the Chieftain's family. How dare he linger in his father's well-appointed keep, reaping the benefits of MacKay brutality while his clan starved and his crops wilted?

Shirtless beneath the MacKay tartan, *his* flesh glowed a healthy bronze, stretched taut over thick, rangy, well-fed muscle. Her mother's skin was now a shiny mass of webbed scars hanging off weak, hungry muscles and old, brittle bones.

His chamber was warm and dry with thick, new furs on the large bed and sturdy, dark wood furniture like the desk he currently occupied.

Katriona snarled as she approached him. The lazy bastard propped his head against a fist and the back of his chair, full lips slightly parted in deep repose. In his lax hand, a quill bled black ink onto a large ledger volume. The circles beneath his eyes were likely from drink rather than exhaustion. His ledger must be a work of fiction, and padded with unfair taxes.

Objectively, Katriona calculated the markedly vast physical differences between Rory and his older twin Angus. Rory outweighed Angus by a few stone, at least. Also Rory's square jaw, bronze hair, and high cheekbones branded him a McCrimmon, like his mother, whereas Angus, Laird of the MacKay clan and his son, Angus the younger, had long, cruel features, dirty red hair, and bad teeth.

Watching the firelight play across his strong face, Katriona knew that Rory had not been there with his twin the night she and her sisters had died. She would have remembered his handsome face. Even so, she'd found his cursed blood with her magic and before this night was through, he'd be begging for his own life, as she'd begged for hers.

She'd pierce his ears with her cry before she ripped his soul from his body and send it straight to hell. Justice would be a sweet victory she could take to her mother, and perhaps then, she and her sisters could finally rest.

"My Laird!"

Katriona shrank into the shadows as a gangly teen with knobby knees sprouting from beneath his kilt burst into the room. He waved a missive with a broken seal above his wild brown hair.

Rory leapt from his desk and drew his sword, pointing it at the boy's eye with unerring accuracy.

The lad skidded to a halt mere inches from the lethal point and both men stood for a moment, their chests heaving.

Rory lowered his sword and ran a hand over his face. "Forgive me, Baird, I must have drifted off."

"It's all right. Angus would have cut me for certain." The boy tapped a finger to a scar stretching from his chin to his ear.

A muscle twitched in Rory's braw neck. "What brings ye?"

"This." Baird shoved the letter to him. "I canna read, but Lorne told me it was important. A messenger arrived with it not five minutes ago. He's waiting in the hall for yer response."

Rory took the paper and quickly scanned the missive. "Fucking Lowlanders." He crumpled the note and tossed into the fire.

"What is it, Laird?" Baird's voice cracked on the question.

Rory glared into the flames, his fist clenching tight on his sword.

Katriona frowned. 'Twas the second time the boy had called Rory *Laird*. Yet he was merely the youngest son of the current Laird, Angus. Perhaps they bestowed upon him the honorary title while his brother and father were off terrorizing the Highlands?

"Laird Fraser said he wouldna make the journey until spring." Rory slid his sword back to its scabbard. "Tis only Candlemas."

Katriona found herself momentarily distracted by the play of torchlight and shadow across the muscles of his back.

"Fraser?" Baird squawked. "He's coming now?"

"According to the missive, he'll be here as soon as tomorrow."

"But isna that good news? He'll bring yer betrothed, Lady Kathryn, with him, along with her dowry."

Rory's face darkened from exhausted to irate. "Aye. But look around ye lad, we're not ready to host one of the richest men in Scotland."

It didn't matter. Katriona's lips cracked into a wicked smile. After tonight, the Fraser and his poor daughter, Kathryn, would arrive in time to attend Rory's funeral. And, if her sisters had any luck, they could mourn the deaths of all three worthless MacKay nobles.

"I'll get Lorne to rouse the house, Laird, we'll work through the night to ready yer keep. We'll do whatever it takes."

Katriona's stomach twisted at the loyal veneration in the young lad's eyes. Didn't he understand the evil this man and his family wrought upon their clan?

"I thank ye, Baird." Rory's eyes gentled. "And tell yer brother to give the messenger our Highland hospitality. I'll be down to help in a moment."

"Right away." Baird sprang for the door, but paused with his hand on the knob. "There's—one other thing," he said, with obvious reluctance.

"Aye?" Rory lifted his eyes to the ceiling as though praying for strength.

"Some of the men want to go after the washer woman. Everyone's saying she's a witch. That she killed her own girls in that fire and deserves to burn."

Don't you bloody dare. Katriona thought, her heart pounding as she fought a surge of her deadly magic. She couldn't kill the innocent. She had to wait for the boy to leave.

"Does 'everyone' happen to be Bridget and Ennis?" Rory asked.

Baird looked down. "They said they spied a blue light coming from her ruins. That she was heard talking with demons."

Katriona scowled. She'd been talking with her murdered daughters. Ones who dared any man to attack their home again.

Rory absently waved a hand at the boy. "Tell Lorne and the men to leave the woman be. She's survived a terrible accident and lost her entire family." He slammed the ledger closed, his wide shoulders dropping as though laden with a heavy weight. "'Tis enough to drive anyone a little mad."

"Yes, Laird." Baird dipped his head and quit the room, his footsteps fading down the hall.

A terrible *accident?*

Cold fury wound its way through Katriona's soul, weaving dark bonds of hatred with her magic.

A little *mad?*

Power vibrated in whatever matter that manifested into her miasma of blue and white until she threw the full force of her glow into the room. Behind that, she emitted a keen so shrill and horrid that Rory's hands flew to his ears.

She reveled in the shock and disbelief on his face.

"Stop!" he ordered. "What is this?"

Rory gritted his teeth against the unnatural, ear-shattering scream. He'd never heard anything of the like. It grated on skin and soul in equal parts like every offensive sound in the land warred for supremacy. The scraping of metal against stone, the bagpipes played by a deaf man, and the scream of an angry bairn couldn't compete with such a noise.

"Ye've been cursed with a Banshee for yer crimes, Rory MacKay." Fractals of magic shattered her voice until it came at him from every corner of the room. "I am the harbinger of your death and the reaper of your tainted soul."

Rory opened his eyes. Blinding blue and white light assaulted his vision, but he forced himself to gaze upon it. Whether his eyes adjusted or the light abated, he couldn't tell, but a form appeared in its center. Dark robes whipping about it in a non-existent wind, the image drew closer, congealing into that of a terrifyingly beautiful woman.

A Banshee.

Her long, dark hair tossed about her and blue glowed from enraged eyes. She floated toward him above the rushes, an unhurried specter intent on making his punishment as slow and painful as possible.

Why now? When he was so close to mending everything. Rory had not thought to be called into account for his crimes until death. On the heels of his incredulity, a feeling of bittersweet relief uncurled inside. Perhaps the cursed sword hanging over the head of his entire clan would vanish with his death.

"Why do you not bleed?" the terrible voices demanded. "My shriek should drive you to your knees and fracture your mind!"

Rory lowered his hands from his ears. He wondered the same thing. According to legend, he should be bleeding from all orafices before she reached in and ripped his soul from his flesh.

"Perhaps my soul is already broken, my lady," he murmured. "Ye canna wreak damage already wrought."

The glow intensified again as the shrill scream bombarded him. "You would do well to fear me, MacKay! The pain I will inflict is like nothing you've ever imagined and is no less than you deserve!"

The apparition shoved her ghostly face close to his.

Rory froze, unblinking. He *knew* this woman. Knew every detail of her face, every curve of her body. The thick, dark hair had lost its luster in this form. No sunlight to catch its sheen, only the blast of otherworldly white to overwhelm it. Sharp, cat-like green eyes lost any of their femininity, glowing with hard anger and deadly intent. And yet, her delicate face remained unmistakable.

"Katriona?" No. Not *her*.

The power of her magic snapped and arced between them with chilling force.

"*You* don't have the privilege of uttering my name," she screamed. "Not after what has been done."

Rory stood frozen in place, searching his memory for what sins could have called upon this curse. He'd tried, Goddammit. He'd tried so bloody hard to stop the evil spreading through his clan. Pushed to the brink, he'd done one thing to stain his soul for eternity.

"Is this because of Angus?" he asked.

His heart petrified before her bitter laugh. "Why weren't you there that night, Rory?" Her arctic lips burned his ear as they brushed it. "Didn't you want your turn with Kylah? Didn't you want to hear our screams as the flesh melted from our bones?"

What madness was she spouting? "I never even *looked* at your sister. It was Angus who loved—" Rory's heart began to race, a sick knowledge knotting in his belly. Suddenly he couldn't breathe.

Angus. What did ye do?

"*Everyone* looked at Kylah."

"*She* wasn't the one I wanted." Rory tried to track her movements but the very air around her transparent form snaked and twisted in wretched vibrations. Like bones rubbing against one another and flesh tearing. One moment she leaned and whispered darkly in his ear. The next she was behind him. Then on the ceiling, her joints twisted in unnatural angles as though holding to the stones.

"Angus made my mother watch as he took my sister's virginity and then threw her to his men. They'd spent themselves on her and had already lit the washhouse on fire by the time Kamdyn and I returned from the woods, or we would have suffered the same fate."

Her every word drove a spike through his chest until Rory thought he might die from the pressure alone.

"Instead, they doused the three of us in whisky and locked us all inside." In the space of a blink, her face floated in front of his again, which meant her feet were at least a span off the floor. "They didn't touch my mother with liquor," she snarled. "*She* burned more slowly. And for every excruciating minute she suffered, you and your family shall endure an eternity."

Rory swallowed the contents of his stomach crawling up the back of his throat. He wished his brother alive so he could tear him apart with his own hands. He hadn't the stones to do it before.

He would now.

His twin created this creature of vengeance. Banshees arose from a soul so tortured and wronged that the Fae took pity and gave them a chance to reap justice. Rory gazed into the woman's eyes, so alight with hatred, and despaired.

For a glimmering moment, he'd begun to hope for the future. He'd thought that, with enough sacrifice on his part, he could heal the wounds created by his father and brother. He could pull the MacKay clan from the dregs of their massive defeats and mend broken clan alliances.

He'd been a fool to hope. The very word should have been ripped from his vocabulary decades ago.

The weight on his shoulders finally buckled his strong knees and they hit the floor.

"Do it," he rasped. "Take yer vengeance."

The creature cried and a thousand nails rained down upon his exposed skull, but a blast of cold air was all that touched his skin.

"Get up," she snarled.

Rory shook his head, affixing his gaze on the glowing coals of the fire. "I'll not ask yer forgiveness. It isna deserved. I'll burn for the sins of the Lairds before me if it puts ye to rest."

"Get *up!*" she screamed. "You'll not take this moment from me! *I* burned. My sisters burned. My mother burned. But not you, Rory MacKay. You'll beg me for a lot more than forgiveness before I strip the flesh from your bones!"

Rory looked up at her, a determined calm settling over him. "I've never begged for my life," he informed her. Though he'd had plenty of chances. "I'll not be going to now. Maybe I deserve this. Not only for what my brother did to ye, but also for what I did to him."

Katriona paused. "What did you do to him?" she demanded.

"I had him assassinated." There. He'd said it. His most evil act and darkest secret.

Some of the weight abated.

"No." The fear and pain conveyed in that one word caused him to wince. The wind died down to a breeze. "No, it can't be. Where is your father? Is he not away raiding?" Her voice almost sounded human.

Confused, Rory shook his head. "He was killed in the Battle of Harlaw by the Berserker, Roderick MacLauchlan." She'd died right before then, but if she'd lingered in this world, how did she not know this?

"Two dead?" she whispered, a frantic light pulsing from her. "But there are *three*. Three of us. Three MacKays. Three deaths to keen before we can rest.

"I'm sorry," Rory murmured, wishing that words existed to express the depth of his regret. "Mine is the only life I can offer ye."

Her scream rent the night as she rushed toward him. Searing cold infused his body as she grasped his shoulders and opened her mouth. He felt a tear. Not in a physical way, but like the fabric of his very essence unraveled. The pain paralyzed him in place.

But the relief still lingered inside him, and soon, she would have her revenge.

Chapter Two

He wasn't dying. *Why* wasn't he dying?

Katriona blasted him with renewed effort, drawing all remnants of her magic and forcing it from her fingers into his body.

His chiseled features twisted into a grimace, but he made no torturous sound of agony. No blood leaked from anywhere. She'd been promised *blood* and damn it she *would* be satisfied.

"Why do you not die?" she demanded. "How do you resist me?"

The Laird blinked his liquid brown eyes open and looked across at her, his brows drawn in puzzlement rather than pain.

"I doona know, Katriona." The sound of her name on his lips riveted her. The way he said it, like silk snagging on gravel, echoed through the stone room as powerful as any of her screams. "I've never been able to resist ye before."

What the bloody hell did he mean by that? Katriona glared at him, her thoughts racing through her options. His sword was inches from where her hands rested on his chest, but she couldn't very well wrap her hand around it and shove it though his body. As a spirit, she wasn't corporeal, and therefore couldn't move anyth—

Katriona gasped. *Her hands rested on his chest.*

Smooth, warm flesh flexed under her fingertips. The quick pace of his heart thumped a strong rhythm beneath her palm and his ribs expanded with deep breaths. Dumbfounded, Katriona moved her hands across the expanse of his torso. As with any inanimate object, she reached right through the tartan slung over his shoulder, but once her hand hit skin, it was as tangible as when she'd been alive.

And smooth, very smooth.

"What sorcery is this?" she breathed. "How can I feel you?"

Large, calloused hands covered hers, their warmth spreading up the perpetually cold miasma of her arms. The light she cast illuminated golden striations in the darkness of his umber eyes. The sorrow she read in them interrupted her rage and held her captive for a soft moment.

"Again, I doona know, lass." One of his hands released hers. The back of his fingers found the curve of her cheek. "I never thought I'd see yer face again," he murmured.

At his touch, a dangerous heat threatened her frigid wrath, revealing the weak spots in the wall of ice she'd built around her humanity. If he found one crack, the entire thing could shatter completely. This wasn't going at all how she'd planned. He was supposed to be *dead.* Or at least writhing on the ground in anguish.

Panic surged and she smothered it with anger, slapping his hand away and jolting him with magic.

He winced as though she'd shocked him, but still didn't cry out.

"You're the worst one of the lot, *Laird,*" she sneered. "At least your father and brother didn't hide their evil behind honeyed words and false compassion." Her cheek burned where his fingers had touched, almost as though he'd branded her.

It fed her rage.

She didn't want to notice how solid his flesh had been beneath her fingertips. Or for his touch to remind her that it had been nigh on a year since she'd had human contact of any kind. The fact that the vibrant timbre of his voice slid awareness to places she'd ignored when she was alive irritated her to no end.

She was the powerful one now, no longer helpless against the whims of stronger men. How *dare* he affect her like this?

"I will return," she vowed. "And when I do, I'll bring your fate with me."

A pottery bowl sailed through Katriona and shattered inside of the blackened, hollowed- out shell that used to be their fireplace.

"Already *dead*?" her mother screeched. "*How*?"

Katriona floated over piles of scorched stone and rubble, evading the small fire pit in the open room. A light, misting rain dampened inside the structure where the ceiling had burned away and exposed them all to the Highland sky. "He said his father and brother were killed by the MacLauchlan Berserkers only recently." She didn't examine why she left out the part where Rory had ordered his twin's death.

"*Lies!*" Spittle collected at the corners of Elspeth MacKay's scarred and disfigured lips. "Deceit falls from the mouths of Angus's kin like mud from a Firbolg."

"But Mother, it's true." Kamdyn hovered over the tiny, uncomfortable cot in the only corner of the ruined structure that maintained a roof. Her sweet face, rounded with the softness of youth, mirrored the anxiety they all felt. "Kylah and I both searched for Angus and his father. We only found their graves."

"How *could* you allow him time to spout his poison Katriona? Why didn't you kill him right away?"

"I *tried*," Katriona pulsed with frustration, her blue glow intensifying with her emotions. "He wouldn't die. He just— stood there."

"You mean, he's still *alive*?" Kamden cried, her glow increasing, as well. "What if he comes after us?"

"There's nothing more any of them can do to us now," Kylah murmured from her corner.

They all three turned to look at her in surprise. Her slim, delicate body leaned against the short remnant of what used to be the front wall. Knees pulled up to her chest, she almost disappeared into her flowing, ghostly blue dress. The steady rain pattered through her and colored the rock beneath her still body a darker grey.

Her glow was the dimmest of them all.

"He could come after Mother," Kamdyn worried. "Someone knows she's here because food, furs, wood, and medicine arrive every week.

None of them knew the identity of their Good Samaritan, as the deliveries were always during the witching hour, when the sisters were drawn from this plane into an empty nether.

"Could Cliodnah have tricked us?" Katriona asked.

Kamdyn shrugged, her thick waves of strawberry hair floating around her visage as though she was submerged in water. "It's possible, I suppose. The Fae are known to use us mortals for their sport."

"You dare question my integrity?" A disembodied voice shook the earth.

Kamdyn squeaked, and they all turned toward the center of their stone and earth ruin where a form slowly manifested.

"She meant nothing by it, my lady." Elspeth threw her body in front of Kamdyn's specter. "She's young and speaks without thought."

Any moisture in the air around the Faerie queen froze to glistening crystals, catching the light from the fire and winking like faraway stars. The heavier drops of rain in her vicinity solidified and fell to the rubble below her feet, the resulting noise a musical tinkling of halcyon glass upon stone.

Many a man mistook a visit from the Scottish Banshee queen as that of an angel as her silver robes and lily-white hair flowed with an invisible breeze and radiated an innate luminescence. Of this, she took gleeful advantage, wreaking havoc with the blindly pious and simple-minded.

"Your Majesty." Katriona took to one knee, hoping to distract Cliodnah from her ire. "To what do we owe the pleasure of your visit?"

Despite her symmetrical perfection, Cliodnah's unnatural eyes detracted from her beauty. Their movement didn't seem to focus as a mortal's might, but slid from vision to vision as though impeded by tar. Far too large for the ocular cavity, her pupils disappeared from time to time into her eye-lids, which proved to be most unnerving. Katriona tracked them as they followed the torpid movements of her neck before finally resting on her.

"Nearly a year has passed since I granted your mother's request and bestowed upon you the powers of a Banshee." The Fae spoke like she moved, as though immortality had banished any sense of urgency. Every syllable carefully ennunciated. Every thought clearly expressed in her flawless features before moving along to the next. "Did I fail to mention that if your vengeance is not exacted within one rotation of the Earth in her orbit that you will fail to ever be released from my service?"

"Nay, my lady," each of the sisters chorused.

"Why, then, do you delay?"

"'Tis impossible, my queen, as two of our three intended victims have already died." A jolt of panic ran through Katriona as she thought of Rory's immunity to her magic. "The other is not susceptible to my powers," she admitted.

"Interesting." Cliodnah's voice never changed inflection. Katriona was unable to ever ascertain the veracity of her words.

"How is this possible?" Katriona ventured. "Was there fault in how I used my magic?"

"Unlikely." The queen drifted closer, the chill that was a Banshees constant companion intensified at her approach. "Fae magic only requires intent to employ. However, two possibilities abide in which a mortal can resist the lethal touch of a Banshee."

The MacKay women held their collective breaths. The only sound in their vicinity the rhythmic shattering of insignificant ice drops.

"And they are?" Katriona prompted when she was certain her mother's lungs would burst.

"If a human is blessed by a Deity, or they are one of *An Dìoladh*."

"The returned?" Kamdyn's rampant curiosity obviously overcame her better judgment. "What does that mean?"

Katriona's heart sank. She knew what it meant because her father, a blacksmith, had loved to tell his two little girls stories and myths around the fire at the end of a long day. He'd been kicked in the head by an unruly stallion before Kamdyn was born, and their broken-hearted mother had never repeated his lively tales.

"One who has walked in the Otherworld, child, and then returned to their body to live out their days."

"You mean—someone who's died?" Kamdyn whispered, her eyes round as an owl's.

"And then had their life restored to them, yes," the queen confirmed. "It is rare among your kind, but occurs from time to time."

"Is Rory MacKay blessed by a Deity?" Katriona demanded.

"He is not," Cliodnah answered. "Of this I am certain."

"Then he is one of these—these *An Dìoladh*."

"That is the only possible explanation."

"How *else* can he be killed?" It was all Katriona cared about. Her vengeance. Justice.

"By no means of the Fae or Sidhe." The queen's words froze the useless heart in Katriona's chest. "He may only die by a natural course like any other man."

"What about my younger daughters?" Elspeth clutched her hands together as though at prayer, or supplication. "Their vengeance is denied, but their victims are dead. May they be released now to their final rest in the Otherworld?"

"It is impossible." The condescension in the Faerie's voice spilled resentment like hot tar in Katriona's chest. "If they are unable to exact their vengeance, then their souls are contracted for my use indefinitely. One of the wronged ones must do the deed."

"No." In horror, Elspeth dropped to her knees. "What have I done?"

"There is no justice in this!" Katriona hissed. "We cannot kill someone already dead."

Cliodnah made a dismissive gesture, agitating the frost in her atmosphere. "That does not concern me. They were alive when you came to me seeking vengeance. You should have acted quickly and exacted your justice then."

"Our mother was near to dying!" Kylah contended. "We could not leave her."

"So you stood helplessly by and let your retribution escape you." The Faerie queen, ever cold and unaffected, began to fade from view. "Unless you can find a way to regain your mortality, I'll return by the Summer Solstice to collect you."

Katriona's frustrated cry echoed in the emptiness. As she watched the last of the frost settle and disappear into the ashes and stone, the sound of Kamden and her mother's frightened sobs gnawed at the edges of her sanity. Kylah's constant, broken silence became more maddening and excruciating than any Banshees shriek.

She could not linger here another moment.

What she could do, is lay the blame at the feet of the man who deserved it.

Rory MacKay might be immune to her magic, but he was not unaffected by it. He was still mortal. He could still die.

And before her soul was claimed by the Faerie queen, Katriona would see him dead by any natural course she could devise.

Chapter Three

"Ye look like ye're about to meet the Reaper instead of yer bride." Lorne MacKay slapped Rory on the shoulder with a heavy glove. "Ye'll like to scare her away by scowling at her so."

Rory shook off the trance and adjusted the MacKay badge on his heavy fur cloak. "Aye well, I'm not of a mind to have a bride just now. I've other things in need of attention."

Like Katriona MacKay.

Squinting through the MacKay banners down the Road of Wrath that stretched along the river Naver and then angled west to Durness, Rory searched for any sign of movement. The runner had heralded the arrival of Clan Fraser a short while ago, and it seemed all those of Durness, and the surrounding villages of Strathnaver and its men-at-arms stood at the ready to receive him.

Lorne snorted, scratching his thick, blonde beard with a meaty hand. "What *'other things'?* The clan wants for Kathryn Fraser's dowry and Laird Fraser wants Angus's thousand men."

"Thousand traitors," Rory muttered.

"I still think ye should have slaughtered them when ye had the chance." Lorne spat on the ground.

Rory thought of Angus's twenty or so closest men, butchered single-handedly by Connor MacLauchlan, Laird of the Lachlan clan. Connor had received the last of Rory's gold from the deal, and also a wife, Lindsay Ross, who was technically supposed to have been promised to Angus.

They all found out what happened to a man who stood in between a Berserker and his mate. The picture of his twin's crushed and broken body reared in Rory's mind, and he squelched the complicated emotions surging through him.

"Had I massacred them all, I would have made enemies of a thousand MacKay families. It wouldna have done anything to foster unity in the clan. At least indenturing them to Fraser gives them a chance to live and fight for Scotland. Maybe regain some of the honor they've lost."

"Aye, ye've appeased a thousand families with yer mercy, and still three thousand more MacKays call for justice against them," Lorne argued.

"Canna justice and mercy go hand in hand?" Rory asked. "At least this way, they have a chance to claim their lives, or for their deaths to mean something. And the money we receive for their swords can be put toward reparations for their crimes against their own people." Even as the words left his mouth, Rory wondered if he still believed them. He'd heard of and ultimately seen some of the atrocities committed by his father and brother and their men, but none had affected him like Katriona's tale.

Burned alive. Her sister violated. Her mother forced to watch.

How did Angus become so twisted? Someone he'd shared a womb with. A life with. How did they grow to be so different? And why did any of those who followed his evil brother deserve to live?

Because the MacKay coffers had been drained by his family's warmongering, and they needed money if they were to survive another harsh winter. Because the families of those men were *still* MacKays, most of them innocent.

"It seems ye have something else weighing on ye," Lorne correctly observed.

Rory sighed and glanced around, meeting the eyes of the watchful Fraser runner who stood only paces away. He leaned down closer to Lorne.

As wide and thick as a centuries-old tree, Lorne MacKay stood no taller than Rory's chin. Though Rory stood eyes taller and a span thicker than most men, he knew better than to ever make Lorne feel the disparity in their stature.

"I've a Banshee," he muttered.

Lorne's laugh was booming and sudden, startling many of those gathered nearby. "Did I hear you wrong or did ye say ye had—oof!"

Rory's swift and sharp elbow to the ribs cut him off. "I didna tell ye to cry it to the entire clan, ye daft arse."

"I'm sorry," Lorne wiped a tear of mirth from his eye. "It's just ye're so serious, I didna expect ye to say something so outrageous."

"I'm *not*—" Rory glanced at those of his clan that were now regarding the men with piqued curiosity, and lowered his voice. "I'm not in jest," he insisted. "She came to me last night, after yer younger brother, Baird, left my chamber,"

"That's impossible." Lorne swatted the air in front of his face, still speaking too loud for Rory's comfort. "Ye'd not be standing here if ye were speaking the truth. We'd have found yer shriveled body in yer chambers this morn."

"That's just it; she *tried* to kill me, but couldna." Rory remembered the look of pure shock on her transparent face. He felt the sensation of her cool hands on his flesh. That memory would be with him for all his days.

"Ye had a dream, Laird, a nightmare. Many a warrior does before his wedding," Lorne said sagely. "Marriage is not so hard. Just remember some flowers, a kiss, and a good long tup rights just about any wrong." He shouldered Rory in the arm and pointed toward the sapphire waters of the Kyle. "There's the Fraser Vanguard."

Indeed, a train of wagons surrounded by kilted knights appeared around the Kinloch pass.

"It wasna a dream," Rory said, his eyes tracking the progress of the Frasers. "It was Katriona MacKay. The washerwoman's eldest daughter."

"The one who died in the fire last spring?"

"Aye," Rory confirmed, debating on whether or not to reveal the cause of the fire.

Lorne's eyes narrowed. "Didna ye always have eyes for her? And Angus for the sister who was too pretty for her own good, what was her name? Krista, Kayleigh—"

Rory elbowed his Steward and most trusted friend a second time. "Kylah, and keep yer voice *down*. What if she lurks nearby?"

"Yer bleeding serious?" Lorne's mouth dropped open and he stared at Rory as though he'd sprouted a tail and started dancing a jig to an English ditty. "Ye've lost yer fucking senses, on today of all days." He threw a hand toward the approaching clan.

"If ye doona keep yer bloody voice down, I'm going to run ye through in front of all these people and feed yer corpse to the Frasers for their supper," Rory threatened through gritted teeth. He sent what he hoped was an encouraging smile to the dour-faced Fraser runner, who was now regarding them both with suspicion, though Rory was fair certain he couldn't hear their conversation.

Yet.

Maybe Lorne should have stayed back in Argyle to aid the MacLauchlans. Rory scowled at the man.

"Just promise not to let it show that ye've cracked until *after* the wedding." Lorne ignored his empty threat.

"I'm sorry I mentioned it to ye," Rory groused.

"Well that makes two of us." Lorne answered Rory's scowl with one of his own. "Now keep yer daft hidden and woo yer bride's father. The contract isna signed as of yet."

Lorne had a point. Rory could only focus on one crisis at a time.

Rory went to rest his hand on his sword and found the scabbard empty. He felt naked without it, but had removed it as a gesture of goodwill to his new in-laws. He sent his second-in-command a look that spoke volumes as the gilded, well-guarded wagon in the middle creaked to a stop.

The Fraser colors of vibrant red, green, and the impudent violet of Gallic royalty whipped about in the chilly February wind, its sound as loud as thunder in the crisp, silent morning. A burly, dark-haired clansman dismounted and rushed to open the latch to the coach's door and lower the step rail.

A man with the dimensions of a barrel of scotch stepped onto the rail, mightily testing its resilience. Alistair Jean Roche Fraser, Laird of the Lowland Frasers, surveyed the gathered crowd of a few hundred souls with dark eyes more suited to a mischievous goat rather than the laird of a powerful clan.

His gaze snagged on Rory and his jowls lifted in a quivery smile. "Laird MacKay!" His jolly voice echoed across the moors. "They told me to expect a braw lad, but I didna know you were as tall as an oak!"

"Laird Fraser." Rory stepped forward and clasped the man's forearm. It was more solid than expected for a man of sixty-plus years. "Welcome to Durness."

"Is it true what I heard, that you *gave* Dun Keep back to Argyll and the MacLauchlans banished ye all the way back here to the edge of the world?"

The man didn't mince words; he and Lorne would surely get along. Rory checked his temper. "Strathnaver is our home and MacKay lands stretch from Caithness all the way through Reay. We've bountiful oceans, plentiful kin, and fertile soil. My father and brother overreached our boundaries and brought war to our clan when I would have peace in the Highlands. Angus took Dun Keep from its rightful owners and I merely restored it and any pilfered Argyle lands.

"And as for the MacLauchlan's, they're my friends and allies, currently holding yer thousand soldiers in good faith to be delivered upon signing of our contract." Rory realized that 'friend' might be too strong a word for the relationship he'd forged with the MacLauchlan Berserkers, but in his opinion, this Lowlander with French blood could stay out of their Highland affairs.

"Did these wild Highlanders treat ye well, Albert?" Frasier used the French pronunciation, dropping the 'T'.

The runner stepped forward, his wide shoulders at odds with his diminutive chin. "Aye, Laird." Something in the icy grey of the runner's eyes disturbed Rory. It seemed as though his hospitable treatment somehow disappointed the man.

Fraser nodded in a strong movement, his plentiful chins quivered like the leavings cook scraped from a boiled broth. "Very well, MacKay, I present to you Kathryn Fraser, soon to be your wife."

"Oh my," Kamdyn exclaimed. "She's very pretty. Maybe even as beautiful as Kylah."

"Yes, I can *see* that," Katriona snapped. She'd watched the buxom, flaxen-haired woman appear from the coach like a Norse goddess. What she'd not been able to look away from, was the sharp flare of masculine appreciation in Rory's expressive eyes.

She and Kamdyn hovered at the edge of the large crowd, able to pick through the cacophony with their exemplary hearing and hone in on the happenings with the Laird and his intended.

"Ye'll have fine, strong sons to war with the Sutherlands," the Fraser was saying.

Katriona decided to dislike him right away.

Rory took the woman's elegant hand and helped her down from the coach before bowing over her knuckles in a show of respect.

The cheers from the MacKay clan shook all of Strathnaver, and Katriona could see in the eyes of the people a small flare of something that had been absent for a good long while.

Hope.

Though the MacKays had long been one of the strongest, largest clans in the north since the last of the twelve Druidh Chieftains combined the northern clans, they'd been plagued with war, cruel leadership, and economic difficulties for centuries.

Katriona could see the fervent wish that Rory would be different than his predecessors, and this marriage of wealth would be the beginning of that. But for how long? Until *Laird* MacKay started building a new castle and funding a larger army with his wife's money? Until the children's bodies lay starving in the square? And the cries of the hungry mixed with sea storms that whipped through the moors?

She refused to allow it.

Rory still hadn't released the hand of the woman who stood silently by him. They made a magnificent picture. Both handsome and regal. Her delicate golden beauty complemented his strong, bronzed, imposing features. They looked like they were born to be Highland royalty, wrapped in fine furs and crowned with fine metals earned with the blood of their people.

"We've been cooped up in a coach for some days," Laird Fraser swept his short arm to encompass the wide sky, his accent tempered by years in the Lowlands surrounded by the

English. "Perhaps a small tour of your home and lands would help us stretch the legs and work up an appetite."

Rory motioned for some saddled horses to be brought forward. His, a large bay stallion accompanied by Lorne's speckled war-horse, and two other gentle-looking mares. "I thought ye and yer father might be interested in inspecting the grounds of yer new home." He spoke directly to Kathryn. "Do ye ride?"

"I ride very well," the woman murmured, a heated meaning glowing from eyes that matched the blue of the Highland sky.

"Do ye have a mount for Albert, here?" Frasier boomed. "No offense meant to ye, but the man has long been a personal guard to my daughter, and she is rarely without him."

If Rory felt any irritation, he hid it well. "Of course. I'll have one saddled right away." Rory motioned to Baird, who jumped into action and sprang up the hill to the stables like a fleeing rabbit.

Katriona's lip curled in disgust and she motioned for Kamdyn to follow her. Stealing through the crowd, they were invisible to all and only tangible as the kiss of a death-chill on someone's flesh. As she passed, women held their children closer and ducked into the protection of their men. The elderly narrowed their eyes and crossed themselves or spoke a quick incantation against evil in the olde language.

But they were all safe from her. She was dangerous to one man, and that was if she could only find out how to kill him. While she still wanted too. Because she did.

Didn't she?

Rory put his hands around Kathryn Frasier's waist and lifted her onto her mare, not letting go until she settled into the saddle.

Yes, she definitely wanted to kill him.

"Thank you, Laird," Kathryn murmured, her hands resting on Rory's forearms.

When he released her and turned to take the reins of his own mount, the color in his cheeks intensified.

Katriona could feel a wail building inside her, but she didn't let it escape in front of the gathered crowd. Though the people wouldn't be able to see her, they'd hear her Banshee cry. And these weren't just Rory's people. They were hers too. She couldn't bring herself to frighten them.

Besides, she didn't know where the cry came from. Or why it had built of its own accord. She hadn't been particularly angry. She'd been watching Rory MacKay put his large, strong hands on his betrothed, thinking about the last time she'd seen him blush.

It had been two years ago, when the MacKay warriors had returned from besting the Sutherlands at Dingwall. The men had scattered to their villages, some to Cape Wrath, and others to Kinlochburvie, Farr, and Balligill. But Angus and Rory MacKay had returned with their soldiers to Durness.

Katriona, Kylah, and Kamdyn had been working with their mother in the washhouse they'd converted from their father's smithy. Bedecked with war-braids, weapons, and the blood of their enemies, ten loud MacKays had converged upon the washhouse. One service Elspeth MacKay supplied above cleaning linen and wool was the care and upkeep of armor, learned from years with her husband. She had the proper oils and such on hand and her family saw a great deal of income after a battle.

"Ye canna hail Rory as the battle's hero," Angus bellowed as he and the men crowded inside. "He had his sword and all I had was a bow. Did ye count the number of corpses with arrows in them?" Angus's thin, stringy hair had no blood in it. His tartan soiled with nothing but dirt and food.

"Doesna matter," one of the men diplomatically pointed out. "The battle's won, we'll celebrate tonight!"

The men had dropped their armor off with Katriona and then crowded around the large metal basin to vie for Kylah's dainty, beauteous attentions and Kamdyn's youthful, fresh smiles.

All except for Rory MacKay.

His tartan and sword had been bloodier than the others, his chest and arms thicker, he'd towered over them, his eyes bright with a post-battle intensity. Ducking through her entry last, he'd hung behind the crop of men, but towered over them.

Her mother had left Katriona alone by the entry shelves of the washhouse with him to go and run interference for her two younger daughters.

"Do you all intend to pay, or simply gawk?" she'd asked him, impatient with the extra work and maybe a little irate at the lack of attention. Katriona had always known she wasn't as beautiful as her sisters, and with each year she grew older as they bloomed. She'd been attractive in her own way, catching the eyes of many lads. Though each time they'd lost interest the moment Kylah entered a room.

"I'll cover expenses for the men." Rory's voice had sounded dark and warm as the air in the washhouse, and Katriona had to wipe a bloom of sweat from her brow.

His large, intense umber eyes had captured hers, unsettling her more than a little. Katriona was used to men's notice bouncing off of her to hone in on her sister. But not Rory. Big and silent, he'd stared at her while she piled soiled armor, tartans, and such onto the shelves, trying to remember which belonged to whom.

"This is Eagan's," he'd corrected when she'd added a coat of mail to a wrong pile. Bending past her to lift it, he put it over near Eagan's things. "And this," taking an unwieldy and soiled tartan from her, he folded it and placed it on another pile. "Is Bran's."

"You don't have to help me," she'd snapped, embarrassed that his regard had thrown her off. She never forgot orders. Ever. But with his huge body taking up most of the entryway, there'd barely been enough room to breathe, let alone think.

"I want to," he'd rumbled, stepping even closer, crowding her and overwhelming her senses.

Backing away from him, her toe had tangled with someone's leather sword belt and she'd pitched to the side, falling toward a boiling rinse cauldron over a bellow-fed fire.

In a lightning-fast movement, he'd caught her, his arms locking around her like bands of iron, but not pulling her into his dirty chest. Frozen like they'd been, bent over the dirt floor, Katriona could distinctly recall what he'd smelled like. Earth, blood, sweat, and something sharper, very distinctly *male*.

Katriona had liked it, despite herself. Her body had responded to it in a way that had vexed and excited her. She'd been entranced by his bold and grungy face suspended above hers.

Their lips parted. Their breath mingled. And every part of Katriona's body had come alive in that moment.

"Sod it, Rory, are ye goin' ta take her virginity here in front of us and her mother?" Angus's cruel, bawdy taunt had broken the spell. "Because ye'd have ta marry the spinster for certain if there be witnesses."

He'd blushed then, too, as he'd pulled her upright and steadied her on her feet before turning away. He'd murmured something about payment, tossed coin on the table, and left.

The feast that night had been the first time Angus asked for Kylah's hand in marriage. Their mother had refused.

"I'll never give any of ye to Angus or Rory MacKay," she'd vowed. "There's something wrong with that family. A streak of cruelty and evil. I don't want you going near them, promise me."

They'd promised, of course.

But Katriona had never forgotten those few brief moments in Rory MacKays arms.

And now they steadied another.

Chapter Four

"The sheep are dying." Lorne strode into the great room of the keep where Rory shared a post-feast toddy with Kathryn and her father. "Maybe fifteen of Kevin's herd and there are reports of fresh milk curdling in the village of Tongue."

The serving woman, Bridget, paused in her pouring of whiskey and shuddered, her abundant cleavage drawing Fraser's notice. "I swear to ye, Laird, it's that washer-woman, Elspeth. She's put some kind of Fae curse on the clan like she promised to do." Crossing herself, Bridget also made olde signs to ward off evil before running fingers through her glossy brown hair and straightening her gown. Rory imagined a lot of women felt compelled to do such while standing next to a beauty like Kathryn Fraser.

"Perhaps we can address this *tomorrow*," Rory hissed at Lorne. "It's half 'till midnight and I have *guests*." The last word he forced through his teeth. What was his steward thinking? Next he'd be telling them about the Banshee.

"What's this?" Kathryn's soft, honeyed voice poured over them all. "Are you plagued with a witch?" She turned from handing a pastry to Albert, her lovely blue eyes alight with gentle curiosity.

"Nay," was Rory's instinctive denial, but then he thought the better of it. "Maybe." It would be foolish to admit it to his intended, lest she change her mind. "I doona know." What was it about beautiful women that turned him into an idiot?

"If ye ask me, ye should finish burning her and let the devil take her instead of—"

"*Thank ye*, Bridget, that will be all." Rory dismissed her with a warning look. "Make sure to carry yer charge on yer way home."

"Finish?" Fraser's eyes widened.

"The washer woman was wounded in a fire last year, she had extensive burns," Rory explained. "Some say she's gone a little daft since and was heard making curses in the square." He remembered seeing her charred and blistered face last summer as she wandered into Durness and pointed to Angus promising retribution on him and his clan. Rory had never seen such hatred on the face of another. Such loss.

Angus had been of a mind to kick dirt in her blistering skin and Rory had to distract him from it. That had been the first time he'd truly hated his twin brother.

Now he knew why. Perhaps some part of him, deep down, had sensed Angus's responsibility.

His guilt.

Rory shook himself, returning to the moment.

"Maybe you should look to getting an inquisitor up here," Fraser suggested over a swallow of Rory's most expensive scotch. "He could interrogate her, just to be certain."

Alarm rippled through Rory. He'd heard stories from Glasgow, Aberdeen, and Inverness about inquisitors terrorizing entire clans, called to start one fire, but igniting hundreds. Then installing a monastery or church to lord over the lands. He'd die before bringing that kind of evil upon his clan. Some of them still followed the olde ways. Hell, Rory himself still paid homage to the olde Gods and had delayed building any kind of church on his lands, despite the inquiries from some of his Christian people.

There were too many Berserksers, Druids, Shapeshifters and Banshees about the Highlands to go inviting that kind of trouble.

"I'm certain there's no need of that." He tried to pacify his soon-to-be father-in-law. "I'll pay call upon Kevin tomorrow and see if it's a possible illness that sometimes strikes the herds. Maybe rotted grain or the like. And we'll need to substantiate the claims of the milk before making any decisions. Milk *does* tend to curdle if left out for too long, curse or no curse."

"It's just that ye mentioned Katriona—"

"*Haud yer Wheesht.*" Rory struggled to keep his voice calm and his fingers from Lorne's throat. Hadn't the man just lectured him this afternoon about caution? Had everyone lost their mind? "I'll deal with this in the morning." Rory pointed to the door and glared at his steward.

Lorne wisely and silently escaped the hall.

"Katriona?" Kathryn's golden brow arched, but her eyes remained gentle.

For some reason, Rory didn't like the sound of Katriona's name on Kathryn's lips. It sounded wrong, somehow. Like a forgotten platitude or a broken vow.

"Is this going to be a problem, MacKay?" Fraser queried with a frown.

"Nay." Rory grappled with his temper. "Nay, Katriona was Elspeth's daughter, she died in the fire." And perhaps now took her wrath out on sheep because she somehow failed to kill *him*?

Rory reached for Kathryn's hand and pulled her to her feet. He had to admit he liked the way the firelight threw strands of red into her golden hair. "It's been a long day for ye," he murmured. "Why don't ye and yer father retire and refresh from yer journey."

A familiar pang of guilt stabbed him low in the belly. He kept looking at her perfect, lovely face and thinking that he still liked stormy green eyes over her gentle blue. He'd been making comparisons like that all day. While Kathryn's body and features pleased him greatly, she didn't stir him. Not like—

"My laird is kind to me." She curtsied, her soft hand still encased in his. "I find this match very agreeable."

Albert stood and moved to her side, drawing Rory's attention. "I'll see ye safely to yer chambers," he bowed. Though his name was French, his brogue was Scots. And his eyes glowed at Rory with an intense dislike in his impassive Gallic face.

Kathryn's face remained placid, seemingly oblivious to any masculine tension.

"Aye." Fraser stood and clapped him on the shoulder. "We'll talk about signing a contract in the morning, and after the wedding, I'll be off to collect my thousand men."

Single-minded, Fraser was.

"Very well." Rory bowed and brushed his lips over Kathryn's soft knuckles. "Sweet dreams, lady."

A complicated slew of emotion tightened in his chest. A bud of affection, perhaps, for his intended. A turbulent mixture of excitement and dread for what, or who, the night may bring. If Katriona appeared to him, he'd have to question her regarding the sheep. Despite the legitimacy of her fury, he couldn't have her threaten the livelihood of his clan.

Something would have to be done.

"*When* did you die?" Katriona demanded, pitching herself out of the grey nether and into Rory's bedchamber at the precise stroke of midnight.

Water sloshed above the rim of the bath and onto the stone floor as Rory flailed into a seated position in the tub without a modicum of grace. He stared at her for a full minute, his mouth agape, swiping water out of his eyes as though to rid them of her. "Wh—What?"

In spite of herself, Katriona felt the corners of her mouth twitch with mirth and she hastily flattened her lips into a thin line. Since the tub was placed next to the glowing fire in the hearth and Katriona hovered in the farthest, coldest corner of the chamber, she couldn't see into the water's obscure depths.

What she could see, though, rendered her as momentarily speechless as Rory. Backlit by flames, his eyes seemed to glow just as she knew hers did. Shadows darkened the valleys cut into his large, war-honed body by cords of muscle encased in bronzed flesh. Rivulets of water caught the light as they sluiced in distracting pathways over his chest and torso.

When he raised two thick arms to brush his wet, shoulder-length hair back, his body flexed and morphed in ways that boggled the mind.

Something warm and slick clenched deep within her, contrasting with her constant chill. "You... died." Katriona blinked. Once. Twice. Trying to regain her purpose.

"Woman, as you can see, *I* am not the one who is dead." He raised his brows at her.

She threw up her hands. "I didn't say you *were* dead, I said you *have* died. It's why I can't kill you." She dared a pace closer, reminding herself that fire could no longer hurt her. "Yet," she added for measure. "You're one of the *An Dìoladh*."

"I am?" His baffled expression was infuriatingly endearing.

"How can you not remember *dying*?" she exploded. "It's generally a marked occasion!"

Rory shrugged, the water rippling with the movement of his heavy shoulders, a sly sort of smile lifting the corners of his sensual mouth. "I doona know if you ken much about a man, but it's difficult to produce a memory whilst naked in front of a beautiful woman."

"You can tell me now, or I'll start keening and not stop until dawn," she threatened. Had he just called her beautiful? She was still trying her best to ignore the fact that he was naked.

He smirked. "Ye mean, ye'll stay with me all night? I've often thought about ye here, in my chamber."

"Trust me," she hissed. "I will *not* be pleasant company."

To her utter shock, something dark and dangerous flared in his eyes. An excitement borne of wicked deviance. "Ye'll be punishing, then?" His voice had changed, hailing from somewhere lower, controlled by something still hidden in the steaming water. "Maybe, try to kill me again with yer touch?"

Katriona stared at him in astonished disbelief. He sounded—eager. Had he lost his bloody mind? Curious wonderment drew her slowly closer to the bath. Her glow intensified, but she didn't feel the rush of anger that usually preceded such an event. A rush of something else perhaps, but she couldn't afford to examine what it was. For some reason, she had a sudden and intense fear that Laird Rory MacKay wasn't the one in danger.

"You do not realize what you're saying." Had her voice been altered as well? "I will not be kind."

His tongue wet his lower lip as though preparing for a much longed for confection. "Ye may be as cruel as ye wish."

"If I touch you, it'll be painful," she warned.

"Aye." The word sounded like an entreaty. "I remember the pain to be exquisite." One large, rough hand disappeared below the water. His recently moistened lower lip caught his teeth after a loud exhale.

Katriona became transfixed by the ripples in the spot where his hand had vanished.

"What if I really kill you this time?" Why on earth would that be a problem? Wasn't that the entire meaning of her current existence? Why was her heart hammering and her breath sawing in an out of her lungs as though she still depended upon it for survival?

"Ye won't." He motioned for her to come closer and she complied, stopping at the edge of the tub, hovering near his shoulders

"How do you know?" Her voice lowered to a whisper.

"Because last night, when ye put yer hands on my flesh, I'd never felt so alive." He surged forward, his strong arms closing around her, and pulled her down into the water.

Chapter Five

Katriona jolted him right away, more out of alarm than menace, her hands against his chest releasing currents of her deadly Banshee magic. His body bowed beneath her, every sinewy muscle going taut, his arms clenching her so tight that they would have crushed her had she still been alive.

His animalistic cry echoed off the stone walls in ragged, masculine tones, vibrating through her as powerfully as she knew the pain poured through him. One part, in particular, ground against her as he arced. She could feel the thick throbbing heat of it against her belly, even through her thin robes.

Her clothing and hair remained dry, nor was she bound by the solid barrier of the tub. But she did feel the sensation of the water's warmth enveloping her. The only tangible, corporeal matter in her entire world thus far remained the heated flesh of Rory MacKay.

She reigned in her magic and Rory folded back down to settle at the bottom of the tub. He didn't release her though, but held her firmly against him, his eyes burning down into hers.

Katriona gasped. This was as close to a fire as she'd allowed herself to come in almost a year. But at the moment, she couldn't decide which threw off more heat, the flames in the hearth or the man beneath her. Her body molded against his, fitting into the hollows and crevices created by his sleek muscle.

Her thighs tucked against his, her breasts crushed to his chest. He was so solid. So hard and smooth.

So... alive.

"Release me," she commanded, though her voice didn't carry the authority it should have.

"Nay," he rasped through labored breaths.

"Release me *now* or I'll—"

"Yer threats do nothing but tempt me, Katriona." His gaze roved her face, her hair that swayed in an invisible, ethereal breeze, as though he could devour her with his eyes.

"Tempt you, to what?" she breathed.

"To do this." He opened his mouth over hers in a bruising kiss, his arms tightening around her once more.

Katriona froze against him, more a prisoner of sensation than of his arms.

Fierce. The only word that truly described his lips. Fiercely passionate. Fiercely possessive. His growl vibrated against her stunned mouth as it built from deep inside of him. Clawing its way out from an abyss long forgotten.

For what seemed like an eternity, but may have been a blink, Katriona didn't dare move. Urges long ignored and pleasure long denied thrummed through her, eclipsing the pain and rage that had been her driving force the past year.

For the first time since she could remember, she felt warm, wanted—vital.

Her thighs split over his hips and he surged between them. Her hands moved from his chest, up his neck and plunged into his sleek hair. When his rough, wet tongue sought entrance, she granted it without hesitation, meeting it with her own, returning stroke for stroke.

His hands, however, angled down, relaxing their hold on her ribs and following the curve of her back in a sensual, insistent caress before gripping the flesh of her bottom and pressing her harder against his length.

She gasped into his mouth at the unexpected pleasure of their contact. Though he was not inside her, his body found the sensitive place that ached for him. Sang for him. And he ground himself against it with a slow, demanding rhythm.

Pressure built. Her loins clenched and Katriona caught herself wondering if the thick length of his manhood would feel just as searing inside of her.

Rory's lips strayed from hers, exploring the curve of her chin, the column of her neck.

Her hands gripped the hard, straining muscles of his shoulders as though preparing for that searing pleasure that could only be seen on the far horizon, but barreled toward her with all the awesome power and inevitability of stampeding wild horses.

"Christ." Rory's moaned expletive ended with a nip on the sensitive skin at the hollow of her throat. "I canna believe ye're here with me."

Katriona couldn't believe it herself. Grinding beneath her, feasting on her skin was Rory MacKay. The man she'd sworn to kill. The twin of the brute who murdered her sisters. The same blood as the monster who'd violated Kylah...

Reality permeated the haze of warm passion.

The Laird who would be married in a few days' time.

Nay. This was *wrong*. Even now, her sisters lurked among ruins with her mother in the perpetual cold. Trusting her to find a way to carry out her duty.

"Wait." Her command came out as a groan. "I shouldn't."

"You will." He thrust against her, harder this time, the echoes of pleasure growing stronger.

"*No*." She forced a surge of magic into his shoulders and he instantly bowed beneath her.

"Katriona," he panted. "Stop... Not yet... Ye haven't..."

She was relentless. If she stopped now, she'd give into the violent instincts of her traitorous body to follow every moist thrum of thrilling sensation he elicited in her. She just couldn't allow it.

"Kat..." his plea gasped from between clenched teeth, his amber eyes glowing with desperation. "I can't..."

Waves of water sloshed over the rim of the tub as his powerful body heaved and bucked. Raw, torturous sounds ripped from deep in his throat and his eyes clenched shut as every muscle bulged and strained.

Between her legs, he pulsed hotter, larger, in the exact same rhythm his entire body did. This was different than the other times she'd jolted him. Perhaps this time, she'd succeeded in truly hurting him.

He was beautiful like this, Katriona noted almost dispassionately. He was like an animal. Stripped away of all artifice. No code of honor. No past or future. Just pure, desperate sensation coursing through a large, potent mass of sinew and flesh.

In this moment he belonged to her.

Katriona closed her eyes, a wave of pain and loss suddenly squelching her other senses. All moments were fleeting, and disappeared before their time.

With a final jerk, Rory collapsed as though released from a bond, though her power still flowed into him. Spontaneous twitches of muscle belied that he still felt pain, but his face relaxed and his head lolled against the rim of the tub.

Katriona realized she'd been jolting him long enough to kill a hundred men, at least. Releasing him, she drew back, looking down into his achingly handsome, strong features.

"Ye didna find yer pleasure," he accused in a husky voice, chiding her softly from behind heavy lids. "Let me—"

"Nay." Katriona wrenched herself away from him. His arms tightened as though to hold her prisoner, but she used her Banshee ability to levitate away from him, above the water.

"Nay, that shouldn't have happened." She'd not meant to cause him such extreme pleasure; he'd found it on his own.

"Why not?"

"Because I'm here to *kill* you, not kiss you," she snapped.

A lazy smile slanted across his lips. Katriona tried not to look at them, to remember how they felt on hers. "Well, if ye canna do one, what's wrong with the other? I've wanted to do that for longer than ye can imagine."

"With the woman you are bound to marry a few doors away?"

Rory winced, a hand coming up to rub new lines that appeared in his forehead. "All of that was set into motion before yesterday, before I knew ye were still—"

"*Alive?*" she bit out. "Because I'm not, Rory. I'm dead. And there's nothing in our past or future *but* death. *Yours* if I have my way." Despite what they'd just experienced, the debt of vengeance still had to be paid. The blood of her sisters called for it.

And hers still did too, didn't it?

"But... ye canna kill me. Ye said so yerself."

"When did you die?" She repeated her earlier question. How in the bloody hell had they strayed so far from her purpose?

"What does it matter?" He sat forward in the bath, all the remnants of pleasure drained from his features and shadows took its place.

A part of Katriona mourned the loss. Her emotions felt much like the water in the tub, displaced by Rory's unrelenting mass until they spilled over.

"*Tell me,*" she keened, her Banshee voice splitting the air between them like a blade.

Rory cringed and held up his hands. "All right, I'll tell ye what I think happened," he promised.

Katriona crossed her arms, valiantly keeping her eyes on his face and away from the enticing curve of each individual stomach muscle as they flexed and glistened with his movement. She'd never forget what it had been like to have all that power beneath her. At her mercy. And that fact irritated her to no end.

"I was a lad, maybe all of sixteen or so," Rory began. "Angus and I were boar hunting on Cape Wrath."

Lip curling at his brother's name, Katriona bit back a snarl.

"I'd had so much to drink the night before and it'd been the first time I'd—" Rory's gaze snagged on hers. "We'll I'll say my head wasna on the task." He shifted in the water, his eyes sharpening.

"We'd cornered the boar between a rock crevice and a sea cliff. We had to climb down to kill it. I lost my grip on a mossy hand-hold and fell some distance onto the rocks below hitting my head and breaking my arm."

A bleak distance blanketed the observant clarity in his features. "I remember floating above it all, looking down at my brother and wondering why he was so afraid. He skidded down the rocks, screaming my name. Then, he hoisted me over his shoulder and carried me up the cliff face to the safety of the grasses." Rory shook his head and let out a mystified breath. "I weighed at least a stone more than he, even then. It should have been impossible for him to lift me, but I'll be buggered if he didna." A sad, wry laugh burst from his chest, and his gentle sorrow released something inside of Katriona that reminded her of when the frozen Highland lochs thawed and broke into jagged pieces of floating ice.

"It was in that moment I truly I realized that I was watching him try to save my life, from *outside* my skin. I felt the pull of my body, but also the presence of a nether world. It terrified me, that dark unknown, and I knew I wasna done here, that I had to live. So, when Angus jumped on his horse and went for help, I decided I needed to be *inside* my body when they returned." Rory shrugged. "That's the last thing I remember for a full month. Maybe more. That entire summer's a wee hazy." He reached up and massaged the back of his scalp, perhaps finding a familiar scar beneath his thick, wet hair. "I was told that I let everyone know what I saw. Maybe I even heard that word before, *An Dìoladh*, though I canna remember it."

Katriona snorted. "Perhaps your head wound was worse than you thought if you remember watching the likes of Angus save your life."

Rory's eyes narrowed on her face. "Angus was always so angry. So incredibly cruel. But he shared a womb with me. He laughed only with *me*. He rode, hunted with, and fought beside me. He *loved* me. And regardless of what happened after... that day he saved my life." His gaze slid to the fire. "It ended up being one of his biggest mistakes."

"His *biggest mistakes* were viciously raping Kylah and burning my family alive. Or raiding and pillaging across the Highlands, wreaking unspeakable terrors upon those who wouldn't cower to his demands," Katriona hissed. "Or how about dividing our clan and making us weak, turning kin against kin until every death was a MacKay death." Katriona advanced. "How *dare* you mourn him."

Rory stood, proud and completely nude. His jaw locked and a storm gathered in his eyes. "I ordered his *death*, Katriona." His low voice a dark contrast to her Banshee wails. "My own brother. *I* put a stop to his evil." Stepping out of the bath, he reached for a plaid and wrapped it around his hips, hiding his glorious male flesh from view. "That doesna mean I doona mourn the child Angus was, or the man he could have been."

Katriona could see the pain and shame etched into the lines around his eyes. The weight of his deeds straining the muscles of his heavy shoulders. She felt a swell of pity for him, but tried to crush it beneath a wall of ice.

"Our father he was... cruel to us both, but Angus got the worst of it. I suppose because he was the eldest and next in line to be Laird." Rory squeezed at his forehead again, a now familiar sign he experienced unpleasant memories. "The degradation that we—the humiliation... It's no wonder he became a creature of pain and perversion."

"You excuse him in *my* presence?" Aghast, Katriona recoiled farther away from him.

"Not an excuse." He held up his hand as though to ward off her anger. "I just—"

"Just *nothing*." Katriona could feel the Banshee rage gurgle from deep inside what little soul she had left, squelching what tendrils of warmth remained from his touch. "You were subject to the same upbringing as your brother. Based on your logic, don't you have the potential for the *same* evil?"

"Aye, it's possible. But I *choose* to be different. I want my clan to be strong and prosperous." Rory hit a fist to his chest, amber flames flaring in his eyes in response to the frost forming in hers. "I want the word of a MacKay to mean something in the Highlands again. And, most of all, I want to pay for my *own* sins and not the deeds of the Lairds before me!"

"You *enjoyed* the pain my magic wrought, didn't you?" Katriona sneered. "It brought you pleasure? Is that not a perversion? Do you enjoy inflicting pain with the same excitement that you receive from it?"

Muscles heaving with fuming breaths, he advanced on her. "You *know* I would never."

Katriona let out a dry sound that may have been called a laugh if it wasn't so full of contempt. "I know no such thing. What other sins do you hide from the fools in our clan who love and trust you? What price will they ultimately pay for their innocent willingness to forgive?" What price would she pay?

Or her sisters? And was it already too late for them all? For even as she hurled accusations at him and watched the darkness gather on his features, she yearned to be back in the warmth of the water with him, forgetting anything about the past and the future. Living, as it were, only for the next moment and the new sensation it would bring them. A part of her knew she was being unfair, but she'd rather it be so than be deceived by a MacKay Laird.

"Ye really have the audacity to lecture me about the well being of my clan?" His voice gained volume, as did the heat of his glare. "When ye let yer anger at me and mine punish the *innocent* ye seem so worried about?"

Was he really turning an accusation on *her*? "*We* were not finished living either, but the choice was ripped from us. We died innocent, and we *remain* innocent!"

"Tell that to Kevin when he's starving without his herd. Or the village over the hills from *yer* washhouse where the milk is spoiling. I mourn for what befell ye and yer family, but yer Fae curse is spilling into the lives of Strathnaver and I'll not have it!" Rory stalked forward and only then had Katriona realized that she'd been drifting back in the wake of his anger. "I'll do whatever it takes to stop ye."

Stunned, confused, and enraged, Katriona warded him off by releasing a wailing keen of such incredible pitch that the tub shattered. Rory dropped to his knees, holding the sides of his head and baring his teeth at her. She watched in despair as the water that had brought her the first touch of warmth she'd felt in as long as she could remember flooded the chamber, soiled and chilled by the stones.

Rory hated the sound of her cry more than just about any other on the earth. It reverberated through his body with its otherworldly force, shriveling him up until he curled in upon himself. No one had wielded the power to drive him to his knees since he was a small boy, and perhaps that galled him the most.

A loud crash and a tortured bellow told him that someone had burst through the door and was now reaping the full brunt of Katriona's wails.

A bright light flashed across Rory's vision, momentarily blinding him, and then the wail abruptly stopped. He caught his collapsing weight on his hands, blinking rapidly to rid himself of blind spots.

He expected Katriona to be gone when he finally gathered himself enough to look up, but her absence screamed as loud as she had. Too much had been said and left unsaid between them. How would they ever bridge the chasm between their worlds? How would wrongs be righted, ties severed, and wounds healed?

The impossibility of it all hung like a lead weight in his chest.

Rory let his head drop in defeat, staring at the inch of bathwater surrounding him and soaking the stones of his floor, spreading out toward the open doorway.

"Holy Christ, ye've a Banshee!" Lorne yelled into the silence while using the doorway to pull himself to his feet.

"I fucking told ye that this afternoon," Rory snarled.

A small but steady trickle of blood leaked from Lorne's ears and one nostril, which he unceremoniously wiped with the back of his hand. "Wha'?," he cried. "I've ringing in my ears like ye wouldna believe."

Rory hoped like hell the damage wasn't permanent.

Lorne staggered to his side, helping Rory to stand. "Did she get close enough to touch ye?" he boomed. "How did ye survive?"

Rory shook his head to clear it. She'd touched him deeper and more thoroughly than any other. Aftershocks of her power singed across his nerves even still, reminding him of the excruciating bliss her touch and her body had manipulated from him. And though he'd been lost in a place of pleasure tinged with pain, through the surprise in her emerald eyes, he'd glimpsed a hint of something deeper. More familiar.

Possession.

"*An Dìoladh.*" A husky, feminine murmur sounded from the doorway.

"Huh?" Lorne shouted. "Speak up, lass!"

"Kathryn." Rory nearly choked on the word, waving at his steward to be quiet. Albert rushed around the doorjamb brandishing a sword that seemed a mite too large for him. He pulled up right behind Kathryn, his un-tucked tunic and disheveled dark hair matched the sleep-hazed alarm in his dark eyes.

"That's why you lived, isn't it?" Kathryn continued as though she hadn't noted his arrival. "Because Fae magic cannot affect one of *The Returned* or *The Rewarded.*" Her sky-blue eyes glittered with soft curiosity tinged with concern. Clad only in a thin white nightgown and slippers, Kathryn hovered on the edge of the pool of water. Her soft, graceful hands clasped in front of her as she took in the chaos.

Rory admired her calm demeanor, thankful that he had the presence of mind to cover in his tartan at least when he and Katriona had been arguing. "I'm sorry this disturbed you, my lady."

"The bloody hell is this, MacKay?" Fraser shouldered past his guard and daughter, his slipper squishing into cold, soiled water. His face turned a deeper shade of red. "Someone tell me what cursed noise awoke me. I felt as though my head would split in two!"

"They've a Banshee, Papa," Kathryn informed him as though she was discussing a new hound, putting a hand on his shoulder and drawing him back from the water.

"A— a Banshee?" His beady eyes widened to an almost normal size, eyelids disappearing into the sleep-swollen bags beneath. "I wouldn't believe such nonsense had I not heard it for myself!"

"A remnant of my brother Angus's short and violent reign, sir." Rory stepped forward, aware that his skin and hair still was still slick with moisture.

Kathryn seemed to have noticed, her gaze sliding down his body along with chilly droplets from his hair. So did Albert, who glared poison at him through narrowed eyes.

"Are we in danger?" Albert demanded. "Should we be gone from here?"

Rory froze, feeling as though everything he needed was slipping through his fingers and spilling to the floor. Not just for his future, but for the survival of their clan. What if the Frasers left? What if Katriona's vengeance caused everyone to starve?

"Don't be silly, Albert," Kathryn chided. "Everyone knows a Banshee is no danger to anyone else until her vengeance is complete. If her aim was your brother, Laird, then she's harmless as anything but a nuisance. If you were her intended victim, then she'll fail to kill you and give up eventually."

"Ye call this harmless?" Lorne's voice boomed. I'm going to have to read yer lips for who knows how long!"

Kathryn shrugged delicate shoulders. "Are you closely related to the Laird?"

The men looked at each other. "Second cousins, I believe," Rory supplied.

"Well, there you have it." She looked pleased. "Perhaps you're a wee more susceptible because of your blood, but still in no real danger."

"The danger of goin' deaf seems danger enough," Lorne muttered.

Rory ignored him. "How do ye know I'm *An Dìoladh?*" He could kiss her for her level head. But wouldn't, of course. Not with the sweet taste of Katriona still lingering on his lips.

Shame heated his chilled skin. How could he dally with Katriona when a woman like this was waiting for him? She was one of the innocent. Still alive. Still hopeful. Obviously prone to optimism. This was what he wanted.

Wasn't it?

"Even we Lowlanders enjoy Highland gossip." She gifted him with a self-effacing smile that enhanced her sweet, golden loveliness. "A bard of Inverness was there the day you awoke all those years ago. He wrote a lyric entitled 'Rory's Return.'"

Rory blinked. "There's a song about me?"

"Aye, didn't you know?" She looked at him through shy lashes and Rory summoned a smile for her. "Maybe I'll sing it for you sometime." His fiancé was such a beauty. But when she looked at him with soft suggestion he felt—nothing. No stir of arousal. No flicker of anticipation.

Albert snorted.

"Yes yes, very good." Fraser swatted at Albert and shooed at his daughter. "Let the Laird get cleaned up. We'll discuss this in the morning." Before leaving, he shot a serious look at Rory that told him he wasn't in the clear just yet, thousand men or not.

Once the door shut behind them, Rory turned to Lorne. "Are ye all right?"

Lorne nodded, itching at his ear. "Aye, it's starting to get better," he said in a more normal register.

"Thank ye, for rushing in when ye did. How was it that ye were so close to my chamber?"

Shadows appeared in Lorne's eyes and his arms dropped to his side. "I didna want to say with yer lady here and all, but I was coming to wake ye about a different matter altogether."

Rory's heart dropped into his stomach.

"More disturbing news from the clan," Lorne stated reluctantly. "A flock of crows flew into Achfery and old Hamish MacKay died at his own supper table thirteen minutes after they arrived. And more herds are said to be struck dead or ill in the Balkins. The clan elders want to meet tomorrow night to discuss what is to be done."

A headache burned behind Rory's eyes and he pinched the bridge of his nose.

"Think ye it has to do with the Banshee?" Lorne asked. "Or her mother?"

"I'm starting to believe it's so," Rory sighed. "Did ye know that Angus burned them to death?"

Lorne lifted a hand to the back of his neck. "I had my suspicions, what with his frustration over the middle one and her refusal of him. He... really went a violent kind of mad toward the end there."

Rory could do nothing but nod.

"What do ye want to do about this?" Lorne asked.

Katriona's face swam in front of Rory's eyelids. Her rage covered a pain wrought by anyone's greatest terror realized and the memory of her flesh melting from her bones in a fire his own brother ignited. Once there had been warmth behind the bright green of her gaze, an endearing vulnerability. A need to be loved for who she was and not overlooked.

That need had spoken to Rory in a very powerful way. He'd often fantasized of gathering the courage to offer to fill that need.

His brother had stopped him, of course. Truth be told, he dared not bring a woman into the same household as his family. Though he'd grown large and strong enough to deter any danger from his father, he'd always worry about the safety of a wife.

No woman should have to live like that.

The mistrust and fear of her family had also seemed like an insurmountable obstacle. He'd known they regarded him the same as both his father and brother.

Monster and marauder.

Despite his best efforts, nothing had changed.

"Should we send 'round for the old washer woman?" Lorne suggested.

Rory thought of their dire situation. If the herds died, his clan starved. If they were weak, their enemies the Sutherlands would sweep through with destruction like they'd never seen and leave their bones for the MacLeods to pick over.

But could he submit an old woman to burn for the second time in her life to appease the masses? Didn't that make him as much a monster as his brother and father? What if it was one of Katriona's sisters wreaking the curse upon the land and he angered them further? Kathryn could very well be mistaken regarding their harmlessness.

"Nay," Rory gritted out. His mind was made up. The Banshees had to be dealt with, and he only knew of one man powerful enough to rid him of them.

"Send for the Druid."

Chapter Six

The washhouse nestled beneath a gently sloped but tall hill on the banks of Loch Caladail. The icy sea wind that blew from Cape Durness screamed through the craggy limestone gorge on the opposite side of the knoll and broke upon the hill, buffeting the ruins from the worst of the foul weather.

Katriona turned to Kylah, who perched next to her atop the large pile of unused firewood, watching their mother fitfully sleep in the unused hearth beneath a warm pile of old furs. "She cannot go on living like this," Katriona muttered. "I'm surprised she lasted the winter without a fire."

"'Tis her hatred that keeps her alive." Kylah didn't take her eyes from Elspeth to reply. "And the warm food and layers of clothing that are left."

"And us." Kamdyn supplied from the stony arch that was all that was left of their doorway. "She doesn't want to leave us behind."

Katriona didn't tell Kamdyn the dark thoughts she'd been harboring about their mother during the last few days. Elspeth had been inconsolable after the death of their father for months. She hadn't been strong enough to cope with losing her daughters the way she did. She'd cast a spell and struck a deal with a Faerie to keep her daughters from leaving *her* alone. Not the other way around.

"Any sign of it?" she asked after the bundle of food and supplies delivered regularly under their alder tree. Every day except for Sundays.

Kamdyn shook her head, her lovely copper hair stirring with the movement. This had been the second time she'd gone to check, and the tree remained empty.

It was only Thursday.

"You never did tell us if you had any luck at the Laird's keep today." Kylah still didn't meet her eyes, but she'd had trouble with eye contact since that horrible night. Her gaze rarely left the ground. Her voice rarely rose above a whisper. She was truly a shade, lurking about in the shadow of her grief and pain and, Katriona suspected, her shame.

Katriona herself battled shame as she felt the full weight of her sisters' expectant stares. How could she confess to them that she'd not only failed them, but she'd further betrayed their purpose by allowing Rory to kiss her? Worse than that, she'd kissed him back.

And liked it.

More than liked it. Even now, in the chilly wee hours of a misty Highland spring morning, the heat of Rory's mouth still lingered on her lips. She felt—singed by an invisible brand, weakened by the soft emotions threatening to leach his warmth into her cold heart.

And yet, a part of her became angrier at the thought of what had happened between them in his chambers. He'd waited until she was *dead* to act upon his desire for her, to introduce her to yearnings never to be fulfilled and pleasures always to be denied. Then he'd shown her the love he'd borne his evil brother and ended their interlude with ridiculous accusations.

Rory obviously didn't understand Fae curses.

"Katriona?" Kamdyn's worried prompting brought her back to the grey-tinged present. "You look so bleak. Did he do something to harm you?"

"Nay," Katriona answered gently. "What can he do to harm me now? It was I who hurt him." *And he'd liked it.*

"But he still resisted you?" Kylah asked. Her soft green light pulsed brighter, but the emotion never reached her lovely almond eyes.

Rory absolutely hadn't resisted her. "I was again unable to kill him," Katriona evaded.

"What happened?" Kylah persisted.

"Someone's coming." Kamdyn's worried proclamation saved Katriona from having to decide whether to lie to her family or worse, tell them the truth.

"Who is it?" she demanded.

"I don't know, but I see a lantern there, through the mist." Kamdyn pointed to where the road, more like a well-worn path a few spans from their ruins, led around the Loch toward the wide and shallow waters of the Kyle of Durness. "There have been rumblings in the village of witchcraft," Kamdyn worried. "I overheard someone talking about coming for mother the night before last."

"They won't harm her," Katriona vowed.

"But we're powerless against anyone until we carry out our vengeance, and there's no chance of that now," Kylah despaired.

"We're still Banshees, are we not?" Katriona hissed.

"Aye," Kamdyn nodded and Kylah lifted a dainty shoulder.

"We might not be able to kill them, but we *can* frighten years from their lives."

Kylah's gaze sharpened with interest.

"I don't know..." Kamdyn's reluctant voice irritated Katriona. Normally, her sister's sweet nature was endearing, but tonight she needed to be strong.

"Do you want something to happen to Mother?" she snapped.

"Nay." Kamdyn's eyes brightened with tears. "I just... I don't have any practice frightening others. What if I bungle it?"

"Just don't."   Katriona drifted through the burnt-out window and let her Banshee rage brighten the blue aura around her. As when they were alive, it fell to her to handle the situation.

Some things never changed.

Katriona opened her mouth to prepare for the loudest, most terrifying keen she could muster. However, instead of the torch-carrying mob they'd feared, the mist-concealed road revealed one lone lantern now perched on the ground next to the hollowed-out alder. Bending to stuff a familiar bundle inside was Bridget MacKay, lead housemaid for the Laird's keep.

Her presence stunned each of the sisters into absolute silence.

"If I didn't need the extra wages, I'd set this bundle ablaze," she murmured to herself in a grumpy brogue. When she finished stowing the package, she straightened her cloak, held a hand to her lower back as though it ached, and turned.

The frightened scream she produced could have put every one of the Banshees to shame.

"*Haud yer Wheesht,*" Katriona ordered. "You'll wake my mother."

Bridget's scream cut off immediately, but her mouth dropped open and clamped shut a few times, reminding Katriona of a daft lake trout. "D-don't kill me," she begged. "Katriona... I had nothing to do with—anything. I'm just taking care of Elspeth." She gestured to the bundle.

"Why do you leave this here?" Katriona demanded. "I've heard you murmur against my mother in the village."

"I meant no harm by it!" Unflattering wrinkles appeared as her face crumpled, proving her older than the eight and twenty years she claimed to her dwindling number of male admirers. "I just do as I'm bade to do. Please don't hurt me, I have family in Keoldale-upon-the-Kyle who depend on me. I walk this road home every night and bring the package I'm paid to deliver. I've been doing it for nigh on a year now."

"Paid by *whom?*" Katriona's heart sank as she'd already guessed the answer.

"By the Laird, Rory MacKay."

Katriona barely registered the astonished gasps of her sisters. They'd never known. *She'd* never known who'd shown their mother this mercy. They'd only ever been grateful. It made sense. Bridget generally walked home earlier, during the witching hour.

This changed everything.

"Laird, I wouldna believed if I didna see it for meself!" Carraig MacKay was a gnarled fisherman with a flair for the dramatic, yet his words still carried a heavy weight. "I stayed out until the tempest drove me to shore, and every time I pulled in my net, I'd caught nothing but dead fish."

The murmurs of the gathering MacKays swelled within the hall and Rory caught words not swallowed by the thick tapestries. *Curse. Witch.* And *Banshee.*

Such news always traveled with astonishing speed through the Highlands.

"Aye, and now what has stricken the sheep, spread to the cattle!" Hugh MacKay called.

"Forget about the cattle." Saoirse MacKay, the butcher's wife, swatted a chubby hand at Hugh. "The olde and the bairns are sick with a mysterious fever."

Rory surveyed his clan council with a grim sense of urgency. In truth, he'd given anything to trade places with Lorne. All his steward had to do was cross the wide and icy Kyle and ride hard through the sea gale to the west until he hit the Faerie mound called *Cearbhaig.* Then, he'd angle around it to the right until he found the golden sands where the *allt dubh* or "The River Black" met with the ocean. Then he'd have to paddle a span around treacherous black rock cliffs until he reached the "Black Caves" wherein lived the most feared and reviled man in all the Highlands.

Easier than facing the expectant stares of his clan.

Checking the time, Rory calculated that Lorne had been gone all of twenty four hours. It now neared midnight, and if he survived the journey and never rested, Lorne still couldn't be expected back with the Druid for at least another five hours . . . at the very least.

That was if the arrogant bastard agreed to be summoned at all.

"Is it true ye have a Banshee?" Carraig lifted a brow that had never quite separated into two.

Rory sat back in his tall chair and pinched the bridge of his nose. He keenly felt the presence of Kathryn Fraser and her father standing close behind him. Not Albert, though he kept the man in his line of sight. One didn't put such a man behind him and expect to keep his head.

Seeing no reason to deny Carraig's question, he answered, "Aye, I've a Banshee, but I've sent for someone to take care of it."

"How is it that yer no' dead?" Saoirse demanded.

Carraig bristled. "Ye daft woman, *this* is Rory MacKay. His knack for survival is *legendary*." Sweeping his arm to address all assembled, he lifted his salt-roughened voice. "First he returned from the brink o' death when he was but a lad. Then, he led the charge in the skirmishes wi' the Sutherlands at a mere twenty and three, a war that lasted seven grueling years. He returned from each battle with nary a scratch, bathed in the blood of our enemies."

Rory rolled his eyes; the man should have been a bard instead of a common fisherman.

"And now!" the old man continued, rushing forward and clapping him on the shoulder. "Through a stroke of luck for him and our clan, he's the second-born-son-turned-Laird who survived a Banshee."

"What about the rest of *us*?" Saoirse cried. "*We* might not survive yer Banshee."

Rory ignored the *stroke of luck* comment. He was fair certain neither Connor nor Roderick MacLauchlan's sword arm was named "luck."

"I canna be certain the clan's difficulties are caused by the Banshee," he assured the crowd. "Even so, I'm taking measures to be rid of them."

"Them?" Hugh bellowed. "Ye mean there's more than one?"

"Aye." Saoirse swung at Hugh's burly arm as though she gripped a meat cleaver. "Didn't ye hear Bridget's tale when she came into town this morning? She saw them, the Washerwoman sisters, lurking in the ruins with their bedeviled old mother. She barely escaped with her life."

"That's not exactly how she told it," Carraig corrected her. And if *he* cried an embellishment, then something must be rotten.

"I always thought Elspeth MacKay was a witch," Saoirse mumbled.

"Yer just sayin' that because yer husband asked for her hand first, but she refused him for Diarmudh, the braw smithy," Hugh laughed. "He had to settle for you instead." His bright orange hair flashed as he ducked her fist again.

"What's yer plan to fix this, Laird?" Carraig prompted him, a supportive smile on his face. "Ye said ye'd sent for someone?"

Rory loved and resented the kind old fisherman for the devotion and trust he read in his eyes. What if his plan failed? He found himself equally conflicted regarding Katriona and her sisters. They had every right to be what they were, but why did they insist on taking their anger out on their entire clan? What if the bairns started to die of the fever? What kind of woman would allow such a thing?

"I summoned the Druid."

Rory's announcement was met with shocked silence.

"Do you think that wise?" Fraser stepped forward. "Shouldn't you send for a proper cleric to get rid of the Demons?"

Rory bristled a bit at the man's calling Katriona names. He wasn't a part of this. He didn't get a say in how it was handled. And, as soon as he and Kathryn were married on the morn, Fraser would be off toward MacLauchlan country to collect his thousand men.

The betrothal contract between him and Kathryn had been signed after a long discussion and a little more bartering over the dowry. What with the Banshee troubles, Laird Fraser seemed to think that affected the price of grain.

Miserly old bugger.

"They're not demons," Rory corrected. "They're creatures of the Fae now. Souls yet to be laid to rest."

The tall doors to the hall burst open with all the force of the storm raging outside.

Rory surged to his feet as a timely flash of lightning silhouetted three black shadows against the silver-streaked sky. The most astonishing sight wasn't the Druid himself but his unlikely companions.

Flanked on either side by a magnificent red stag and a light-footed she-wolf, Daroch MacLeod didn't just step into the dry, torch-lit hall, he advanced upon it.

As was their custom, many of the five gathered elders of the clan council made various signs of protection against him. Some olde, some new.

A mocking sneer twisted Daroch's sinister features into something jarring and unseemly.

Unease tightened in Rory's gut, but he was a desperate man.

"Ye're all fools if ye think that those signs ye make protect ye from anything." His words were lent a spectacular darkness by his harsh voice. "Most especially me."

The silver wolf at his side let out a low, threatening growl.

"MacLeod." Unwilling to be intimidated, Rory stepped out of his place at the head of the council table by way of greeting.

The Druid's eyes were an unsettling color, too light to be called brown, too dark to be called green. They were like him, situated in some abandoned, unthinkable in-between. They became lost behind the shocking array of tattoos claiming the left side of his face and reaching across the boundaries of his strong nose and cruel brow as though to portray the inevitability of their accessing his right side eventually.

Rory had only laid eyes on the man twice before in his adult life, and he'd known him to darken his flesh with the black silt of the *Allt Dubh*. He valiantly tried not to stare at the markings now, likely uncovered by the violent storm from the looks of the smudged streaks on his right cheek. He couldn't tell if the man's long, snarled hair was truly black or made so by the same means.

"My God, MacKay," Fraser sputtered from behind him. "What is the meaning of this—this profane sacrilege?"

"Calm down, Father," Kathryn's soft voice sounded closer and Rory turned to see her glide forward to rest an elegant hand on her father's arm. "'Tis how things are done here in the Highlands still. Not everyone's ways are your own."

Bestowing his intended with a warm and grateful smile, Rory turned his attention back to the Druid.

Daroch MacLeod regarded Kathryn with an intensity that Rory didn't appreciate.

"I had not expected ye for some hours, yet, but I thank ye for coming."

The Druid stared at Kathryn for a moment longer than was appropriate before turning his startling attention back to Rory. "I had some companions to aid me with swiftness." MacLeod turned to the wolf first and bent to it, touching it firmly beneath the throat and motioning to the door with his eyes.

The wolf's golden glare touched upon every soul within the room before turning and padding back the way it had entered, and fading into the stormy darkness.

Next, the Druid turned to the stag. Pressing his forehead to that of the powerful animal and pushing it back one step toward the door.

The stag looked like it would argue, but in one dexterous bound, he leapt away from Daroch and also plunged into the night, leaving a departing pile of scat at the top of the entry stairs.

Saoirse huffed, as though the animal had made a personal remark.

Maybe it had.

"Where's Lorne?" Rory asked.

"What did ye do to him?" Saoirse demanded.

The Druid silenced her with a shrewd look tinged with wildness. "Ye'll be dead within two years." The dispassionate tone of his voice directly contrasted with his demeanor.

Saoirse gasped, "Ye just cursed me! Everyone heard it. I'll see ye burned for that!"

Daroch sighed. "Yer hands tell me ye're a butcher's woman, but the condition of yer skin and eyes and the ingredients on yer collar prove ye're too often at the Baker's. Due to yer sheer size, it's obvious that ye visit the pastries rather than the man who makes them, but I predict that if ye do not stop gorging yerself, yer pancreas will give out and ye'll be dead within two years."

Saoirse paled, then reddened. "My—what?"

"Pancreas," The Druid's lip curled. "Likely that wrapped foot will rot first and poison yer blood, but either way, yer fate remains the same."

Her chins doubled as her mouth dropped open in silent protest. Closed. Then opened again.

"Yes, eat more fish. That should help." Twin strings of swansea, whelk and eigg shells clinked together from the knotted braids at Daroch's temple as he dismissed Saoirse and surveyed the assembled council, his swiftly moving regard leaving no detail uncalculated.

"You just cursed her!" Fraser thrust his stubby finger at the Druid.

"I just *warned* her." Daroch's eyes flashed as they collided not with Fraser's but his daughter, Kathryn's. "She has it within her power to change her fate by eating fibrous tubers, vegetables, and fresh meats, though I doubt she'll do it."

Dismissing the subject as inconsequential, the Druid addressed Rory. "Yer man was foolish enough to come to collect me with one horse. I left him in my residence with an assurance of *my* safe return and enough food for the appropriate time of my absence." His gaze touched Rory's, glittering with untold secrets and unrepentant derision. "There's no way out, unless one is an excellent swimmer, which he's not."

Rory's temper warred with his desperation. Yet, he forced as much diplomacy into his voice as he could muster. "Was that necessary?"

The Druid's face remained impassive. "That remains to be seen, doesn' it?"

"Ye have nothing to fear from me if you give me yer word he willna be harmed," Rory vowed.

"I give ye my word as a Druid."

"I'd rather take yer word as a man," Rory countered. "I know nothing of Druids, or their words."

"Obviously, or ye wouldna have called upon me to rid ye of a Banshee," Daroch sneered.

"Lorne told ye of my curse?" Rory asked.

The Druid shook his head, upsetting the musical shells again. "Nay, but she lurks right behind ye."

Chapter Seven

Kylah MacKay froze beneath the sudden regard of the entire great room. Why had she come to this place?

She'd felt the hollow echoes of intense pain and barely-leashed fury call to her as she emerged from the swirling grey of the cold Fae nether. It reminded her of what she was supposed to be feeling. What she couldn't make herself feel. Drifting in a span of endless numb ambivalence, the strains of this new and potent force of emotion drew her toward it with undeniable power. So she'd followed it.

And it radiated from somewhere in this room.

She scanned those closest to her. Lowland strangers. They were frightened, all but one.

Rory MacKay stood in front of them at the head of the table. His handsome bronzed features swiftly flicking through a display of shock, hope, disappointment— then pity and shame.

He knew what his brother had done to her. And he felt— sorrow.

He fed and cared for her mother, as much as he knew she'd allow from the likes of his family. The question remained, why?

Unsure of how to process this, Kylah became abruptly grateful that Rory had been absent that night. He stood taller and wider than all her assailants. His powerful arms would have caused her the most pain. His deep, heavy chest would have robbed her of the most air. His gentle, warm brown eyes would have confused her and given her the most hope for mercy. Indeed, she would have plead with him most fervently, cried and begged and gifted him with the loss of her dignity as well as her innocence.

Aye, better that he hadn't been there. Because hope was dangerous, and Angus had taken that from her first. Before he'd taken everything else.

The council table, full of familiar faces from her life, sat in stunned stillness. No one blinked. No one breathed. They just stared.

And Kylah wanted to scream at them all, if only to draw a reaction.

But she didn't. She hadn't screamed since the smoke billowing from her melting flesh had choked off her voice. It went against everything she'd become in the afterlife, certainly. And yet, she couldn't bring herself to do it. She didn't have the energy to produce one.

Then she saw *him*.

Sodden, torn layers of linen robes held together by a belt of vines draped over enormous, unimaginable power, whether natural or unnatural had yet to be shown. The relentless downpour streaked grime from his face, revealing a beauty touched by the Gods and then forsaken by them. The dark tattoo crawled up the muscles of his neck and knotted across the left side of his face drawing the eye away from his hard, full mouth to his severe eyes.

His gaze went past observant to intrusive.

Penetrating.

And all that keen intellect hidden by sinister markings of earth and ink concentrated on *her*.

Kylah swore the source of the beckoning misery came from him, but she had to be mistaken. Though his hair and tense stance bespoke an untamed element, his fearless stare revealed an indifferent petrifaction that rivaled her own.

"That's not..." Rory let out a loud hiss through his throat. "That's only one of them."

"Never heard of a silent Banshee before," Carraig, the fisherman breathed.

Hugh elbowed him, though he still hadn't blinked.

Kylah ignored them all. Her entire being focused on the man Rory had called to rid his clan of them.

Could the druid do it? Could he free them from their curse?

"Ye've wasted yer time." The druid's voice was like the man; harsh, dark, and arresting. "I willna help ye, MacKay."

"If it's a matter of payment—" Rory began.

"Nay," the druid interrupted, his notice swinging to the Laird. "Banshees are Cliodnah's creatures, and I doona cross purposes with the Fae." After tossing her a look that should have meant something, the man gave his back to the hall and melted into the storm.

Kylah felt released from a dangerous captivity, and she relaxed shoulders she hadn't been aware she'd tensed before her mind snagged on something the terrifying Druid had said.

Or rather, hadn't said. He'd told the Laird he *would* not help him.

He didn't say he could not.

Chapter Eight

"It was you." Katriona lurked in her usual dark corner closest to the bed, though it seemed less safe than in the past. She avoided glancing at the soft-looking furs and imagining Rory's tremendous body stretched beneath them. Instead she noted the worry lines etched on his forehead had deepened to match the pinched grooves sprouting from his eyes. They'd lost their amber fire, the irises dulled to a burnished bronze as though aged for centuries in the space of a few nights.

A wry smile played with one corner of his mouth as he shut the door, but he didn't look at her. "Tell me what I've done now." He undid the clasp of his Laird's badge and let his plaid drop from where it draped from his shoulder and fell across a sculpted chest. "Though I have to warn ye, I'm short on apologies or offers of reparations." His voice lacked the bitterness his words implied, carrying instead a deep soul-weary note that tugged at her heart.

"Why didn't you tell me it was you who'd been leaving food and supplies for my mother all this time?" Katriona knew she was bungling this. She'd meant to make peace, but for some reason, everything she said still escaped her lips as an accusation. "She wouldn't have survived without your help."

He found his bitterness in a dry chuckle as he bent to remove his boots. "I thought ye knew. Bridget has been paid to leave the supplies on her way home for months. Did ye think it was out of the kindness of *her* heart?"

Katriona caught the skeptical glance he tossed in her direction. "My sisters and I are pulled into a different plane during the witching hour," she explained. "That happens to coincide with Bridget's nightly journey home. Mother doesn't venture out of the ruins at night. We never knew."

He chuffed again. "Explains why she's not mentioned seeing ye until now." He discarded his sword from around his hips. Clad in only his kilt, Rory crossed to the fire, as though knowing its proximity protected him from her nearness.

Katriona drifted forward, drawn as always by his compelling presence and the hope of his touch. She watched him as he stared into the flames, his gentle eyes hardened by acrimony. His posture wary and features guarded.

She hated to see him like this. These were the moments that created wicked, compassionless men. Someone at the end of their rope, exhausting all the resources of kindness and equitable integrity and still losing ground, grasping for a foothold, for another elusive option. Often the answers that presented themselves were chained to the kind of sins that stained one's soul. Katriona would have given anything to know what he contemplated in the flames.

"Why?" It was a dangerous question, but she had to ask.

"Ye know why," he told the fire.

She feared the knowledge. Exalted in it. Doubted it. But he was right. It was the reason she'd sought him out in his chamber, though something kept her from truly accepting it.

"I need to hear you say it." She hovered ever closer, heedless of the flames.

He turned on her then, eyes flashing back to life. "You want me to say it was because I was a good and benevolent Laird who pitied one of the suffering in my clan, but that had nothing to do with it." He seized her shoulders, giving her a shake that would have rattled her bones had she still been alive. "I *loved* you. Gods help me but I did. For *years*. I rose every morning just to watch ye bring yer basket of deliveries to the village. I rode to the loch every evening hoping to glimpse ye emptying the wash basins. I adored yer laugh. Yer smile. The bossy, temperamental way ye loved yer sisters." He thrust her away from him, gesturing angrily with his hands. "I was never truly allowed to mourn yer loss, but I did. I mourned ye. And I thought of the only thing ye might have me do if ye'd been my woman, to care for and protect yer kin. I had Bridget deliver the goods because I knew yer mother had no love for my family, even before I knew about... what Angus had done."

Katriona trembled. Stunned by his unrepentant revelation. So many questions flowed through her, they crowded on her tongue and paralyzed it until one escaped. "You— mourned me?"

You loved me?

Did he love her still? It seemed impossible, after everything she'd done to him. Tried to do. After all the pain and death that stood between them.

"*Yes.*" He turned from her then, an astonishing glint of moisture clinging to his lashes. "Ye wanted me punished, Katriona, and ye'll have yer wish. I'll marry another in the morn, and promise my love to her, but the poor lass has no chance of ever receiving it. I'll lose ye again. I'll mourn ye again. And I fear that once was already too much to bear."

"Rory," she begged. Tears burned her throat and blurred her vision. Katriona put up a hand against his turned back to stanch the flow of his words and her tumultuous feelings, but he couldn't see it. She doubted it would have made any difference.

"I'm no better than my own kin," he hissed. "For it doesna matter how many herds are cursed, or people die, I'll not stop yearning for ye. I'll be surrounded by a ruined clan and a tarnished name and still my selfish heart will beat for ye. And because of the cruelty of my brother, the Fae, the fucking *Gods*, I'll be forever denied."

"*Nay.*" The word escaped on a gasp before the torrent released by the thawing of her frigid heart clogged her throat.

Rory went unnaturally still. Even the taut muscles of his back ceased moving with the force of his breath. He was waiting. He'd said everything he was going to say, and now he waited on her to redeem or destroy him.

Katriona swallowed around the raw emotion in her throat. "Not forever. Tonight... Tonight, I'll deny you nothing."

Nothing stood forgiven or forgotten between them. Nor did it have overmuch to do with how he cared for her mother, though that remained a part of it.

He'd been right, it *was* cruel. That he loved her. That the most beautiful, desirable man in all the highlands and beyond could pledge to her a heart so pure and true despite everything he'd been through. That she could have loved him just as passionately had she lived, and still, she'd fallen hopelessly in her afterlife.

Tomorrow they'd do what they must. She'd leave him and he'd marry another in a desperate attempt to save and strengthen their clan. Because despite what he claimed he'd always been a good and decent man.

He was the Laird the MacKay had always hoped for.

He was the man *she'd* hoped for, and in life she'd been too blind or too afraid to see it.

"Doona promise what ye canna give me, Katriona." The command escaped his lips as a plea. "If yer mine tonight, I'll demand much from ye, as it must keep me for a lifetime."

Rory turned to look at her and what he saw stole the breath from his lungs. He understood that others in his clan had often compared Katriona with her sisters and found her wanting. But to him—tonight—as always, she shone brighter than they ever did. The strength of her soul illuminated her features, demonstrated the lethal Fae power she wielded like a whip.

A dark and dangerous lust speared him. He'd barely survive the night, if luck was with him. Remembering the feel of her magic painfully animating him, made him hard and heavy with such a feral intensity, his stomach clenched and roiled.

Sea green eyes alight with heat and electric potency glowed from the pale incandescence of her skin. Reaching up to undo the clasp at her breast, Katriona released his gaze so he could track her ghostly robes as they hugged each blessed curve before revealing all to his hungry eyes. It disappeared into the nebulous mist at her feet, taking the last vestiges of his control with it.

"It is you who must be certain, Rory," she countered. Her dark hair swirled around pale shoulders, blown by unearthly wind. "For once I have hold of you, you'll be at my mercy." She drifted forward, her glow intensifying. "And when have you known me to be merciful?"

An alien sound escaped his raw throat. Something between a gasp and a growl. Every muscle tensed in anticipation the instant before he lunged.

The moment their flesh connected, Katriona became a part of him. She coalesced into something less ethereal and more corporeal. Her strong legs wrapped around his middle, her arms clasping him to her smooth, chilly body. Hands plunged into his hair, fingers raking his scalp as their mouths met in an explosive melding of need.

Her tongue met his with matching desire, sparring wetly as he staggered the few paces to his bed.

"Have ye been taken before?" he asked, needing to know what care to use with her. Because, though a feral beast of demanding lust was about to swallow them both, he couldn't bring himself to cause *her* fear or pain.

At least, not until she begged him for it.

"Aye," she admitted, pulling back a little, but allowing their breath to mingle. "In moments of desperate, spinsterish loneliness, I gave myself to another."

Rory closed his eyes, awash with equal parts relief and jealousy. He didn't have to worry about maidenly concerns, but he instantly hated anyone else who'd tasted of her passion.

He tossed her toward the bed, loving the way her glow reflected like sunshine on the animal furs. He would erase from her memory any thoughts of another, filling her with himself.

As the night sped toward inevitability, Rory felt parts of himself stripping away with his boots and kilt. He bared to her not his body, but his soul.

Nay, perhaps it didn't go that deep. Or perhaps it went deeper. All the learned artifice of titles, responsibilities and birthrights— indeed, courtesy, dignity, formality, and propriety, lay in shreds at his feet. Kicked beneath the bed he was about to debase.

Damn his soul, but he didn't care.

Rory rose above her, electrified by the lightning that flashed within her eyes.

His growl was the answering thunder as he took her lips again and settled atop her.

Distantly, he knew what was happening. Piece by piece, he was being disassembled by Katriona. When she took his mouth with her tongue, he lost the title of Laird. When she bit his lower lip, he forgot his family name. When she scored his back with her nails, his childhood disappeared.

He was born into this moment. With little promises of pain sweetened by unparalleled pleasure, she ripped away his being, leaving only a creature of base instinct. Driven solely by need and lust and hunger.

"I must have ye," he rasped, forcing a knee between her perfect, pale thighs.

"When have I let you have anything you wanted?" She bared her teeth in a predatory smile before surging her hips beneath him, unsettling his balance, and using that propulsion to roll on top of him.

Her legs wedged over his hips, grinding his cock against her sex. There she was wet, and she was warm. The heat of her shocked him compared to the coolness of her touch.

"I will do the taking, for once, MacKay." Her hand on his chest held him prisoner beneath her. Her small, pert breasts tantalizing his eyes as she lifted her hips.

He rose to meet her, to fill her body with him, to drive himself home.

The white hot burn of her power sliced straight to his cock and ripped a cry of panic from him. Not because of the pain, but because he feared the gathering of release he could already feel in his belly.

Her eyebrow rose. "This moment is mine," she informed him.

He lifted heavy arms and wrapped them around her ribs. "Ye said ye'd deny me nothing," he reminded her.

She made a soft sound and lowered her succulent mouth to suck at his earlobe. "I lied," she whispered before her sharp teeth bit down, eliciting a hiss from him before she drew back "It is *I* who will not be denied."

She took him then, sheathing him in one rapacious thrust.

Rory trembled with the effort it took to let her adjust to the feel of him inside her body. Her mouth fell open. Her breathing labored, she held him down, flexing her powerful inner muscles around his hard flesh.

If her magic couldn't kill him, this just might.

He knew it would be like this with her. No womanly self-consciousness. No coy batting of eyelashes and pouting of lips.

Just frank, open appreciation of the pleasure he could give her. She gave no quarter, no mercy, and expected none in return.

She'd accept no less than all of him.

The hungry animal he'd become began to writhe beneath her, moaning warnings and demands.

She put both hands on his chest, leaning all her weight upon it, her hair falling forward, blotting out every feature but those bright, Banshee eyes.

"This is what you want?" she asked, lifting and impaling herself again.

"*Aye*," he gasped, his fists curling at his sides.

She did it again. And again. In excruciatingly slow movements, stretching her feminine skin around him and testing the angles of his penetration with soft, surprised notes of pleasure.

Rory had thought she'd reduced him to as witless a life form as was possible before this, but he'd been wrong. His head lashed from side to side, sometimes lifting and straining to seek her mouth, which she held out of his reach with a throaty laugh that vibrated through her body.

Rory cursed her. He praised her. He said things he never thought a man should say. And still she maintained her slow pleasuring of herself upon him, never creating enough friction. Never allowing him to rise above a throbbing, aching, torturous desire.

"Kat..." he groaned, sweat blooming on his skin. "I... need..."

This time the darkness in her laugh matched his own. "I know what you need," she purred.

She reared back, opening herself to his gaze and speeding her thrusts until she rode him like the wild thing he'd become. With pure, vicious intent, her hand dropped to his hips and with the same power with which she'd taken him apart, she proceeded to recreate him.

His first release was a transformation. He became naught but flesh and fire, flayed open by a thousand white hot needles contracting each muscle until it seized with pleasure that surpassed the pain; and when it became too much, it subsided but only enough to allow him the option of awareness.

And yet, Katriona stayed true to her word. She continued her relentless assault on his body, on the organ that remained hot and hard and straight within her. A sadistic pride shone on her face, a wildness he'd not seen before.

She fell forward, both her hands landing on his chest, her radiant body thrusting and contracting with punishing force.

Rory opened his mouth to stop her, to tell her it was too much, that he needed to recover, but only throaty commands escaped him.

Harder.

Faster.

Fuck me.

Own me.

She took none of his directions, or all of them. He couldn't tell. But the force of a release teased his nerves and he strained every muscle to find it.

"Do it again," he begged.

Her smile chilled him. Soothed him. Frightened and excited him beyond capacity.

She used both hands this time.

Rory became more than his flesh. He became the pain. He melded with the agony ripping through him. It no longer held him prisoner. It released him from any bond he'd ever submitted to, and the ones he fought. He grasped Katriona's hips with punishing fingers, slamming upward until their bones connected.

She squeaked in surprise, a high-pitched sound of sex and submission. Yes. They would both dominate each other before this night was through.

They ground together, their sounds frenzied and unnatural as Rory forced her to find her pleasure. Her eyes widened with surprise. With the loss of control and a momentary trepidation of what was to come. But then her head whipped back and she let a keen that split the sky and caused the stones of his manor to quake. She clenched around him, pulsing with release heightened by the vestiges of her own punishing magic.

Watching her, Rory gave himself over to his own pleasure. His muscles jerking and quivering with the force of her magic and the strength of his release. He emptied himself into her, drilling home with powerful thrusts until her cries became human again.

And so did he. Returning to himself with more clarity than he'd ever before possessed.

Katriona collapsed atop of him, her forehead resting against the base of his neck, her hair spreading about his chest and ribs in soft waves. "I love you too," she panted.

His heart was broken, but it sang.

They'd always been meant for this. And duty. Death. Even the Fae couldn't keep them from the other's arms.

At least not tonight.

Chapter Nine

Until the pounding began on the locked chamber door, Katriona was only aware of their labored breathing scissoring through the stillness of the night.

"Rory!" Lorne bellowed though the heavy oak. "That keen was heard in the Lowlands! Are ye all right? Are ye slain?" A loud crash shook the rafters, as though the large man had hurled his body against the barrier. "Rory MacKay, answer me, damn you!"

"Go away," Rory groaned from where he lay still trapped and spent beneath her.

"It's my fault," she whispered. "They heard my scream." Lifting herself away from Rory's slick, magnificent body, she ghosted to the dark corner so Lorne would be unable to see her.

"If ye're dead in there, I'm going to…" Lorne paused, then the door trembled again beneath the force of his weight. "*Rory!*"

The Laird in question heaved himself from the bed. "Lorne, get ye back to bed! I'm unharmed."

A few beats passed. "I'd rather see for meself, if ye doona mind," came the muffled, dour reply.

Rory unlatched and wrenched open the door, but only wide enough to reveal his rumpled head and bare chest. "There, do ye see? Now go to bed, the Banshee is gone."

A smile found Katriona as she watched the firelight play off the golden skin of his muscular backside. It was a might paler than the rest of him, rarely seeing the sun, and for some reason, it endeared that part of his anatomy to her greatly.

"This plague of Banshees is going to end me before it's through," Lorne muttered. "I sent all the Fraser's back to their quarters for their safety."

"Tell them that everything's fine. They can go back to sleep," Rory assured him.

"What have ye been doing in there?" Lorne's voice turned suspicious and Katriona smothered a giggle. "I'd guess ye had yer intended with ye for a tup, but I just spied the lass in the hall in white as virginal as the holy mother."

Rory sighed so hard he seemed to deflate. "I've gotten little sleep tonight." The admission sounded like a complaint, but Katriona could hear the slight bit of mirth behind it.

"Aye well, refresh yerself for the nuptials tomorrow."

Rory nodded and shut the chamber door. "I plan to." he turned back to Katriona with his eyes full of mischief.

"I don't want to talk about the wedding tomorrow." Katriona's thoughts escaped her before she could rein them in.

"Nor do I." The gleam dulled and suddenly his heart shone through.

Katriona could see he felt all that she did. That he saw the same endless, lonely span of years stretched before them. Their arms full of purpose, but achingly, despairingly empty.

"Kat—" his voice broke, but he strode toward her, reaching out. "I need—"

She went to him, her needs mirroring his. Folding herself into his embrace, she lay her cheek on his chest and clung to his waist, listening to the sure, strong beat of his heart. She did her best to not let her emotions spiral out of control. The injustice of it all galled her, frustrated her. She could drown in "only if" and "should have been."

She raised her face and kissed him, her breath choked off by a lump of misery and loss.

Luckily, she didn't need to breathe. She was already dead. An insurmountable barrier to a life with the man she wanted.

Rory pulled away and cupped her face with tender, roughened hands. "Let me make love to ye, Katriona. We've enough of pain and punishment and much more yet to come by our parting. Let me show ye with my hands and mouth how very much ye mean to me."

And he did. Their tears sometimes turned their kisses salty. The slow, tender sweetness of his regard became its own kind of torture. And he did not release her until the stars began to disappear, succumbing to the silver light of dawn.

Rory smothered another yawn behind his hand, earning him a sharp jab with Lorne's elbow. "If I was yer wife, I'd kill ye for yawning through the entire ceremony and now the bride's dance."

He turned to meet Lorne's disapproving scowl. "If ye were my wife, I'd save ye the trouble and kill myself."

Lorne harrumphed, and then shuddered. "What will ye do if one of the Banshees show during yer wedding night?"

Clearing his throat, Rory found the soft blue eyes of his wife as she pranced in a circle with the other lassies, and bared his teeth in what he hoped was an encouraging smile.

Her full lips lifted, as well, much to the cheers and pleasure of the MacKay clan, feasting upon meat her dowry had supplied.

"They won't." A sharp pang stabbed Rory in the chest where a dull ache had opened a gaping void he feared he would never be rid of. Maybe, in time, the ache would subside. Maybe he'd fill the emptiness with children and bounty and a successful rule of one of the Highlands' largest clans.

But in every darkened corner, in every screaming wind, he'd search for Katriona's eerie blue glow and mourn.

"How do ye know?" Lorne asked.

Because she promised I'd never see her again...

Doing his level best to show the assembly that his eyes were only for the lovely, light-footed Kathryn, Rory quelled the pain threatening to overwhelm him. For no pleasure followed this damage, only more torment.

He wondered how much he should convey to his Steward. "I've struck a bargain," he admitted.

"With the *Banshees*?" Lorne's astounded voice rose over the raucous music and Rory took his turn elbowing the man. "Doona ye ken that any bargain struck with a Fae creature is well nigh a curse?"

Rory frowned. He was cursed from birth. Cursed with a greedy, violent father. Cursed with a deviant, selfish brother. Cursed with dying herds and spreading plague, and bloody Banshees. Cursed to live forever without the love of his life. The worst curse of all would be pretending to love his wife, because she didn't deserve to be married to a man who pined for another.

Why not add another curse to the pile?

Standing upon the dais in his great hall, Rory could see every cheery face alight with warmth and ruddy from the closeness of so many bodies. More than five hundred MacKay packed into Durness for the festivities, though not all of them could be contained in his hall alone. Rowdy pipes, strings, and drums lifted the pulse of dancing and laughter to deafening. Movement became more animated as Highland scotch and ale flowed from bottomless spouts. Bawdy calls and whoops kept rhythm with the dancing women as they lifted their skirts and kicked out their ankles, producing a feminine thunder upon the floor.

In the middle of it all, Kathryn spun and leapt, danced and clapped with the vitality of a happy bride. Her golden locks spilled down her back from intricate braids and her face glowed with unmatched beauty and youthful vigor.

"Ye're the envy of every man in Durness, nay, of all that lays West of Strathnaver." Lorne clapped him on the back.

Rory smirked and tugged at the cuffs of his shirt, trying not to choke on the irony.

As she whirled through a circle, Kathryn waved to the only other scowling shadow in the room.

Albert.

"I doona like the look of that man," Lorne said darkly. "I'm confused as to why he didna depart with Fraser right after the ceremony to collect his men."

Rory shrugged. His apathy on the subject couldn't be greater.

"Though it was mighty unprecedented for the father of the bride not to at least stay for the feasting. Especially *that* one." Lorne snorted. "Never pegged him to miss a meal."

A chuckle escaped Rory in spite of himself. "Fraser has something up his sleeve with Albany and Stewart, though I doona ken what it is, nor do I want to. Albert is here to ensure that Kathryn settles in and plans to wander off within the week. 'Tis common among such rushed marriages so the lass doesna feel abandoned."

"No ladies' maid or such attendants?" Lorne scratched his thick beard.

"None that I know of. She can pick from a number of lasses in her new clan."

Lorne looked from Rory to Kathryn to the French-Scotsman and back. "Doona ye ever wonder if it's not as simple as all that?"

Albert's eyes burned at him from across the hall and Rory could feel a ripple of doubt wrinkle his brow. "Maybe neither of us come to this marriage with a free heart," he conceded. "But look around ye. My clan is fed. There are crops to be planted.

And, Gods willing, we'll make it through this last of the frozen season with replenished coffers and hope of better years than the last have been."

"Here. Here!" Lorne raised his tankard and drank deeply. Wiping his mouth on the cuff of his sleeve he heaved a great sigh. "Ye're a good man, Rory MacKay. Ye'll be a fine Laird. The finest this great clan has seen in ages."

Rory squeezed the shoulder of his friend. Judging from the past few Lairds, the standard wasn't so hard to surpass.

"Aye, 'tis a rare husband I've found." Kathryn's small hand wound into Rory's and he looked down into her smiling blue eyes.

Her beauty impressed him once more and, objectively, he was still a little stunned at the ease in which this advantageous marriage had come to pass.

All it has cost him was his heart.

Another yawn seized him with such intensity, his jaw cracked. "Ye'll haveta forgive me, my dear." He took Lorne's warning into account. "I'm afraid I didna sleep well last night."

A pang of guilt followed his admission, tingeing his cheeks with heat.

"Not to worry," Kathryn patted his hand. "You're certain to get enough sleep tonight to make up for the lack."

Lorne choked on his drink, some of it dribbling from the sides of his lip. He tried to catch it with his sleeve as he dissolved into a fit of uncontrollable coughing.

Rory clapped him soundly on the back. A knot of dread forming in his belly as he studied his dainty bride, shimmering in a gown the color of heather fields in August. What an odd thing to say on one's wedding night. Perhaps she truly was sheltered and completely ignorant of what was expected of her.

Puffing his cheeks out on a beleaguered breath, Rory realized the night would likely be longer and more taxing than even he had anticipated.

Katriona had thought Rory was the glutton for punishment, but she called that notion into doubt whilst lurking in the corner of his chamber. The music drifting from below shook the stones with merriment. And each burst of laughter drove black daggers into her still and silent heart.

For once she wasn't where she *should* be, at home to greet the Fae queen as summoned by her mother. She'd already bade farewell to her mother and sisters, after delivering the news of the bargain she'd struck with Rory. He'd provide a safe and warm home for Elspeth and her Banshee daughters for all the rest of her days. He'd make known the deeds of his brother against her family and publically clear her of any heresy or witchcraft. The washhouse would be rebuilt into a smithy and some other braw MacKay would work it.

In return, none of the Banshee sisters would harm an innocent MacKay. They would move along, searching for peace and finality in the afterlife.

And Katriona planned to do just that. Which was why, at this moment, Elspeth worked a spell to call Cliodnah to Katriona's side. So, upon the stroke of the witching hour, Katriona would pledge her soul to the Fae queen, giving her sisters a better chance of at least one of them breaking the curse and reclaiming a life.

Because life wasn't worth fighting for anymore, not without the man she loved. Drifting over to the bed, she floated into it, unable to touch it without touching Rory. She morosely wondered if he would be plagued with visions of their night together while he made love to his new bride upon it.

"You mortals are prone to such morbid thoughts."

Katriona started and turned to find Cliodnah by the fireplace, soaking in the warmth. The dancing crystals of frost winked and sparkled in the light of the flames turning silver to gold.

"Do the Fae not ever fall in love?" Katriona asked.

A brief flash of intensity sliced through the Queen's silver eyes before vanishing. "We avoid it," she droned. "Love and hate are too often used as excuses for stupidity and are corrosive to the superior immortal psyche."

Katriona couldn't think of an argument or an agreement, so she silently drifted to the Queen's side. "You're here to collect me, I gather, but would you grant me leave to abide until the witching hour?"

"I suppose that's only a handful of minutes." Cliodnah's gossamer gown rippled as she attempted a shrug, which still seemed too unsettling a movement for someone so inhuman.

"Thank yo—"

The door opened, and Katriona shrank back, too startled to cloak herself in magic.

Kathryn preceded Rory into the chamber, though both of their gazes skipped right past her and the Faerie Queen.

"My presence shields us from their notice. They will not see either of us unless I will it," Cliodnah explained. "This is your mark. The *An Dioladh*."

Katriona nodded, her words choked off by emotion as her eyes devoured the sight of his grim face.

"You turned your hatred to love in such a short time." The Queen conveyed mild amusement in her cold voice.

"Aye," Katriona whispered.

"Such is more common among your kind than you'd believe."

Katriona ignored the wry mockery of the Queen as she studied Rory's new wife. Her fair Anglo coloring must have come from a Teutonic mother, though the dainty sharpness of her beauty was decidedly Gallic. Thick lashes splayed from such lovely cat-like eyes and brushed the sweeping line of her cheek bone every time she gave a coy blink.

"Shall I undress you, my Laird?" She clasped her hands in front of her, watching Rory expectantly.

He blanched, then turned to stare at the fire.

At Katriona.

Or through her, rather. She wondered if he could feel the presence of her soul. If he could sense the pain and the love emanating from her.

Gods, this was torture. She should leave. This wasn't a memory she wanted to taint her eternity with. Rory with another woman in his arms.

In his bed.

"Kathryn," Rory hesitated, his big hands balled at his side. "I know coming here has to be a shock to ye. A new home, a new clan, a stranger for a husband. I'm amenable to letting ye adjust to yer life as mistress of this clan before..." He gestured to the bed and a deep red hue crept beneath his bronzed skin.

Aye! Not tonight. Not when his bed was still warm from their own love-making.

"That's kind of ye, husband, but in truth, ye have what I want and I'd like it tonight." Kathryn smiled shyly, which enhanced her unnatural beauty.

Katriona wanted to rearrange the features of her face, if only a little.

Rory's eyes flew wide and all the new color drained from his face and he sputtered for words but was ultimately unable to find any.

Katriona's eyes narrowed. Perhaps more than a little. Perhaps a great deal.

Cliodnah made a musical sound of amusement. "Jealousy. Now that's an emotion the Fae know quite well."

Kathryn sidled closer to Rory, who stood as though paralyzed. "Now, my Laird, let me make this easier for both of us." She reached out and undid his sword belt with deft, elegant fingers, easing it from his lean hips with practiced ease.

Rory grimaced and Katriona took comfort in his obvious discomfiture. He didn't want this golden paragon. He loved *her*.

Next his tartan was released from his shoulders, and then his loose, billowing shirt until the burnished expanse of his torso impressed more than the woman he knew stood watching.

"Oh my..." The Queen breathed behind her. "Now this *is* interesting."

Katriona turned to beg Cliodnah to take her away, but something stopped her. Perhaps it was a calculating brightness in Kathryn's normally gentle, somewhat vacant expression. Or the way her heart-shaped lips formed soundless words behind Rory's back.

"I have something for you," Kathryn's sweet conversational voice grated on Katriona's nerves.

She really couldn't watch this, nor could she look away.

"I had wine brought." Kathryn's eyes gleamed with feminine appreciation as she circled Rory and then turned toward the door. "A special vintage."

Katriona's fingers curled until her nails turned into claws.

"*Sit down and do not move,*" Kathryn ordered in a voice much darker than before.

Rory abruptly sank to the bed, his arms locked to his sides. His expression of apprehension instantly turned to alarm.

"What is this?" he demanded. "*Kathryn.*"

"What's happening?" Katriona asked.

"Can't you feel it?" Cliodnah condescended. "Magic."

Kathryn opened the door and Albert strode in, balancing a tray with a pitcher and two goblets. "From his own kitchen, my lady, with the cook's blessing for the merry couple." His sneer turned Katriona's veins into rivers of ice and she hurtled herself into their midst with a mighty keen.

Albert walked through her, his spine shuddering from a chill, but nothing else about his smug demeanor registered her presence. He set the tray on the bedside table and advanced on Rory.

Kationa screamed at him again. "Touch him and you die," she threatened.

No one turned to look at her.

"Kathryn, release me," Rory ordered, his muscles straining and bulging, but not moving one whit. He eyed his sword belt lying helplessly against the far wall as though salvation rested with it.

"Did I not tell you that my presence keeps you hidden from them?" The Queen asked.

"Please!" Katriona begged. "Do something."

Cliodnah shook her head. "This is none of my concern, I'm here to collect you."

Kathryn was pouring the wine into the two goblets.

The night sped toward the witching hour and Katriona knew she was running out of time. "Leave me until eleven. Give me long enough to scare them away."

Cliodnah pouted. "But I'm curious to see what unfolds."

"*Please!*" Katriona shouted.

The Queen held her hand up as though to silence an unruly child.

Kathryn pulled a vial out of the long sleeve of her lovely lavender dress. With a sickly sweet smile, she poured it into the goblet closest her. "I took a risk prompting father to let me marry you on the mere rumor that you were *An Dioladh*." She stirred whatever foul concoction she'd added to the deep red liquid. "Imagine my delight when your survival of your Banshee confirmed it."

Rory bared his teeth in a snarl at a taunting Albert, who bravely nicked his skin with the point of a sharp dirk. "'Tis a small man without honor who would wound an opponent who couldna defend himself."

Albert returned his sneer, opening up a small cut on the meat of Rory's shoulder. "Men with honor are rarely men with power," he countered. "And I owe you blood for each time you touched *my* woman." His next nick to Rory's shoulder was only deep enough to draw a welling of blood. Rory didn't so much as flinch, but his eyes burned with promises of retribution.

Helpless panic raced through Katriona. Each wound on Rory's flesh was relatively small, and still they stung her.

"I beg of you, my Queen!" she dropped to her knees. "Intervene and I shall do whatever you ask."

Cliodnah barely spared her a glance. "You'll do whatever I ask, regardless. And I am enjoying the spectacle."

"Aye, but... but..." Katriona quickly flipped through her childhood memories, trying desperately to find anything her father had said about the Fae and their mysterious ways. "Have mercy upon him, I love him. Dear Gods I love him so much, I can't bear to see this."

The Fae Queen's eyes softened on her. "I am sorry, but I promised another long ago that I would not interfere in the matters of mortals here in the Highlands. If I do, I'll owe him a boon."

"Interfere? But what about *us*? You turned us into Banshees," Katriona argued.

"Ah, but that was a deal struck by your mother who summoned me. A different situation than this." She motioned to the bed.

Katriona rushed to Rory, reaching for his straining hand but grasping onto nothing, a gut-wrenching, helpless fear overtaking her. "Then I must merely watch them kill him?" she sobbed.

Cliodnah shook her head, but did not move. "Maybe the nether will be kind and take you before then."

Chapter Ten

"I doona understand." Rory fought to stay calm, but frenzy crawled like a wild thing through his veins. He'd hated and feared being bound more than anything, even as a child. This was worse, for no mortal bounds held him, but some kind of treacherous magic. "Why do this to me?"

He gritted his teeth as the blade-happy bastard sliced into his chest. Luckily, Rory had a high tolerance for pain. But that tolerance didn't extend to traitorous Lowlanders, and if he ever managed to free himself, he was taking Albert's head and displaying it on a pike in the great hall.

And maybe his *sweet* wife's too. Perhaps there was more of his father and brother in him than he'd first thought because the idea of choking the breath from her delicate throat was making him hard.

"That's enough, love," Kathryn chided, clinking the spoon against the side of the goblet and setting it on the tray. Turning toward him, she eyed his naked chest with interest. "You are breathtaking. It is a shame I didn't have the time to lie with you as wife just once before I do this." She reached out and ran her hand over the grooves of his stomach.

His gut roiled with disgust. He'd rather get another slice from Albert than a caress from her.

"Kathryn!" Albert growled.

"Do shut up, Albert," Kathryn ordered softly. The large man complied with a sullen frown.

"As for your question," she continued. "As you're now aware, I'm a dark and powerful witch, and becoming a powerful witch often creates powerful enemies." She stroked the flat of Albert's dagger with her finger, and then sliced the pad at the tip. "Among my enemies are quite a few different castes of Faerie and you, my love, possess something that can eternally protect me from them." She drew her bleeding finger down his torso, creating a runic symbol.

Everywhere she touched burned like acid.

When she pulled back, she stuck her finger in her mouth and sucked at the wound. The flesh came away healed, as though she'd never cut herself to begin with.

"Ye were behind all of it," Rory hissed. "Weren't ye? The curdled milk, the diseased herds, the dead fish, and the sudden plague, that was all yer doing!"

"Perhaps you should reform your pagan ways." Kathryn turned back with an ironic smile and picked up both goblets, handing the one closest to her to Albert. "If you had a priest to read you your bible, you'd have recognized the omens of dark witchcraft."

The terrible accusations he'd flung at Katriona came back to haunt him. Of course she wouldn't punish the innocent for the crimes of his family. His clan was her clan. She'd lived among and loved them all. He'd watched her do tiny extra kindnesses for all those she and her mother served.

Gods he wished he would see her again. That he could tell her he was sorry. That he knew better now. That he should have known all along.

"This potion will separate your soul from your body, husband." Kathryn nodded to Albert. "And then it will pass to this amulet," she took a necklace from the bodice of her dress, and the rune shone silver despite the golden glow of the fire. "I'll speak the words *róin m'anam* and then I'll become *An Dioladh*."

Rory strained with all his might against the strength of whatever spell she used to incapacitate him. "Think of what ye do!" he warned. "Ye leave my clan without a Laird. How will they survive?"

"As your widow, I'll have *de facto* rights over the clan. It will pass to my father, I imagine."

"I'll die before I let a *Lowlander* have them," he vowed.

"Aye." Kathryn's lovely eyes flared with an azure fire as she took a long sip of her own goblet. "I rather expect you will."

Albert shoved his neck back and plugged his nose, dumping the wine into his open mouth. Rory did his best to close his throat. But it burned in his lungs and clogged in his sinuses and, in the end, his body betrayed him. The muscles of his throat contracted in a swallow and despair threatened to overtake him.

He even inhaled some and was racked with chest-rattling coughs as he tried to choke up whatever he could. He spat it in Albert's face, and received an elbow to the jaw.

Well worth it.

Kathryn laughed, a merry, musical sound so contrasted with her dark soul and all the more chilling for it.

A deep, primitive rage welled within Rory until all he could see were violent images of their slow and torturous deaths. Despite his carefully cultivated humanity, Rory was still a MacKay, Son and brother to two of the vilest warlords the highlands had yet seen. All of his heritage culminated into one pulsating burst of hate and violence. He couldn't voice threats, because words wouldn't be able to properly express the debauched fantasies he harbored.

All his life, Katriona had kept him decent. Without even knowing it, her kindness, her work ethic, the way her family conducted themselves toward one another had set an example which he'd striven to emulate, despite his upbringing. She'd *taught* him how to love. How to put the needs of his clan above his own.

But now she was gone. And lessons in humanity could be quickly lost to a man stripped of options. His sputtering quieted, but his eyes still watered as he watched Kathryn lift her goblet in a mocking toast, and tip her head back to drink deeply.

"I'll wait until morning to call for your men and play the confused, grieving widow" she taunted. "Albert and I will share our wedding night while your body cools on the stones." Picking up her amulet, she rolled it in her lovely fingers, letting it catch the firelight. "I wonder... How aware will you be trapped in my—"

Her eyes widened, a dawning realization was followed by frantic panic that didn't have time to manifest before her breath hissed from her throat and ended in a disgusting gurgle before her body crumpled to the floor.

"Kathryn," Albert whispered, and lunged for her, crouching over her lifeless body.

Rory couldn't believe his luck. After all her calculating, could she do something so ridiculous as to drink from the wrong glass? But he could swear she hadn't. He'd watched her put the potion in the goblet closest to her and force that very one down his own throat.

As abruptly as the spell had taken him, Rory's limbs were released, flowing with unspent ferocity.

Luckily, he had a perfect outlet. Honing in on Albert, he stood, testing his strength and balance, pleased to find no residual effects from her evil magic.

Albert noted his movement and slowly straightened to his formidable height, dirk still clutched in his hand.

"Make no sudden movements. I stand between you and your sword," he threatened.

Rory made some quick mental calculations of his opponent. Shorter than him, less brawny, but his lean, muscled body was likely adept at speed and accuracy. This man knew how to kill and had done so many times.

But so had he. "I doona need my sword to kill ye."

"Don't underestimate me, Laird, I'm the hero of Stewart. I've killed more English than you've seen in a lifetime."

Rory scoffed, "And I've killed many stag, but I wouldna be braggin' of it. The English are easy to kill." Advancing on Albert, his eyes tracked the dirk. "But there exists no world wherein the likes of *ye* would best a Highlander."

Albert moved with even more speed than he'd credited the man, and Rory barely dodged the slash to his throat. As they danced in a slash and parry, Rory kept his hands loose in front of him, quickly learning the Lowlander's movements. He took a nick to the forearm but counted it as a victory because he watched as Albert's eyes foreshadowed his next attack. He feinted high, but slashed low, aiming for the lethal vein in Rory's thigh.

Aye, the man was fast, but Rory was faster, and he caught the fist in which Albert held the long dirk in a viper grip, and landed a devastating punch to his throat.

Albert's eyes bulged, and he clutched at his throat while he fought for air.

Using the Lowlander's momentum to turn him and shove him against the wall, Rory's other hand smashed into Albert's elbow, forcing it to bend, pointing the dagger toward the traitor's neck.

Trembling and straining, much in the way Rory had against his magical bonds, Albert desperately fought Rory's superior strength as Rory inched the dagger toward flesh.

Their eyes locked and the dark part of Rory's soul rejoiced in the defeat he read in the other man's gaze.

"I do ye a favor," he growled. "I'm sending ye to join yer woman in the afterlife."

Rory didn't find the man's hand covering his throat much of a barrier as he slid the dirk between two knuckles and didn't stop until the hilt met flesh.

Wet gurgles escaped Albert's opened throat, but his skewered hand blocked the spray of any blood.

Rory let him drop to the stones.

Katriona felt physical pain for the first time in nigh on a year. Her shoulder and the side of her head throbbed from impact as she pushed herself from the stones. Holding her hand to her forehead, she groaned and accomplished a somewhat steady sitting position.

The first thing she registered was Rory standing proud and victorious over the treacherous Albert's dead body. At her sound, he spun to her, the gentle, umber eyes she'd come to love had been replaced with hard, sinister intent. He stormed to her with long, predatory strides, seized her by the shoulders in a bruising grip, and dragged her to her feet.

"Rory!" she cried. "You're alive!" Thank the Gods. He was her living, breathing miracle and now they could be together.

"Aye," he hissed. "And I'm deciding whether to kill my first woman with my bare hands or to let my clan burn ye alive."

Fear sliced through her. "Rory! It's *me*, Katriona."

He shook her roughly, doing no good for her already pounding head. "Ye have no right to even *speak* that name to me, witch!" He shoved her toward the door.

"Look at me!" she cried. "My love, *please*, look at me."

He jerked her toward him, snarling down at her, his features alight with a lethal temper. "Now is not the time to test me, woman, I'll—" His breath escaped him as his eyes locked onto hers. The hand that held her began to quake. "They're...

green," he gasped. "What magic is this?" He regarded her as he would a coiled serpent.

"Faerie magic." Katriona smiled and lifted her hand to point toward the fireplace where Cliodnah stood, unveiled, clutching the spitting, struggling spirit of Kathryn Frasier.

Rory's mouth dropped open and he squeezed his eyes shut, opened them, looked over at Katriona, then back toward the Fae Queen. His mouth looked as though it formed words, but none came.

"When Cliodnah heard that Kathryn was an enemy to the Fae, she decided to switch the goblets," Katriona explained. "Once Kathryn's soul was released, I seized the opportunity and leapt into her body." Katriona held an unfamiliar hand in front of her eyes, a joy bubbling through her veins that she'd never again thought possible. "This one's shorter than what I'm used to so, I'll need you on hand to reach for high things."

The man she loved turned to her, his hand tightening even more on her arm. His wounds had ceased bleeding. He appeared a fierce warrior, his features stark and lethal, though his eyes glittered with unshed moisture.

He moaned her name and crushed her to him.

"You can't call me that anymore," she chided against his warm chest. "It'll confuse everyone."

"My body is *not* yours!" Kathryn sputtered, still writhing in the queen's effortless grasp. "I can still take it from you! And mark me, you simple bitch, I will find the way!"

"Witching hour approaches." Cliodnah's lips twitched with delight. "I do appreciate when something unexpected happens." She nodded to Katriona and Rory. "For it so rarely does. I'll consider this an even trade. Enjoy what's left of your mortal life."

Katriona's smile widened at the dawning of a memory. "What were those words again? *Róin m'anam.*" She didn't feel the magical melding of soul or anything that could verify that the spell had any real merit.

But, judging by Kathryn's screams as she faded into the nether, she supposed the ancient words had done their job binding her soul with a new body. She pulled away from Rory, who was still apparently struck speechless.

She realized they were already married, technically. "I'm yours," she murmured. "If you'll have me in this body." She looked down at the form of the woman who'd betrayed him.

Rory gently took her face in his hands, his eyes boring into hers with such fervent intensity that tears welled in response.

"I didna love ye for yer body," he vowed. "It was yer soul I so treasured all this time." He took her mouth in a swift and burning kiss. This time, her warmth matched his and their heat ignited a flame that would last an eternity.

Rory pulled back, his breath much quicker than before.

"I canna express my joy at having ye here with me." He clutched her closely and his brow furrowed. "Though, I doona like the idea of calling ye Kathryn in front of people. Ye're nothing like her, and I'd just as soon not utter her name again."

Katriona had to admit she adored the fact that he felt that way. She bit her lip and regarded his dark eyes that were again gentle and so full of emotion. "In our most intimate moments you called me *Kat*," she remembered. "I think I would like it if you addressed me as such from now on."

That seemed to please him. "My Kat," he murmured. "Whom I like to stroke until she purrs with contentment."

Katriona's body warmed to the heated promise in his voice.

"I have to go for Lorne," he sighed, reaching down and wiping at the symbol drawn on his torso in blood with his tartan. "I need to move the body from my chamber."

Katriona nodded. "We'll say he attacked in a fit of jealous rage."

"Aye," Rory agreed, tucking her into his side as though he was loath to let release her, even for a moment.

"Then we should hie to the stables," Katriona suggested.

"Oh?" Rory's eyebrows lifted. "Are ye of a mind to take a midnight journey?"

Katriona shook her head and ran a finger over Rory's beloved lips. "I'm without any particular power now. But in the stables, we'll find all kinds of straps and whips and whatever apparatus may catch our fancy."

Rory's entire body tensed, a groan vibrating up from deep in his chest.

"You see," she continued, enjoying the quiver of yearning her body experienced in answer to his. "I mean to have my wedding night, husband. I'm afraid you won't get the sleep you were promised."

"I'll be all right." Rory steered her once more toward the door, his stride hurried and full of purpose. "I can sleep when I'm *dead.*"

A Highland Historical Novella
by the Bestselling Author of *Unleashed*

KERRIGAN BYRNE

"A mouth-watering hero in a story spiced with vengance.
Kerrigan Byrne will keep you on the edge of your seat."
                    –Anna Robbins, author of *Sunkissed*

REDEEMED

Redemption can be found
in the most unlikely places...

Redeemed

a highland historical novella

Chapter One

The question hung in the air like the heavy, inescapable stench of charred flesh or rotted meat. Everyone's eyes held the same breathless and hopeful expectation as they stared at her.

Kylah worried a part of her cheek with her teeth. What was she supposed to be feeling at this moment? What was the acceptable response they expected her to convey? She supposed she could react one of two ways.

Anger and betrayal. *How could you, my sister, marry the brother of the vile Laird who murdered us all? He carries their poisonous blood in his veins. I'll never forgive you for this...* et cetera and so on.

Or she could side with her youngest sister, Kamdyn, and her mother, Elspeth. *I trust your judgment and am ready to give the new MacKay Laird a chance to make you happy and right the wrongs done to our family...* Heaping platitudes of magnanimous forgiveness and such until everyone's worries were laid to rest.

Kylah studied the pale green glow she cast on the warm rugs and tapestries littering her mother's new cottage. Since she'd refused to move into the keep with the MacKay Laird, Rory had bequeathed to Elspeth a lovely warm home close to the castle so her eldest, Katriona, or Kathryn as she was now known, would be able to visit her family often. A kindness Kylah supposed she should be grateful for on her mother's behalf. She no longer had to worry about her comfort and survival. Elspeth now had a living daughter to care for her.

Gratitude. Relief. Yet more emotion she was supposed to experience but didn't.

She searched her soul for the warmth of sisterly affection and compassion, or the heat of rage brought on by the pain of disloyalty. But found—emptiness.

Less than that. She stood at the edge of a black, gaping abyss and kept squinting and straining to see the bottom like a bloody fool. She couldn't very well reach into it and pluck out an answer. It contained nothing.

She was nothing.

No one.

Therefore, why did her opinion even matter? Why was it her responsibility to grant them absolution for something they were going to do regardless? Because she was the only one who had been violently raped before she died?

"Kylah, dear, whatever you're thinking you can just say it outright." Kamdyn drifted toward her and leaned the specter of her shoulder next to Kylah's to show support. In fact, their outlines overlapped as the dead could no longer touch the living. Or each other. They just floated above the floor, little more than ghosts. Ineffectual Banshees. "What do you feel about Laird Rory and Katriona being married?" she repeated the question.

Kylah flicked a glance at the Laird in question. Even stone-faced and grim, Rory MacKay didn't resemble his twin brother Angus in the slightest. With the tall, broad frame of a mythic warrior, his handsome features consisted of different variations of bronze. Light hair, amber-hued eyes, and sun-kissed skin had once contrasted with the ugly pallor of his brother's ruddy complexion. Rory wore pity and remorse like a cloak, but hid defiance beneath it like a concealed dirk. He didn't take responsibility for his brother's actions, though they shamed and angered him.

Katriona stood next to her husband, hand clutched within his large palm, her eyes pleading for understanding. Kylah latched on to them, for Katriona's eyes were the only thing that remained her own. The rest of her body had once belonged to Kathryn Frasier, Rory's bride. Where she'd once favored her sisters, tall and slim with long, mahogany hair, she now resembled a Nordic princess. Blond curls tangled down her back, tamed with a circlet and braids. Pale skin touched with a golden hue covered lush curves most women only dreamed of possessing.

Katriona had never been a great beauty, but Kylah missed the honest angles of her sister's expressive face. The one she'd had before it was melted away in the fire Rory's brother had ignited.

Elspeth was the hardest to look at. And not because of the shiny, painful burn scars on her face, but the softer way she regarded Rory MacKay. With a little kindness, he'd won over her mother, but Kylah and Kamdyn remained unconvinced.

Elspeth reached out to Kylah, like she'd done so many times in the months since she'd spoken the olde words that'd turned her murdered daughters into Banshees. "Kylah, love, don't you want your sister—"

"It's fine." Kylah drifted back from her mother and attempted to force inflection into her answer, but from the looks on their faces, she'd failed utterly.

"Fine?" Kamdyn echoed. "Are you certain? You don't sound—"

"I said its fine," Kylah insisted. "I can feel that he loves her, and that she loves him. Is anything we say going to change that? Or have any effect on how they've chosen to live their lives together?"

Katriona and Rory looked at each other. His strong hand tightened around hers, and his solemn eyes softened with unabashed affection.

"Nay," Katriona murmured. "But we came here to explain. It happened so fast. We wanted to give you all a chance to express your feelings or concerns over what has transpired."

"I have none."

Katriona's brow wrinkled. A familiar expression on a foreign face. "None of which, feelings or concerns?"

Either. Both. She could pick one. "I've told you it's all right." Kylah hoped those words fared better than *fine*. They were all she had to give them.

"Your feelings have to be more complicated than that, sister."

"They're not."

"But dearheart..." Elspeth stepped forward once more and Kylah again retreated. It was a struggle to look at her mother. Not because of Elspeth's disfigured face, but because of the hurt and pity etched into her gaze. Her mother always reminded Kylah of that night. Because she'd been forced to watch. And Kylah relived those terrible moments before her death through the unspeakable horror in her mother's eyes.

Chapter Two

Spring had come early to the Highlands, and though Kylah could feel no heat, the setting sun gave off an illusion of warmth that proved almost as effective. Drifting aimlessly, she sought to lose herself among the emerald moors to the north and west of Durness. But even without the wild pulse of the waves to guide her, every dark loch, craggy knoll, and mossy plane on MacKay lands was achingly familiar. She'd explored them all as a girl, marked them, and learned of their names from sweet Carraig MacKay, the fisherman.

She wondered if she'd made a clean escape from her mother's home. Thinking back on it, she couldn't exactly remember what she'd said before plunging through the walls and into the rare Highland sunshine.

In the narrow alley, Hugh MacKay had accidentally walked through her, and the strange contact unsettled them both. Hugh, because he'd felt an icy and invisible chill reach into his bones despite the warm sunlight. And Kylah because it had felt as though he might rip away another part of her soul as they disengaged.

Another man inside her without her permission. More contact than she was willing to allow. Durness was too full of people. Of memories. Of emotions and desires not her own. Contentment and hope swelled within her clan at the dawn of a new spring. Their Laird had money and there were crops to be planted. The plague of witchcraft had passed on the night of

Rory's wedding, as suddenly as it had appeared. Everyone rejoiced.

Kylah couldn't bear it, so she'd sought the solitude of the wilderness.

Reaching the swift waters of the Kyle, she levitated over and idly wondered why some people considered walking on water so bloody miraculous. All one needed was a bit if Faerie magic. Her constant aura reached the western shore before she did and Kylah grimaced as she watched it spread out on the rocks before her, casting the growing shadows in her sickly green glow. Her sisters' auras had always been a bright and eerie blue. Why not hers?

Kylah's head snapped up from where she contemplated the ground. A strong ocean wind ruffled the grasses of the moor and brought with it a faint call of something she'd encountered before and never forgotten. A response rose inside her with a dark and powerful allure, drawing her toward the phenomenon before she made the conscious decision to follow it.

Highland streams and lochs flew past her with more speed than the swiftest horse. The *Cearbhag* River split around the *Cearbhag* Dune and crawled through the golden shore of the tiny bay of the same name. The *Allt Dubh* or River Black spilled across the same sands where both rivers were claimed by the roiling waves of the ocean. Named for the fine dark silt embedded beneath the clear waters, the River Black was notorious across the Highlands for a singular reason that had nothing to do with its rare earth.

And everything to do with the infamous man who lurked along its banks.

Beyond the beach, the land lifted to the large and ancient cliff face. Kylah followed the precipice, her insides rolling and crashing in time with the loud incoming tide that was hurling itself against the stones.

She'd reached the edge of the world. Or at least, the edge of Scotland. *Cape Wrath,* it was named, by the numberless hordes of Norsemen who'd tried to overtake her inhospitable shores. Time and time again they were driven back by the perilous sea and the remarkable clans strong and formidable enough to carve out a life here. They then chose other beaches from which to launch their assaults.

It was wrath which drew her all the way out here. It pulsed from the black rock. From the waves. From—somewhere beneath her. Not only wrath, but a hopeless misery, a cold fury stewed and stormed with rebellious opposition to the lovely sunset.

Kylah stepped off the edge of the cliff and dropped to the ocean below. Enormous sprays of water clashing with stone showered through her as she surveyed the rocks.

There.

To the left of the jagged rock, a shadowed cleft slashed through the cliff face. To the naked eye, it appeared shallow, but if one noted the break in the agitated water as it flowed deep into the gap, it would be recognized as a sheltered ocean cave.

This was what she'd been looking for.

As she floated past the entrance, the black sea that had churned beneath her calmed in contrast to the stirring hatred emanating from the depths of the cavern. Her weak glow acted as an insufficient lantern as the twilit Highland sky disappeared, replaced by smooth rock hollowed out by untold millennia of tides.

The place had an ancient, sacred grief beneath all the darkness. As though evil had overrun a holy place. Beyond the narrow passage, the water smoothed into a clear pool that reflected her light back at her as it became shallower, until the stone rose above the water and created a shelf.

Kylah drifted to the ledge and peered into the shadows. She couldn't tell how far back the cavern extended, and didn't care. She liked the illusion of blackness pressing in on all sides, threatening to overwhelm her pitiful glow. Turning, she sank to her knees and let the yawning darkness of the grotto engulf her.

Her face reflected back at her in the still waters, and it captivated her. This was the first time she'd seen herself since she'd died. The features in the water belonged to her, but were unrecognizable. The same heavy-lashed green eyes responded to her blink, but remained dull and vacant.

Kylah brought trembling fingers to her face, almost stunned that her reflection did the same. Despite the unflattering pale green glow, and the sunken pallor she'd adopted in death, she was still beautiful. Stunningly so. She'd once considered herself fortunate to have possessed such prominent cheek bones and a delicate chin.

She reached out a hand and slapped at the pool. Of course, nothing happened. No ripples interrupted her perfect nose. She did it again. Deeper this time, harder, a sound frustration escaping her throat when, again, her hand passed through the water without creating the slightest ripple.

A bleak yet passionate rage oozed from walls she could not see, snaking toward her like an unseen predator. *This.* This was the emotion she needed to conjure. This strange antithesis of unfulfilled pain bordering on hysteric madness. This manic loneliness. It surged through her with a sensation she'd thought lost within the husk of her flesh now turned to ashes.

Her hands curled to fists as she flailed at the water. The face that remained unharmed still crumpled into an accusatory snarl as it hurled raw grunts that echoed about the cavern.

Never in her life had she raised her voice. Not in anger, nor silliness, nor competition. People stopped when she spoke in her silky tones to listen to her. They watched her lips move and hung on every word.

The night of her death, they'd silenced her with their hands, smothering her frightened pleas. She'd tried to scream once the flames had begun to devour her, but peals of smoke had mercifully stopped her breath and filled her throat.

She'd never screamed.

They did. Not. Let. Her. Scream.

In the water, her pupils disappeared, swallowed by a frighteningly powerful illumination. Her glow coalesced into tentacles of light that lashed into the darkened corners of the grotto. Her grunts became cries, and her cries became a wail. Then her scream fractured into many. Until one was a roar and another a screech, and yet another a keen that reached such a pitch that it shook the stones and vibrated through the water. Now ripples distorted her reflection and drowned out the sounds of the ocean. To her it was a lovely symphonic melody, crafted of hatred and vengeance. She drew on whatever sinister emotion she could grasp as it was flung at her from somewhere in the darkness and intensified it. As she endlessly screamed, she also reveled. She grieved. She cursed.

It felt marvelous.

A loud crack reverberated off the stone walls and sliced through her keen. Kylah could *feel* its percussion carve through the vibrations her pitch created, and the sensation stunned her to stillness.

"*Haud yer Wheesht*, woman!" The deep command issued from everywhere and nowhere. It could have come from the Gods, if she hadn't known better.

But she did. She recognized the voice immediately and knew who lurked in the darkness behind her without turning to look.

The Druid, Daroch McLeod.

Kylah squeezed her eyes shut. What was *he* doing in here? This cave was nigh impossible to get to. She'd thought she was alone.

"Ye shouldna be here." His growl lashed at her from the walls like a cornered predator, accusing her of trespassing in a succession of echoes. "*Leave.*"

"Why?" she breathed, watching her glow crawl back toward her, the intensity of terrible emotions smothered by a simple, pervasive curiosity.

"Because ye doona belong here." His voice favored the cavern in which they stood. Cold. Dark. A mysterious, unfathomable chasm hidden among wild peril.

"But I was... called here." She'd meant to insist, but her chest suddenly felt too small to call forth much volume.

"Nay. Ye werena. Now go away," he clipped

Kylah scowled. Who was he to tell her where to go? And so rudely! Anguish nigh forgotten, she whirled to face him, but was met with only darkness.

"Why?" she demanded. "Why do you want me to go away?" Not the most brilliant of questions, but valid nonetheless.

The blackness was silent for so long, she wondered if he'd been the one to retreat. "Because I—doona want to look at ye."

Kylah gasped. She'd expected him to reference her Banshee keen, or her glow disturbing the darkness he so obviously desired. But his answer shocked and incensed her so completely she would have been struck dumb if she'd still been alive. What did her looks have to do with anything?

"Why not?" she asked the darkness.

"Why would I?"

She narrowed her eyes and crossed her arms. "I've been told that I'm quite pleasant to look at." And that was being modest. "In fact, I'm... well, I'm quite beautiful." Lud, she'd never said it out loud before. "Why would that offend you so?"

His amplified snort grated on nerves she thought long dead. "Beauty is nothing to be proud of. It's no great feat or accomplishment, only a happenstance of birth. It doesna make ye intelligent, interesting, nor desirable company. Now again, I say *be gone.*" The stones augmented his command and likewise fractured his voice into many, which all told her to leave more than once.

"Nay." There was a refreshing truth in his words, Kylah begrudgingly admitted to herself. No matter how indecorous the manner in which they were stated. But she wasn't going to do what he told her to. If there was one advantage to being dead, it was free reign to lurk where you liked.

Through the omnipresent darkness, Kylah knew exactly where the Druid stood, and exactly what she was doing here.

"It was you," she murmured, advancing into the darkness. "I thought this god forsaken *place* drew me here. But, nay, the anguish and loss doesn't belong to these stones... It's yours."

The Druid was suddenly in front of her. His unsettling face shoved close to hers, his mud-streaked features pulled into the most terrifying snarl she'd ever seen.

"Get. *Out!*"

Chapter Three

If Kylah had still been alive, she would have fled. She would have obeyed. As it was, she still found herself retreating a few paces until she floated over the grotto.

The Druid stalked her to the water's edge, his hulking body swathed in the shadows beyond the reach of her dim light. In a swift movement, his staff of petrified birch cracked against the earth, causing that percussive vibration to ripple through her again.

It was the closest sensation to being touched Kylah had felt in almost a year.

She closed her eyes and let out a breath. "Do that again," she murmured.

He didn't.

Seized by the need to see more of him, she drifted closer. Her glow crawled up tattered, ancient grey robes lashed to an enormous body by weathered, knotted vines. Shells of swansea, whelk and eigg clung to where he'd fastened them into his hair from the temple, where warriors would have donned war braids.

Kylah met a scowl so intense she had to suppress an absurd and surprising smile. Never in her life had she been the cause of such an expression.

Why would it amuse her so?

The angles of his face remained inscrutable, hidden behind a layer of silt from the *Allt Dubh*. The rest of his hair caked to his head and fell down his back, contained by the same dried mud. Kylah searched her memory for what she knew lay beneath the mask. She didn't have to go far. The image lurked at the surface of her mind's eye more often than she cared to admit. Compelling, savage features carved by a primordial artist and defaced by some undisclosed blasphemy. Dark blue tattoos of a forgotten, ancient design covered the entire left side of his face, but were concealed beneath the silt.

The only clarity belonged to his eyes, which glittered at her with unmistakable hostility. It rolled off his impossibly wide shoulders with all the force of a physical shove.

"I'm sorry if my scream disturbed you, I thought I was alone," she explained. "I promise to stay at a more pleasing register."

He ignored her peace offering. "I know I'm not the soul ye're after, Banshee, so there's no reason for ye to linger here unless ye're just entertained by disturbing my peace."

Kylah found herself distracted by his white, even teeth bared in a disgusted sneer. She was, in all honesty, vastly entertained. But couldn't exactly say why.

"How do you know you're not the one I'm after?"

"I'm not bleeding, am I?" He rolled his eyes before giving her his back and slinking into the darkness. "Yer intended victim's head would have burst during that wasted keen."

"The keen wasn't wasted," she shrugged. "It helped *me*."

"I doona care," the blackness coolly informed her. "Now go away."

Kylah drifted forward, hoping to find him again with her glow. "You still don't know you're not the one I'm after. What if you are *An Dioladh* and therefore immune? Like a Faerie creature or blessed by the Gods? You're a Druid, aren't you?"

"Druids are *not* Faeries." He spat the word as though it tasted foul. "Nor are we cleric or Paladin to any god, contrary to misguided opinion."

"Oh?" Intrigued, Kylah reached the back of the spare cavern and she started to follow the wall to the left. "You still could be *An Dioladh.*"

"Nay. I couldna," he said shortly. She couldn't pinpoint where the Druid's voice hailed from in the dark. It was like he threw it off the walls and caught it from a different location each time he spoke.

"But how can you be certain?"

An inhuman sound split the darkness and the staff arced through her in a vicious lash one second before the entire bulk of the Druid flew into and all the way through her with astounding speed. He glanced off the stone wall with a heavy leather boot and, in a flurry of robes, used the momentum to twist his leg behind him in what would have been a powerful and devastating kick to her temple.

His boot sailed through her head and he landed with surprising dexterity for such a large and encumbered man.

Kylah's hand flew to her chest. "You just... you could have..." Her entire body arced and vibrated with an unseen force and, though she'd not felt him at all, the impact of his intrusion was so potent she'd lost all sense of reason.

"Nay." He said the word slowly, as though speaking to a dim-witted child. "I *couldna.*"

"But..." She couldn't collect her wits. He'd just attacked her. A woman! A dead and lethal woman, certainly. But, even so.

His eyes narrowed as they traveled the length of her specter in a cold and calculating manner, as though searching for a weakness, any chink in her armor he could use to his advantage. Obviously unimpressed with what he saw, he lifted an eyebrow, creating fissures in the mud there.

"But... You are a *Druid,*" she repeated lamely, as though that should explain everything. The word had always held such mystic allure to the superstitious Highlanders, spoken in whispers of awe and fear alongside ancient words like Shape-shifter, Dragon, and Berserker.

"And *ye* are a fool." He disappeared again.

Kylah blinked. "I'm not a fool, I'm a Banshee."

"The two are not mutually exclusive." His voice now came from—inside the rock? That couldn't be right.

She ignored his insult and pressed her ear to the wall. "We're both creatures of magic, you have to admit that."

"*Wrong*." The rock told her. "Ye're a creature of magic. I'm a being of power."

Kylah drew back and frowned. The rock or the man? This had to be the most confusing conversation she'd ever had.

And the most fascinating.

Along the left wall, she'd reached the water's edge so she trailed back to the center and started searching along the right.

And found nothing.

Disappointed, she looked back and a gleam in the black rock caught her notice. Embedded in the wall, just wide enough for a body to hide was an overlay of stone virtually invisible from anywhere in the cave except for where she stood now.

"Hello." Investigating it, Kylah realized it must take a small miracle for someone the Druid's size to fit. No magic, indeed. After following it, she realized the crevice angled rather sharply to the right, and since one couldn't turn around in the space, one simply must angle with it and change direction before being dumped into a cavern twice as large as the first.

"Wha—" Kylah gasped, her mind incapable of processing the strange and complex stone and metal tools and contraptions displayed in front of her backlit by a roaring fire at the rear of the chasm. Abruptly she was grateful she didn't actually have to blink, or her over stimulated eyes would have surely shriveled in their sockets.

A movement to her left warned her before a rock hurtled through her and broke against the wall. "Get... the *fuck*... out!" the Druid roared. "Ye canna be here."

"Why?" Guilt for imposing upon his solitude caused her to cringe. She'd never before been in the habit forcing her company on others, but then, she'd never had to. She couldn't very well leave without learning more about this... this... she didn't even know what to call the things in front of her. Kylah drifted toward a table of sorts crafted of stone and weighted with numberless round bowls of various sizes, colors and materials, avoiding the infuriated Druid. He looked more terrifying in the firelight. Menace roiled off of him. She could feel it in her Banshee way, inexplicably drawn to the strength of his rage.

Letting out a frustrated sound, he pulled chilly calm about him like a cloak. "Ye ask that question more often than a toddling child."

Kylah didn't like the condescension in his voice. "Well, it's a simple question, isn't it? I apologized for the scream, so *why* do you so passionately dismiss my presence? It's not like I can upset anything here." She slapped at a stone bowl and the Druid flinched, though they both knew it would remain undamaged. "Tell me the reason, and I'll decide if it's valid or not." She leaned down to inspect the unfamiliar powder that glittered in her light.

"The why of it doesna matter," the Druid countered. "My will should be deterrent enough,"

"Not to me."

"Then I question yer intelligence." He stalked to the table, hovering and glowering, as though warning her not to touch anything. An intimidation tactic, maybe? He was so tall as to tower over most men, maybe as tall as Katriona's new husband. And possibly thicker, judging by the width of his robes.

Kylah wrinkled her nose and levitated to meet him at eye level. "I'm not stupid, I'm dead. What have I to fear from you?"

The Druid gave a derisive snort and shoved away from the table, "Considering what ye are, more than ye realize."

What did that mean? Kylah looked over his shoulder to a cauldron left boiling over a second fire in the middle of the room. She looked up. The ceiling of the cave disappeared into the darkness. Where did the smoke from the fires go? How did he get the fodder for them?

She stepped around him and moved to an adjacent slab of balanced rock, ignoring his growl. This one stacked with smaller pieces of earth that varied in size, shape and color and seemed to be organized accordingly.

"You said that I'm a creature of magic, and you're a being of power. What is the difference?"

He remained silent, but she could feel exactly where he was behind her. His body radiated so many complex, stimulating sensations that he stood as a point of reference no matter what he surrounded himself with.

"Is not magic a kind of power?" she prompted, turning to face him.

He put up a hand. "Patience, woman, I'm trying to answer in the right terms."

"Which would be?"

"The simplest," he said imperiously.

Kylah bristled. "You've yet to offer me a simple answer."

He grunted and crossed his arms. "We've yet to *touch* complexity."

She adopted his exact posture. "Well then, go on, touch it."

His nostrils flared on a long exhale, and his eyes flared with something else, though the light was squelched as quickly as it appeared. "Magic is the manipulation of elements by creatures not bound by the laws of our plane." His lip curled again, as though it couldn't help itself. "Faeries, Demons, Shape-shifters,

Berserkers, those who would call themselves deities and so forth. It is merely power we don't yet understand.

"My power, Druid power, is gained by testing the elements of our Earth, our plane, through exhausting all variables and learning to control them for definitive use."

Kylah nodded, though she wished she had swallowed her pride and asked for a more simplified answer. "What sort of uses? What do you seek from this knowledge? This... Control?"

He turned his head to stare at a row of strange tools all hung on hand-crafted hooks littering the far wall, offering what Kylah knew to be the unadorned side of his face. She yearned to uncover it. To make a study of it whilst his notice was elsewhere.

"Truth is what I seek," he murmured. "What else is there?"

"Oh lots of things," she ticked them off on her fingers. "Beauty, freedom, life, love, family—"

His derisive snort interrupted her. "Doona be ridiculous. Beauty is but an illusion that subjectively changes with perception and cannot be trusted." He gave her a pointed look, but continued. "Freedom, also a perception, can be granted and taken at the whim of another, generally one with more power. Same as life, as I'm sure you're well aware."

Kylah flinched.

"And *love*," he scoffed. "Love is an indefinable, variant weakness that can be used against you." He vehemently shook his head, upsetting the braids at his temple. "Nay, I want for none of those things."

Kylah couldn't disagree with him on any particular point. Which unsettled her. All those "things" had been violently taken from her, by someone with a great deal more power.

Except... "What about family?"

A muscle flexed in his jaw, upsetting more of his mask. "I doona have a conception of what that word means, so I dare not speculate on it."

Kylah thought on her mother and sisters, a stab of remorse staining their last interaction. Though she'd lived, for lack of a better word, the last year through a haze of broken apathy, she'd not taken for granted the omnipresent love and support of her family. She couldn't always pull her mind from the constant fog to interact with them. But in life, and death, they'd always done what they could for each other. Though at times she had to admit, it hadn't always been enough.

She closed her eyes, letting the pity she felt for the Druid overtake the welling of pain and terror that lurked below her surface, closer now that she'd called it forth in the cavern's antechamber.

"No family?" At her words a blast of helpless tormented rage hit her with an almost physical force.

From him? Had to be.

But the Druid merely shook his head and waved a hand as if to expel the word. "But truth. Truth is constant. No one can change it. It just *is*." His voice rose, every word perfectly annunciated. "Whether we believe it or not. Accept it or not. Whether we're ignorant of it or able to wield it. It remains as is. When it is tested, the outcome is certain. Every time. Without fail."

Kylah thought about his words. "If that is truth, then I believe love can be truth."

His eyes disappeared into his lids a second time. "Aye, well, we've already established that ye're a fool."

"No we haven't," she corrected. "You've assumed that I'm a fool, but your theory has yet to be tested."

He stared at her with a face void of expression for a long moment, and then blinked. "Let's just agree that the evidence suggests."

"Maybe so," she shrugged. "But you can't call *truth* until you have definitive proof after exhausting all the variables." Kylah couldn't hide her victorious smile. The first of its kind in almost a year. She thought she saw the corner of his own mouth twitch before he turned away from her, busying himself with the bowls.

She had him. But was smart enough not to say so. Which, in her opinion, was a strong *variable* in her favor.

Chapter Four

He couldn't stand to look at her. It was too... She was so... Well, descriptive words had never served his purposes; therefore he elected to avoid them.

Ignoring alarming, unnecessary physical responses, Daroch carefully inspected the bowl of fine black powder upon which she'd demonstrated her ethereal lack of material mass. It consisted of the combustible mixture of sulfur, charcoal, and a purified solution boiled from ashes of wood. If he dropped the bowl, Cape Wrath would be leveled in the explosion. From what he could tell, the interaction with her miasma had no significant impact on either force.

Interesting. Unsurprising, but interesting.

"What are you cooking over there?" Her voice reached through his robes and touched his spine with an unwanted thrill.

He sighed. On second thought, he should just drop the bowl and be done with it. An inexplicable tremor in his hand caused Daroch to set the powder down.

"Oh I see! You're melting copper and tin to make bronze. What are you going to use it for?"

It took Daroch several moments to process her question. Who ever heard of a Banshee with a melodic voice? Also, how was it one woman could be gifted with such— symmetrical features—and also a... dammit he would *not* use the word 'beautiful' to describe anything about her. Least of all her voice. Pleasing? Lyrical?

Sensuous.

He bit his lip. Hard.

"I'm fashioning a... conducting an experiment." Gods be damned, in trying to distract himself, he'd nearly given her the honest answer, which could have meant the end of everything he worked for. A woman with a little knowledge was more dangerous than a horde of Berserker warriors. They would be the sword, the death bringers. But she, *she* would be the blood, the inciting incident. He had to get her out of here before she ruined everything.

"Would that experiment have anything to do with the raw iron on this table? Or the gold and silver? Or all these powders and tools and—"

"Nay," he lied. It had everything to do with all of it. It was his life's work. His reason for existence. And the greatest kept secret in the Highlands.

Until now.

"Good, because you overworked this other iron here, though it's still too crude. It looks like the blast temperatures were too low but you still got enough oxygen in the metal to—"

"What are ye, a secret alchemist?" he clipped and turned around, forgetting in his exasperation that he'd planned on not looking at her.

"Nay." Her glow caused metal beside her to glisten and Daroch focused his eyes on that, rather than her lithe form barely concealed in ghostly, transpicuous robes. "I'm the daughter of Diarmudh MacKay, the best blacksmith in the Highlands."

Surprisingly, Daroch had heard of the man. "Didna he die some fifteen years hence?"

"Eighteen." The Banshee turned from where she inspected the metal and caught his gaze with a sad smile. Damn it all, he wasn't supposed to be looking. "But I was his favorite, and spent many hours in the smithy with him, black as a Demon, singing songs not fit for a wee girl while he worked all sorts of metals."

"Demons aren't black." Daroch corrected while he studied her. "Ye're not old enough for that."

"I was four when he was kicked in the head by an unruly horse." Grief shadowed her delicate features and Daroch had to clench his jaw and consider numerical figures to distract himself from a dangerous softening somewhere in the region of his lungs.

"Anyway, I remember everything he taught me. Especially about alloys." She was coming closer, and Daroch found that he wanted to retreat from her. "You know, we turned it into a washhouse after his death, my mother and sisters. It was... burned." This time, it was she who averted her eyes. "But the forge remains, though the bellows would need repairing. I'm certain you could use it."

Daroch gaped at her. "Why?" The irony of his asking her the question wasn't lost on him.

"Why what?"

"Why would ye offer me the use of yer beloved father's smithy when I've been..."

"An unmitigated arse?" she helpfully supplied.

Daroch scowled at her. "Unwelcoming."

She shrugged, setting her long auburn curls to flowing about her body as though she were under water. The effect was disturbingly lovely. "All this interests me, and I've nothing better to do."

Something about her answer displeased him, but Daroch couldn't identify it. Deciding he needed to busy his body before it betrayed him further, he snatched a tool and smothered one of the fires with loose earth, noting that the Banshee didn't drift into that section of the cave until the flames had died.

Intrigued, he sank to his pallet by the dying embers of his cook fire and took the last of his dried fish from where it warmed on the rocks, trying to figure out how to inspect her without looking at her.

She stayed where she was, looking very young and very lost.

A cold pit formed low in his belly and he suddenly wasn't hungry. Not for food, in any case. "Doona ye have someone *else* to torment? A vengeance to reap or some such Banshee justice to meet out on a deserving villain that will result in ye *leaving*?"

"Nay, not really." She hugged her arms to her middle.

"I'm going to sleep now," he informed her presenting her with his back and lying on the pallet facing the glowing coals. Wide awake.

"So early?" She sounded disappointed. And closer. "Can I... watch you?"

He bit back a savage curse. Her words reached through the layers of his robes, the silt, his flesh, and straight to his cock.

One hundred years. One hundred years since a woman had watched him. Objectified him.

"If ye stay, ye'll watch me do more than sleep," he ground out.

Her glow vanished, leaving him in frigid darkness but for the dying embers which he stared at for hours.

Chapter Five

He must have gone into the sea. Kylah inventoried the belongings in front of her. Freshly laundered, still-damp Druid robes and a dark pair of trews flapped in the ever-present wind, secured to the cliff's ledge by heavy stones. Beside them, a birch staff and a pair of gigantic knee boots were neatly lined up next to an iron sword that Kylah recognized from his cave the night before.

She peeked over the cliff and shook her head. Situated somewhere between the point at Cape Wrath and the sands of the *Allt Dubh*, this bluff plummeted dangerously into deep water, yet no rocks jutted from the seafloor to catch an unwary diver. Still, she'd have been certain the drop would kill a man, but the ceaseless sensation of unfathomable, swirling emotion called to her from deep beneath the waves.

The Druid *was* down there, and had been for some time.

Rare sunlight warmed the spring chill, and the sea was calmer than usual, lapping against the cliffs with small white breaks instead of volatile surges. Kylah could see rather far into the blue gulf, but had no sign of the man.

No one could hold their breath for that long.

She stepped off the cliff and dropped into the water, barely registering the change in temperature after plunging into the sea. To someone whose life still heated their flesh, the icy chill of the ocean would feel like a thousand needles driven into skin by a relentless hammer. Kylah couldn't fathom how Daroch McLeod could stand it.

Maybe he couldn't. Mayhap the frigid sea had frozen his limbs and stolen the life-giving heat from his body. Spurred by the thought, Kylah followed the signature of emotion reaching through the space separating them, roiling beneath her translucent skin and dancing along veins no longer filled with blood.

In this ghostly form, the water didn't hinder her movement and Kylah didn't let the wonders of the sea distract her as she drove herself ever deeper and farther from shore. Until a strong movement from just ahead and beneath her caught a shaft of sunlight that pierced deeper than the rest. She froze just in time to see the Druid plunge a several-pronged wooden spear into a school of sea bass and emerge with a large catch.

Kylah could picture the pleasure of victory on his features, though he'd yet to face her. The sea seemed to be his element. His heavy body rippled and flowed with the currents, uncovered by all but a loincloth secured to his strong hips. Two straps crisscrossed his wide shoulders. One belonging to a burgeoning bag obviously full of the day's catch, and the other a bladder of some kind with a long spout, which he secured around his mouth and took a long pull into his lungs. Holding it there, he placed the wriggling bass in his other bag and then had to angle his body deeper to fight buyancy. His hair flowed around him with suspended movement, much like hers always did.

In awe of his ingenuity, Kylah went to him.

"Ingenious!" she exclaimed, pointing to his bladder full of air. "What an extraordinary idea."

He recoiled from her; his tattoos reflected the shaft of light. A group of bubbles burst from his mouth and escaped toward the surface on a surprised gasp. One hand went to his throat as the other frantically groped for the bladder with air in it. He found it and sucked in another breath, but his body was caught in some powerful spasm and those bubbles escaped from his mouth in two short bursts.

Seized by panic, Kylah reached for him out of habit, but her clutching fingers only passed through him and seemed to make the situation worse.

He surged upward with a powerful kick, but they both knew he'd never reach the surface in time.

"I'm sorry," she whimpered as his eyes flared and his muscles started to spasm and jerk. "Daroch, no." This was all her fault. He was going to drown because of her. She'd never forgive herself. She'd thought that burning to death was the worst possible way to die. But as she watched his eyes latch on to the surface of the sea, so close and yet too far, she realized that drowning must be equally frightening and horrific.

His eyes rolled back beneath his lids and he went unnaturally still.

"No," Kylah groaned as her hands reached for him again. "No, keep trying. It's too early for you to give up."

The tattoos on the side of his face rippled with a dim light, catching her notice. The undulation flowed down the knotted work that covered the entire left side of his body until a pulse of power exploded from his form and broke over her to expand in a circular arc through the sea.

No, not power. Magic.

Kylah watched it go, and then turned back to his still form.

What in the in the name of the Gods...

A high-pitched ticking answered from somewhere to the left. Kylah turned to it in time to watch two swift black shadows dart through the water with synchronized movements. She had to wait until they slowed enough to situate themselves beneath the Druid's arms to recognize just what they were.

Seals! Kylah rejoiced. Somehow he'd called them to his rescue and they lifted his bulk from the depths and shot him toward the surface with their sleek, swift bodies.

Kylah followed, able to keep pace with the animals until they broke the surface. While the Druid sputtered and choked up an alarming amount of sea water, the seals scolded and barked their displeasure at Kylah.

"I'm sorry," she told them. "I didn't think I would startle him."

"Ye didna *think*," Daroch rasped, tugging at his ears.

One seal blew a very rude noise at her with its wee pink tongue as they started to tow Daroch toward the rocks.

"No. Well, yes. That is, I figured you would see me as I came at you sideways and I do tend to glow," she rambled. "I wouldn't at all put you in danger on purpose. You *must* believe me."

The Druid glowered at her. "I was a more than a little preoccupied," he quipped. "And it's not lack of foresight on my part if I wasna on the lookout for a Banshee in the middle of the ocean at midday! I'm only a man." They reached the cliffs and the Druid touched his nose to each of the seals' in a surprisingly sweet manner before he pulled himself out of the water and onto a narrow ledge.

Kylah's retort died an instant and vicious death in her throat.

Not one living soul would glimpse Daroch McLeod standing on that ledge, surveying the ocean as though he owned it, and mistake him for a mere man. Nay, they would invoke the Sea God, Llyr, and tremble. Surely a man so savagely, brutally rendered could only exist in a mythic Pantheon.

Kylah's gaze skimmed across runic tattoos that took on a wicked cast in the midday sunlight. They wrapped and knotted upward from his powerful left leg to splay indolently across a vast expanse of rippled torso and flare beneath his ribcage, then circle the flat of his nipple to claim the entire left side of his immense chest. There, the black and blue of the symbols vied for supremacy in an intricate design before stretching across one wide shoulder, reaching up the cords of his neck, and cutting across his clenched jaw before ending with sharp points over his intense left eye. His long, thick arm was also covered in runes to the wrist.

Her gaze darted back to his hips where the runes were half concealed by an animal skin loin-cloth secured by a leather strap. They drew her eyes like a sin, disappearing beneath each part of the scant covering, suggesting that they obscured more than she could ever wish to see, both in front of him and behind.

Something clenched deep within her belly. Something wet and warm and ready. The completely foreign sensation perplexed her, terrified her. It made her intensely aware of *that* place. The one she vowed to forever ignore.

Something beneath the cloth flexed and twitched and the Druid made a dangerous, guttural sound.

"I'm sorry," Kylah breathed. Though wasn't sure if she apologized because she'd been caught staring or because she'd almost drowned him. Her eyes flew to his face, which didn't help with the alarming ache building inside of her. Kylah had always known she was a beautiful woman, but she realized that until this moment she'd never beheld true beauty.

Daroch's beauty was cruel. His brow was high-born and lined with scorn, his nose straight but flared with arrogance, his lips full, but pulled tight into a malevolent sneer. His eyes evoked the sea in a storm, swirling with grey, brown, and green and occasionally flashing with silver.

"Ye have no idea what ye've done, woman." Those eyes accused her now, as he reached into his bag laden with fish and threw a reward to his two lingering rescuers.

Kylah swallowed. "I'm really, *very* sorry. I—I—don't know how to make it up to you."

His eyes swept the expanse of ocean again with cautious expectation. "In a few moments, ye may not ever have to worry about trying." With that cryptic statement, he turned to the stone and began to climb, using small fissures and juts in the rock to hoist his considerable body up the cliff face.

This must be something he did quite often, Kylah considered as she watched his muscles strain and cord with more interest then they likely merited. Perhaps it was how he'd built such a large, strong body. Kylah found herself transfixed by the movement of the tattoos reaching around his back. His shoulders and arms bulged. His legs propelled him with surprising strength and dexterity and she realized that if she remained at this angle for much longer, his loin cloth would no longer shield him from her view.

"You're wrong, you know." She levitated to eye-level with him.

"Not... a good... *time,*" he gritted out as he looked up as though to determine the distance he had left to climb.

"Oh, yes, right. I'll wait." Kylah decided to be silent, not wanting to be the reason he fell to his death. It wouldn't do to be the cause of another disaster before she'd even amended for the first.

A little more than halfway, another ledge jutted from the cliff that was large enough for him to stand on. It took hoisting his entire body with just the strength of his arms, but once he swung his foot up and found purchase, he was able to rest for a moment and adjust his burden.

Shaking his arms, Daroch sent her a cranky look before latching on to the rock again. "Well, out with it. How is it that I am wrong?" With a grunt, he tackled the increasingly precarious cliff with renewed vigor.

"You're not *merely* a man," Kylah gently accused. "You said in the cave, that I was a creature of magic and you were a being of power. But that isn't true, is it? You just used magic to save yourself. I felt it."

A strong gust of wind tossed his dark, wet hair and the Druid clung to the rock, waiting for it to pass. "Aye, and it may have been thc death of me." The tattoos made the grim set of his face seem sinister. He looked over at her then, as she floated beside him. His calculating eyes searched every inch of her, snagging on places she'd not expected. Her feet. Her legs. Her breasts. The exposed column of her throat. When his gaze finally met hers, it held a naked mixture of desolation and heat. "Maybe I should have just let ye drown me."

While he hoisted himself closer to the top, Kylah tried to control the unnecessary breathlessness that squeezed her chest.

A small tingle ran up her spine that had nothing to do with the mostly naked Druid.

Kylah looked up. Daroch was only a few hand-holds from the bluff.

And something malicious waited for them at the top.

Chapter Six

"Wait." Frigid goose bumps erupted on Daroch's shoulder as he grasped the grassy ledge, signaling that the Banshee had reached for his skin. "Someone's up there." Her warning killed the sensation reaching toward his loin-cloth.

"Who?" he asked. And why didn't he have his fucking shamrock amulet? The years had made him reckless.

"I don't know." She sounded worried. "But he looks like death incarnate."

"So it's true. The Druid slave still lives after all these centuries." The wind whipped the mocking words over the cliff.

Daroch grited his teeth as hatred impaled him with all the force of Dagda's spear. They would send *him*.

"Ly Erg." Daroch kept his voice cold to hide the inferno raging through him. He used it to surge to the ground and roll to his feet. "Ye still kneel at the foot of *her* throne and jump to do her bidding, while I answer to no one. I ask ye this. Which of us is still a slave?"

"Centuries?" Kylah breathed.

"Stay out of this Banshee. Your Queen commands it." The militant Fae pointed a permanently blood-stained finger at Kylah and she shrank back.

"W-why?"

Daroch couldn't smother an ironic smirk at her favorite question. Apparently, the Banshee Queen's executioner found it as irritating as he did.

Ly Erg's imperious voice had the distinct unhurried pacing of an immortal and the cruel anticipation of someone who loved to kill. "Because it's none of your concern. Now be gone."

Daroch grunted. "Good *bloody* luck with that command," he muttered. He divested himself of his satchel of fish and bladder of air. He may not live long enough to eat.

Calculating odds, his mind flew through a series of observations as he tested his muscles. His body was moderately fatigued from swimming, fishing, and climbing, running at about seventy percent maximum strength and, due to the extra adrenaline dump from almost dying, sixty five percent of maximum agility without extra stores of energy.

"You're not going to hurt him, are you?" The desperate note in the Banshee's voice thrummed something soft in the center of Daroch's chest that he thrust aside with cold estimations.

"I've already hurt him." Ly Erg bragged, drawing the curved, long-handled sword from a scabbard decorated with intricate Fae Symbols. "I'm here to *finish* him."

Ly Erg's Fae strength amounted to roughly four hundred percent of Daroch's own maximum. But since the hubristic nancy bastard insisted upon appearing the part of soldier, his constant armor of Faerie mail did slow him down to comparable speed.

What the Banshee Queen's sometimes consort didn't realize, was the magic runes on Daroch's sword allowed it to slice through Fae mail like hot iron through flesh. He just needed to get to it, and because of the angle he'd climbed up the rocks, his possessions were on the other side of Ly Erg.

Fucking Faeries.

"Why must you finish him? He's not threatening anyone." The Banshee drifted into the space between them.

She may or may not know it, but her incessant curiosity was helping him, for once, giving him the time to work on a stratagem.   Daroch reached his Druid sense out to the surrounding moors, calling for help. A stag lingered nearby and answered his call.   A mother fox hunted by a loch, but she declined for obvious reasons. As did the flock of ravens feasting on a kill left by a pack of wolves that'd unfortunately moved out of his range. Sheep grazed on a nearby hill. Useless. Though a serpent or two slithered through the grasses to his aid.

Strength and cunning. He would need both.

"Is that what he's convinced you of, that he's no threat?" The Fae soldier's silver eyes lit with mild amusement, contrasting with the shimmering gold of his braided hair. "That makes you twice the fool. Think about what you risk. In three more months you'll no longer be a dead woman, but a lower caste of the Fae." His sneer turned lecherous. "I've had untold millennia to think of ways to punish unruly girls like you." Ly Erg ineffectually slashed through the Banshee with his curved blade, drawing a dark growl from Daroch's throat that surprised none more than himself.

Where had *that* come from?

The Banshee trembled, but held her ground. "The Fae can't just go around killing innocent humans," she argued. "The Queen, Cliodnah, told me there was a pact struck with the Gods."

"All pacts are not ironclad," Ly Erg sneered. "And this *human* is no innocent. He spends his time trying to work a way to slaughter all of our kind, and our seers have told us he is close."

The Banshee gasped, turning to him with those lovely, wounded eyes. "Is that true?"

Daroch could feel his animal guardians drawing near, power and strength surged through his veins until he nearly burst with male aggression as the stag bounded toward them. Clarity and cunning sharpened his senses as the snakes wove sacred, ancient knots into the grasses.

"Aye," he snarled. "Every last one of ye."

The Faerie attacked. Though he was stronger and faster, Ly Erg telegraphed every move he was about to make before he followed through. By not focusing on any one part of his opponent, Daroch was able to see all of him and use the acumen lent by the snakes to predict his attacks.

Ly Erg slashed and sliced, mostly carving the air as Daroch dodged and lunged around him. Taking a calculated risk, he curled and dove past the enraged Faerie, paying for it with a shallow slice to the thigh, but unfolding from the roll with his sword brandished in front of him.

"You think that will make a difference to the outcome of this battle?" The Fae soldier scoffed. "Since finding out it cuts us, all your human weapons have become iron." He hacked at Daroch with bone-jarring force. "Still doesn't kill us," he mocked. "Just stings a little."

Daroch recovered, twisting away from Ly Erg, and sliced upward, slashing the Faerie's torso through the armor. He reveled in the momentary look of shock as the Fae inspected his precious armor and the blood pouring from the deep wound. "That mail might protect ye from Fae blades, but not *mine*." The runes on his blade pulsed with power and light, even in the midday sun.

Ly Erg's skin made terrible, wet sounds as it knit together. "Fortunate, then, that *I* require no protection from you." His offensive was swift and brutal, yet methodical enough to be learned from centuries of bloodshed. Daroch had to adjust his style to deflect and avoid his devastating blows to conserve strength. For he fought Ly Erg, the most lethal Fae in the history of mankind. One who had slaughtered so many ancients that his hands were forever stained with blood so as to alert an unsuspecting human to not be fooled by his beauty or artifice.

This Faerie lived for the kill. And hated all humanity.

Daroch most of all.

Thrusting when Ly Erg sliced, Daroch made him pay for every offensive. But the wounds he inflicted instantly healed, while the few nicks and cuts Daroch received remained open and bleeding. His strength was failing, his limited magic waning. The angles he used to his advantage were slower to manifest themselves. His calculated odds for survival fell lower and lower out of his favor.

As it was wont to do during mortal combat, time slowed and sound only reached his ears as though he were still submerged in the sea. He couldn't go on like this, and Ly Erg was likely only toying with him. Perhaps the time had come. He could roll over and submit. All of this would be over, one way or the other.

Only one other time in her memory had Kylah felt so helpless. This was all her fault. She wrung her hands and pulsed with terrified light. Though he may desire her death, she didn't want the Druid to die. Not because of her. If she were to scream now, she might distract him. Her impotence infuriated her and the feeling was fed by the hatred pulsating from the two warriors in front of her.

Daroch was magnificent, his every movement fluid and dynamic. She could see the sinew of each muscle respond to his commands, directing superhuman power into each blow.

The battle lasted for hours, or only minutes, the flurry of parries and blows eliciting gasps and strangled sounds from her.

Until the moment all the keen intelligence went out of Daroch's eyes. All skill and method seemed to drain out of him as he leapt at the Faerie with a shout of pure madness.

With a victorious smile, Ly Erg easily deflected the blow that would have flayed open any man and heaved the Druid to the ground.

Daroch landed heavily and was still for a few moments, his sword fell to the soft earth just out of reach. With a cough and a groan, he pushed himself up from the moss, his arms straining and causing the tattoos on his shoulder to ripple.

"Daroch," she whispered before she could stop herself. He froze at the sound of his name leaving her lips and turned his head toward her. The shells at his temple ran across his cheek with the movement until his eyes finally found hers.

"This is fitting, is it not?" Ly Erg stood over him. "You dying on your hands and knees where you always belonged. Too bad *she's* not here to watch. You remember, Druid, how she loved to watch before joining in?" The Fae used two hands to raise his lethal sword above his head.

Kylah saw it then. Daroch had kept it from his eyes until this very moment. All the humiliation, rage, anger, misery, and loss she'd detected inside of him shone hotter than the sun above them. The emotion lashed out at her, reaching into her soul and amalgamating with her own memories until she trembled from the force of it.

Her mouth dropped open. Her eyes darted toward the sword and back to him. If he lunged for it. If he only had a moment. A distraction.

He nodded to her and she let it loose, a keen so powerful the serpents died and the Stag retreated in astounding leaps. His pain fed her wail until the sea raged with it, the sky darkened with it, and the Fae froze for the moment they needed.

Daroch lunged for his sword, surged upward, and in a powerful arc, sent Ly Erg's beautiful head soaring over the cliff into the depths of the Sea.

Chapter Seven

"We did it!" The Banshee cheered as Daroch kicked the Faerie's lifeless body over the cliff. His blood still flowed with untempered fury and he didn't trust himself to speak. "Well, *you* did it." She joined him where he stood and they silently watched Ly Erg's long fall into the ocean far below. "You slaughtered him."

"He's not dead, the head will grow back." Daroch spat over the cliff and turned away, inspecting the damage done by Ly Erg's curved blade. Less than he'd expected. Only his thigh still bled.

"Oh." Her deflated voice drew his notice. He found the worried wrinkle between her delicately shaped brows oddly adorable. Still simmering with heat and aggression, the blood pounding through his veins naturally looked for a different outlet, and raced south. Averting his gaze, he set to collecting his belongings.

"How long does it take for a Faerie to grow his head back?" She still squinted over the edge, looking for a sign of the Executioner.

Daroch strapped his satchel of fish onto his shoulder and considered her question. "Maybe a day or so. Once he can, he'll return to the Isle of the Fae to finish recovering." Stooping to pick up his sword, he strapped it to his hips with the vine belt and grabbed his staff.

"Then he'll be after you again?"

"Likely." He set off down the hill toward Lake Shamrock. There he would find what he needed and some bog myrtle for the wound on his thigh.

"Why?"

Gritting his teeth, Daroch turned on the Banshee who followed close behind him. "You know *why*. Because I'm going to find a way to kill the Fae." He stepped closer and narrowed his eyes so she'd catch his meaning. "*All* of them."

Her eyes fixed on the string of shells at his temple and followed the long strand down to his chest. "Why?"

If she asked that question one more fucking time... "Knowing my intent, do I still have the use of yer father's forge?"

Her gaze flicked to his sword and her face became very serious. "What did he mean by what he said before you beheaded him?" she whispered. "About you being on your hands and knees?"

Something snapped inside him. "Answer *my* question for once!" he roared, his hands aching to grasp her wee shoulders and shake her senseless. "Are ye going to help me or not, knowing one of my weapons might one day kill ye?"

She retreated a step. Regarding him for a long, silent moment, she finally said, "I... I think I will. Yes."

It occurred to Daroch in that moment that he neither needed her help nor her permission to use her father's forge. If it was truly abandoned, he could walk in and use it whenever he liked. He opened his mouth to inform her thus.

"What is yer name, Banshee?" His question stunned them both.

"Kylah MacKay."

Kylah. Lovely, feminine. Like her.

"Ye made a dangerous enemy today, Kylah MacKay."

"I know." Her iridescent face shone with earnest regret. "I'm sorry to cause you all that trouble. I'll do what I can to make amends."

That foreign, soft emotion bloomed in his chest, soothing the cold fury pulsing there. "I didna mean me, lass. I meant Ly Erg."

A dark shadow crossed her illuminated features. "He doesn't frighten me." She drifted around him and took a slow pace down the bluff.

Daroch followed her, for once, catching her easily. "He should. Ye doona ken what he's capable of."

"Yes, I do." Her eyes remained fixed on the fragrant fields of blooming spring buds. "I really feel so terrible that he found you because of me. That's how he did it isn't it, because you had to use your magic?"

"Aye, well, no permanent harm befell me." If Daroch were completely honest with himself, it wasn't her presence that had surprised him into gasping water into his lungs. It had been her beatific smile. She'd taken his breath with her loveliness, and it happened to be in a place where air was in short supply. His brows drew together. "Let's forget it ever happened."

She nodded, seeming eager to do just that. "Where are we going?" she asked.

"Lake Shamrock."

Her mouth formed a relentlessly familiar shape.

"*Because*," he cut her off. "I need a shamrock and some bog myrtle."

"Bog myrtle for your wound," she seemed pleased with herself. "I should have thought of that... but a shamrock? wh—"

"*Because* when one is holding a shamrock, one can see a Faerie, whether they want ye to or not," he answered quickly trying to stay a step ahead of the dreaded word. "Who knows what they'll send after me next? Or when."

She was thoughtful for a blessedly silent moment. "May I ask you something?"

A harsh laugh escaped Daroch's throat. "Did ye just ask a question about asking a question?"

It was her turn to look exasperated. "Well?"

"When has it stopped ye before?" Daroch motioned for her to proceed, shocked to discover that he wasn't as aggravated at the lass's questions as he'd previously been. He wouldna say he was enjoying himself. Nay. He wouldna say that.

"How old are you?"

Daroch frowned. "That's actually a good question. One to which I doona know the answer."

"Well, it's not that complicated, in what year were you born?"

He furrowed his brow, trying to remember. "About... sixty four."

"Thirteen hundred and sixty four?" she asked, aghast.

"Nay lass," he smirked. "Sixty and four, about twenty years before Agricola and Caledonia."

"The *Romans*?" she nearly shrieked.

He winced.

"That makes no sense at all. You say you're not a man of magic, yet you are. You say you aren't blessed by gods or a Faerie creature, and yet you're centuries over a *thousand years*! I can't believe all this, and I'm a bloody *Banshee*." She swung a slap at his shoulder, but of course it only resulted in chilly goose bumps.

"Did yer father ever tell ye Faerie stories when ye were a wee lass?"

She sobered a little, her eyes becoming wistful. "All the time."

"Did he ever mention what happened when an unsuspecting human ventured into a Faerie ring and spent a night in the land of the Fae?"

"He said that a man would spend one night in Faerie and come back in time to meet his grandchildren all grown. That time doesn't pass there like it does—ohhhhhh." Comprehension dawned and her eyes went round as an owl's.

"Imagine what a month or so would do to ye."

"Dear me!" she exclaimed. "In what time did you return to Scotland?"

Daroch focused on the pain in his leg so as to deny the hollow ache lancing through his chest. What time had he returned? In a time where the Druids had mysteriously disappeared leaving not a trace to prove their advanced existence. To a time where the united people of the holy emerald isles had divided into warring clans living in hovels while their English overlords oppressed and objectified them. To a time when everyone he knew and loved was long dead and forgotten and he'd taken on the clan McLeod because they'd been the first to shelter him and show him kindness. "In time to ride with Robert the Bruce against the English," he answered darkly. "I was the mood for warfare right about then."

"A hundred years at least!" she put a hand to her forehead in disbelief. "And you've been so young and..." she gestured at him with a helpless hand and Daroch found himself mighty interested as to what descriptive word she would pull out of that inquisitive brain of hers. "And... vigorous this whole time?" Her pale translucent cheeks tinged a becoming shade of pink.

She thought him vigorous, did she? Heat crept up his collar from beneath his robes and he cleared his throat. "My theory is the food I ate and drank in Faerie had properties that slowed the aging process down, though I seem to have aged about fifteen years in the last twenty, so I also theorize that the process is accelerating again."

"Oh? So that would place you at about five and thirty, I'd wager, though your physique is far better than that of any man I know of that age." Her blush intensified.

A niggling warmth swelled inside him and Daroch squelched it the best way he knew how. Intellectual distraction. "I find it fascinating that ye blush." He squinted at her creamy complexion, the tinge still prominent through her ever-present green hue. "Blushing is usually a body's reaction to emotional stimuli through the thermo dilation of blood veins. But yer heart doesna beat. Yer blood doesna flow. So how does blushing occur?" The temptation to reach out and touch her skin became so overwhelming, he passed a finger through her cheek.

Startled, she jumped back from him and batted at his hand like a wee kitten. Both of their attempts at contact were predictably unsuccessful. More was the pity, in his case. Which caused him pause. He hadn't wanted to touch a woman in over one hundred years. Why had that suddenly changed?

"Now who is asking silly questions?" she huffed, clearly disconcerted. "It's magic, who knows how it works, only that it does? Everything seems to work as it did before except that I don't eat or drink anymore, of course. But when I cry, tears flow. When I spit... well it's strange but it... happens. Mostly."

The erotic possibilities of her admission slammed into him.

Gods be damned.

"And only lately, I've started to feel my heart beating. Very fast, in most cases, like it's going to jump out of my chest." She pressed a dainty hand to her breast and speared him with eyes the color of Irish moss.

"Do ye," his brows lifted. "And when does this occur?"

"Only when I'm around you."

Daroch's own heart threw itself against his ribcage. Something had to be done about this.

She was no longer harmless.

He truly was a man out of time. Kylah studied Daroch as he foraged through the unused piles of peat bricks and coal in the ruins of her family home and washhouse. He'd been strangely quiet after her admission and his withdrawal depressed her. As he'd reapplied his layer of silt at the Allt Dubh, it had been like he donned an extra layer of armor *against* her. When she'd asked him why he wore the mud, he'd simply barked, "Protection." As if she was supposed to know what that meant. She'd tried to pry it out of him as he stored his satchel of fish in the frigid river, but he paid her no heed.

When he'd gathered shamrocks from the loch and dressed his wound with herbs, he'd been strangely modest, hiding most of his action beneath his robes.

He'd been so bloody adamant about wanting the truth, hadn't he? Well she'd been honest with him. What did she have to lose by the admission? More to the point, why would he be disturbed by it? *She* didn't particularly like the idea that the only thing to break the bleak apathy surrounding her this past year was a miserly *old* Druid with an infuriating air of superiority. But there it was. He awakened sensation inside of her. Evoked her natural curiosities. Fascinated and distressed her.

Made her forget...

Most men would have welcomed her questions, taking any occasion to impress her with ceaseless conversation on their favorite topics. Namely themselves. But nay, not he, not Daroch *mud-face* McLeod. What did he do when he'd garnered her interest? Ordered her to leave! Thrown things at her—well—through her, but even so. Treated her as though her company was undesirable.

And yet the question remained: *Why!?*

"Yes, brighten yer glow until I can get these bricks started." He stacked them in his arms.

Kylah made a sound of irritation which he either didn't recognize or ignored.

"This is all new and fine material. If ye lost everything in the fire, where did ye get it?" he asked.

"Laird MacKay had it delivered to my mother as we resided here until recently."

He turned to her then, the surprise on his face evident, even through the mask. "She remained... here?" He looked around as though seeing the place for the first time.

The large circular room had accommodated the smithy's waiting customers and, later, the washhouse. Blackened stones, earth, charred beams and ash covered the ground. The once vaulted ceilings were non-existent but for one corner which had been where her mother had stacked the cot upon which she'd slept. A wall of stone lay where the arch to the small room that housed her father's forge had been. That room remained mostly intact, though the bricks were now black instead of earth and all that remained of the ceiling was a fine layer of ash over everything.

Kylah never ventured into that room.

"How did she survive?"

The corner closest to the burned-out entry had become Kylah's by edict of the amount of time she spent there. Kylah lurked there now, feeling on edge as she considered the Druid's question.

"The Laird sent food, bread, cheese, potatoes, jerky, things that didn't need to be cooked. Animal furs, and that." She gestured to the makings for a long-lasting fire.

"There's a year's worth of fire here, she never lit one? Even in the winter?" His skeptical voice grated on her already raw nerves.

"Never." She cast a pointed look at the state of the building. "She had somewhat of an aversion to fire."

His brows lifted, but he wisely remained silent as he maneuvered through the rubble with his arms full of coal and disappeared into the back. "The bellows are not too damaged," he called to her. "I'll need to go into town for the textiles to repair it. 'Tis a fine forge yer father built."

"Aye," she agreed, still unable to look at it.

He appeared in the entry, returning for another load for the fire. "If I'm lucky, yer father will have a safe place in the fireclay where a few of his tools would be kept untouched by rust and such."

Kylah searched her memory. "Behind the row of anvils, beneath the slack tub." At least he was speaking to her now.

He disappeared into the room again with another armful of coal. "Show me," he ordered.

"Nay." Her refusal was instantaneous.

His head reappeared in the entry. "Nay? What do ye mean, 'Nay?'"

"Have you never heard the word before?" she asked, stunning them both with the ire in her voice.

His hazel eyes turned stormy and he stood atop the rubble, glowering down at her from across the wide ashen floor. "What's gotten into ye, woman?"

"*Me?* What's gotten into me, you ask?" Kylah watched her green glow crawl across the ashes, though she didn't move from where she stood. "You've been naught but churlish and ill-tempered with me this entire afternoon. *If* you've acknowledged me at all."

"Ye did almost get me killed. Twice in the space of an hour, which is a feat, even for a Banshee," he replied archly.

"That's not why you've been insufferable, and we both know it," she sneered.

"I've lived in solitude for a hundred years." He crossed large, defensive arms over his broad chest and Kylah had to force herself not to remember what that chest looked like without the robes. "Ye canna invade every moment of my life, demand every detail of my history, and uncover all my secrets expecting me to *like* it."

Anger covered the flash of hurt and truth in his words. "Well, Daroch McLeod, if you want your solitude so badly you may have it. I will not venture into *that* room. You're safe from my odious presence there, so do what you will."

Were she not in such a temper, she'd have found his expression of absolute befuddlement endearing. He looked behind him into the forge room, then back at her. "Why doona ye go in there? Because it's where yer father—"

"It has nothing to *do* with my father!" she exploded, her glow pulsing further into the waning twilight.

"Then, why—"

"You don't get to ask why! That's *my* question." At this point, Kylah realized she was being childish and ridiculous. But she'd never in her life lost her temper. She'd never felt this kind of organic, indignant anger before. Never had a deserving outlet for it. And since the horrible day she died, she'd only ever lurked in her corner, staring at that damnable forge, reliving the horrors that befell her there.

Every memory created by a loving man and father in that room had been defiled, replaced by the image of another man's hatred. His domination. His sweat. Her pain. Her blood. Screams. Flames.

"Keep your secrets, Daroch McLeod." A tear snaked from Kylah's eye and burned its way down her cheek. "And I'll keep mine."

She'd vanished again. The evening seemed darker without her, and not just for the absence of her ever-present glow. Daroch inspected the ruins of the quaint washhouse with renewed intent. What would keep her from entering the forge? What harm could befall her there?

The living structure just off the business had been made of wood rather than stone, so only the blackened outlines of two bedrooms and the cook hearth of a kitchen remained. They told Daroch nothing, except that if anyone had been trapped there, they'd have perished.

Beneath a mulberry bush, a stone cross and two small wooden ones were lined neatly by the pond. Perhaps his wee Banshee was buried there. His nose pricked to the smell of the heather blooms mixing with the mulberry as he made his way to the tiny, well-kept graveyard.

He ran a finger across the stone engraving of Diarmudh MacKay. His cross was done in the olde way. Not to symbolize the Christian sacrifice, but in the way of the Druids, symbolizing the great balance of science and magic. Of earth and the sky. The body and the soul. Man and woman. Life and death. Twined together with sacred, eternal knots.

Sinking onto his haunches, he found the next two graves to be small, shallow, and relatively fresh, only recently overtaken by moss and grass. The markers were rough hewn and wooden. They read *Katriona MacKay* and *Kamdyn MacKay* in shaky, hand-carved script. The graves were small enough for young children.

Only their bones rested here. Daroch shook his head. That must have been all that was left after the fire. He stood and scanned the outlying area, capturing each detail in its entirety.

What about Kylah's bones? Where did they rest?

His gaze landed back on the ruins and a cold spear pierced his chest.

He knew exactly where they were.

Returning to the entry, Daroch studied what used to be the washhouse. The patterns in the char along the walls and floor implied fire accelerant of some kind. Not pitch, so likely alcohol based. He could mark where the large wooden tubs had stood and noted the metal remains of various tools and instruments of their trade strewn every which way among the ashes.

As though they'd been upended and tossed in violent chaos.

Violent enough to spawn the creation of three Banshees.

Heart accelerating, Daroch's eyes flew to the ruined archway and the forge beyond. His boots sounded very loud as they disturbed the ashes, creating the echoes of a ghastly, unspeakable horror. By the time he reached the forge, his breath sawed out of his lungs in great bursts. His nostrils flared, and his mind retreated from what he was certain to find there.

The room fared better than the rest. Daroch's eyes skimmed past burnt tools, a great forge covered in the fine layer of ash, anvils specialized to make everything from nails to horseshoes to armor.

The back window cut into the stone wall behind the forge was broken. The sunset illuminated the heather-strewn hill that offered some protection from the harsh Highland weather, and sparkled off jagged edges of glass.

Something strange drew Daroch to it and he crossed the room with swift strides. Reaching out, he pried one of the glass fragments from the casing and inspected the dark, dried stain on the sharp point.

Blood.

Someone had escaped through the window. Upon further inspection he surmised that the window had not been broken by the heat of the fire, but by the force of a blunt object. But what? He looked at the floor to the corner on his right and then turned to the left to search the dark nook created by the back wall and the forge.

All the breath in his lungs released in a great whoosh as Daroch's knees fell to the ashes.

Bones. *Her* bones.

"Gods," he rasped through a throat closing with alarming pressure.

Huddled there, as though playing a children's hiding game, the legs were curled into the chest. The arms circled the drawn up knees, but the wrists...

Daroch turned from the sight, sucking in a bracing breath before he could face it again.

The wrists were secured with small iron chains. Likely forged in this very room. The tiny bones of the fingers clasped together in supplication.

He closed his eyes again, but gruesome, hideous images flashed behind his lids. The worst of which was her soft green eyes, round with terror, begging for mercy. His own eyes burned, and a suspicious sheen clouded his vision when he opened them again.

Daroch blinked it away. A band of wrath encircled his lungs. His heart fell like a heavy brick to the pit of his stomach. He wanted to scream. He wanted to vomit.

He wanted to run.

Instead, he forced himself to look at her. To bear witness to her unjust death. Her skull sat on slim, delicate shoulders, regarding him from small, empty sockets. Her teeth smiled at him in the most macabre way and a shudder overtook him.

"Och lass," he whispered. "What did they do to ye?" Reaching to her, Daroch's finger trembled as he gingerly wiped at the green patina of ash that covered her bones and rubbed it between his finger and thumb. Peat moss, oil, and pitch, identical to the bricks he'd been loading into the forge.

Huddled in the tiny nook, she would have been spared the fire. Likely, the smoke would have filled her lungs, but she'd have died before feeling the burn of the flames. Daroch had a sick suspicion the blaze hadn't been lit in one room of the house. Nay, the fucking villains had used live women as tinder.

I never venture in there.

His stomach protested again and he snarled. What other secrets of hers did this room contain that had been erased by the fire? Why hadn't her bones been laid into the earth? Why was she stuffed back here like so much forgotten slag?

Who had done this?

Daroch picked up a peat brick and crushed it in his fist. The first time he'd laid eyes on Kylah MacKay was in the great hall of Laird MacKay's Castle. Rory MacKay had been plagued with Banshees and summoned Daroch for help. The self-same Laird who sent these peat bricks. He hurled another one through the window.

Banshees were creatures of vengeance. Daroch looked down at her bones, every part of him aching for her. He'd know, of course, that Kylah must have died horribly. He'd just forced himself not to think of it. Not to care. She wasn't his problem, after all. She wasn't his fault.

She wasn't his to lose. To avenge. But the fact that she remained a Banshee this long after her death meant she was unable to claim her vengeance.

And that was something they had in common.

Chapter Eight

The witching hour fell before Daroch found himself at the doors of the MacKay keep. He beat on them with his staff. "Open up, MacKay," he demanded.

A familiar, fair-haired man with the dimensions of a tree trunk threw open the heavy door and held Daroch at sword point. "*You*, Druid!" he accused.

"Yes. Brilliant deduction. Now get me yer Laird," Daroch ordered.

The man sputtered before rushing him, sword aimed at his throat.

Daroch side-stepped his attack easily, and thunked him soundly between the shoulder blades with his staff, sending the man sprawling face-first into the dirt.

The man was likely still sore at the hours he'd spent as Daroch's guest some weeks past. The curses that were spat from his mouth along with the mud validated the theory.

Perhaps *guest* was too kind a word.

Shrugging, Daroch slipped through the open door and slammed it closed, barring it against the angry MacKay steward and turned to find another sword held just as directly to his throat.

"Druid," the soft, low voice of Rory MacKay held a lethal note Daroch instantly respected.

"Laird," he returned the man's greeting, meeting Rory's deadly amber gaze with one of his own. "If I were ye, I'd look into finding more competent protection."

"Lorne is one of the most capable, deadly warriors to see a battlefield." Rory glanced at the door, but only for a moment, a look of resigned respect teasing good humor into his brawny features. "I imagine he's still cross with ye for leaving him stranded when I sent him for ye."

"Lower yer sword," Daroch commanded slowly. He would not trade good natured conversation with the man who may have murdered three innocent women.

Rory instantly sobered, stepping closer and narrowing his eyes, the dangerous tip of his weapon pressing against Daroch's jugular with precision. "State yer business, Druid, before I run ye through."

For a moment of pure male instinct, Daroch wanted to test the man. Rory's name was heralded as one of the best warriors in the Highlands that didn't claim to be Berserker or Shape shifter. Daroch rarely ventured out of his cave and he'd still heard of the man. They stood remarkably similar in height, and though Daroch's shoulders and arms were wider, the Laird's trunk was thicker.

"Why run me through, when ye can tie me up and set me on fire?" Daroch put a winter's worth of chill in the words and watched as the Laird's face transformed.

Rory lowered his sword as though it had become too heavy to lift. Shame and regret darkened his eyes and he turned away, treading the few steps to the council table to settle his bulk into the Chieftain's chair.

"I thought I was a cold-hearted bastard," Daroch advanced on him, shaking with the strength of his rage. "But three innocent lasses, burned *alive*. Do ye ken the pain of it? Have ye no compassion at all, no humanity? Why have the Banshees not reaped their vengeance?"

A hollow, wry sound escaped the Laird. "Believe me they tried, but the man responsible is already dead by my own order. I stole their vengeance from them, but not their lives."

Daroch hit the table with his staff. "Doona lie to me! I *vow* I'll see ye burn as they did. I can prove the bricks used to raze the washhouse to the ground came from this very castle."

"Set to blaze by my twin brother, Angus, and his men." Rory put his knuckles on the table and rose to his feet, bringing their faces flush. "All of whom are dead upon *my* command."

Daroch searched the man for signs of deceit. His breath was steady, his eyes undilated and clear, the pulse thrumming in his temple slightly elevated, but none more than had been at Daroch's threat. He spoke the truth.

Aggression sizzled in the air between them for a tense moment.

"Who are ye to storm my castle and accuse me of such atrocities? What business is it of yers?" Rory's voice lowered to a more reasonable register, but his meaning was apparent.

"I'm—" Daroch paused. No one. He was nothing to these Banshees or to their Laird. If he truly was a smart man, he'd be relieved Kylah had finally left him alone and go about his business. But he couldn't. The ghostly lass had reached her wee glow into his darkness and illuminated something he'd long forgotten he'd even possessed.

His heart.

"I'm buggered." He sank into the chair behind him and tossed his head against the wooden back. He was so close. So close to reaping a vengeance of his own. He couldn't afford a comely distraction like her. Not now. "Ye requested that I help eliminate a Banshee back when ye were tormented with them. How did ye end up ridding yerself of her?"

The Laird threw his bronze lion's mane back and laughed so hard he fisted his hands in his blue and green plaid. "It's quite the story," he choked out between guffaws. "But the long and short of it is I married her."

Daroch gaped. Perhaps the Laird had gone mad.

"Moved their mother and the entire lot next door for the time being." Rory wiped a tear of mirth from the corner of his eye.

"Ye... jest?" Daroch asked dubiously.

"Serious as a Banshee's curse." The Laird still chuckled as he took his seat again and regarded Daroch over long, steepled fingers. "I'm assuming Kylah's been yer unwelcome companion these past couple of days."

Daroch nodded, squirming at the word *unwelcome*.

"Her mother's been worried."

"I thought ye were after some black magic by marrying the Frasier witch," Daroch recalled. "How did ye end up married to a Banshee?"

"I had no idea Kathryn Frasier was a witch when we married. To be fair, both women tried to kill me," he said good naturedly. "But Katriona couldna because I've already died once and came back so I was immune to her Banshee powers."

"Ye're *An Dioladh*," Daroch observed.

"Aye. But Kathryn attempted to poison me on our wedding night and ended up poisoning herself. Katriona took advantage of an empty body and..." he waved his hand, as though that explained the rest.

Daroch gaped for a second time in as many minutes. "So Katriona is now Kathryn."

"To everyone but her family." Rory confirmed. "And ye now, though I canna ken why I told ye."

"Do ye love her?" Daroch's question surprised them both.

"Aye," Rory's lips curved into a secret smile. "I always have." His smile disappeared as quickly as it had materialized. "Kylah took the news of our marriage understandably hard, though, if ye'll excuse my saying so, I doona understand why she sought ye out."

Daroch ignored his question. "Kylah disapproves of yer marriage... because of who yer brother was?"

Any sign of good humor abandoned the Laird's face as shadows encroached. "Because of what he did to her."

"Ye mean, burning her and her family alive?"

The Laird's eyes darkened and the skin around his lips turned white.

A sick, heavy dread landed in Daroch's chest. "Tell me," he breathed.

Rory winced. "What has she told ye?"

Daroch shook his head. "Nothing. I only know what I saw in the ruins. Her bones. The ashes... They never put her in the ground. She was just... *left* there. Bound and discarded."

The Laird closed his eyes for a long moment, and when they opened again, the pain and shame in their depths shaped the dread in Daroch's chest into a sharp, jagged point.

"I loved Katriona MacKay since I was a boy," the Laird admitted. "And Angus he... he loved Kylah because she was such a beauty. But Angus didna love like a man should love. His love was possession, nay, oppression and dominance. He was a covetous, violent, and sick man."

Daroch's hand tightened on the birch staff until it was white. His teeth clenched so hard his jaw ached. His mind refused the Laird's words, shunning where they were about to take him.

"Kylah and her mother rejected his offer of marriage on numerous occasions, but once my father died and Angus became Laird, he offered one last time. Ordered it, more like."

"Nay," Daroch whispered.

Rory's throat worked over a difficult swallow before he continued. "Upon receiving her rejection, he took his two closest friends with him to the washhouse. Only Kylah and her mother were home..."

"*Nay,*" Daroch shook his head violently, rejecting what came next.

"From what I could tell, Angus and his men were there for an hour or so before Katriona and Kamdyn returned. Before... the fires were set. My wife told me she didna see anything, but they had Kylah and her mother in the back room with the forge and they made her mother watch while they—"

A roar crawled up Daroch's throat and he surged upward, grabbing the heavy table and tipping it over, reveling in the sound of splintering wood.

Rory was also on his feet, hand at the hilt of his sword but surprisingly, the Laird made no move to stop him.

Daroch grasped the chair he'd been sitting on with both hands and hurled it at the stone wall. It shattered as though made of glass instead of oak.

"Angus was brutally slaughtered by the Berserker Laird, Connor MacLauchlan." Rory insisted, putting a staying hand out. "They all were. They didna die... well."

"Good!" Daroch barked. "I will curse their bones. I will submit their names to the Gods and mark the rest of my flesh to pay for their eternal suffering."

Rory jaw worked over raw emotion and Daroch realized for the first time he truly spoke of the man's brother. His twin. The Laird's shame made sense now. And, though he pitied the man, he was glad to see it.

"Ye care for her," Rory murmured.

The Laird's statement stunned Daroch into silence. He looked at the destroyed table. The shattered chair. Down at his own trembling hands.

Fuck.

"They should have had their vengeance," he growled.

"I know." Rory put his hand on Daroch's shoulder, his first human contact in a hundred years. Daroch didn't shrug him off, but took a strange, surprising comfort in the gesture. "Angus is eternally burning in hell for what he's done. But the pact is struck, and the two younger lasses will belong to the

Banshee Queen come the Solstice. Unless there's something ye can do."

Daroch choked on his own impotence. "There is naught I can do unless the Queen breaks her pact first." He let out an exhausted sigh, the entirety of his day catching up with him in a single moment.

Rory nodded in understanding and for an added first, Daroch had to fight another feeling he'd thought had deserted him a millennia ago.

Embarrassment.

"I'm... sorry about yer table."

"It was my father's table." Rory shrugged, but his voice held a curious dark note. "Better suited to firewood anyway. It's high time I crafted my own legacy as Laird of this clan."

"Aye," Daroch agreed and turned to the door, wondering if Lorne lurked behind it.

"Katriona is afraid to lose her sisters to the Fae," Rory admitted.

Daroch turned to him, his intent deadly serious. "She should be." He plunged into the night, which was empty of angry stewards or glowing, inquisitive Banshees. Looking around the dark streets of Durness, he noted the changes in the village since last he came. Roofs were newer, structures reinforced, and the energy of the place had changed from one of fear and strife to one of hope and careful optimism. Rory was a good man, a good Laird. Different than his brother had been.

A blue glow from the window of a cozy, thatched cottage caught his eye. Right next to the castle. Kylah's home.

He had to see her.

Daroch found himself in front of the door before he remembered the strides it took to get there. He knocked louder than he should have this time of night.

"Who- who's there?" a brittle voice inquired.

"The Druid. I need to see Kylah."

Daroch jumped back when a wee young face burst from the sturdy wood of the closed door followed by slender shoulders. "What do you want with Kylah?" the young Banshee's voice demanded with a shake of her strawberry curls.

"I need to speak with her," he hedged.

"She's not here, you may go." The girl disappeared back behind the door.

Daroch frowned. Being dismissed felt... well he felt a little ashamed for how many times he'd uttered that command to Kylah. And with much less civility. He put his palm on the door. Then his forehead. "I-I put her bones in the ground." He didn't recognize the husky voice as his own. "Will ye tell her that? I removed the chains... and she rests next to her father."

After a quiet moment, several latches released and the door swung inward. Instead of the young Banshee, a stooped creature draped in soft robes and furs appeared.

"You did what I could not bring myself to do." A gnarled hand pushed the hood back from a face so disfigured by scars Rory could barely stand to look at it. Soft green eyes flooded with tears that rolled down ribbed, mangled cheeks. "I couldn't make myself go back in that room." She clutched at his robes as she fell to her knees, burying her face in them and sobbing. "And I hate myself for leaving her there!"

"Oh, mama." The young Banshee drifted into the entry, hovering helplessly.

Daroch bled for the woman. He could not condemn her weakness. Not after what she'd suffered. He leaned his staff on the cottage and scooped the lady up, carrying her inside. The house was small but comfortable. A fire lay prepared, but not lit, in the large stone hearth. No lanterns glowed. The only light provided by the blue glow of the youngest MacKay sister.

"Kamdyn, is it?" he asked.

"Aye, ye can put her here." She gestured to the large bed, likely brought down from the castle.

Daroch bent and set the frail woman down gently and covered her with a mountain of furs.

"I thank ye, Druid, for putting my wee one to rest." the old woman touched the silt on his face, then brought a hand to her own face.

Daroch didn't trust his voice, so he only nodded. Straightening, he looked around. "She's really not here," he noted with disappointment.

"Hasn't been for days." Worry glimmered in Kamdyn's eyes. A familiar green turned aquamarine by her blue glow.

"She's been with me," he informed her.

The freckled nose wrinkled. "On purpose?"

A wry laugh wrung from his heavy chest. "No one's more mystified by it than I. I made it abundantly clear her presence wasna wanted."

Kamdyn smirked, wisdom beyond her years shone behind her pretty features. "Perhaps 'tis why she sought you out. *Everyone* wants Kylah." Her face fell. "*Wanted*, that is. Also, she may have been drawn to the pain and loneliness in your heart. For I think 'tis what she needed to feel."

Daroch found himself in front of the door, ready to flee from a harmless wee ghost. "What do ye know of my heart?" he thundered.

"Not a thing," she admitted gently. "But we are Banshees. We're drawn to sadness, anger, and loss. Thus is our nature."

Daroch couldn't think of a thing to say, so he turned from the young girl who saw too much and shut the door quietly behind him.

"Thank you, Druid, for what you did," the wee Banshee called after him.

He didn't turn to acknowledge her, but melted into the moonless highland night.

Chapter Nine

It took Kylah until the next evening to gather the courage to see him. She stood for untold hours staring at her grave, at her name so meticulously carved into a marker with strange and lovely runes surrounding it.

Daroch had found her remains. He'd laid her bones to rest. He'd visited her home and comforted her mother. He'd fascinated and excited Kamdyn, who'd vigorously regaled her with every detail of their short interaction.

"You must go to him, Kylah." After a hearty and warm welcome home, Kamdyn had rushed her out the door so fast it left Kylah slightly dazed. "He *needs* you."

Needed her? Her youngest sister obviously knew nothing about the man. But even so, the pull to see him again was almost magnetic in its inevitability.

Kylah lurked in the small crevice that opened into his cave, masking herself from his notice. He wore a vest-like leather tunic that bared his arms to the shoulders and fell to his feet. It split at the waist in many different places, allowing for movement and showing the stag skin trews he wore beneath as he purposefully strode from one place to another. His skin was free of silt and glowed in the firelight like honey poured over iron beneath the ancient markings. His long hair fell clean to the middle of his back in a thick, ebony braid.

Kylah gawked as he carefully poured what appeared to be liquid metal into a clear bowl of water and marked the change in water level.

"I can see ye, Banshee," he informed her, though he'd never once looked in her direction.

"How?" she asked, incensed at being caught staring.

"Shamrock, remember?"

Drat. Kylah scowled. She'd forgotten.

Drifting toward him, she watched as he recorded his findings on a parchment with ink and quill. Kylah wished she'd learned to read, but they'd never had the time whilst running the washhouse. Katriona learned her figures to keep track of the money, but Kylah had never been bothered to.

"What are you doing?"

He still didn't look up. "I'm measuring mercury."

"You're what?"

He moved back to the clear bowl. "Everything that exists on this planet is made up of tiny, invisible particles of material," he explained. "An object with the same mass might still have more or less of those particular materials than another. By measuring how a submerged object displaces a volume of liquid equal to the volume of the object, one can calculate the density of this material."

Kylah studied the clear bowl and frowned. "Then *I* no longer exist.

"Doona be ridiculous, of course ye do."

"I don't have this— material. I don't displace anything. Not air. Not water. Not even you." She reached out and passed a hand through his thick arm to make her point. "Therefore, I no longer exist. Not really."

He looked up at her then and his eyes widened, snagged by a major change in her appearance.

"Blue." She held her hands out for inspection, casting her soft new glow wider against the black stone of his cave. "Your doing, I think."

The Druid remained silent, setting his parchment and quill down and picking up a large shell from an adjacent table.

"I want to show ye something." He walked to the fissure and disappeared into it.

Kylah barreled right through the stone. She followed him to the edge of the grotto, her light reflecting off the softly lapping water. Something about the way he fit his lips around the opening of the shell and blew caused a curious tightening of everything beneath her belly button. Two long calls and one short emitted from the shell, echoing in the cavern and yet muffled by the water. He lowered the shell and listened.

Kylah remained utterly still. What was he showing her? What was she supposed to infer?

His arms flexed as he raised the shell again, but a high-pitched whistle followed by a series of ticks exploded into the cave. A smooth grey body jumped from the grotto, glistening as it executed a perfect flip and dove back into the water with barely a splash.

Daroch turned to Kylah, his lip curling in a devastating half-smile as he waded in to the knee and greeted the dolphin who came up to him with a welcoming cry.

He ran his large hand over the smooth skin and the creature chattered and groaned in obvious pleasure.

Kylah bet her soul the dolphin was female.

Entranced, she moved to lurk just behind his shoulder and was startled to find the dolphin noticed her.

"Hello," she whispered, awed by the rare moment. A gift from the Druid she'd never be able to return. The dolphin's ever-present smile seemed to widen as it rolled and nodded, spouting water until she laughed.

"Impressed as I am by your animal ken, I have to admit I don't understand what you're trying to express to me," she murmured, watching Daroch launch the incredible creature back into the deeper water of the grotto.

"Did ye know sound is one of the most powerful forces in the Universe?" he asked. "In fact, most of my Druid ancestors believed sound was the material by which the Universe was created."

Kylah shook her head, though he wasn't facing her.

"It's actually a wave. A mechanical vibration that can travel through *any* form of matter," He gestured around them. "Air. Water. Stone. It leaves nothing untouched or unaffected." He turned and waded back toward her, his wide shoulders turning with the effort of walking through the water. "Creatures like the one I just summoned use sound to navigate and to detect danger. We all use sound to communicate. To perceive. To identify. To seduce."

He didn't stop until he loomed in front of her, and Kylah could only stare at his deep chest, a curious lump in her throat and an even more perplexing heat in her loins.

"Every powerful force produces its own identifiable sound. The wind, the sea, a storm... And ye, Kylah, ye are a creature of pure, dynamic resonance."

She turned from him, her heart surging beneath her breast. Something in his words resonated, all right, and she thrummed with the power of it.

"To a Druid, the understanding of it goes even deeper than that," he murmured.

"Deeper?" she breathed, catching her lip in her teeth.

"Every soul, every scream, every emotion leaves an echo in this world. Every conscious being is made of energy. Every heart beats with it. Every thought is shaped by it. And that energy canna be created or destroyed. Not by magic. Not by death. Not even by the Gods. It can only be manipulated or changed. Therefore, everyone who ever existed still continues to do so, in one way or another."

Though they weren't touching, Kylah could *feel* the energy he spoke of leaping off his potent, vital form and melding with hers. The sensation was like no other, arcing between them as though charged with lightning. His tattoos glowed blue in her light, seeming to rise off his skin and pulse with magic.

Kylah tilted her head back to look into his eyes and what she saw in their brindled depths caused her to jump away from him.

"You *know*," she gasped. She didn't have to clarify. He'd somehow found out about Angus, about her darkest and most terrifying shame. About the violent loss of her innocence and the hour of hell she'd endured before her death.

His eyes closed in a protracted blink, and when they opened she saw none of the pity she feared. She couldn't feel it, either. But she did feel the anger, the sorrow, the helpless, masculine rage that burned within him, searching for the absolution of retribution and finding none. It roared at her from his aura, from his eyes, from the tension in his dangerous body.

It drew her back toward him. "You don't have to worry about vengeance, for there is none to be had." She heaved a great sigh. "And besides, it's not your responsibility to exact."

"I *know* that." His demeanor darkened into something vicious and altogether frightening. "In here, I know that." He tapped his finger to his temple. "But in here..." He pressed his fist to his heart, but didn't finish his sentence.

Kylah reached out and put her ghostly, iridescent hand over his fist. "Sometimes, I'm sad that I cannot touch you. At first, I was glad of it, because I didn't have to be afraid. But now..."

He shuddered as her hand passed through his to settle by where his heart beat. Kylah could almost feel the power of it, the strong, steady rhythm accelerating along with the shallower breaths he took.

"Ye should be grateful for it still," he murmured, then blinked, as though stunned he'd said it aloud.

"Why?" she frowned.

"Ye have good reason to fear me."

"Because you're going to find a way to kill the Fae, possibly even me?" She met his eyes and saw something in them that transfixed and repelled her with equal force.

"That," he said in a low, rumbling growl. "And because despite everything, I desire ye, Kylah. Just as much as that MacKay bastard wanted ye, probably even more."

Kylah snatched her hand back, horrified. "But-but you said that beauty doesn't matter. That it doesn't *mean* anything! You told me you *didn't* want me."

A muscle in his jaw jumped and he turned his face, the tattoo flexing with the clench of his teeth. "I know what I said."

"You *lied*?" she gasped. "You, who seek and regard truth above all else?"

"*Aye*," he hissed, advancing on her. "But I didna lie to ye, I lied to myself, which is the greater sin."

Kylah shrank back, forgetting that he posed no physical threat. Right now, he was the most dangerous being on the planet. How could he? How could he make her care for him, make her *trust* him? Lure her into a false sense of security, make her *feel* again. He'd delighted and soothed her with his poetic knowledge about the Universe and her place within it and then he tells her *this*. It changed everything.

"You would hurt me like they did?" she accused, suddenly feeling very small. Like she wanted to crawl inside of herself until the moon let go of the earth and the sun evaporated the sea. She wanted to die. Again. "You would humiliate me? Bind me? Expose me and—"

"*Nay*," he rasped, reaching out like she was a cornered, skittish animal he was trying to tame. "Never. I wouldna cause he pain for the world, but teach ye all the pleasures a woman's body is capable of."

She squinted at him, weighing the earnestness of his expression, the desire in his voice, the veracity of his words.

Never had he looked so open. So naked.

"What do ye mean by 'pleasure?'" she ventured.

"Och, Kylah, a woman's pleasure is a very powerful, very complicated thing. But once attained it is... indescribable to behold." He ran the backs of his knuckles down what would have been the curve of her cheek.

Kylah's eyes fluttered closed and if she concentrated very hard, she could almost feel his touch.

Almost.

Her curiosity tempered her anger at him, anger that should have been stronger than it was. She had to admit that beneath the fear, beneath the dark memories and instinctive revolt, relief resided there. He'd noted her beauty, as she'd noticed his. He was not immune to her, as she was so entirely affected by him. "Where does one find it?" she whispered. "How?"

His lids lowered by half, a knowing smirk toying with the edges of lips that appeared much more full than any time previous. "The incidentals differ for every woman, but it culminates in the same place for all of them."

Kylah had a feeling she knew which place that was, for at his low, silken words it clenched and ached with a foreign awareness. She couldn't think of that place. She couldn't face it. It couldn't exist.

"I don't believe you," she breathlessly denied.

He chuckled. A dark, threatening sound that washed over her like a cauldron of boiling tar, scalding skin that no longer existed with a heat that was not unpleasant. "I could prove it to ye."

"Nay, you cannot!" she quickly reminded him, holding up a hand to ward him off. "You can't touch me."

"Aye, but..." his brow quirked.

But what? He could not touch her. He couldn't *teach* her. There was no way around it, to her immense relief. There simply was no *but*.

"Ye can touch yerself, can ye not?" he rumbled. "Ye can feel yer own... flesh?"

Her hand flew to her throat in absolute shock. She felt its pressure as sure as when she was alive. In response to that realization, she jerked it to her side again, and hid both hands in the flowing folds of her robes.

His face gave the notion of a triumphant smile without the slightest movement of his lips. Though his tattoo did wrinkle devilishly beside his eye. He stepped closer, bending his head so it was right next to her ear. "What do ye say, lass, are ye up for... an experiment?"

Chapter Ten

Kylah swallowed. Failed. And did it again. She was attempting to swallow her heart which kept trying to escape through her throat. What if she could do it? And yet, what if she couldn't? How awful would that be... for both of them?

She pulled back a little and looked at him. He was so certain. Self-assured to the point of arrogance. He knew so much about pleasure, did he? What if...

"What if it doesn't work?" she worried aloud. "What if—they've broken me?"

"That's really up to ye, isn't it?" The gentleness in his dappled eyes softened the hard truth of his words.

A storm brewed within her. How could she be broken if she did not allow herself to be so? How could she let the pain they inflicted upon her ruin any chance at pleasure? If it existed, didn't she deserve it? Didn't she need it more than most? If it was to be had, if it was a part of her body, she should be claiming it. Owning it.

"Tell me what to do."

His nostrils flared at her whispered order, but he held completely still. He took a few breaths deep into his chest and let them out slowly, his gaze conflicted and intense.

"S-should I be... undressed?" The idea left her cold and terrified.

His brows drew together. "Eventually, but ye often doona start out that way."

"Oh." she felt suddenly very awkward, and moved closer to his imposing body, instinctively seeking his warmth.

"Gods how I wish I could touch ye," he groaned.

The same desperation he expressed vibrated through her body. "Tell me what would happen if you could. If you *were*. Where would you begin?"

"That's easy, lass," he said huskily. "I would start with yer infuriating, tempting mouth."

She covered her mouth with diffidence. "Infuriating?"

He grunted with amusement. "Aye. I'd stop yer incessant questions with my own lips as I'm tempted to do time and again."

"Oh?" she asked from behind her hand. How long had he been *tempted* to do so?

"Move your fingertips," he cajoled. "Run them across the ridges of your lips where they meet yer skin." She did so, discovering that her mouth felt fuller and warmer to her now than it ever had. Keeping her touch feather-light, she traced the two peaks beneath her nose and enjoyed the sensation of her breath escaping through parted fingers. Her lower lip had more sensation in it than her upper and she lingered there, looking to him for further direction.

His eyes hungrily tracked each movement of her fingers and in a moment of impulse, she slipped one into her mouth and wet it on her tongue. She took the soft hiss of breath through his teeth as an affirmation.

When he spoke again, his voice was tight and low. "Next, I'd explore yer jaw, and the hollow of your throat. It can be very sensitive there."

Kylah ran the backs of her fingers across her jaw, mirroring the action he'd attempted to perpetrate only moments before, before dropping beneath her chin. She sucked in her breath. It was like the entire surface of her skin awakened and came alive. Starting with the skin on her cheek and spreading downward in a wave of delicate sensation. Her chest became flushed, her nipples constricted, her belly tightened and beneath it, a shameless quiver began, stunning her into stillness.

"What de ye feel, Kylah?" he prodded.

She searched her mind, which had somehow deserted her. "Awake?" No. That didn't seem quite right. "Aware."

"Yes," he sounded pleased, but she couldn't look at him. "That is the beginning, now ye must discover more."

She swallowed hard again, feeling her throat work beneath her fingertips. "What would you—discover next?" she queried.

That dark chuckle speared through her again, weakening her knees.

"I'd run my hands over yer shoulders and down yer arms, taking yer robes with them."

"Really?" Her brows fell together in puzzlement. "To be frank, I thought you would go straight for my... my breasts." She finished in a whisper.

"Oh, I'll get to them," he vowed. "But they have to ask for it, first."

Ask for it? "I don't know what you mean."

"Yer shoulders," he reminded. "Slowly. Feel the softness of the skin there."

She followed his dictate, undoing a few clasps and sliding her ghostly robes from her shoulders with her fingertips, taking a moment to feel the soft glide of her fingers over smooth and velvety skin. It was lovely. It relaxed and revitalized her all at once.

"Lower," he pressed.

Her robes hung onto her nipples, almost exposing them to his eyes that appeared to glow in her intensifying light.

"I-I'm frightened," she admitted. Even though this time there was no tearing and rending of garments. No violence. No pain. There was still danger. Danger of degradation. Of shame and rejection. Of judgment and failure. She couldn't bring herself to bare her body to the greedy eyes of a man. "Maybe I should just lie down."

"Excellent idea." He locked eyes with her, and they simultaneously lowered their bodies to the smooth stone of the grotto. His hazel gaze remained steady on her own. Never once wavering, never drifting to other parts of her bared flesh. He sustained her, strengthened her, staying with her until she was prostrate on her back and he on his side next to her, his head propped onto one palm supported by his elbow.

"All right." She let out a shaky breath. "All right, what would you do next? Now that I'm lying down."

He took more breaths, as though choosing his words very carefully. "When you open your robes, doona focus on what ye expose of yerself. Just run your fingers along the underside of yer wrist and forearm."

She frowned at him again. It seemed as though he focused on the strangest parts. No other man had ever even *mentioned* her wrists or forearms. Never looked at them. Touched them. They were mundane parts with no particular erotic draw. "Are you entirely certain—?"

"Do it. Just with your nails. Score it lightly." He gave her an impatient look that dispelled much of her earlier tension and brought a smile to her lips.

She lifted her shoulders off the ground, and shrugged her robes away, scoring her tender skin with her nails.

Pleasure. There it was. A hollow, aching pleasure skittering along her skin in such a way, that if she tried to define where it was, it would disappear. The acute response danced along her nerve endings with such intensity that her back arched and her thighs clenched.

"Now," he stated tightly. "They're asking for it now."

"What?" she tried to latch onto his words through the gathering fog in her brain. She was more concerned about what was going on below.

"Yer breasts," he gritted out. "Yer incredible breasts. They're begging to be touched."

They were? She glanced down. They *were*. She was certain of it now. The pert mounds with small, pink tips quivered with her unsteady breath. She risked a glance back up at Daroch, who was staring at them in a most peculiar way. As though he'd never seen their like before. He swallowed convulsively. Once. Twice. His tattoo intensifying the movement of his throat.

"I don't know if I can," she whispered to him.

"Oh, ye can lass." His command sounded more like a plea. "Ye *must*." His chest now scissored with breaths that flared his nostrils with every intake.

"How?"

He dragged his eyes away from her breasts and back to hers and with a blink, the gentleness had returned. "Close yer eyes," he murmured. "Doona think about what ye *should* be doing. Let yer body tell ye what it wants ye to do."

Kylah snapped her eyes shut and instantly felt better. "What it wants *you* to do," she corrected breathlessly, feeling braver now, protected by the darkness behind her eyelids.

"Christ woman," he cursed. More breaths. Not as deep and slow as before, and their increased pattern did something else to Kylah that she'd not expected. It sped her own breaths to match his. Daroch was enjoying this, though he'd not admit it to her. He garnered a pleasure of his own from teaching her this.

She wondered what it was. What it felt like for him.

The ache between her thighs intensified and her breath hitched. She reached her trembling hand to hover over her bare chest and awaited his dark instruction.

"Palm it," he commanded, shorter and less gentle than before.

She did.

"Lift it," he gritted out. "Feel the weight of it."

The longer she touched that part of her, the heavier it felt. All the sensation seemed to be concentrated in the jutting, demanding nipple.

"Run your thumb across yer nipple," he growled.

She complied, softly, slowly.

Pleasure. There it was again. But now, it was tangible. It was there, in her breast. It still bloomed along her skin, particularly in a southerly direction. It was in the panting breaths and the tense muscles of the Druid beside her.

Her other hand flew to her belly as though to contain the swarm of butterflies unleashed within. She gasped as a sudden hot, slick sensation flooded her loins. That place between her thighs suddenly felt uncomfortably warm and alarmingly wet.

She clenched her eyes tighter. "Daroch?" she whimpered.

"Aye?" He sounded pleased again, but also leashed. Restrained, somehow. It ratcheted her anxiety higher.

"Something's happening," she confessed. "Something... there."

A small rustling of fabrics told her that he leaned closer and she had the overwhelming urge to curl into his chest and hide from herself.

"Is it wet?" His tone had turned into silk being rent with bare hands and it reached all the way through her, landing in that place with a wicked vibration. "Is it slick, and swollen, and aching?"

She trembled and turned her head away from him. "*Yes.*"

"Then ye are ready."

She wanted to deny it. But she didn't. She wanted to run from it. But she couldn't. Her body had taken complete control of her mind and the whole of it seemed to be ruled by her sex. And her sex seemed to want to be ruled...

By *him.*

She unhooked the rest of her robes, until they were splayed open beneath her, baring her entire body. Her teeth were clenched, her limbs trembling. Unbidden memories and fears seemed to want to worm their way into the darkness behind her eyelids so she opened them and focused on the stone as her face still turned away from him.

"Find that moisture, Kylah, and there ye'll find yer pleasure."

Slowly, the fingers that rested on the quivering muscles of her belly crept lower and lower still. Through downy curls protecting that most secret part of her, and dipping into her soft, warm sex.

A sharp gasp seemed to escape them both at the same time and mingled with the gentle lapping of the grotto onto the smooth stone.

She was soft and delicately fleshy. Slick and warm and... wanting. Kylah's hips arched and her thighs parted slightly of their own accord.

"Daroch?" she turned her face toward him as her finger brushed against something so intense, her eyes flew wide and their hot gazes collided with all the force of a physical touch.

"I'm here, lass."

"Cover my hand," she begged.

He did. The pressure such that his hand settled into hers. Overtook it. And yet, touched it not at all.

"I can... almost..." He caught his lip in his teeth, his eyes boring down at her, more needs and shadows in their depths than she could ever attempt to count.

She nodded, her fingers seeking out the slick moisture once more, exploring it and the sensitive flesh beneath it.

"Find that place that makes you gasp each time you touch it," he murmured. "Circle it, caress it..." He stopped, dropped his head and seemed to be trying to gather his will.

Kylah took his advice as best she could. Pleasure stabbed at her each time her fingers delicately danced over the small bud of sensation. She'd found it. She reveled in it. She pulsed with it, and each time she found it, the pleasure seemed to bloom wider and throb until in a long and singular moment, instinct seized her, and she no longer needed the Druid's promptings to know what it was she sought.

A rhythm of sorts found her. A circular pressure that tightened every muscle in her thighs and curled her toes. Her breaths became irregular pants. Her eyelids fluttered open, and closed, and open again. Her head tossed from side to side. Seeking him, retreating, then finding him again.

Daroch was right there with her, hovering above her ear, saying dark, wicked things to her in a language long dead, belonging to a people long forgotten. Incantations of sin and sex and possession. The timbre of his voice prompted a perturbing perception to uncurl deep in her very core, to reach out from inside her and seize upon her being.

Pleasure and demand built and competed until wretched little cries ripped from her lips. Just when she felt as though her body could take no more. Like the Fates had pulled her thread too tightly and their tools hovered to snip it into pieces, a wave of pure, unadulterated ecstasy crashed through her with indescribable force.

Her thighs clamped together and she was helpless to do aught but survive the blissful shocks jolting through her. She was dimly aware of the pulsing of her glow, the pitch of her cries. It was the pleasure Daroch had promised and more. It was experiment and atonement. Bliss and blasphemy. Sin and redemption. It was completion. The realization that no one could truly know themselves until they'd known themselves in such a way. Could never truly be a lover, until they'd thus loved.

But as her sense of self seemed to gather back from whence it had shattered, she felt as though something was missing. The kiss of cold spring air on her skin. The warmth of his breath hitting the flesh she bared to him. The satisfaction of something—mutual.

She peered up at Daroch's intense, savagely handsome face and offered him a lazy smile. Everything seemed different in this moment. What once had been cold, black stone now felt close and cozy, much like a sanctuary. What had been a dark place where the very walls had mourned now was full of wicked secrets and echoes of delight. "Now you," she murmured. "Don't you need to find your own... pleasure?"

His jaw locked and he abruptly rolled away from her. "Nay."

She sat up, clutching her robes in front of her. "Why not? I'll be here with you. I want to learn what brings you satisfaction. I want to watch—"

"Doona say that!" he whirled on her, a wild spark of something cruel igniting in his eyes. "*Never* say that to me."

Kylah blinked, disoriented by his abrupt change. "A-all right. Tell me why."

"Why?" Daroch pinned her with his icy stare. "*Why?*" He began pacing like a caged animal, the strips of his tunic flaring about his powerful legs. "It's perverse and repulsive, that's *why*." His lip curled and caused his tattoo to bunch into a demonic shape. "It's unnatural, and—and debasing, beneath our *human* dignity."

"But..." Kylah proceeded very carefully. "Isn't it what you just did with me?"

For the first time since she'd laid eyes on him, his jaw went slack. He went perfectly still but for the breath lifting his chest. His unblinking eyes discomfited her, so she levitated to a standing position and tried to modestly rearrange her robes.

"Tell me what's wrong," she nudged gently. The warmth of her release drained from her limbs like the water of a bath, leaving her cold and trembling and searching for cover.

He plunged both hands into his bound hair, gripping it in frustration. The movement did fascinating things to the muscles in his arms, but Kylah ignored them, focusing on the unraveling man before her.

She floated toward him, reaching out, "Daroch, I'm sorry if I said something to ruin—"

"Don't." He held up his hand, a mask of chilly courtesy settling over his features. "You did nothing. I—have a lot of work to do."

Her head snapped back as though he'd slapped her. "Work?" She gaped at him.

"Aye," he turned from her and strode toward the hidden crevice. "I've already wasted enough time tonight."

Dumbfounded, Kylah stared at the stone wall he just disappeared into. *Wasted time?* Anger smothered a bloom of hurt and confusion. Why would he entice her to do something so intensely intimate and then cruelly abjure it? *Perverse? Repulsive?* She wrapped her arms around her middle.

A deafening crash sounded from his lair. Then another.

Kylah prepared to plunge through the stone and see just what the bloody hell he was doing. And, while she was at it, she would give him the tongue lashing of his life. How *dare* he provoke such a lovely, intimate moment and then go and—

His angry roar preceded the unmistakable shattering of glass. Then wood. After that, a clatter of steel kept her feet planted, as it were, right where she was.

"Oh Daroch." A tear slipped down her cheek. She suddenly understood what had just happened. This had nothing to do with her. And everything to do with his obsessive quest vengeance.

Chapter Eleven

She'd found him again. Daroch had known it was just a matter of time before her now-blue light chased away his shadow. He sat on the point of Cape Wrath in the moonless darkness, contemplating the stars through a breathtaking display of northern lights.

He'd been thinking of her. The dramatic blues and greens curtaining the sky, dancing seductively with each other just out of reach of the human scope, conjured her specter to his thoughts. Not that she hadn't been lurking there since the previous night.

Nay. He sighed. Since he'd heard her heart-rending scream in his cave, she hadn't left him for a moment. Like a tune tripping through one's mind uninvited, or a desire that drove every action, there Kylah was. Unattainable and ever-present. Glowing and chattering and filling the lonely darkness.

Or reminding him of it. Every time his body hardened, remembering the glorious beauty of her pleasure, the image of her stricken astonishment while she held her robes together pricked his conscience with a thousand tiny barbed needles.

She silently settled herself on his left side, and he winced. Most people, especially women, shrank from the peculiarity of his runic tattoos. But not his Banshee. She studied them. Sometimes overtly, her rapt curiosity painfully obvious on her lovely, expressive face.

He was too much of a coward to look at her now. He'd be able to read exactly what she was thinking. And he didn't want to know.

He knew too much. Always had.

"They're so beautiful," she breathed, turning her face up to watch the lights bend and snap across the sky.

There was that word. Beauty.

Kylah scooted almost imperceptibly closer to him. "My father used to say that Biera, the Queen of Winter, was a selfish and power hungry goddess. He said that she causes the storms and sea gales in January and February because she wants to prolong her reign. In ancient times the Spirit of Spring went to Bel, the Summer God, and asked for his help. In turn Bel sent the lights in March as a warning to Biera that her reign is absolutely ended. But to balance this, he also sends them in October and November to tell her that she may begin winter early in the Highlands."

Daroch shifted, still unable to look at her, but studied his hands which were now cast in a jewel blue. "Winter doesna start until December."

"According to legend, Crom Dubh is the powerful, carnal god of harvest and death." Kylah repeated her father's story with the deftness and drama of any bard. "He emerges from his underworld domain early in August and angers Bel. They compete for power and for the favor of Danu, their mistress, and goddess of all creation. Bel calls in Beira as early as he dares, hoping that winter will overshadow the debauched revelry of the harvest and send the sensual Crom Dubh back to his lonely Underworld and away from Danu's bed."

"Yer father told ye all this when ye were four?" Daroch chanced an irate glance at her and instantly wished he hadn't. All he could see was her fingers disappearing into her soft mouth. Then drifting lower, obeying his commands as though they were his own hands.

He cleared his throat, smothering a groan as his cock twitched and threatened to take over the situation.

She shrugged, "He was a bawdy blacksmith, or so my mother says in the rare moments she mentions him. And I believe it. I mean, she did spend nearly three of the six years of their marriage pregnant with us." Her voice became wistful, but he could also hear a smile in it. "I asked her once if he'd ever been disappointed that none of us had been a boy. She told me that she'd asked him that very question not long before he died, because she was pregnant with Kamdyn and was worried it was another girl. Do you know what he told her?"

Daroch shook his head, surprised by how much he wanted to know.

"He said he hoped all their children were girls so she would let him keep trying for a boy."

He couldn't pull back the half-hearted sound of amusement that escaped his throat. Her father sounded like someone he would have liked to know. Someone who loved his family. Took pride in his work. Cultivated a reputation for fairness and strength. A man with a life. Who knew who he was and what he wanted and worked hard for it. A man like Daroch had strived to become once. Long ago.

"Do you pray to them, the ancient gods?" she asked.

He snorted. "Hardly."

"Why not?" She gestured to the shimmering lights flaring ever brighter in the sky. "Bal is a vengeful god. His magic is right there, closer to the earth than any other time. It is said he also holds no love for the Fae. Perhaps he would help you as you're a Druid and all."

Daroch looked at her then. The earnest kindness in her steady gaze shamed him, which stirred his temper. She was supposed to be angry with him, dammit. She was supposed to be here to scream and rant at him as was a woman's way when she had been so wrongly scorned.

"Because yer father's gods and legends are all ignorant superstitions with no basis in reality," he challenged her.

"Oh?" she lifted one eyebrow, but also quirked the corner of her lips. "Enlighten me."

He planned to. As soon as he could form a memory or thought that didn't pertain to her generous mouth.

"Ah." His eyes dropped lower, to the breasts lifted higher by her arms crossed beneath them. If he studied them very hard, he could make out the darker shade of her small pink nipples. "Um."

"The *lights*?" she reminded, her voice warm with amusement.

He wrenched his gaze toward the sky, seeking salvation there. "These lights are actually produced by incredibly powerful winds emitted by a flare from the sun."

"Well that makes sense," she agreed. "Bal is the God of the sun."

"No, no" he gestured impatiently. "The sun has nothing to do with a deity. The Sun is merely a star, a very close star burning so hot and so big that we are pulled toward it in our planetary orbit."

She gave him a silent, skeptical look.

He threw up his hands, running into his biggest annoyance of the modern century. "How is it possible that we Druids, and Anaxagoras and Copernicus were discovering this more than a *thousand* years ago and it's still not—" He cut of his own digression with a tight sound, rubbing at his temples. "Regardless, let me explain the lights." He drew in a deep, slow breath. "The Earth's core is made of molten alloy. As our planet spins around the Sun, it creates magnetic fields that emanate outward and protects us from this dangerous solar wind. When the highly charged winds flare at their mightiest, they can sometimes make their way through this magnetic field and they encounter our oxygen and nitrogen and other atmospheric elements. Thus, that interaction manifests itself in the far northern and far southern points of our world, as those are key magnetic points of opposition."

He glanced back at her, to gauge her comprehension.

She was looking at him as though he'd lost his mind. "That seems... unlikely." She wrinkled her nose.

He grunted. "More unlikely than deities and magic?"

"You forget," she chided gently. "I'm a creature of magic. And so are you."

Too exasperated to sit anymore, he stood in one fluid move. "Trust me, I havena forgotten," he insisted. "But I doona believe that magic is mystical. Just a greater understanding of what we doona yet know. No magic is absolute and no magical creature indestructible. The laws of the Universe tend to balance such things."

She shrugged. "If you say so."

"Argh!" He threw his hands up and stormed away from her, angling south across the moor. She was so damned adorable. So sweet and wounded and... "What are ye doing here anyway, besides being an insufferable Harpy?"

"Not Harpy," she corrected, keeping perfect pace with him. "Banshee. And I'm here to apologize for last night."

He snapped his head to look at her. "What the bloody hell do *ye* have to be sorry for?"

"What I said—what we did— upset you." She offered him a conciliatory smile. "And I regret it, because everything before that was..." She delicately cleared her throat and looked away from him, her cheeks tinged with that becoming heat.

"Aye, that it was," he agreed gently. Because the lass was absolutely correct, whatever it had been defied words. The most erotic experience of his life. And he'd not even been an active part of it. How was it possible? And he'd acted like a fool. He'd tainted the experience with his own weakness. "It is

I who was wrong," he admitted. "Which is rare." The addendum eased the peculiarity of the admission.

Her melodious laugh was a delicate explosion of delight. It rippled across the sky as remarkable as the northern lights. All the moisture in Daroch's mouth dried and bloomed in his palms, which he rubbed on his trews.

"It did help, you know." They skirted a marsh pond and still angled south, the only sounds other than their voices were Daroch's heavy boots on the soft earth. "It was... I felt... Anyway, I understand more now about lovemaking versus violence. Pleasure versus pain. I know myself better, if that makes any sense."

A tight sound vibrated in his throat. "I *hate* that ye ever... that it's ever been anything other than pleasure for ye."

She was silent a long while. So long that Daroch could hear the cogs turning behind her ears. "I get the sense that perhaps it has not always been pleasure for you either."

He refused to discuss it. "Aye, well, not everyone's senses can be acute."

"Stop implying I'm stupid every time I'm right about something you don't want me to know," she snapped. "It's a loathsome tendency and it reveals more than it protects."

Daroch gaped at her. Christ, she was too perceptive sometimes. He preferred to be surrounded by idiots. They were easier to fool, to intimidate, and to control. "Ye're right... Forgive me."

She smiled and he was instantaneously gifted with the return of her good humor, "That's twice in one night." Her elbow passed through him with a few ghostly nudges. "One for the history books, is it not?"

His lips trembled with a poorly repressed smile. "Most definitely."

"So you've never..." she pressed.

"Never... what?"

"Never—you know." She waved a hand a looked away, he blush intensifying.

"I doona know," he smirked. "I'm a Druid, I'm no mind reader."

"Oh for heaven's sake," she elbowed at him again. "What we did! What *I* did." Her hands flew to her face to cover glowing cheeks. "I don't even know what to *call* it. But in all your centuries, you've never... done that?"

Daroch chuffed. "Exactly the opposite, I spent a great deal of my tender years perfecting the art."

Her hands dropped to her sides. "On women?"

The sharp note in her voice didn't escape his notice. Daroch took one look at her stricken expression and a laugh burst from him. Slowly at first, as though remembering how to abide, then with more vigor. "On myself," he managed between spasms of amusement. He put a hand on his ribs as they subsided. "Until the lasses would let me," he admitted honestly. "Then most of my untried efforts were focused on them."

Her eyes had gone round and luminous, and she watched him laugh as though witnessing something rarer than the lights above them. The speed at which they narrowed with displeasure was equally astounding.

"Them?" she turned the word over on her tongue and frowned. "I question the moral character of any woman who would let you."

"*Ye* did," he chuckled.

"Don't be ridiculous, that was different," she insisted.

"'Tis what most of the lasses say," he taunted.

"Most..." Her frown deepened. "How many were there?"

He grinned, thoroughly enjoying himself, and shrugged. "I was a pretty lad."

She huffed, clearly incensed.

"If it makes ye feel better, they're all long dead now." He sped his walk to hide his smug smile, knowing she'd chase him, and looking forward to it.

"*Oh are they?* All scores and scores of them? You're horrid," she accused, catching him easily. "I could just kick you."

He chortled. "Nay, ye couldna if ye tried!" And for some reason, that sent him into more fits of mirth.

She scowled. Though obviously fighting a begrudging smile. Her shoulders began to shake as small gasps escaped through her nose first. Before long, they'd stopped walking and were both bent over, holding onto their sides as humor held them prisoner. Their laughter tangled with the sea breeze and was carried across the moors by ribbons of celestial color.

Kylah straightened first, taking a sighing breath while Daroch wiped a tear of amusement from his eye.

"Our humor is dark." Her voice was still warmed by laughter.

"It matches our thoughts," he mused. "Our pasts."

"Aye," she murmured.

Their eyes locked.

She blinked.

He swallowed.

Daroch felt something very powerful sizzle in the air between them. It vibrated on a frequency that could only be found in silence, but contained untold volumes. Its language consisted of internalized desires floating upon words like "maybe" and "what if." It was the surge of rebellion against fate that turned a fleeing man's galloping horse in the opposite direction. It changed the courses of exploring sea fleets and sometimes, the fates of entire civilizations.

So charged with this energy, Daroch took a step toward her.

She retreated, tucking a glossy auburn curl behind her ear. "Where are we going?" she asked with false brightness, turning toward their previous course and setting off slowly, taking her glow with her. "What business have you this evening?"

He fell into step beside her, letting the moment pass with a mixture of relief and disappointment. "If you believe it, I'm on my way to finish milking my fig trees."

"I'm sorry," she gawked at him in utter disbelief. "I thought you just said you were on your way to milk—"

"Fig trees." He veered left and climbed a dark hill.

"I don't... I don't know what you mean." She levitated herself up the hill. "Is that a euphemism for something?"

They crested the hill and he gestured toward a neat row of short, exotic trees silhouetted against the glowing night sky nestled at the opposite base. "I chanced upon a Grecian apothecary's apprentice some forty years ago who was exploring the Highlands as bade by his master for a certain strain of Meadowsweet herb. I was in possession of a large quantity of the stuff as I'd used it for inflammation caused by a broken foot. The apprentice traded me these saplings not just for the fruit, but for what else it contains."

Reaching the trees, Daroch circled them and pointed to taps set into shallow bark. Beneath them, wooden bowls caught the sticky leavings.

"What is it?" Kylah bent over a bowl, inspecting the sap-like content with her usual all encompassing curiosity.

"I call it *Arborlatix* which, in Latin, roughly translates to tree milk." He picked up a bowl. "This is the first year I've really been able to cultivate enough of it to be useful."

"What's it for?"

Daroch took a tightly worked leather bag from his robes and a smooth wooden scoop, and began to patiently transfer the contents from bowl to bag. "Look," he murmured, holding up the substance that ran from the scoop a touch slower than honey. "It's a rather complex polymer emulsion that's made of the tree's sugars, proteins, starches, tannins, and resin. Mixed with other elements, it can do a vast number of things, not the least of which is protecting other substances from water and erosion." He moved to the next bowl where she crouched. "It could be of great use to me."

Bending toward her, he reached for the bowl, bringing their faces dangerously close.

Kylah stumbled backward, as though to avoid the contact and the bowl beneath the tree behind her tipped over, the contents spilling onto the ground. She snatched her hand away and hissed, cradling it to her body.

Their gazes collided. She began to tremble.

"What just happened?" he asked very slowly, his heart rate flaring along with the fear in her eyes.

"I-It burned me," she whispered, very slowly extending the quivering hand out to him. "It burns still."

Daroch barely heard her for all the roaring in his ears. He knelt beside her and reached for her injured hand. He turned it over in his palm studying the effects of the substance. The soft blue glow was nearly indistinguishable now and the pink, irritated flesh of her dainty hand was as corporeal as his own. It seemed as though she'd immersed the entire thing in the *Arborlatix*. On any other matter, the substance would have stuck like a glove, but not Kylah. When she'd snatched it away, none of the stuff adhered to her hand, but the result was extraordinary.

He could feel her skin. It was as soft as he imagined it to be. He ran a thumb across her palm and, though it was cold, it was *real*.

She gasped and tried to jerk it away.

"How bad does it pain ye, lass?" he asked.

"I-It's not like fire, but it burns and stings fiercely... and itches." She flexed her palm and affixed her worried gaze on him. "What will it do to me?"

Daroch had no idea, and he tried to keep the concern from his features. "Is it getting worse or better?"

She waited, wiggling her fingers. "Better, I think." Her mouth was touched by a tremulous smile. "You touched me." Kneeling closer to him, she lifted her hand to his face, brushing her feather-light fingers over that tattoos on his cheek. "I can touch you."

Daroch closed his eyes. He'd thought any touch from Kylah MacKay would go straight to his cock, but it didn't. It settled in the empty chamber of his chest and lodged there.

"Do you know what this means?" she whispered.

He knew what he wished it meant. "But wouldn't dipping ye in the entire lot be exquisitely painful? I very much doubt ye'd like—"

"Nay, Daroch." Her eyes glimmered with bleak sadness and unshed tears. Her chin quivered and her breath caught on a silent sob. Not one of wonder, but of dread.

The knowledge knifed through his lungs, rendering them useless. This discovery changed everything.

"It means that now you can kill me." Her trembling intensified. "You may claim your vengeance."

"Stay here," he gently commanded. "I'm going to get ye something that might soothe yer skin." Daroch's mind raced through the possibilities and his blood thrummed with excitement as he turned and followed the line of the hill to the mossy swamp where he would find what he needed.

After all these years.

Kylah wasn't exactly a full blown Fae creature yet, only a specter of their magic. If the *Arborlatix* had this strong of an effect on her, then he could only imagine what it would do to an actual Faerie. If contact with the stuff created such a reaction, then a weapon coated in it could do incredible damage. It would cut through them like their weapons sliced through humans during the great hunts millennia ago, before the pact had been struck.

His lip curled. One hundred years. He'd thought of nothing but revenge and justice. He'd been close to despair when the wee Banshee had startled him with her invasive wail only a few short days ago.

It was because of *her* that he would be granted his vengeance.

Plunging his hands into the marshes, he gathered mud and herbs to soothe and coat her skin. If the sensation was, indeed, improving, he hypothesized that the ghostly part of her, the part that was still human, protected her from long-lasting complications with the *Arborlatix*. The thought of her in any pain or discomfort displeased him greatly and a part of him still strove to reject the soft feelings that any thought of her produced.

Now you can kill me.

Daroch very much doubted it. She was still technically dead. He probably couldn't truly kill her until she'd been turned into a Fae. He froze. Kylah was frightened of him now. She'd trembled while she touched him. At first, he'd assumed it was because she realized the scope of the meaning of their discovery to him... but she couldn't, could she? He'd never shared with her his reason for hating the Fae so intensely. Not in its entirety.

From the beginning, he'd never posed a threat to her. He could not touch her and therefore could not do her violence. But all that had just changed hadn't it? In three short months, she'd become a true Banshee. Not just a creature of finite power for reaping their own personal vengeance, but a soldier of the Banshee Queen. An assassin.

Daroch closed his eyes, a peculiar desolation settling in his gut. He couldn't let that happen. If he could release her from her curse, even by exacting a final death, would that be a killing or a kindness? Could he look at her face, so intensely lovely and so inquisitive, and plunge a weapon into her flesh? This one would burn. It would penetrate her delicate skin and likely kill her.

He'd be no better in her eyes than Angus MacKay.

Daroch growled. Faeries used Banshees to exact harsh and excruciating punishments on those deemed worthy by them and the gods. Innocents would suffer at her hand, and she'd have no say in whom she killed. In who lived or died. She would merely be a creature of death and blood and torment. Her innate curiosity would be warped and twisted into something perverse and lethal.

Daroch stood, a grim despondency settling into his chest, smothering the light and warmth her touch had ignited there.

He had a decision to make.

Turning back with the poultice he'd made, he trudged out of the swamp and climbed the hill toward his tiny fig orchard. The witching hour had fallen upon the night. New and devilish shadows writhed in the light cast by the north. All traces of laughter and softness vanished.

And, he discovered as he crested the rise, so had she.

Chapter Twelve

Kylah floated in the ether of the witching hour. Upon first becoming a Banshee, she'd been frightened and confused by the daily ritual of spending every hour prior to midnight in a grey nothingness. No sound permeated the eerie, absolute stillness. No light, and yet, no darkness. She had no body but pure consciousness. There was no pain here. Her hand didn't exist, though it had been greatly improving before she'd left the copse of deadly trees.

After a while, she'd come to yearn for this place night after night. She and her sisters all existed in a similar plane, but never had a trace of each other whilst trapped here. She never had to hide her thoughts and emotions. Or lack thereof. She could hover in this present absence and simply exist. Or not. She wasn't sure.

Tonight she took sanctuary in this place for a different reason altogether. Not because she blended with the stark nothingness, but because she pulsed with so many different emotions, fears, and desires she could barely contain them all.

Cliodnah appeared in front of her. Kylah would have gasped, had she a voice to produce the sound. She'd only ever laid eyes on the Banshee Queen in her own world. There, the Fae was frigid and resplendent in arctic silver-white, often turning the moisture in the air around her into glimmering crystals of frost, no matter the season.

Here in this plane, she was a being of so much color, that if Kylah had been in possession of her eyes, she didn't believe they would have contained or comprehended the spectrum. The flawless symmetry of her features was unnatural in its exactness and lent her beauty an unfinished quality which she hid behind layers of glimmering color and riotous translucent robes. She didn't walk so much as glide through the nether until she filled the same space that contained Kylah.

Behind the Queen, a smaller, more delicate Fae hovered unobtrusively. She often had accompanied Cliodnah to their meetings and Kylah had the impression she was some kind of attendant or Faerie lady-in-waiting. Her robes were more substantial than the one's draping the Queen's seductive body, and the spectrum was limited to indescribable, uncommon shades of blue.

"Your Majesty." Kylah didn't so much speak as reverberate with the intention to do so. "I've never seen you here before. How lovely you are."

"Banshee." Cliodhah's voice was at once atypical and familiar. The infinitely slow, methodically annunciated immortal lack of inflection was at once chilling and strangely melodic. "I've come to discuss our pact."

Fear speared through Kylah. "I understood I had three months more, my lady."

Pupils twice the size of a human's slid to pin her with a disdainful glare. "My consort, Ly Erg, tells me you are oft in the company of the Druid of Cape Wrath."

Kylah was suddenly glad she didn't require breathing for survival. "Yes, majesty." She decided not to elaborate.

"I believe you have captivated him," The Queen remarked with an infinitesimal level of amusement.

"The Druid?"

"Ly Erg." The Queen's lip lifted in the terrifying ghost of a smile, but didn't leave Kylah a chance to contemplate the horror of her announcement. "For a hundred years, the Druid has hidden himself in the earth somewhere, away from our notice.

Only recently have we felt his powers stir. This, we think, is largely your doing."

Did she mean the royal "we", or that Kylah had garnered the notice of the entirety of the Fae? The possibilities frightened her beyond her wits.

Cliodnah waved her hand, disturbing the swirling grey until it congealed with a foreign sound like vines snapping in a heavy storm. There appeared in front of them a vision of Daroch crouched naked and bathing in the grotto. The lower half of his body remained concealed by the dark water, but his tattooed torso was burnished blue and gold by a fire he'd kept dark while Kylah had been with him.

He'd done that in deference to her, she realized. Regardless of his many verbal dismissals, he'd never once lit a flame in her presence, knowing she feared them.

Perhaps he cared, in his own way.

Kylah, the Queen, and her lovely blue attendant silently played voyeur to Daroch's private bath. He scrubbed his slick body and long hair with a sort of spongy, colored salt that bubbled and then dissolved in the water. When his skin glowed raw, he took a wicked-looking dirk and gripped the string of shells that hung close to his right eye. Kylah felt like wincing as he took three preparatory breaths before shearing it off.

"What is this?" she whispered.

"'Tis how the ancient Druids prepared for war," Cliodnah didn't look away from him and Kylah noted the uncloaked lust dripping from her voice. She resented it. She wanted to hide Daroch from the Queen's view. He didn't want to be watched, this she understood absolutely. "He left the Faerie realm promising retribution for his bondage. I fear he has finally found the means to turn his threat into reality."

"It was you," Kylah gaped, horrified. "*You* kept him prisoner in Faerie."

The Queen made a foreign gesture that would have been the human equivalent of a shrug. "Look at him. He's a paragon of masculinity. One of the most perfectly crafted human beings I've seen in millennia. As a youth, he was an especially gifted and powerful Druid. I had to claim him before another Faerie Queen did."

There were more of them? Kylah's fear spiked.

"There are more castes of the Fae than there are different races of you humans." Cliodnah seemed to read Kylah's mind without tearing her hungry eyes from Daroch, which added to her disquiet. "I am Queen of the Banshees, alone, and only answer to *Elphame*, or Maeve, as your myths call her. She is chief among the Council of Queens."

Kylah watched the water embrace Daroch, watched his lips move in silent incantations. He'd sheared his hair to above his shoulders and away from his eyes. He looked more brutal somehow. More stark and ancient and feral. Reaching for a sharp needle and a bowl of blue ink, the muscles in his magnificent body flexed and strained with his fluid movements. He dipped the needle in the ink, and let the wooden bowl float nearby as he reached across his chest to the one empty space on the entire left side of his body.

The one above his heart.

With a series of deep punctures, he painstakingly stabbed the needle into his flesh again and again, all the while his lips whispered magical things in a language no longer spoken. He'd whispered those words into her ear as she'd come apart.

Kylah could hardly bear them now. "What did you mean when you said you'd claimed him?" She already suspected, already knew, but wanted to hear her Faerie liege say the words.

The Queen turned to look at her then, but her attendant first caught Kylah's eye. It was the look of disapproval on the blue Faerie's face that drew Kylah's notice. Not directed at Kylah, but at her Queen.

"Things have not always been as they are now between the Fae, your Gods, and humans." Cliodnah could have been called wistful, if such a thing were possible for the Fae. "Untold thousands of years ago we, the Fae, and your deities united in war against an ancient evil for supremacy of this world. After we conquered, we tried to share this plane but ultimately began to war amongst ourselves. The Gods had already created many different kinds of warriors to fight evil, and we had blessed many humans with our own Fae gifts. We used these humans as our pawns and as our fodder. As the spoils of war and as slaves."

Kylah felt as though she might be sick, but knew it was impossible, so she suffered through the Queen's horrible, dispassionate tale.

"Boredom is an unpleasant side effect of immortality. There are many pleasures that humans afforded us that angered your Gods. There were hunts and experiments and magical debauchery that your mind couldn't even envisage." The Queen's eyes were wide and held an exhilaration that terrified Kylah beyond comprehension. Cliodhah wasn't glad these times were over. She yearned for them.

She was bored, now.

"I claimed the Druid at the end of these times, when I knew a pact would be decided upon by a court of your Gods and our Queen." She turned her attention back to Daroch, who precisely punctured his flesh and paused every so often to clear the blood with sea water.

He never even flinched.

"Faeries *love* consorting with human men. They fuck like savages. Like they have no time left because their lives are so brittle and finite. Their fear smells delicious and tastes even better."

Kylah didn't even want to consider what the Queen meant by that last statement so she, too, kept her eyes locked on Daroch.

"A long and complicated pact was decided upon by your Gods and our Queen that took hundreds of years to write. But the gist of it is that we can no longer meddle among you humans, not without your consent or that of the Gods. The consequences are very— detailed."

The drop of blood running down Daroch's chest was the tear of regret Kylah could not produce. She traced it as she addressed the Queen. "Why are you telling me this?" she whispered, horrified.

Cliodnah reached her hand out to Daroch's specter and made a wanton sound so inhuman that Kylah's very essence shrank from it. She was glad she hadn't mentioned the Arborlatix and vowed never to do so. It was the only advantage he had over the Fae and now she hoped he had opportunity to use it.

"Times were different when the Druid was my—guest," the Queen murmured.

"When he was your prisoner, you mean." Kylah knew she was being bold, but it didn't matter. This Banshee Queen ruthlessly stole Daroch's life from him. Plucked him from his home, his time, and...

"I will not argue semantics with a *human*." The Queen's lip curled in a very human gesture of distaste. "I'm here to offer you more than that. I'm here to give you the chance to save not only your existence, but that of your sister Kamdyn as well."

The Queen was silent for a moment to allow her offer to sink in.

"How?" Kylah whispered, though she had a sinking fear she knew.

"I want you to kill Daroch McLeod."

Chapter Thirteen

"You know I will not do this." Kylah refused to entertain the idea. No matter the danger Daroch posed to her and the Fae, perhaps they deserved what retribution he was about to exact.

"I know nothing of the sort," Cliodnah said imperiously. "I know that I am your Queen and you will do as I command you to do."

"I cannot." She employed a different tactic. "I cannot touch him nor use my Banshee powers on him."

The Queen's mocking gaze raked Kylah as though she still had a corporeal form. "It is simple as this, Banshee. I will grant you the form and powers of the Fae. You will find the Druid and use your Banshee magic to slay him. To reward you, I will create you and your sister as one of us, granting you untold power and immortality."

"And if I refuse?" Kylah asked.

"You and your sister, Kamdyn, will be thrown to Ly Erg as his pets for the remainder of your contract with me." The Queen ventured closer. "Three months can seem an eternity, as you well know."

Terror stabbed at Kylah. Not only for herself, but for her sweet, innocent sister. She wouldn't survive the kind of debauchery that lurked in Ly Erg's unnatural eyes. Neither of them would.

She turned back to Daroch. How had he survived? "What did you do to him?" she whispered. Watching an intricate outline of a triquetra appear in the ink over his chest.

The Queen scoffed. "The appropriate question would be, what *haven't* I done to him? He was mine to do with as I wished. He did what I desired, when I desired it and he did it because I promised I wouldn't harm the Druids and keep his sect intact."

"But... the Druids disappeared."

The Queen's smile chilled the very core of her. "When one enters into a pact with a Faerie, they must pay very close attention to how it is worded. Of course *I* didn't harm any of the Druids. But Ly Erg eradicated entire villages of them and their kin. A Druid sect only needs five Druids to work their powers, and Daroch's had close to forty. I slaughtered all but four and then I returned and forced him to lick their blood from my flesh. I made him thank me for sparing his life and theirs."

Kylah wept for him. Her soul bled for him. "Why?" she whispered the burning question. She wanted to sob it. To scream it. But she didn't dare. What would the Queen do to him? To her sister?

"Why not?" was Cliodnah's dispassionate answer. "At the time, they were our enemy, favored of the Gods with which we were at war, and granted their magic."

"But Daroch told me they're not clerics of the Gods."

"The distinction is... minute," the Queen said. "They are still a holy race and now they are no more. But for one. I only gave him up because *Elphamae* found that I kept him in violation of the terms of the pact and she made me put him back from whence I'd taken him. But now that he is a danger to all those within our race, I believe that she will forgive this latest breach."

Please do not make me do this," Kylah begged. "Why not just send an army of Ly Erg's to kill him? Wouldn't that have been the easy solution all along?"

Cliodnah laughed, not the evil, maniacal sound Kylah expected from someone so cold and cruel, but a soft, enchanting melody of amusement. "You simple creature. You think we would not have? His cave is protected by powerful runes and denies us entry. I cannot even watch him in his inner sanctum behind that stone wall he disappears into. Besides, the pact forbids me to touch him unless he uses his Druid magic. Ly Erg failed in this, with no small thanks to you. Also, because of the help I gave your sister, Katriona, I broke the terms of *Elphame's* pact not to interfere in human affairs, and I now owe him a boon." The Queen speared Kylah with a very meaningful look. "Upon which he cannot collect if he is dead."

It took Daroch an entire night and half the day to process the Arborlatix down to a glossy, clear substance that would coat his weapons without dulling them. Turned out, he wouldn't need the MacKay's forge after all.

Sitting in only his trews by the fire, he let the rhythmic slice of the whet stone on his Druid sword lull him. Scanning the cave that had been home and sanctuary to him for nigh on a century, his eyes kept darting to the fissure in the rock that often contained a soft green or blue glow. Funny, that Kylah generally used the opening still when she could simply glide through the wall. That corner of the cave remained dark for too many hours now. He'd even left the lanterns unlit, just in case.

In case of what? In case she wanted to pay him a social call? He looked down at his sword, tested its edge with his thumb and was pleased at the shallow slice he received.

Perfect.

He glanced at the entry once again. Where had she gone? Why wasn't she here asking 'why this' and 'why that' until he was forced to order her to leave? What if she never bothered him again?

The thought left him feeling much like the entry to his cave. Dark, hollow, and empty. Daroch steeled his resolve. These thoughts weren't relevant to his cause. There was little likelihood he'd survive this to see her again, regardless. For when morning dawned the next day, he was reaping vengeance like none the Fae had yet to see. Never in this epoch had any but the Gods possessed weapons that would vanquish a Faerie. Humans had been at the mercy of powerful, apathetic beings for much too long.

It was time that changed.

He plunged his sword into the long cylindrical tube of Arborlatix and let the substance coat the steel. Pulling it free, he doused it in ice-cold sea water, letting the salt and temperature harden the substance around the weapon.

Holding it up to the firelight from the blaze next to his pallet of furs, he let the flames illuminate the glossy sheen of the coating.

Excellent.

He wished to show it to Kylah. But she would fear it now, wouldn't she? It was a weapon against her, as well as his enemies.

"It's incredible, what you've discovered." The melodic voice echoed out of the darkness

Daroch leapt toward it, brandishing the blade at the ready and squinting into the shadows. No blue glow. Had he conjured her words by wishing for them?

Kylah stepped from the darkness into the edges of the soft firelight. Absent her blue glow, her creamy skin was tinged with a soft peach. Auburn curls fell heavily around her shoulders and down to the small of her back. Her lovely green eyes flickered with flecks of gold, and her translucent robes dragged on the earth as she moved toward him. Stepped. On the ground. Not floated, not drifted.

Walked.

Daroch nearly dropped his sword. Of course. He should have known they'd come at him sideways. That they'd find his greatest weakness and use it against him. Use *her* against him.

The way she looked at him heated his skin more than the fire ever could. Even if he stood within it. He almost hated her for it. That she could make him want her with such intensity even as she became one of his enemies.

"Ye're here to kill me," he said with much less emotion then he felt. He was already dying on the inside, in small increments while other parts of him stirred and came to life.

"I could say the same for you." She gestured toward the sword he held still gleaming with the deadly coating of what he hoped amounted to Fae poison. She took a small step toward him. Then another. Her throat worked over a difficult swallow, as was her habit when about to do something that terrified her.

Daroch's heart began to pound. This was his chance. The Queen had turned her into a full Banshee. She was a lower caste of Fae and if he ever needed to test the effectiveness of the *Arborlatix*, now was the time. He could slice through her before she held out her wee Banshee hand and sent her deadly currents through his body.

She was close, too close. One more step and she'd be in reach of his blade. Three more and she'd be inside his guard. It would all be over.

He had to act now.

Daroch lunged. He was distantly aware of his sword clattering to the earth as his lips captured Kylah's mouth and he roughly pulled her shock-stiffened body against his. Her lips were shockingly warm. Pliant and soft, yet utterly still.

Daroch knew she was afraid. Knew she could kill him at any moment and bring his piteous existence to an end. He should soothe her. He should take care with her. But instead he kissed her as though he were Annwn, the hellhound escaped from the underworld to run his prey to ground. He kissed her like he did everything else in his life, with single-minded and exacting thoroughness.

Her hands went to his shoulders and fluttered there like deadly butterfly wings. Daroch's heat shot even higher and his entire body hummed with lust heightened by the threat of pain and death. It was not unlike the moment he stood at the edge of the cape staring down at the ocean before he dove in. An exhilaration tinged by a fear born of instinct to survive, unmatched in its intensity before this moment. And if it was to be his last, he refused to die without tasting her.

He licked at the seam of her mouth, warning her before he claimed it. Thrusting his tongue into the moist heat behind her lips, he let out a groan. She was here. She was real. And he could touch her. Hold her. Claim her as his own.

The moment the thought manifested in the miasma of lust that had become his brain, Kylah came alive in his arms. She returned his kiss with a desperate, wanton innocence. Wrapping herself around him and clinging to him, her mouth became hot, hungry and timidly inquisitive.

Should he have expected anything else?

He drank from her deeply, tangling his tongue with hers in a dance of wet experimentation and exploration. He was distantly aware that he'd conjured a storm in this moment. The inevitability of its arrival hung thick and heavy in the air between them and the ominous clouds rolled in the distance, promising to unleash the full force of their thunderous power.

They were both out of breath when he tore his mouth from hers. She let out a whimper of protestation and Daroch thrilled to the gleam of firelight on her moist and swollen lips.

Their foreheads touched and for a moment, and they simply shared wordless, panting breaths while soaking in the foreign sensation of touch and taste and the swell of a frightening and demanding passion.

"If ye doona kill me now, I'm going to take ye, Kylah." He'd meant it as a warning, as a threat, but the fervent need in his voice lowered the timbre to the equivalent of a vocal caress.

She nodded against his forehead. "Just... don't hold me down," she admonished in a whisper.

He nodded against hers. "If ye doona watch," he requested.

She closed her eyes.

He lifted her into his arms.

Carrying her to his pallet of furs, he kicked some loose dirt over the fire, dousing the flames and leaving only glowing coals in the pit. Daroch hoped it would be enough. He wanted some light to see her by and she no longer provided it.

He realized his double standard—his weakness—but it couldn't be helped.

Setting her on her feet, he pulled her against him again. She kept her eyes closed as her face turned up to his. Her dark auburn lashes fanned across her cheek and he kissed them lightly, touching her lips with a shy smile. A part of him wanted to see the soft, expressive liquid green burn as he brought her pleasure, but he feared that her gaze would cool the heated blood pulsing through his cock.

Her mouth parted, and he took the invitation, sealing his lips over hers and plundering her honeyed recesses with a hunger borne of a hundred years. Her nipples hardened against his chest, but the curves of her body softened and melted into the hard angles of his.

He cupped her precious face in his hands, feeling the delicate skin of her jaw before drawing his fingers down the column of her neck to her collar bone. His hands trembled as he pushed her robes away from her shoulders and let them glide down the lovely curves of her body.

Kylah squeaked against his mouth and pressed her naked skin firmly into his, her eyes squeezing shut.

Daroch pulled back. "Are ye frightened, little Banshee?" he murmured.

She pressed her face into his neck, and shook her head 'no' as she trembled against him.

He smiled against her temple, pressing a kiss in the downy curls there. He'd forgotten all about women. How complicated and contradictory they were. How creatures so soft and delicate could be so strong and resilient. Even if they had to start by pretending.

Against the velvet skin of her slim back, his hands felt big and unwieldy. He dropped his lips to her neck as his fingers explored the dip of her waist, the flare of her hip, and the curve of her bottom

She let out a sigh against his ear, turning her face to press her lips to his jaw, then his neck, then the sinew where his throat connected to his shoulder. Her hands also traversed the muscles of his back, their feather-light touch tickling along sensitized skin until he was certain he'd go mad.

Daroch realized he couldn't see her. Couldn't be certain that her eyes were shut. He pulled back, his skin instantly missing the contact.

True to her word, her lids fluttered against her cheek, but they never parted.

"Lie down," he ordered thickly, thinking the better of pushing her to the ground.

Kylah nodded and sank to her knees on the furs before stretching herself out on her back.

Daroch stood above her, tremors wracking his own body borne of epic amounts of restraint and dominant desire warring within him. He'd never had anything so lovely displayed before him. Never had a question or experiment consumed him with such absolute obsession. He needed to know this woman. Needed to touch every inch of her, learn every recess and secret she possessed. To learn and master every desire and fantasy she could conjure and surpass it. To overcome every fear. To revel in every pleasure.

He needed... her.

"Daroch?" Kylah's voice had become uncertain. "Are you..."

"I'm here," he soothed, quickly divesting himself of his trews and joining her on the furs. She instinctively reached for him, pulling his mouth down to hers. "You may take me now," she consented against him.

A renewed wave of lust pounded through him at her words.

"I must taste you first." He kissed her throat, her chest, and headed to the softness of her quivering, magnificent breasts. Yes, he must taste those.

"Nay," she whispered. "Take first, taste later."

Heat seared straight to his loins at her words, but he forced himself to wait. "Kylah, it'll be better for you if I—"

"I'm losing my nerve." She opened her eyes then, they were liquid pools of vulnerability. "But I want you inside me. Please... do it now."

For a brief moment Daroch was completely paralyzed between primal desire and fear. What should he do? She'd opened her eyes. She was looking at him with expectation and want. And in order for him to take her, she couldn't be. She needed him now. But he hadn't prepared her for him.

"Do you trust me?" he asked her.

Kylah's eyes widened, but she gave a slight nod.

Daroch lifted himself away from her, and nudged her to lie on her stomach. The sight stole his breath. Her hair curtained her face hiding her and, more important, himself. He settled atop her pressing his lips against the blades of her shoulders as his hot length came into contact with the soft skin of her thigh. The sensation ripped through him and he drew a sharp breath through his teeth.

She gasped and tensed beneath him, and he was careful not to burden her with his weight. Daroch held his breath as he eased her legs apart and positioned the throbbing length of him at the aperture of her thighs. He could feel the wet heat of her and every muscle in his body clenched.

"Kylah," he gasped.

"Yes," she demanded on her own tortured hiss.

Daroch let out a raw sound. He'd meant to go slowly. To ease inside and let her body adjust to him. But in a desperate moment he found himself buried to the root and pulsing with a white-hot pressure. She was so tight, almost unbearably so. Had he not known better, he'd have thought her a virgin. But she was also slick, her body welcoming him and bearing down against him all at once.

He whispered her name again, moaned it, dropping his forehead onto her back. It bloomed with sweat, his or hers, he couldn't be sure. "Gods... *fuck*... are ye...Did I...?"

He felt her flesh tighten around him and he wheezed out another pained gasp, but he dared not move, no matter what his body screamed at him to do.

"Don't stop." Her voice was muffled by her hair, but the words were unmistakable.

She was right. There was no stopping now. His second thrust was slow and difficult. Her body tried to clamp down and Daroch felt a sheen of sweat break out over his brow as he slowly plowed to the hilt. The muscles of her thighs and bottom tensed and he could hear her soft hitches of breath. He griped her hip as he withdrew and thrust again. And again. Each time sweeter and more exquisite than the last.

Finally, her body relaxed and arched, a small mewl of need escaping into the cave. It was all he needed to hear.

Emboldened, Daroch reached his long arm around her hips, forcing them to bend only a little, but not bringing her to her knees. He needed enough room to delve his fingers into the soft curls of her sex and find the sweet flesh he'd been denied before.

The moment he touched it, a tight sound burst from her, then another, this one higher in pitch. The strokes of his fingers matched those of his body and with every thrust he drove her higher and higher until she arched her back and cried out her pleasure in desperate gasps. She bucked beneath Daroch's surging body, the muscles of her sex clenching around him and milking him, and he valiantly tried to fight the release that screamed up the base of his shaft. He mustn't... not yet.

He focused on his breathing. Her pleasure. On the wet, rhythmic sounds of their flesh coming together.

His careful control broke. His hand left her, and he gripped both of her hips as he came deep inside of her. The pleasure wasn't confined to his cock, it pulsed through every vein, cycled through every breath, until he felt it in the pads of his fingertips where he clutched her soft flesh, and in the seams of his lips where he muffled his roar against her back. It was a consummation in its purest form, for no part of him was left unaffected as he spilled his release into her warm depths.

Daroch didn't allow his body to collapse on top of her when the spasms passed. He held his weight on trembling arms. He allowed her room to move so she didn't feel trapped beneath him. The only sound in the cave came from their labored breaths and Daroch couldn't for the life of him think of what to do next.

A myriad of likely scenarios flooded his mind. He couldn't bring himself to do aught but calculate the odds of this ending well in the least. All of the variables came out against his favor.

"Daroch?" Her voice was husky and it vibrated to where he still remained joined with her, sending little aftershocks through him.

He squeezed his own eyes shut, praying to the Gods she didn't reject him before he'd even withdrawn from her body.

"Daroch, I can hear you thinking," her voice grew stronger. "Stop it at once and kiss me."

His heart clenched, though the rest of him relaxed in relief. That he *could* do. He leaned down and turned her chin and shoulder to meet his mouth with a tender kiss. A lover's kiss. For his lover she now was. The first in a century. The first one he'd wanted in as many years, and the first woman, he realized, he didn't want to let go of. Even though she was now a Fae creature.

And his enemy.

Chapter Fourteen

The moment Daroch withdrew from her body Kylah missed him. Now that she possessed a form, every tactile sensation she'd taken for granted in her life now felt like the kiss of the sun after a freezing rain. She reveled in it all. The slight rasp of the calluses on his palms. The abrasion of his evening beard on her tender skin. The smooth glide of his cock inside of her. It took on new and treasured perspective beyond what it would have in life.

She'd been unsure if she was ready to receive him into her body, despite the burning desire to do so. Now she was certain she didn't want to let him go.

Daroch collapsed to his back between her and the fire pit and rolled Kylah to tuck into the crook of his arm and chest, splaying her naked body over his. She contemplated the tattoos on his chest and torso, her finger fluttering over the new one above his heart. The skin, still raised and a bit inflamed, seemed to be healing.

She traced the tri-point knotted design without touching it while soaking in the warmth of his hard, strong body. "Why did you put this here?"

Daroch's muscles bunched and flexed as he lifted his head and shoulders to observe his torso. "The Triquetra has a myriad of meanings, for example—"

"I was raised a Highlander," Kylah reminded him. "I know what it means to us, I'm asking what it means to *you*."

Daroch was silent, but he pulled her in tighter against him. "It reminds me of the three of ye sisters. Of the power that exists in that number. And of the vengeance you'll never truly taste."

Any reply she could muster stuck in a throat thick with emotion. Kylah moved on to trace different runes with her finger, watching as her hand worked its way down the patterns of his torso. He let out a satiated moan that rumbled through him like a purr and she decided she would never tire of touching him. Everything about him, it seemed, was more interesting than any other person she'd been acquainted with. Even his skin.

He murmured her name, taking her exploring hand in his own. "Are ye... all right? Did I frighten ye?"

Kylah thought about it. "I was frightened, but not of you." She kissed his chest, flicking her tongue across the nipple. "And then, I wasn't afraid anymore, because I was flying."

Daroch brought her palm to his lips and kissed it. "Flying, were ye?" She felt his lips curve into a smile. "Careful not to say such things too often, lass, I'll become intolerably conceited."

She nudged him and grinned. "*Become*?"

"Aye, there's the spirit," he chuckled.

Kylah watched as Daroch twined his fingers with hers, their tangled movements naught but black shadows back-lit by the glowing coals. Her heart expanded until it pressed painfully against her ribs and threatened her breath. Beneath all those cold calculations and inner volumes of burdensome cosmic knowledge was a tender man. Wounded and angry and lonely. She could still feel it inside of him. Though Daroch was sated and content for the moment, a dark purpose still burned in the soul encapsulated beneath all the hard sinew and complex runes.

Sobering, she asked, "What about you? Are you afraid?"

"I fear nothing," he rumbled.

"You're a terrible liar," she accused, rising onto an elbow to look down into his face. Beneath the insolent tattoo was near-perfect symmetry. A beauty unmatched in any man real or imagined. Though arrogance lifted his brow. Sardonic brackets pulled his mouth thinner than it should be and his eyes constantly narrowed in a wary, aloof way that most would consider uninviting. The line of his strong jaw thrust forward in impudent estimation that would make the most self assured of men squirm.

But if he were to ever truly smile, his magnificence would rival that of the Gods.

"Quantify that statement," he challenged. "What do ye suppose I fear? You?" His brow lifted.

"Aye. I know you fear me and not because I can kill you, either. But more than that, I think you fear my Queen."

He jerked as though she'd slapped him.

"It's why you tattooed your face, isn't it? There is plenty of space left on your body for the marks. And why you covered yourself with silt and robes. You were hiding from her desire until you could take your vengeance for what she did to you."

"I work with and study corrosive elements and live in a cave rife with salt water. I wear the silt as protection for my skin." He'd retreated into the Alchemist side of his nature, all traces of the tender lover tightly covered by an almost defensive logic. "The tattoos are required of me to work the magic that protects my sanctuary from the Fae. The greater the sacrifice, the more powerful the spell."

"Yes, but why—"

Daroch sat up abruptly, presenting her with his wide back. "Ye ask *why* like its yer right to know everything. Why canna ye just leave me be?"

Kylah flinched. "Is that what you want? For me to leave you?"

"Aye," he said irritably, then glanced back at her reclined, naked body. "Nay." He turned from her and plunged his hands through his shorter mane with a sound of aggravation. "I... I want..." He fell silent. His back expanding and contracting with labored breaths.

Kylah rose and put a hand on his back. The muscles quivered beneath her touch, but he didn't pull away. "You know everything about... how I died, do you not? My torment was revealed to you."

He didn't answer her, but she sensed a change in his intense emotion. His head turned toward his shoulder.

"I know what they did to you, Daroch. Perhaps not all the details but Cliodnah told me *horrible* things, ordered me to kill you, and then made me what I am."

Daroch met her eyes then. Without her slightly improved Fae sight, she wouldn't have been able to make out the greens and golds shot with rust and brown as he intently contemplated every detail of her face.

"What are ye going to do?" he asked in an expressionless voice.

Kylah put his fingers against the roughness of his jaw and pulled his mouth close for a gentle kiss. "I'm going to help you get the justice you deserve."

His eyes narrowed. "Why?"

"Because the Faerie Queen threatened my family," Kylah said matter-of-factly. "And because I love you."

Daroch leapt to his feet and Kylah again admired the speed and grace with which he moved. No mean feat for a man of his size and strength.

"Nay," he insisted in a trembling voice. "Ye doona."

Kylah also got to her feet, but she padded to the wood pile, affording him some much needed space. "I do," she insisted gently as she fetched a few logs to set atop the glowing coals. "I have from the first night I set eyes on you in the Laird's keep, though I only recently realized."

His wild look was so absurdly out of character that Kylah had to stifle a pitying smile. Poor man, this would take him a while to digest.

"Ye doona know what ye're saying, woman. Y-Ye're not making any sense." He stammered.

"Love isn't supposed to make sense." Lord but men were so dense at times.

His features darkened and he shook a very paternal finger at her, as though gearing up for a lecture. As he was completely nude, Kylah wanted to inform him that the effect was ruined, but decided against it. "Ye know how I feel about love," he thundered. "Try and be logical."

"Now you're just being silly," she admonished with a patronizing shake of her head. "Love isn't logical. It cannot be measured, contained, or aptly described or recorded. It is simply powerful, undeniable, *pure* emotion. And is as necessary as any sustenance the body craves. Only it is also craved by the soul."

"Nonsense," he blustered, the color in his face draining as though he came to a frightening realization.

"Oh?" She continued building a fire in front of him. "Prove it."

He started toward her, then apparently thought the better of it and his feet remained planted on the furs. "I'm not the one making a claim, the burden of proof lies with ye." He crossed his arms over his chest.

"Fair enough." Kylah forced herself not to jump back as the kindling caught fire and licked at the larger dry wood she'd placed in the pit. Light flared between them and illuminated his glorious nakedness. For such an intelligent man, he was quite oblivious. It was one of the many things she loved about him.

Skirting the fire, Kylah went to him. He regarded her approach as one might a dangerous predator, but stood his ground. She cupped his jaw in her hands and felt it clench, working over the strong emotions vibrating from his very core. "I do love you, Daroch McLeod, and I *will* prove it."

"How?" Kylah never believed that such a large man could produce such a small whisper.

She shrugged. "I haven't figured that out just yet, but I'll get to it. Vengeance is a good place to start."

"Nay. How can ye know... and still love—" his voice broke on the last word and her heart shattered along with it. Though nearly imperceptible, the words were full of shame, of pain and torment compounded by a century of isolation.

"Daroch, you removed my chains and my shame. Held my defiled *bones* in your hands. No matter how many clothes you shed in front of my eyes, no matter what I discover about your past, you will never be so exposed, so *naked* as that." She pulled his face closer to hers. "Do you understand?"

His eyes glittered with the flames behind her, but burned with something from so deep within him she was shocked he'd brought it to the surface for her to see.

"You never have to cause to be ashamed before me," she smiled gently and touched her forehead to his again. "Or behind me, as the case has most recently been."

He stared at her, still as stone but for the flare of his nostrils.

And then he was on her. Mouth fused to hers and wild-hewn body taut with every imaginable sort of strain, he reached down and seized her thighs in his large, strong hands and lifted her against his turgid erection.

Kylah closed her eyes and let his tongue force its way into her mouth. She wrapped her legs around his lean waist and ground herself against him, sharing her heat and coating him in slick desire.

With a growl he sank to his knees with her clamped around his body, never breaking the contact of their lips. Only when he'd laid her beneath him did he pull back. .

Kylah arched her hips in shameless invitation.

"Look at me," he ordered darkly.

Blinking her eyes open in shock, she met a stare so hot and intense it should have scorched the flesh from her bones.

Again.

He thrust forward then, and she gasped at the power of his invasion. Her untried body was swollen and sensitive and she felt every thick inch that filled her.

He cursed in a language unfamiliar to her and the word was dark with such ragged lust it stabbed at the core of her just as powerfully as he did. His broad body pushed her knees farther apart as he pressed her into the furs and he shuddered as though experiencing a pleasure so intense it bordered on pain.

But Daroch's eyes never left hers. Something had been breached within him. Some wall or fortress erected so tall and strong that the collapse was brutal and devastating. Any sign of restraint evaporated as he pounded into her with deep, insistent thrusts.

Kylah felt her body respond in kind. Opening to him, her hips leaving the earth to meet his in a grinding climb toward a peak that she now knew and desired with a wanton, wicked hunger.

But she did look at him. It was why she'd built a dreaded fire. She wanted to watch his magnificent body surge and retract. To note every sinew and cord bunch and release. To find individual beads of sweat as they formed and rolled down into deep grooves between his muscles. She gloried at the intent in his savage eyes, at being the focus of something so rare and exacting.

Her climax didn't build with waves of pleasure, but rocketed her into bliss before she was prepared and ripped a banshee scream from her lips.

Daroch smothered it with a kiss as his thrusts became impossibly faster, stronger, and he grew within her before tearing his mouth from hers to unleash a ragged cry of his own.

Chapter Fifteen

Daroch stood at the edge of Cape Wrath and let the sea winds lift the jagged edges of his long vest and flow through his sheared hair. He leaned against his staff, the end having been sharpened to a spear point and the whole thing coated with the Arborlatix. He'd even blunted the top into a rounded carving of the ancient tree of life. Closing his eyes, Daroch connected with each of the guardians he'd called upon to aid him against the Fae.

The pack of wolves paced a wide perimeter around the cape, lending strength, unity, and a predatory ferocity that surged around and through him with feral intensity.

A pair of black polecats tangled with each other nearby, leaping almost imperceptibly from rock to borough and gifting him with supernatural speed and unmatched, observant reflexes.

A conspiracy of ravens circled above calling eerily down to them. They lent a certain darkness to his intent. A fortitude of will and wisdom. Theirs was a sight and perspective that differed from all other creation. A potent understanding of the need for adversity and finality. They were the harbingers of death and the arbiters of new beginnings. Their portent declared that this ended here.

One way or the other.

He sensed Kylah's approach, but did not acknowledge her as she drew beside him. Despite everything, the strength he gained from her presence was more potent than what he'd derived from any creature in the past. It was as though he overflowed with it, and it unsettled him more than he cared to admit.

"Kamdyn is safe within the protection of your cave behind the runes," she informed him.

He nodded, though his gaze remained fixed on the sea. If he looked at her now, he might say things he couldn't take back. Things she could use against him. He might use words and platitudes that he didn't believe in, only for lack of sufficient verbiage to describe his complicated emotions.

The previous night had become a haze of lust and sex and recovery that had only dwindled when fatigue forced exhausted, trembling muscles to sleep. Barely a word was spoken between them and those that were only served as carnal encouragement. Kylah had taken him any way he'd wanted her to. She never issued commands or made demands of him, only desperate, passionate pleas that made him feel powerful and dominant. She'd allowed him to drive their pleasure in any direction he desired it.

And he'd desired it all.

He'd taken her with his mouth. With his hands. With his body, and sometimes intense combinations thereof. And in doing so, systematically shattered any physical barrier or taboo left between them. Only when she begged him for respite did he tuck her against his sated, exhausted body and allow sleep to overtake them both.

She loved him. Or thought she did, if ever there were such a thing. She trusted him. Desired him. Stood by him here at the end and risked everything she held dear to fight for his justice despite being denied her own.

Foreign and intense emotion rushed into his throat until it was thoroughly blocked. He couldn't have formed words if he tried.

Kylah's hand wound its way into his and gripped it with a strength that surprised him enough to command his attention.

War braids tangled at her temple and the ancient blue war paint of their Woad ancestors marked her lovely features in a fashion very similar to his own. Dressed in a loose blue shift and kirtle, she clutched a long, deadly dirk that he'd given her this morning, coated in a substance ultimately dangerous to her.

"Do ye know how to use that?" he rasped, wishing he'd said something better, more meaningful.

Her wee face was fierce as she brought it out in front of her. "Not even a little bit," she admitted with a wry smirk. "But the important part is, I know the sharp bit goes into a Faerie."

Daroch's heart swelled. Her courage put him to shame and a sudden icy fear clutched at him when he thought of all that might befall her in this endeavor.

"Perhaps ye should join yer sister in the cave," he suggested, turning to her and taking her shoulders in his hands. "I can't stand the thought of ye—"

"Perhaps *you* should hold your tongue," her brow lifted along with her lips in a taunting smile. "There's not a force on this earth or in the heavens that would keep me from your side."

His heart jumped into his throat again and suddenly made him bold. "Kylah, I—"

"Do not waste your breath, Druid." The familiar, arctic voice of the Banshee Queen froze the warm words on his tongue and his heart along with them. "It is too late to save her traitorous life and she will die screaming."

Daroch and Kylah turned toward the Fae, who'd appeared upon the green plane behind them, trapping them effectively against the cliff. Dripping with diamonds as brilliant as the sun and robes as pure as fresh snow, they would have resembled wrathful seraphim to anyone who didn't know better.

But Daroch knew. He knew their colors had so many facets and spectra that they could not be contained in this realm. And so they weren't.

Despite the uncommonly warm spring sunlight, little crystals of frost swirled about them as their auras froze what moisture clung to the sea air. They were the absence of warmth. The ironic immortal antithesis of life. And an all-encompassing hatred swelled within Daroch, lent abject ferocity by the snarling wolf pack now flanking the Faeries.

"I thought ye'd bring an army," Daroch sneered as he let go of Kylah's hand to draw his sword. He wished like hell she were somewhere else. Somewhere safe. For, even though only The Queen, Ly Erg, and her hand-maiden stood before him, he knew they were each utterly lethal. Cliodnah and her Banshee companion could kill him with one touch. Probably with only her Banshee scream.

Cliodnah speared him with her empty eyes, and Daroch couldn't stop the shudder of revulsion that clawed down his spine. "To gather an army, I'd have to call a council of Queens. I do not want nor do I need their permission. You humans have a charming saying about forgiveness being easier to obtain."

"My death by your hand would be a direct violation of yer Queen's pact," he taunted. "Because of yer insolence in keeping me, she mentioned me by name in her contract with the Gods."

The frost around her agitated the air as though swirled by a powerful wind, the only outward sign of the Banshee Queen's displeasure. "That is why I brought Ly Erg. He is my assassin when I or my Banshees cannot have a hand in the deed. As you have learned, Druid, since the blood of your people still stain his hands." She reached to Ly Erg and brought a crimson hand to her lips, planting a devoted kiss to the blood.

Her mouth came away clean. The blood never actually touched her, despite that she was swimming in an ocean's worth of innocent dead.

"I just came to *watch*." The Queen's liquid silver eyes ignited with a cruel spark.

Beside him, Kylah gasped.

Daroch's lip curled as he tried to rein in his surging rage and let his logic prevail. "I have defeated Ly Erg countless times. He hardly holds danger for me." Especially not now.

"I have been toying with you, human," Ly Erg scoffed, his new suit of armor gleaming in the sunlight. "As the Queen has never particularly ordered your death before now."

Daroch could not exactly tell if Ly Erg spoke the truth, but it mattered little. Because of his animal guardians, they were more equivalent in combat than ever in the past, and Daroch now held one massive advantage in that regard. Ly Erg didn't fear his weapons.

And that could prove a lethal mistake.

The Queen pointed at Kylah and gestured to her hand-maiden. "Subdue her," she ordered.

The expressionless Fae moved to comply.

Ly Erg slowly advanced toward Daroch. "Know this, Druid, once I have taken your life, I'm going to enjoy punishing your woman. And once I've broken her, I'll start on her sister. I'm going to—"

Daroch attacked, not intending to let Ly Erg finish his threat. He leapt with all the dexterity afforded by the wolves, his staff in his left hand and his sword in his right, poised to rain a final death upon the unsuspecting immortal. Ly Erg barely had time to draw his sword before Daroch was on him. The clash echoed over the moors for miles as their weapons collided with unnatural speed and strength.

Daroch used both weapons in a relentless spinning offensive, forcing the Faerie to block his staff before he followed up with a slash from his sword.

Ly Erg did seem to be more dexterous than in the past, his Fae blade moving with barely traceable speed, still managing to deflect every one of Daroch's blows. Changing strategy, Daroch brought them face to face with a dual-handed attack that caught both his weapons, but took Ly Erg two hands on his hilt to block.

He snarled at the Fae executioner. "Ye'll never taint her with yer touch."

Ly Erg opened his mouth, but rather than hear the Fae's retort, Daroch used a surge of power through his arms to bash at his perfect, cruel features with the blunt head of his staff.

Blood exploded from the Faerie's nose and a satisfying crunch preceded a faint sizzle as the Arborlatix came into contact with Fae cartilage, blood, and bone.

The extent of the damage stunned them both, but Daroch recovered first and leapt away, disengaging their weapons. He growled and began to spin his staff in his left hand to gain momentum for another assault.

Ly Erg spit blood into the grass and leered at him, swiping his sword through the air a few times.

"Why do you not heal?" the Queen demanded of her executioner.

"The Druid has something on his weapons," Ly Erg answered shortly, his silver and gold features sobered and settled into an ugly mask of retribution. "The time for play is over."

"You Faeries are creatures of the forest," Daroch measured his voice carefully, giving away none of the glee he felt as he watched blood continue to leak from his enemy's broken nose. "It seems appropriate, then, that a tree would hold the key to your demise." He advanced again, maintaining his position as the aggressor, his staff whirling through the air as though searching for purpose, his sword poised to strike.

Ly Erg leapt at him, blood staining his teeth and draining from his mouth as he flew through the air, a new and satisfying fear in his silver eyes.

Daroch braced himself, but dangerously underestimated the Fae's strength as he blocked a blow to his staff arm that he should have dodged. His staff went flying as pain exploded in his forearm. The Fae blade sliced through his leather bracer and found purchase in the sinew there. Daroch cursed, and the wolves howled and snarled their displeasure.

Then he saw his moment. It was but a flash of an overextension on the part of Ly Erg, but using his heightened reflexes; Daroch reached over his body and with a vicious stroke of his sword and relieved Ly Erg of his blade by hacking through both of his hands and shearing them from the bone.

They fell uselessly to the highland grasses and rolled before being swiped by chattering polecats and swept somewhere beneath the earth.

Ly Erg looked at the stumps of his hands for an astounded moment before falling to his knees. The ravens cackled like mad from above, lending a discordant cacophony to the shocked stillness.

Daroch reveled in dark victory. "Never again will yer hands claim the lives of the innocent for yer sick amusement." He raised his sword above his head, ignoring the trickle of blood down his arm. "And know that when I take yer head this time, it will be the last."

The Queen's transcendent Banshee scream ripped through him like a white-hot fire, causing him to go half blind. It felt as though his soul was tattered linen caught in the teeth of two competing hounds, each jerking and ripping in the opposite direction. But he managed to draw the last of his remaining faculties and send his blade through the Fae's neck with the ease of a glowing-hot iron through candle wax.

One of the wolves caught the rolling head in his teeth before the entire pack fled the dangerous wail of the Banshee, their sensitive ears unable to stand the unnatural pitch.

Daroch dropped to his own knees, holding his ears and feeling the blood leak through his fingers. His teeth locked and a cry of pain ripped from a throat almost clogged with his own blood. He could feel it leaking like tears from his eyes.

He'd underestimated the willingness of the Queen to flout the consequences of the pact, and that might have been the end of him. And maybe Kylah as well.

Kylah's awe at the defeat of Ly Erg was cut painfully short by her terror for Daroch. Even without his intellectual acumen, she'd known their odds for survival of the day were minimal, but she simply couldn't allow the Queen's second to hold her in an idle, unconcerned grasp while she watched the man she loved die on the ground, writhing in agony.

"Do not move and you may yet live," Cliodnah's hand-maiden whispered.

Kylah refused to listen. Her life didn't matter without Daroch. With a mighty Banshee wail of her own to lend her strength, she pulled the dirk out of her sleeve and slashed at the hand-maiden, who jumped back and released her instantly, peering dubiously at the knife's lethal point.

Once freed, she jerked away and barreled toward the Queen's turned back. She surprised herself as much as Cliodnah when the dirk slid between the Banshee Queen's ribs.

Cliodnah's wail died instantly and her head spun on her shoulders at a frightening and unnatural angle. Turning the rest of her body from Daroch, she caught Kylah's neck in a lightning-fast grip as her silver irises sparked and snapped overtaking the whites of her eye.

"Though you are one of the immortal ones, as your queen I can kill you in slow, immeasurably torturous increments." Her voice fractured from one into many, some with a radiant, high-pitched shrill and others as deep as any man's.

Kylah's limbs struggled in panic, flailing in the air as Cliodnah crushed her neck and her powerful magic snapped through Kylah's body more painfully than her flesh had ignited in the forge a year before. Black stars danced in her periphery, but her heart lifted to see Daroch groan and push himself upright.

Their eyes locked and she poured her heart into them even as she felt her life begin to ebb.

"What makes you think you can mean anything to him?" The Queen demanded. "He fucked me for months. For centuries of your time. How could a lowly, damaged highland washerwoman compete with a Faerie Queen?"

A soft hiss preceded a sickly wet sound as the sharpened point of Daroch's staff punched through Cliodnah's shoulder and chest, stopping inches from Kylah's skin.

Daroch stood panting from where he'd hurled it like a javelin, blood drying on his neck and cheeks where it had leaked from his eyes and ears. The effect was terrifying. He looked like some wrathful, ancient God of the underworld, come to claim his vengeance.

"I may have fucked ye, ye twisted bitch, but I made *love* to her."

Never had Kylah loved him more than at that moment.

The Queen's head snapped back and she keened with the unfamiliar pain of the Arborlatix as it skewered through her. She hurled Kylah toward her hand-maiden with such incredible force, that Kylah would have broken bones upon impact with the earth had she still been human.

"Finish her!" she commanded as she ripped the spear from her body. The contact with the coated weapon singed her palms. She tossed it behind her and advanced on Daroch. "I'm going to slaughter this Druid with my bare hands."

Kylah pitched toward the Fae. She'd left her knife in the Faerie Queen, though it seemed to have little effect. She had nothing with which to defend herself. She didn't want to watch her approaching doom, instead, she pushed herself from the grass as Cliodnah ripped off Daroch's robes, leaving him only in his trews and touched her deadly fingers to the tattoo above his heart.

"This hardly protects you," she snarled at the new and sacred triquetra on his chest. "It will only delay your death and prolong your pain." His body arced violently as she jolted him. His scream was dark and unnatural, filled with incomprehensible torment.

Kylah jumped to her feet, desperate to stop her. His pain pierced her heart. This couldn't be how it ended. There was no justice in this.

Her eyes fell to his staff, discarded by the Queen. It was covered with the Arborlatix, and if she could pierce a vital organ with it, it would surely slow her down.

Kylah reached for it, but the Queen's hand-maiden kicked her hand and snatched it from the ground.

It sizzled in her hands, and the smaller Fae's soft eyes pinched with pain at the edges. She speared Kylah with a look of profound regret that stunned her. "I do what must be done," she murmured.

In a flash of movement, she turned and shoved the spear through her Queen, piercing her lungs.

The Queen's screams died on a wet gurgle, and Daroch slumped to his knees as her power withdrew from his bleeding body. He panted on the ground for a shocked moment as everyone stared at the red and black stain growing around the staff protruding from Cliodnah's chest.

"You are no longer fit to rule," the hand-maiden said dispassionately. "You break our sacred pacts, flout the holy council of Queens, and make light of our immortal words."

The Queen gave a wet cough.

"You would kill this man who was your servant and your slave rather than grant him the boon he is owed."

Daroch's hand tightened on his sword. The Banshee Queen struck her hand-maiden with such force the small faerie nearly flew over the cliff. Cliodnah drifted toward her, slowly pulling the staff through her middle. "You have been little better than a slave to me for millennia," she screamed maniacally. "You *dare* to—"

The Banshee Queen's words died swiftly as her head separated from her elegant neck. She reached the ground in a limp heap before her crystalline flakes had the chance to fall. They settled around her in a ring before melting into the spring grasses.

Daroch spat blood on her white robes, his Druid sword dripping onto her priceless jewels, and promptly collapsed to the grass beside her, still as death.

Chapter Sixteen

The soft, familiar lapping of water against stone told Daroch he was in his grotto. At least, he dared hope he was. He tried to move and pain lanced through him, though he welcomed it as verification that he was yet alive.

"I think he's stirring, Kylah," a young sweet voice pierced the pain in his head. One he'd heard before. But where?

Thank you, Druid, for what you did.

His memory returned to him. Kylah's younger sister, sweet-faced and deceptively innocent looking. She was safe. Alive. Well, not *alive*, exactly.

A cool, wet cloth had been wiping at his face, but it left him, and a hand reached beneath his neck. His soul recognized the touch immediately.

"Drink this. It will help with the pain." Kylah's gentle voice soothed with as much efficiency as any tonic she could give him. But Daroch forced himself to swallow the bitter brew she gave him, testing his mind by identifying each herb by its taste.

That achieved, he decided to risk opening his eyes. Daroch drank in the sight of her, hale and whole and as lovely as she'd ever been. Kylah gazed back at him, her eyes shining with so many emotions, he didn't have the capacity to identify them all. Wouldn't pay heed to the word lurking in his pain-and-tonic-muddled thoughts.

A second head popped into his vision from where he stared up from the flat of his back, a younger, lighter version of Kylah, this one still glowing a luminescent blue and smattered with freckles. "Did you really decapitate two people in one day?" she asked with youthful rapturous awe.

"Kamdyn!" Kylah admonished.

"They werena people," he corrected through a raspy throat. "They were—"

"Faeries." A third head materialized above him and Daroch surged up, causing all three women to leap away from him.

"What the fuck is she doing here?" Daroch struggled to his feet searching for his sword, his staff, anything he could use against the interloper.

"Daroch." Kylah went to him, slipping her hand into his and wrapping the other about his arm as though preparing to support his buckling weight. He tilted a little, as the cave spun around him, but he shoved his woman behind him, ready to deal a final death to the diminutive Fae.

"Get me my sword," he commanded the room at large.

No one moved to obey him. Contrary, bull-headed highland women. Why couldn't they just accept that what he said was always right and do as he bade them?

"I mean you no harm, Druid." The dead Queen's hand-maiden floated above the black waters of the grotto, intricate designs of ice forming in the water below her.

"She helped me bring you home, Daroch." Kylah stepped out from behind him. "Her name is Tah Liah and she has something to offer you."

"I want nothing from a *Faerie*," he growled, fighting feelings of betrayal.

"Not even the restitution you are owed?" The Fae called Tah Liah asked.

Daroch lurched toward her on unsteady feet. "What could you possibly have to offer me that would serve as restitution for all I have lost?" His voice broke on the last word, and Kylah moved to steady him, though there was no need. Rage strengthened his bones and began to erase the damage done by the Banshee Queen and her lethal magic.

"Cliodnah helped Kylah's older sister, Katriona, defeat her Laird's enemies and, in doing so, broke the pact not to interfere in human affairs," Tah Liah explained.

"What does that have to do with me?" Daroch asked.

"According to the contract, if she were to ever again interfere with humans she would owe you, her wrongly captured slave, a great boon. As she is dead by both our hands, the council of Queens will learn of her treachery and by Faerie law, I will succeed her as Queen of the Banshees. As such, I plan to keep our sacred pacts, beginning with the debt she owes you."

Daroch snarled. "I repeat, I want nothing from ye but yer departure from my home."

"Not even a fresh beginning?" The Faerie asked. "Rarely, a Fae is granted the ability to reach through time. I can petition the council of Queens to return you to your own time, to your own people. Your memory of the horrible days you spent with my Queen would be as naught and you would live your life back among the Druids."

Beside him, Kylah gasped, and her fingers tightened their grip on his. Daroch looked down at her and she met his gaze, her liquid green eyes swimming with tears.

"You could go home." she struggled to give him a watery smile and failed, utterly.

Daroch's chest tightened. In the time he'd known her, Kylah's face had become so incredibly dear. Her voice flowed through his thoughts constantly, arguing with him even when she wasn't present. He'd only begun to learn the forbidden mysteries of her body. Of her unconquerable spirit. He'd only basked in her encompassing love for one night.

He wanted—needed—a lifetime.

"Could I use my boon to keep Kylah with me, to restore her life and humanity?"

"Daroch?" she whispered, as though she dare not believe what she heard. "Why?"

Did she truly have to ask?

"You love her," Tah Liah observed.

Daroch shook his head, but pulled Kylah closer. "I doona believe in love. But I canna stand the thought of spending the rest of a century sleeping without her by my side. I couldna return to my time and my people. I couldna live a life without her in it."

A soft and knowing look passed between the new Banshee Queen and the woman he clung to. It puzzled him, but he dare not admit it as a sudden unsettling realization that he was outnumbered by women left him uncomfortably silent.

"It is nearly impossible, what you ask." Tah Liah sounded as though she regretted her words. "The return of a life demands the balance of a human virgin sacrifice, one born of flames. You above all people should know that, Druid."

His hopes fell with a heavy weight. Kylah would never allow the sacrifice of another innocent, not even to solidify their future together.

"What about me?" Kamdyn's quiet voice permeated the somber cave. "I died in a fire, and was... *am* a virgin."

Tah Liah's silver eyes sharpened with interest.

"Kamdyn, *no*," Kylah insisted. "You do not know what you are offering. These Fae, they are cruel and brutal." She turned to Tah Liah. "I mean no offense, but my sister is young and impetuous, and after what happened to Daroch, I cannot allow this."

"All those who are loyal to Cliodnah and Ly Erg will swiftly be dealt with." Tah Liah gestured to Kamdyn. "I will be in need of a hand-maiden and you will be under my protection. I can promise no harm or degradation will befall you at the hands of the Fae, and you will only be set to tasks of the utmost importance. A high place, indeed, for someone who was once mortal."

"Ye're all mortal, now, Faerie." Daroch couldn't keep himself from reminding her. "I will ensure the use of Arborlatix is widespread and prevalent."

Tah Liah speared him with an impatient, meaningful look. "I understand that, and it is more the reason to avoid humans in the future." She turned to Kylah. "You would give up your new found immortality for this Druid?"

Daroch's heart seized. He hadn't thought of it that way. For the moment, Kylah was strong, immortal and he'd rid her life of her enemies.

Kylah glanced from her sister, who smiled and nodded, then to Daroch, and back.

"Without question," she insisted, "I love him with all my heart. But... Kamdyn..."

"Stay with your Druid." Kamdyn went to her. "Mother will have you and Katriona to look after her and as this ghostly Banshee, I can do nothing. I can have... no one." She stole a shy look at Daroch. "Though I know I would have your love, I would truly be alone."

A tear slid down Kylah's cheek. "Oh darling, I didn't even consider that."

"What an adventure this will be for me." Kamdyn's soft green eyes began to sparkle with eager anticipation. "I want to do this, Kylah, for you, for your Druid, and for myself."

Daroch's heart swelled with gratitude, but he couldn't think of a thing to say.

"You're welcome," Kamdyn told him with a smile and turned to kiss the air next to her sister's cheek.

Kylah gave a soft sob, but returned the ghostly kiss.

Kamdyn drifted toward Tah Liah, and took the hand of her new Banshee Queen. It was the last they saw of either of them, as they faded into the nether.

Kylah gave one last sob, and then a gasp as her entire form began to tremble.

"Kylah? What's happening." Daroch clutched her to him, felt her body grow incrementally warmer as Fae flesh became human, fused with blood and mortal energy. He dared not hope. He dared not trust the word of a Faerie.

Suddenly, she pulled back, a radiant smile catching the tears that fell from her eyes. "Could you have imagined, Daroch, when this day dawned that we'd have your vengeance, and then be blessed with my life... *our* lives?"

Daroch felt a smile overtake his own mouth and, for once, he did not fight it. "It truly defies the odds."

"I love you, Daroch McLeod."

Daroch sobered. "I... meant what I said to the Faerie. I canna imagine one single day without ye in it. I feel this— perplexing and primitive drive to possess every part of ye. To be what no other man could possibly be in yer eyes. I want ye to belong to me and to tell me what to do. I want to be the answer to all yer infuriating questions. I want..."

Kylah stilled the movement of his lips by laying a gentle finger on them. "If you said, 'I love you, Kylah', that would encompass all of that and save us a great deal of time that could be spent doing things *other* than talking." Heat flared in her eyes and she made a gesture toward his antechamber.

"I love ye, Kylah." Daroch tested the words and realized nothing he'd ever learned, studied, discovered, or confirmed ever felt more like the absolute truth.

A Highland Historical Novella
by the Bestselling Author of *Unleashed*

KERRIGAN BYRNE

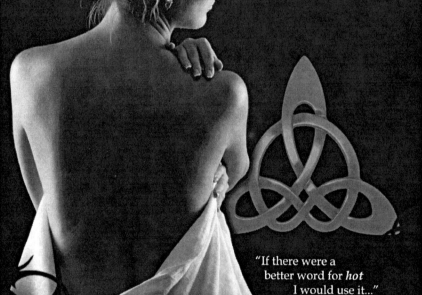

"If there were a
better word for *hot*
I would use it..."
— *Cynthia St. Aubin*

RELUCTANT

Her kiss would be his last...

RELUCTANT

A HIGHLAND HISTORICAL NOVELLA

Chapter One

He was shadow. He was night. He was death and blood and screams.

Grey leached out of his vision as the Berserker rage passed. He melded with the darkness and watched the flames consume what he'd destroyed. The simple homes held together by straw, earth, and pitch caught easily.

Other shadowy figures crept from the flames carrying their plunder. They showed him deference as they melted into the night as though they'd never been.

They would pay him tribute when they returned to the war camp. For a Berserker did not stop his killing to collect his due.

He collected other shadows. Those created by the flames of civilization, but forced to lurk outside of its warmth. Highwaymen, street orphans, discarded soldiers, criminals, the mad and the lost. He organized them. Fed them. Strengthened them. Taught them to take what they could never have had. Showed them the substance of brotherhood was more efficient and profitable than working alone.

The Gods only favored power. If you were not strong enough to keep what you had, you didn't deserve it.

The wails of those left alive, the women and the children, was a familiar and comforting melody that mingled with the roar of the approaching flames. He snarled at the blaze and its illuminating heat, drawing deeper into the night. He did better in the cold. It reminded him that warmth was an illusion and trust was a misconception.

A score of years ago, he'd been abandoned on foreign soil by the weak and deceitful men he'd once called brothers. Though he kept his army, he relied on none. He trusted their fear of him. Had faith in their greed and their anger. But never their hearts. Never their words.

The Highland blackguard named Murdock of Clan Munroe galloped toward him, pulling a dark, riderless stallion.

"It is time, Laird, let us leave this place before the dawn finds it nothing but ashes." Murdock tossed him the reins and tried to still a dancing horse made nervous by the building inferno.

He mounted and galloped after Murdock.

His men called him '*Laird*.' The first time he'd heard the word, he hadn't known what it meant. He'd not known their strange language. But now, he understood. They needed someone to follow. Someone to fear. Someone to blame. Structure to their day and consequence to their insolence.

They called him 'Laird' because he had no name. Not anymore.

He was shadow.

Chapter Two

"His name is Soren and he has to die."

Kamdyn MacKay had yet to speak a word. She had yet to close her mouth.

Finn MacLauchlan had addressed her queen in his short, faded Nordic accent. He had to be the largest, most fearsome looking man she'd ever seen, besides the two dark, gigantic brothers flanking him.

All this time, Kamdyn had thought her brothers-in-law, Laird Rory and the Druid, Daroch, to be in contest for the biggest and most intimidating men she'd ever met. It wasn't that the three Berserkers dwarfed them, per se, it was that the large and ancient warriors consumed the space in which they stood, dominated it even, with a dangerous and predatory energy.

"The three of you are long-mated Berserkers." The Banshee Queen reached over and gently pressed on Kamdyn's chin, forcing her slack jaw shut. "And I hear you are now four as Laird Connor's eldest son has reached manhood and has been blessed by Freya. How is it that four Berserker warriors, three of them approaching a century of life, cannot hunt and kill one unmated rogue?"

A century old? Kamdyn's mouth dropped open again as she studied the Berserkers. Not one of them looked a day older than her brothers-in-law. The five men stood in the great hall of MacKay Castle, each appearing as though they teased the middle years of forty, though Kamdyn was certain that Laird

Rory had seen his fiftieth birthday. Silver threaded through Connor and Roderick's dark hair and even toyed at the temples of Finn's golden locks. Lines of wisdom sprouted from the corners of their eyes and bracketed hard mouths, yet did little to belie the incomparable strength the years still afforded each man on the unofficial council standing before her and the queen.

"We have tried," Laird Connor interjected. "But he is disturbingly elusive." He rubbed a hand over his close-cropped hair. "The people of the Highlands are starting to call him '*The Laird of Shadows.*' It is said he has an ancient Fae relic that protects him from scrying magic."

Kamdyn felt her attention drifting. Each man in this room was *disturbingly* handsome. The MacLauchlan brothers all dressed in their blue, red, and green tartans that accentuated their burnished skin and matching green eyes. Laird Rory MacKay and the Druid Daroch, who'd taken the name of MacKay after marrying her sister, Kylah, each folded heavy, tattooed arms over their blue, green and gold tartans, their intense eyes watching the exchange between Berserker and Banshee with measured interest.

She tried not to wriggle and fidget. Talk of death and retribution bored her. Lord knew in the twenty years she'd spent as the handmaiden to the Banshee Queen she'd heard her fill, but the abundant amount of muscled male flesh in front of her was enough to wrest her attentions away from the conversation.

For some reason, she'd become very *aware* of her virginity. She felt as though she wanted to evoke fantasies about the men present, but in her innocence, she couldn't really do them justice.

Contrary to myth, Faeries were very private regarding sexual matters and, though Kamdyn had been invited to partake in what transpired behind their closed doors, she'd never had the courage to do so. Nor the desire. Faerie men, though beautiful, tended to be somewhat androgynous and held little appeal to her at all. They were nothing like the feast of rampant masculinity before her. For the first time in years, her body stirred and her interest snagged where it was absolutely inappropriate to do so. Mouths. Shoulders. Thighs. The flex of a forearm or the length of strong fingers. These mythic warriors of Freya were certainly a different, arresting breed of man, and they piqued her curiosity.

"My mate, Evelyn, is a seer," the one called Roderick said in his thick brogue. He had long, black hair and a cruel brow over very kind green eyes. "She told us that if one of us were to hunt this *Laird of Shadows*, a Berserker would die before his time."

Finn nodded, rolling his muscled shoulders and allowing his hand to rest on the hilt of his broadsword. "Not one of us is willing to leave our women widows, or our children without fathers. But we cannot allow this Berserker to go on terrorizing the Highlands."

"I thought those blessed by the Gods couldna be killed by Banshees," Laird MacKay interjected.

"No' the Celtic Gods," Roderick explained. "But there's no such rule about the Gods of the North."

"Years ago, a similar delegation was charged between the MacLauchlans and the MacKay." Laird Connor turned and tossed a bag full of coin to Laird Rory, who caught it with a swift hand. Their eyes locked and held. "We knew yer Clan had the ear of the Banshee Queen, and this time, it is *us* who require the taking of a life."

Kamdyn's ears pricked to the meaning in their words. Every person in this room had their fates altered by the other. Even her. She and her sisters had been brutally burned alive by Laird Rory's violent brother, Angus. Roderick MacLauchlan had defeated Rory and Angus's traitor father at the battle of Harlaw. Rory had hired the Berserker Laird, Connor, to kill

Angus, who had become betrothed to Connor's mate. Kamdyn and her sisters had been turned Banshees to reap their own vengeance upon Angus, but Connor's blade was too swift. Though denied their revenge by the Berserkers, the two eldest Banshee sisters, Katriona and Kylah, were able to find their loves and reclaim their mortality through Rory and Daroch. Daroch had exacted his own revenge by killing the previous cruel Banshee Queen, thereby installing her handmaiden, Tah Liah, as the new sovereign.

In order to keep and maintain the happiness of her sisters, their mates, and her beloved Clan, Kamdyn had pledged her immortal soul to the Banshee Queen as sacrifice so Kylah could live with the Druid she loved.

It was all a kind of strange, interwoven knot of destiny. Kamdyn had a distinct impression that the knot was completing itself to form something eternal.

"Keep yer coin." Rory tossed it back. "This Soren, Laird of Shadows, is indiscriminate in his plunder and destruction. He's raided the MacKays and MacLauchlans alike, along with the McLeods, Keiths, Ross, Munroe, even as far south as Clan MacKenzie. He's created twice the problem for me, because every time he raids a Sutherland, I get blamed for it."

Rory was currently embroiled in the flare of a centuries-long dispute with the neighboring Sutherland clan. It seemed every time conditions with the English improved, the Sutherlands turned their war-like ways back toward the MacKay, lusting after their fertile lands and bounteous ocean.

"It is our fault Soren was unleashed upon the Highlands," Finn insisted. "In fact, the fault mostly lies with me."

"How so?" Daroch's hazel eyes sharpened with interest.

"To shorten a long story, I came here from the Berserker temple of Freya in the Northlands to join my brothers," Finn explained. "The others believed that the blessing of the Berserker should not abide in Scotland, and so they sailed here to slaughter us and our mates, ensuring that they'd eliminate our line."

Kylah gasped. Kill the women, too? Just for loving one of these extraordinary men?

"We defeated those who would not submit to us, and have had the Berserker temple under our control all this time. Though during the battle on the long boat, Soren was knocked into the sea, and somehow he survived."

"And has been a thorn in Scotland's arse ever since," Connor groused.

The Banshee Queen held up her hand. "So to mitigate more bloodshed, you request that I send a Banshee to kill this man, Soren?" Her white robes glistened with her movement, sending a shower of tiny frost flakes to the floor. Her crystal eyes took in each of the men. "What do you offer in return for this life?"

Roderick stepped forward. "We figured you'd be interested in reclaiming the Fae relic he has plundered, though if you require aught else, we should be able to provide it."

The queen seemed to take longer than necessary to consider, though the frost about her aura began to swirl in excited flurries. The men started shifting with impatience, but none of them dared to speak. Kamdyn knew that Tah Liah measured everything very carefully with the unhurried manner of an immortal. So she settled in for the wait, wondering who would be chosen to kill the villain.

"I am very much interested in regaining this relic," the queen stated in a voice that conveyed little to no interest at all. "I will send my own handmaiden to procure it, and rid you of this Lord of Shadows."

"It's *Laird* of Shadows," Daroch corrected the Banshee Queen in a voice full of derision. He held little fear or respect for the Fae and was therefore unable to help himself.

Kamdyn felt like a fish pulled from the sea. Her eyes bulged and her mouth opened and closed without drawing any air or making any sound. She couldn't remember once ever taking a life. She had always been the sort to take a spider out of doors to save it from her sister's boot. She'd cried for days when they'd had to eat one of their hens during a particularly long winter. In fact, she'd refused to eat meat for months in protest of the senseless slaughter. As a Banshee, it was understood that she'd been supposed to kill an evil MacKay Laird, but she'd always been secretly thankful she didn't end up having to. Now the queen was sending *her* to take care of this Viking Berserker warlord? This *Laird of Shadows?* What was she *thinking*?

"Ye're sending *this* wee thing to kill the Laird of Shadows?" Connor echoed her thoughts. The Berserkers simultaneously burst into laughter. "I doona think we've properly expressed to ye how dangerous this man is."

Kamdyn scowled at their laughter. She caught Rory cracking a smile and speared her brother-in-law with a withering look.

He pulled his lips into a straight line, but the corner of his mouth trembled furiously.

"I assure you, my handmaiden's touch is as effective as any Banshee's." The queen did not seem amused, but neither did she seem incensed.

"Yes, I am *quite* fatal," Kamdyn insisted, hoping they didn't call her bluff, but resenting their laughter and lack of respect. "And... and... I'm certain that I could even be *lethal*, if I wanted to."

A new wave of masculine chortles crippled the warriors, and Rory lost the battle to his dimpled grin. Even grim Daroch snorted in amusement.

"I'll—I'll do it." Kamdyn regretted the words the moment they escaped her, yet still she plunged deeper into the reckless vow. "I'll kill this marauder and recover the relic. Then we'll see who is laughing."

The two MacKay men sobered and cast uneasy glances at each other.

"We mean no disrespect, wee Banshee." Connor covered his mouth as though to contain his mirth. "It's just ye're such a slip of a girl. Ye look as though ye'd blow away in a strong wind, let alone stand against a Berserker."

"I'll be forty next year," she imperiously informed him. "Though I became a Banshee at eighteen, and am therefore stuck in that form."

The Berserkers peered at her a bit differently then.

"That's no' exactly the case," Daroch chimed in with the information she hoped he'd keep to himself. She should have known the hope was foolish. "She's spent some of that time in Faerie, which means she hasna exactly *lived* all of the years we have, as time passes more slowly there."

"Aye." Rory took the argument a step further, regarding her with brotherly gentleness. "I doona believe she has the heart to do what must be done."

Tah Liah looked back at Kamdyn, spearing her with an arctic, crystalline gaze. "It is my opinion that it is time she learns to use her Banshee magic. She has accepted the terms of this pact, has she not?"

Kamdyn gulped and nodded. Tah Liah had always been good to her. Treated her with patience and fairness, if not affection. Still, she dare not refuse her queen's will. Agreements and contracts were a very sacred thing to this particular Banshee Queen.

"Aye, my lady."

"Then it is settled. Tonight you will end the Laird of Shadows."

Chapter Three

Kamdyn found the Shadow Laird's camp in the Naver forest near Strathnaver. The cloudy night was dark, and their fires glowed in the isolated country like tiny beacons among a maze of stark and gnarled trees. It had to be magic that no one had found them yet, because a force of two hundred or so men was nigh impossible to hide.

She lurked among them, spying on their night time rituals. They laughed, ate like savages, fought amongst themselves, and sang songs that made her ears burn. However, the band of marauders wasn't exactly what she expected. They were clean. Their tents were fine. There seemed to be a subtle organization in their debauched anarchy. A creed maybe? A code by which they lived. Kamdyn struggled to understand it. Who would choose to live like this? There were no women. No color to make their tents cozy or spices to make their meals pleasant. Just pilfered goods and bloodied weapons.

The men spoke about *him* in hushed voices laced with equal parts fear and awe. No matter how loud and raucous they became, when they passed the large tent set away from the camp, tucked into the very corner of the trees, they fell silent, giving it a wide berth and uneasy glances.

There she would find the Laird of Shadows.

And there she would end him.

Kamdyn paused at the entry to the tent, which faced the trees rather than the camp. Becoming corporeal, she adjusted the thin straps of her diaphanous blue robes and hesitated.

Though it was early October, large, soft flakes of snow began to drift slowly to the highland trees and grasses. Not a storm, more a warning that winter approached. At the appearance of the lazy, feathered swirls, a feeling of lost desolation reached out to her. It drifted about the camp, not unlike the snowflakes, leaving none untouched.

Kamdyn watched the pillagers with new eyes. She'd expected evil. She'd expected the kind of violent, selfish brutality that Angus and his men displayed when they'd burned her and her sisters alive.

But she felt none of that from the surrounding men. She felt... Need. Raw, pure, unfulfilled desires. Some so intense and soul-searing, they choked her. The need for love. For acceptance. For food, for blood, revenge, sex, dominance. Some of the men who laughed the loudest were the most empty.

And the emptiness seemed to concentrate at one particular point.

His tent. It was like a chasm. Indeed, they called him the Laird of Shadows, but there had to be light in order to create shadow, didn't there? And in his tent, she could feel none. To her Banshee senses, whatever that tent sheltered was like a gaping wound, nay, like scorched and salted earth. Desolate. Insatiable.

Clenching her fists in preparation, she needlessly filled her lungs with chilly air, and nodded to herself. His name was Soren, and he needed to die. Wasn't that what the Nordic Berserker had said? He'd done terrible things. Killed innocent people. Destroyed livelihoods and homes, and would continue to do so unless she put a stop to it.

Right, then. She squared her shoulders. Time for the Laird of Shadows to face the Reaper—er—Banshee. She thrust aside the flap of the tent and plunged inside.

The hiss of a dagger flying end over end warned her the moment before it imbedded to the hilt just below her rib cage.

Kamdyn let out a shocked cry at the sharp pain. It was more a sound of outrage than anything. Her hands went to where the dirk penetrated her skin.

The Berskerker had a double-sided axe in his hand before he leapt from the pallet of furs on the floor.

He was incredibly massive. He was also incredibly *naked*.

A lone candle flickered at the far edge of the tent on a table strewn with the leavings of a devoured supper. Its flame flared brighter and reflected in the ice-blue eyes that mirrored astonishment back at her.

For a speechless moment, their gazes clashed and held. But Kamdyn couldn't stop her eyes from darting glances at all the foreign parts of him displayed by the dancing candlelight.

Laird of Shadows, indeed. For there were shadows created by the deep grooves and swells of sculpted brawn stretching taut over his thick frame. And there were shadows lurking in his deep-set eyes as they latched onto the hilt of his blade still protruding from her middle.

"You are—a girl," he accused her in a deep, rumbling Nordic accent.

Apparently, brilliance wasn't on the list of dangerous aspects of the Laird of Shadows.

His brutal face was condemning as he again lifted his eyes to hers. His axe lowered and then clattered to the earth as he dropped it. "I thought you were—I do not keep girls in the camp."

"I am a *woman*." She absurdly felt compelled to correct him while trying not to rudely stare at his nudity. Her eyes rested on the torque that encircled the swell of his bicep. "Well, I'm a Faerie. A Banshee. But I *was* a woman. Once. Not that I'm not now. A female, that is. Not a... woman." Kamdyn scowled and squeezed her eyes shut. This was rapidly deteriorating. They hadn't amply prepared her for this. Hadn't told her that the villain would have the sculpted features of Eros and the body of a barbarian god.

"And *you!*" she scolded, latching on to indignation with desperate fingers. "This is why I've been sent here, you know. This unacceptable behavior." Gripping the dirk's bejeweled hilt, she let out a gasp as she pulled it from her body, already feeling the flesh begin to knit back together. "Really, who throws daggers at a guest before ascertaining whether they are friend or foe?"

"Do. Not. Do... *That.*" The dark command held a bewildering pleading note.

"Do what?" she queried, holding the dirk up for inspection. It was long and wicked and since she was so small, it almost stabbed clean through her.

The Berserker's eyes flickered, and shadows of a different sort began to swirl in their depths.

"Bleed." The word was growled from lips peeled back from sharpened teeth. Kamdyn froze in fascination as the black of his pupils deepened and spread until his entire eye was a void, empty of emotion and full of every shade of darkness.

She'd been warned that blood would bring on Berserkergang. That it turned him into a ruthless beast of indiscriminate rage that would kill anyone in his path.

His body arched and he snarled as muscles built and compounded upon each other. He seemed to grow taller, wider, even monstrous. Either that or the tent was shrinking, which Kamdyn very much doubted. The part of him that defined his sex twitched and grew, becoming full and large.

Kamdyn's mouth went dry. Then flooded with moisture.

He'd become some kind of beast. He turned those abysmal eyes on her again and an expression crossed his face that astounded and bewildered her all at once.

On a dog, she would have called it joy. But on the Berserker's feral features, it had to be called something else. He was too savage to smile. To brutal to possess something like hope. Too ruthless to love. She was certain of it.

But to possess, to dominate, to destroy, of these things he was more than capable. Every dark intent she could imagine was blasted toward her by the muddled emotions drowning in the soupy remnants of his tainted soul.

As he stalked her, Kamdyn decided she was almost glad he'd become this monster. It would be less like killing a human. It would be easier to look into the soulless voids that should be his eyes and watch the life ebb from them, taken by her Banshee magic. His murderous intent would soothe the shame at wasting all that masculine beauty.

He leapt for her.

She reached out toward him, bracing for the impact, ready to send her deadly currents through his body.

But didn't. The closer he came, the better she could see just how wrong she'd been. The swirling darkness of the beast's eyes weren't empty at all, just deeper. And what she saw in their depths was a timid, undiscovered tenderness that took her breath away. And a fear of... something. Rejection? That couldn't be right. Her Banshee senses had to be shorting out.

When he seized her, she'd expected him to try to rip her apart with his strong bare hands.

What she hadn't expected was for him to kiss her.

Chapter Four

He didn't just kiss her. He captured her lips with his mouth. Captured her hair with his hand, and crushed her body to his nakedness.

Kamdyn stood frozen. His flesh was so warm beneath her hands, like silk stretched over sun-heated stone. His dangerously hot mouth threatened to melt her where she stood. In fact, her skin felt as though she'd been set ablaze for the second time in her life, but the sensation carried waves of disquieting pleasure scattering through the flames.

He was so strong. Too strong. Strong enough to rend her limbs from her body without using more than two fingers. She could feel it in the unerringly solid band of his arm imprisoning her against him. In the handfuls of hard, meaty muscle on his chest. In the press of his alarmingly thick thighs against her. In the fact that her feet no longer touched the ground, but dangled above it as he devoured her.

He forced his tongue past her lips without seeking entrance. He claimed her mouth as his, thrusting and retreating in a strong, moist action that sent dizzying thrills through her veins.

Arousal slammed into her with a wet and instant rush. All her life, she'd fantasized about being kissed like this. She'd been ashamed of her desires. Of her needs. She'd wanted to drive a man so mad with wanting that he couldn't help himself. She'd wanted to be officially kissed. Thoroughly kissed. And she'd been murdered before she ever had the chance.

His arm allowed her to slowly drop a little, sliding down his body. His sex pulsed between them she could feel the heat of it even through her robes. It made her gasp, though her gasp seemed to resemble a moan and was swallowed by his lips.

It felt glorious to have her mouth ravaged like this. The beast savored her like a doomed man would his last meal, which, she supposed, he was.

Once her feet touched the ground, he released her hair. A ripping sound permeated the pleasure-drugged fog of her thoughts. Cool air kissed the skin of her back. If she didn't act now she'd be as naked as him in a moment.

She wasn't ready for that. Not with *him*. What was she doing? This man was a monster. A murderer! And she was allowing him to kiss her senseless.

Panicking, Kamdyn did the only thing she could think to do. She jolted him with her magic, dropping his giant body into an unceremonious heap on the earth.

Someone was saying his name. Which was odd because he no longer had one. But whoever called for him was distressed. Afraid.

His body hurt everywhere. It felt like someone had tried to rip his soul from him and his skin barely managed to fight them off and contain it.

Who would dare? He swam through a dark current to the front of his eyelids and willed them to open. He would gut the fucker and shove his entrails down his throat while he still lived.

Did the doomed villain now threaten whoever called for him? Did she need his protection?

He furrowed his brow. He protected no one who could not defend themselves. He didn't have time for the weak. For the useless.

Soren. Soren, wake up. Please wake up.

He would protect *her.* The woman who belonged to that voice. He would protect her with his life. With his blood. With his beast. She belonged to him now.

He groaned. Where did these instincts hie from? They screamed through him with an intense ferocity. They were weak. They were soft and humiliating. He wanted rid of them.

Now.

Light exploded into his eye and he could feel his pupil contract. The only illumination came from a lone candle, but even it seemed too much.

"Soren, are you dead? Did I...already?"

His vision swam into focus. Maybe he had died, for never in his life would the angel crouched above him have reached for his face. She was small. Her features so perfectly delicate, he thought they might shatter if touched by a brute like himself.

His vision stung and blurred, reminding him to blink. He tried, but only one eye succeeded, because she held open the other lid with her finger.

"Oh! You're alive. I'm so relieved." Her lilting brogue conveyed pleasure with a voice made of equal parts sweetness and sunshine. Her hair was on fire. Wait. *Nie*, it was just the color of flames and piled on top of her head in a curly sort of disarray. He liked it, but it made him want to find what held it there and release her fire curls down her shoulders.

He scowled and tried to scrub his muddled mind clean of such strange and disconcerting thoughts.

She frowned back at him. The expression didn't look like it belonged on a face such as hers. Clear, sea-green eyes, filled with concern, looked down at him from a face so pale, the pink patches of friction on the flesh around her mouth arrested his notice. He squinted at her moist, swollen lips. A memory tried to struggle to the surface of his murky vision.

The girl's eyes widened and she let go of his eye to cover that soft mouth with her hand.

His scowl deepened and his eyes narrowed before he pushed himself from where he'd landed on the ground.

Once standing, he swayed a little, and the tiny girl popped up to steady him.

Not girl... *woman.* Her voice intruded on his thoughts, but she hadn't spoken it aloud. Not this time.

What the fuck? He held his throbbing head. Was that his dagger on the ground? There was blood on it. Preparing himself to be taken by his Berserker, his addled wits couldn't contain his astonishment when he simply—didn't. A strange and unsettling feeling stirred inside of him, and he turned to the small girl.

"Did you see who attacked me?" he asked testily.

She looked startled. "Um..."

Useless. "What are you doing in my tent?" he demanded, stalling for enough time to recover his senses. He scanned the room for other intruders, but the night was silent and they were alone.

She released him with a sigh and looked down, hiding her face from his view.

He realized he didn't like it when she did that. He reached into his memory. He'd taken a cold bath in the river, eaten two rabbits and a potato cake, then stripped and fallen asleep on his furs.

"I'm here to, well... that is to say... I've been *sent* here to..." She cleared her throat.

"Out with it," he ordered, feeling his blood begin to flow again and settle at one place, in particular.

He looked down at his growing erection. This was her doing. He glared across at her.

She was looking down too, which made him harder.

"You're here to deliver a message, to feed me or to fuck me, which is it?"

Her head snapped back up, a flame of intrigue sparking in her eyes. "That last one?" she breathed. Then shook her head as though to clear it.

Excellent. It was what he was hoping she'd say. He moved toward her and she instantly held up her hand to ward him off.

"No! No. That's a lie. I've been sent here—to kill you."

He paused. Then he snorted, which was the equivalent to an all-out fit of giggles for a man like him. Hadn't she just stated her relief that he lived? "You will not kill me," he informed her, crossing his arms.

She let out another sigh, this one full of sheepish regret. "I'm afraid I have to. There's a contract, you see, and those are very binding. Papers were signed and everything."

His eyes narrowed at her as he studied her lithe form, draped in all but transparent robes. She held the top layer, which he considered to be the most opaque, across her middle with one hand, as though hiding her ribs from him. Perhaps she was a bit daft. Maybe she'd wandered into his tent from the forest. He looked at her bare feet, smooth and unsullied by the earth.

"What papers?" he demanded. Maybe she could give him a clue as to who his enemy was and how he ended up on the ground.

Her nose crinkled, disturbing the light smattering of freckles across the bridge. "I'm ashamed to admit my mind wanders when the terms of the pact are read. They're so boring. But the gist of it is, you're a bad man who does terrible things and I've been sent to deliver your punishment." She gave him a sad sort of smile, her eyes roving over his chest, his arms, his torso and lower. The tiny column of her throat worked over a swallow, and her pink tongue snaked out to lick her lips. "Which is death, if I didn't mention that before."

"You did."

"Oh. Good," she said in a distracted voice, still ogling his naked body with frank, curious appreciation.

A memory knocked at his skull, seeking entrance and finding none.

She'd called him Soren. By the name his father had given him, the one he'd not heard in a score of years, and barely then. The Berserkers at the temple didn't call each other by name. They barely spoke at all.

"Answer this, you mad woman, who dared send you to punish me? Speak their names and I might spare your life." Using the voice he saved for interrogating prisoners and commanding his band of men, he'd meant to strike terror in the woman. No one should be able to find him. He had the *Scáth bhfolach,* which protected him from his enemies. How could one slip of a girl do what entire Clan armies could not? And why didn't she properly fear him? It was starting to get on his nerves.

The girl blinked and seemed to shake herself out of the daze she'd been in. Her eyes snapped with the green fire of a mythical Wyvern.

"*I'm* mad?" she stomped closer, poking a tiny finger at him. "*You* throw very sharp knives through perfectly nice women and then in the next moment you kiss them and threaten to *ravage* them. Are you telling me that's the behavior of a *sane* individual?"

"Nice women?" he thundered. "Did you not just say you're here to kill me?" Suddenly it felt as though someone skewered his temples with a hot poker. Her words unlocked scorching memories that barraged him with a searing pain. "I—kissed you?" He knew he had, his lips now burned with the sweet memory. He just couldn't believe it. The pink skin around her lips had been caused by his roughly stubbled face. He liked the look on her. He wanted to mark her elsewhere. Her breasts. Her thighs. Her—

"That was the least of your sins." The girl rolled her eyes. "But aye, you kissed me, rather vigorously, in fact." She pressed her lips together, and glared at him disapprovingly, but the effect was ruined by the impish twinkle in her eyes.

He'd thrown his dagger right through her middle. His eyes flew to where she hid the blood in the folds of her robe. She'd pulled the knife from her body. He'd gone berserk.

I'm a Faerie. A Banshee. Her voice drifted through his memory.

His Berserker had chosen a Banshee as his mate. He'd claimed her with a kiss, and she'd dropped him near death with the lethal power in her tiny fingers.

"Fuck the Gods," he breathed.

She tisked at him. "I'd say now's not the time to blaspheme against the Gods," she gently censured. "Not when you're about to meet them."

A dry sound of bitter amusement worked its way up his throat. The Gods had fucked *him* time and time again. Why not threaten to return the favor? They were sodomizing his destiny even now. Finally sending him a mate who was bound to end his life.

Chapter Five

"Right, then." Kamdyn glanced around the tent until her gaze snagged on his trunk. She wandered over to it, the warrior's hot glare burning a hole into her back. When she crouched to open the lid, he was suddenly there, slamming it shut.

Kamdyn gasped. She hadn't even seen him move. She didn't dare look at him, as his hips were now at eye level.

"What are you doing?" he barked.

"I *was* getting you something to cover yourself with," she informed the trunk.

He grunted. "If I wanted to cover myself, I'd be covered."

Forgetting herself, she looked over at him. Squeaked. Then locked her eyes back on the trunk. He was so—big.

"I figured that a fearsome leader such as you wouldn't want your men to find you dead *and* naked. I was trying to protect your dignity."

He was silent a protracted moment, and Kamdyn was again blasted with a barrage of very confusing emotions. Or had *she* confused him? She really needed to get better at this.

"I have trews." He pointed to a sodden pile of clothes tucked in a dark corner.

She frowned at them and threw him a very disapproving glare.

"Very well," he said in a low voice, and took his hand from the trunk.

Kamdyn opened it again and looked inside. On the left, gold, silver, and jewels winked at her in the candlelight. Diamonds, rubies, emeralds, and the deepest sapphires the color of Soren's eyes. She fingered the blue stones, inlaid into a silver pendant. He'd taken these things from someone else.

"I'm supposed to recover something from you and return it to my queen," she admitted to him. "A relic."

"The *Scáth bhfolach*," he murmured.

"Aye." She selected a bolt of very fine blue silk from the right side of the trunk and stood.

He was silent again.

When Kamdyn glanced up at him, he was looking down at her with the most peculiar expression. Like she was a problem he needed to solve.

She suddenly felt the absurd need to put him at ease. Just how did one do that when about to execute a fellow?

She glanced around. "Where would you like to... um... you know?"

"Die?" he said wryly.

She nodded and chewed the inside of her cheek, wishing like hell he hadn't said the word.

"Do you want to lie down?" she pointed at the thick, plush pile of furs and pillows on the ground. "Would that be more comfortable?"

"*Nie.*" He crossed his arms again. "I'll die standing, if it's all the same to you."

She should have expected that from one such as him. Nodding again, she unraveled the fabric, hoping she seemed like a capable and efficient executioner. What she needed was to take charge of the situation.

Seizing his hand, she pulled him toward the darkest corner of the tent away from his pallet, fire pit, and table with the candle. She liked the rasp of the calluses on his palm against her hand. It seemed that he wrapped his long fingers around hers in a gentle grip, but the thought was so ludicrous, Kamdyn decided she must have imagined it.

She positioned him near the corner and stepped back. Assessed his placement. Clucked her tongue. Then moved him to the left a little. She was starting to get used to his nakedness. To enjoy it. Which was why he needed to be covered.

"You're being very cooperative, considering," she praised him. "I must say, I'm pleasantly surprised you're not fighting me."

He chuffed. "Can I kill you, little Banshee?"

"I'm afraid not." She cast him an apologetic glance from under her lashes and returned to measuring out a few yards of silk, trying not to stare at the width of his shoulders, or the fascinating cut of the muscles at his hips that led down to his—

"My name is Kamdyn," she blurted, feeling as though he should know the name of his executioner. "And I suppose you *could* hurt me, if you wanted. Would that make things easier for you?"

"*Nie*, Kamdyn." Though the sound of her name spoken with his strong, exotic tongue sent little chills through her, his deep, slow words suddenly carried the emptiness she'd felt before she'd entered his tent. It broke upon her like a wave of darkness, and sudden tears sprang to her eyes. "I could never hurt you now, even if I wanted."

The way he'd worded that seemed odd, but she supposed this wasn't his first language. In truth, she didn't want to hurt him, either. She knew she should. But for the infamous Laird of Shadows, he didn't seem all that unreasonable. Lethal? Certainly. Deadly? Of course. But he was at the very least curious and fascinating company. Kamdyn let out a gigantic deflating breath. She had to do this or she'd go down in history as the worst Banshee ever.

"I was told your name is Soren." It was only good manners to finish the introductions, even with a savage. "Do you have a surname?"

"It was Neilson. But no one has used my name for decades."

"I will," Kamdyn offered. "A name is a very powerful thing. I shall call you Soren."

More silence. Then, "Will you speak it after I am gone?"

She blinked up at him, expecting regret or vulnerability in his eyes. She found none. Only a morbid sort of curiosity. Was this man truly so fearless? "Of course," she murmured at him. "Of *course* I will remember you." She spoke truth. This man would live in her memory until the end of her days. His name would likely spring to her lips often, as would the memory of his kiss.

He broke eye contact first. "Who sent you after me, little Banshee? Do I not have the right to know who wants me dead?"

"Oh, absolutely *everyone* wants you dead." Kamdyn blurted, hoping she sounded stern like her older sister Katriona could be when applying her well-used sharp tongue. Though she had a feeling she fell short of her mark. "You don't do much to ingratiate yourself to people."

He grunted. Then shrugged.

"But it was the Gaelic Berserkers who sought out my queen. Namely Fionngal MacLauchlan."

"You're telling me that Fionngal the Bastard and his two mated Berserker brothers sent *you* to spill my blood rather than claiming it themselves?" He sounded on the verge of laughter, but his implacable features never changed.

"Well, they couldn't *find* you, for one thing. Also, I can kill you without spilling a drop of blood, which is a great deal less messy. Unless you *want* to bleed for sake of legacy and such, then I can make you bleed out of every orifice. We can discuss that later. Can I impose upon you to tear this for me?" She indicated the place where she needed the fabric separated from the rest of the bolt.

He took it from her hands, gripped the silk, and ripped it clean down the middle as though tearing a parchment.

Kamdyn's brows shot up to her hairline. "Thank you." She plucked it from him, trying not to be impressed at his strength. "Lift your arms, if you please."

He complied, the engorged muscles at his sides flexing to create a most impressive V.

Kamdyn bit the inside of her cheek. Hard. "Right, then." She cleared her throat. "Hold still and I'll put this around you."

He raised a russet eyebrow but remained otherwise motionless.

Preparing herself to touch his skin, she went to him and wrapped her arms around his impossibly thick trunk, meaning to hand herself the other corner of blue silk.

His scent suddenly flared thick in her nostrils. River and leather. His skin was warm, hairless, and smooth. Without thinking, she rubbed her cheek on the hard swell of his chest.

All the moisture abandoned her mouth and headed elsewhere.

A deep breath expanded his torso and a low growl rumbled in the chest next to her ear. "Kamdyn." Her name had become a deep and tortured groan. "What are you doing?"

"Sorry." She quickly grasped the corners of the silk and stepped away from him, the movement of her legs causing a delicious friction at the moistened flesh between them. "Slippery," she explained as the held up the fabric, and winced at her choice of words.

His nostrils flared and his wicked features arranged themselves into what could only be called a predatory arrogance.

For the first time since meeting the Laird of Shadows, Kamdyn became inexplicably afraid. Swallowing around a lump in her throat, she wrapped the fabric around his waist and fumbled to secure it with a knot.

Stepping away from him, she inspected her work and frowned.

"Do I look sufficiently dignified for my death?" Soren asked wryly.

He looked like a god trying on his mistress's skirt. "Decidedly not." Kamdyn winced and couldn't hold in a bubble of laughter.

He was staring at her again with that strange intensity. As though he couldn't believe what he saw. He studied the small blood stain on the front of her robes as though it contained the answer to mysteries of the universe.

"We don't bleed overmuch," she explained. "Immortal and all that."

He didn't blink. Not for a long time.

Kamdyn sobered. "I'll fix your wrap, I promise." She reached for the knot and tried to make the fabric more like a tartan. Masculine and fine. "Are you afraid?" she whispered, before she could stop herself.

"What have I to fear?" His voice was so strong, so arrogant.

"Pain," she said incredulously. "Death. Answering for your sins." She absurdly wondered if there was an equivalent to hell for Berserkers, but thought it an inappropriate thing to inquire about, considering the circumstances.

Soren gave another of his nonchalant shrugs. A nearly indiscernible flex of his massive shoulder. "Who gets to decide what is sin?" Ice blue eyes bore down at her.

Kamdyn paused. It *was* an excellent question. Also, she loved the word on his lips. She supposed he was familiar with the concept. Comfortable with it. His existence was a sin, insolent, defiant, and very, *very* wicked.

"Death is inescapable." He didn't wait for her answer. "As is pain. So why fear it?"

Kamdyn had to look away. A tightness in her chest squeezed until she felt her ribs might collapse. "I promise I'll be swift when I...I don't *want* to cause you pain." She finished the knot on her new handiwork, her vision too blurry to know if she'd done it right.

"No matter what, it will hurt. For more reasons than you will ever know." A bleak and desperate ache shot through her and she knew it came from within him. Despite his bravado, the Laird of Shadows didn't want to die. He'd be losing something he profoundly desired—treasured even— and that sense of loss stabbed at her more deeply than his dirk had only moments ago.

"I'm sorry, truly," she whispered, a tear escaping down her cheek.

He reached out and grasped her chin, which had begun to wobble dangerously, and firmly lifted her gaze to face him.

"You've never killed a man, have you little Banshee?" he asked in disbelief, his eyes searching hers for answers to questions she couldn't imagine.

"I've killed *plenty* of men," she lied, pulling away from his grip and dashing at her cheeks. "Scores of them. Hundreds. I'm very old, you know."

He looked at her askance. "Do you weep over them all? These *hundreds* of men."

"Yes." She knew her petulant tone made her sound younger, so she tried to arrange her features into something like his. Cool. Implacable. Deadly.

"I find I like being your first." That infuriating smugness was back in his tone.

"I told you—"

"You're a terrible liar, Kamdyn." His accusation was softened by the first note of gentleness she'd ever heard from his lips.

It deflated her. "I know." Her shoulders sagged and she returned to chewing on the inside of her cheek.

"Have you ever been fucked?"

The question paralyzed her. Did he just ask if she'd been—

"Fucked?" If a whisper could be shrill, hers would have been, but she could do little more than stare at him with what had to have been the most idiotic expression.

His eyes flared brilliantly blue at the word on her lips, along with the flame of the candle. A blaze of lust barraged her like the hot blast of a desert storm. It came from him, but it invaded her. Penetrated her until it had become a part of her own body. Her own need.

"You heard me." He bent down until his face was flush with hers, a predatory triumph playing across his savage features. "I excite you, little Banshee. I can smell it." His nostrils flared again as he filled his cavernous chest as though breathing in the truth of his words.

Kamdyn trembled, then turned her nose to her shoulder and gave a little surreptitious sniff. She couldn't smell a thing, though she didn't dare deny his statement. As they'd already established, she was a terrible liar. He *did* excite her, almost beyond bearing. He also repelled her and fascinated her. He was a villain, indeed the most dangerous marauding warlord to plague the Highlands since Angus MacKay.

Unhitching her knot, he let the blue silk fall from his body, uncovering the evidence of his matching excitement.

"Ye may have known a man, Kamdyn, but I'd bet my soul you've never been well and truly fucked."

"I—um." Kamdyn unabashedly stared at him in stark amazement, unable to tear her eyes from his masculine desire. What was it about Berserkers that turned her into a speechless idiot? It could be that the primal, possessive lust wafting from him called a powerful echo from her own flesh until she couldn't differentiate from his masculine, dominant desire and her own dangerous feminine needs. She chewed on her cheek, frantically trying to formulate a response.

"What say you, little Banshee? Fuck me first. Then kill me."

Chapter Six

Soren stood motionless as his tiny mate silently, blatantly stared at his aroused nakedness. Denial furrowed her delicate brow and doubt telegraphed through her crossed arms and the anxious chewing at her cheek.

But her nipples were hard. He could see them pressing against her robes. Her spine kept arching when she pressed her thighs together in answer to the renewed surges of her arousal that provoked him almost beyond his control.

Soren was many things, but he was first and foremost a predator, and all his instincts were held in a leashed poise, waiting for the exact moment in which to capture his prey.

She was his mate. The answer to every Berserker's most fervent desire, and though she would not accept him as her man, as her own beast, she might accept his body for the night.

He was the Laird of Shadows. The night *belonged* to him, and every dark, shameful, deviant fantasy she'd ever harbored, he would fulfill.

And perhaps a few of his own before he left this world behind.

He only needed her consent.

"All right," Kamdyn nodded, her eyes filled with an emerald storm.

"Say it," he commanded through a mouth drawn so tight it'd gone numb.

"Soren? I—I—" His name trembled from her and need ripped through him with all the strength of a thousand sharp dirks, slashing his control to shreds.

"*Say it,*" he growled through his teeth.

Her lashes feathered over her cheeks as her delicate throat worked over a difficult swallow. Her color heightened until her peach-tinged skin turned a bright pink.

"Fuck me," she whispered.

Her heated womanly aroma intensified along with the scent of her fear as he lunged for her. In a flash of feminine panic, she turned away as though to flee.

But there was no escaping him now.

Seizing her around the middle with one arm, he all but yanked her off her feet and pulled her against him. The curve of her sweet, round ass thrust against the insistent hardness of his cock, her soft thighs pillowing his hard ones.

With his other hand he cupped her jaw, and turned her face toward her right shoulder. "Kiss me, little Banshee," he ordered.

Dropping his head, Soren tried his best not to devour her mouth this time, but to indulge in it. She was the first and last woman he'd ever kiss, and he found the act to be surprisingly sweet. He wanted to fuse their mouths together. To share her breath and give her life.

His life.

And he would, ere this night was over.

The first time his berserker had kissed her, she'd been pliant and submissive in his arms. This time, her hand snaked behind him to plunge into the hair at the nape of his neck and draw him deeper into her mouth. Her tongue met his with equal vigor and even launched a shy exploration of its own.

He swallowed her soft moan as her silk-covered bottom arched against his hips. He felt the unspoken invitation in the marrow of his bones.

A growl tore up his throat and vibrated in the kiss between them.

He didn't break contact with her mouth as he walked forward, each step pumping his painfully hard cock against the cleft of her ass. The silky material of her thin Fae garment chafed his engorged flesh.

When they reached the table, he ripped his lips from hers and bent to clear it with a strong sweep of his arm.

What was left of his dinner and goblet hit the earth with a muffled *whump* and the candle's flame doused before it reached the ground. Soren could re-light it with his fledgling Berserker magic if he wanted to, but he didn't need the light to see her by, and in his lustful frenzy, he didn't spare the consideration.

It was time to claim what belonged to him. This would be the first time of many this night. It would be primal and brutal and savage. He would brand her on the inside and out with his fingers, his cock, and his teeth.

He would leave marks. Reminders of his possession that would hopefully outlive him. Any men she'd had in the past would be erased. With any lovers she would take after his death, Soren would be there. In between her and the flesh of every other man would be *his* memory. In this way, he could achieve immortality.

Kamdyn couldn't contain a ragged gasp when he finished tearing her robes down the back and jerked them from her body, and again when he bent over her, pressing her breasts into the cool wood of the table. In contrast, his giant body was warm against her back.

She felt so exposed. So completely at his mercy. The cold evening autumn air touching her most heated, intimate flesh caused her to clench and shudder.

He surprised her by reaching into her hair and drawing out the clip and comb she'd used to secure it off her neck. He tossed them somewhere in the darkness, it didn't matter where, and plunged one hand into her riot of curls, pressing her cheek against the table.

In unbidden answer, her hips arched back again and a prudish voice in her head told her to control herself.

Kamdyn swiftly silenced that voice, gripped the table, and whimpered.

Gods but she wanted this. It wasn't at all what she'd expected. Instead of a lover's soft caress, his free hand branded its way down the side of her waist, found the flare of her hip, and gripped at the flesh of her offered backside. Instead of preparing her with his fingers and mouth as her sister, Kylah, had described in one wine-filled night of over-sharing, he forced her legs to open wider by nudging her feet apart.

From her prone position, she felt gloriously powerless to do anything but let him do what he would with her. She wasn't gifting him with her virginity, he was claiming it. She would be naught but another conquest. A willing victim. A consenting plunder. Her need had become like an all-consuming hunger she'd never before experienced. It throbbed and demanded. Its intensity overcame her as easily as he did, rendering her helpless before it.

His chest heaved against her shoulders with wild breaths as he bent his knees. Her teeth caught her cheek as she awaited his intrusion.

She'd known it would burn. The heat of his sex had branded her even through her robes. But she hadn't fully prepared herself for the fiery pleasure-pain of his thrust. Her untried body convulsed around him, and she groaned. It was that or scream, which would do neither of them any good as her scream had dastardly consequences.

He cursed in a foreign, guttural language.

Kamdyn heartily agreed with him. Though she felt as though his steely length would cleave her in two, the insatiable void that had suddenly opened up in her womb throbbed and demanded something only he could give.

"More," she whimpered.

"Small," he growled. "So fucking tight." He pressed forward, probing her, torturing her, and still a barrier held that neither of them understood. "Take it, woman," he bit out. "Yield to me."

"I-I can't." No matter how hard she wanted, her body wouldn't cooperate.

Soren withdrew, still pressing himself against her distressed opening, rubbing the thick head of his cock on her creamy desire, spreading the slickness onto his flesh.

"Do it," she insisted. "Hard."

The sound he emitted was rough and raw as he surged forward. She sobbed with equal amounts pain and relief as her virginity yielded and he buried his sex deep within hers. The pain rapidly drained as her immortal flesh healed, leaving only that persistent, feverish need. Which was fortunate because he didn't pause to savor or allow her to adjust, but tightened his hand in her hair and made good on his promise.

He fucked her.

He impaled her with a merciless rhythm that forced her to cling to the table in helpless submission. The sounds he made were low and masculine, a rhythmic percussion to the husky mewls her lungs produced.

Each time she thought she could cede no more, her slick body would yield its heat to him and he'd fill it, demanding she let him farther inside. Kamdyn was desperate to accommodate him, for the deeper he plunged, the higher her pleasure climbed. When the hairs on his strong thighs brushed against the back of her smooth ones, his cock struck something so deep within her that a cry of shock escaped her mouth. It was like he'd prodded her soul. He did it again, and again, until she wanted to give it to him. Her soul. Her body. Anything he wanted if he just never stopped.

He didn't seem capable of stopping. He pounded into her, over her, with ferocious determination. The hand he'd wound in her hair jerked at her scalp, the tension there tight and delicious. The hand at her hip gripped with punishing strength, bruising her skin, but she didn't care. She didn't care about anything but his next invasion. Every time he pulled away from her body was a little death. Every time he returned, she rejoiced.

She wanted to writhe, to seek him, to press back against him, but she couldn't move. Her muscles still tried, instinctually, and when she arched her back slightly, he said something so foul, Kamdyn wasn't sure she knew what it meant.

With that, he quickened his pace from punishing to brutal.

Kamdyn began to tremble uncontrollably. Her muscles seized from her own power as though controlled by some kind of sadistic puppeteer. A stab of pleasure so exquisite held her in its unrelenting grasp. It locked her jaw, grinding her teeth together. Stopped her breath. Bowed her spine beneath him until she feared she would be crushed between it and Soren's heaving body. Each time he entered her, the pleasure pulsed and grew, licking at new nerves like a flame becoming a destructive inferno. This couldn't go on, she realized, this state of unmitigated bliss. It would destroy her.

As the thought congealed in her mind, Soren reared up with a sharp hiss. His hand left her hair and gripped her other hip. A jerky, frenzied note interrupted his otherwise seamless rhythm and Kamdyn became certain he was going to—

Soren froze. Cursed. Growled. Cursed again. And suddenly his weight and heat were gone from her. When Kamdyn found enough strength to turn around, the tent was empty.

Chapter Seven

Blood. More fucking blood. Soren never attempted anything in his life but he was drenched in it an hour after. This time it was *her* blood. Just a small measure, but any was too much. He thought he'd Berserk again. Then remembered that wasn't going to be a problem with her anymore, not with his mate.

He ground his fist into a tree and it splintered, crashing to the ground. Luckily, he was too deep into the forest to worry about any of his men coming to investigate the sound.

Soren was no stranger to the blood of the innocent staining his blade, his hands, his armor.

But never his sex. Never that.

And blood meant that she *was* innocent. Had been, before he took her like an animal. Like a common—

"Soren?"

He whirled to face her, though it took all his fortitude. She stole his breath from a dozen paces away. How had she followed him all the way out here? He'd used his Berserker speed to escape her. To escape what he'd done. He was a coward.

The last vestiges of grey and silver light, the remaining memory of a sun that had set a half hour prior, caused her creamy naked flesh to glow. The flakes of snow still aimlessly drifting like errant feathers, caught in the wild tangles of copper and flame tumbling about her shoulders. Her gentle green eyes shone with concern.

"You're not trying to escape your death, are you?" she asked sadly. "Because I'm afraid you cannot."

Soren stared at her. It was the last thing he'd expected her to say.

"Do it," he rasped. "It is what I deserve. End me now." He watched her small, perfect breasts quiver and bead with the tiny shiver of her taut body. "And then get the fuck out of the cold," he commanded.

She stepped a few paces closer to him and his heart began to pound. "But we weren't—you didn't—finish." Her eyes flitted to his manhood, which hadn't fully lost its erection, despite his distress.

He snarled and turned away from her, bracing his hands on a nearby tree to keep them from snatching her where she stood. "You were untouched," he accused.

"And?"

"And I was a brute." *To my mate,* he finished silently. "I made you bleed." 'Twas the ultimate shame for a Berserker. Even for The Laird of Shadows. He'd held her down, dominated her, pulled her hair and shoved himself inside her like she was an experienced wanton. Which he'd thought she was. He'd thought she'd been dallying with pretty faerie men between her thighs for years.

"You *are* a brute." She was suddenly between him and the tree, her lithe legs wrapped around his torso, her hands gripping his shoulders.

Soren leapt back in surprise, but she remained clasped around him, her small, taut nipples rubbing against his chest with delicious friction.

"How did you—"

She kissed him. Then vanished. Teeth nipped him sharply on the meat of his shoulder. When he turned around to reach for her, she was gone again.

A whistle drew his attention to the highest bough in the forest. She posed there like a nubile goddess, an impish grin touching her lips and twinkling from her eyes.

A realization struck Soren with the weight of a falling tree. His mate was wrapped around him again, her feminine warmth rubbing a slick welcome against his cock. "I could have vanished from your grip at any moment," she whispered his prior realization against his ear in a hot, husky breath. "But I *wanted* to be taken by a brute. By you."

Lust tore through him, evaporating any vestiges of shame or reticence. He looked between their bodies to where he'd stabbed her with a dirk less than an hour before. No scar. No blood. Just taut, lovely skin.

"All my wounds heal," she informed him smugly. "One of the many advantages of being immortal."

Soren seized her tiny waist. Her skin was chilly against his. Relief flooded through him and adrenaline, blood, and lust chased it until he felt like he was on fire.

"I'm going to take you again," he warned, then frowned. "Don't you *dare* disappear."

She hooked small, surprisingly strong arms around his neck and planted a kiss against his rough cheek. "I'm going to have *you* again," she informed him, curling her hips and coating him with more of her slick desire. "And *I'm* not the one who disappeared."

Soren bared his teeth at her. She was so impudent. She didn't fear him in the least, and the fact that had at first irritated him was suddenly so erotic he could barely stand it.

Her hips pulled back just far enough for his sex to find her, but he filled his big hands with the flesh of her ass and held her motionless. His blunt head poised between her folds. "You may be taking my life later, but *I'm* taking your body now."

Her eyes snapped and she writhed against his grip.

"Yes," she hissed, pressing little wet kisses against his jaw.

"Yes. What?" he prodded her, but pulled back when she squirmed to get closer.

"Yes! *Please*, Soren."

The sound of his name as a supplication on her lips was nearly his undoing. Soren began to impale her inch by glorious, maddening inch.

Her breath hitched. Her nails bit into his shoulders, gouging his flesh and into his muscle. Her body shuddered and he began to worry that she'd again have difficulty accepting him completely inside her. But he paused, pulled her back and started feeding himself to her again. This time, with a quivering sigh, he stretched her and filled her completely.

Soren stood like that for a breathless moment. In the middle of the woods with the shadows of night thickening around them, he just let himself be as one with his mate. She was so tiny against him. Light, he imagined, even for a normal man, let alone one of his size and strength. She weighed little more than the flakes of snow brushing his back.

Conversely, the pressure of her core was as tight as a vise around him. The grip of her arms desperate and demanding. She tugged at his hair. Nibbled at his ear lobe. And Soren began to fear that the urge to spill his seed within her might overpower his legendary self-control. It was the most exquisite torture he'd ever experienced.

He pulled her hips back and drove her down on him, giving her what she wanted. What *he* needed.

"Yes," she gasped against his ear. The word became her mantra as he bounced her off his unyielding, thrusting hips. He gritted his teeth. Took deep breaths. She would find her pleasure before him or he would die first.

Soren anchored her hips with one arm, refusing to look at where their bodies slammed together or he'd be lost. He wound his other hand back into her curls, pulling her head away from where her lips worshiped the skin of his neck.

His eyes locked with his mate's and her passion-fogged gaze instantly sharpened. The little explosions of her breath caused by his jarring thrusts hit his face. He used her lovely eyes as a marking point. If he lost himself in them, he wouldn't lose himself into her tight, sleek body.

She'd come to him untouched by another man. Soren still couldn't believe it. No man had previously had these legs wrapped around his waist. He was the only one she'd chosen to accept into her body, out of the doubtless hundreds who'd tried. Kamdyn wasn't only his mate. She was truly *his*. A dark, primitive possessiveness gathered inside of him as encompassing as the encroaching night.

"Soren," she breathed between his merciless thrusts. "Your eyes."

Her red hair disappeared, replaced by a lustrous silver. The green of her eyes became an iridescent, shimmering grey.

When his Berserker growled at her, she cried out. But not in fear. Her head tossed back and her body arched against him. Convulsions began to rake through her, concussing at her core and gripping at his cock.

The beginnings of his orgasm drove him to his knees and he used the new leverage to angle upward inside of her, wringing new and intense cries from her lips.

This time, when Soren became the Berserker, it was unlike any other. It wasn't blood, but another catalyst altogether that brought the beast to the surface. He didn't cede his humanity to it, he shared it. They both took her. They both reveled in her pleasure.

And when he gave her a few more powerful thrusts, it was the beast who roared his release into the night.

Chapter Eight

"You shouldn't kill people." Kamdyn scolded half-heartedly as she lay draped like a limp rug across her Berserker lover. "And you shouldn't take their things." Perhaps she should have opened with that and worked toward the greater sin, which was the part about murder.

The forest floor was soft with moss and leaves where he sprawled on his back beneath her. Tiny shafts of silver moonlight filtered through the trees and kiss of the odd snowflake still let by drifting clouds felt divine.

His sound of amusement was a deep rumble against her ear. "I only kill people who get in the way of what I want." His hand was still curled on her rump and his strong fingers lazily flexed there, testing the supple flesh. "And if things were able to be taken, then they never really belonged to anyone, did they?"

Kamdyn pushed herself up to level the most withering stare she could muster down at him. "That's the most ridiculous thing I ever heard."

"I doubt that." His eyes didn't remind her of ice only because of the color, but because of the cold, remorseless barbarian that lived behind them. The only time his eyes burned with a blue fire was when he was inside of her, but he was that frigid, callous savage now that the flames of passion had been sufficiently fed. "When a Berserker is born at the Temple of Freya, he has nothing more than what is needed to keep him alive. Anything else, he takes by force and guards with his blood. He makes allies and enemies, and power is only held by the strongest."

Kamdyn made a soft sound of distress. "That is terrible. Your mother allowed that?"

"Our mothers are usually whores frequented by our Berserker fathers," he said dispassionately. "They bring us to the temple as infants and leave us for money. Mine is likely dead."

Tears sprang to her eyes. "And your father?"

"Also dead."

It was obvious he would say no more about that, so Kamdyn asked another question she wasn't sure she wanted the answer to. "Berserkers never take— a wife?"

At this, his eyes did spark, and they searched her face with an intensity that left her aching. "*Nie*. When our Berserker decides upon a woman, it is forever. We were denied—any women but whores. A few of us tried to mate with them, but they didn't survive." If his features became any stonier, they would surely crack.

Unable to stand any more, Kamdyn lowered her gaze, tracing the grooves of muscle on his ribcage. "Even still, Highlanders are not Berserkers, they're just people. They don't deserve to be raided and terrorized."

Soren snorted. "Tell that to the *Highland* men in my camp. To the discarded orphans. The outcast bastards. The children of the ill-conceived, the infirm, and the illiterate. There are plenty of us who have no choice but to take what we can from this life. From those who would never give them a kind word or a chance, let alone something to eat or a warm place to sleep. They take what they must to survive."

She'd thought he pillaged because he was from the North and his people were notorious raiders throughout the centuries. Such a thing had never occurred to her, men raiding and pillaging for lack of a better choice.

Her brows drew together. "I don't know anyone who needs fine silks and jewels such as those in your chest to survive."

"They pay homage to me as their Laird and protector, a charming custom, is it not?" He threw her look full of amused challenge.

Sighing with exasperation she shook her head. "Yes but, those things do not *belong* to you. You didn't earn them."

"They are in my possession, so they are mine." Soren smirked and spun one of her curls around his finger. "For such an immortal creature, you know very little about the world."

Kamdyn tossed her piles of hair behind her, wrenching her curl from his toying hand. He frowned at her. "I know that most people work very hard for what they have and they deserve to keep it. I know that every single life is precious— has value and should be respected."

He slanted a look at her so full of meaning it made her pause. "Even mine?"

She blinked down at his swarthy, enigmatic face. *Especially his*, she realized. Despite his crimes, it could be argued that Soren was a protector of those most wronged by civilization. He was most certainly a leader among men, it was no wonder they fell in behind him. He'd given them what they needed, a place to belong.

A Clan.

Without him, most of these men would be raiding highways and pick-pocketing from markets. They would be drinking in the streets and garroting each other in alleyways. Raping women and preying upon children.

Aside from all the horrible stories she'd heard about his fiery, destructive raids, it was known that the Laird of Shadows never allowed rape or buggery. He'd publically skewered one of his men who'd attempted such a horror.

"If you're only taking supplies, why raze villages to the ground?"

A flicker of something akin to a wound disappeared from his features before she had the chance to identify it. She hadn't answered his question, at least not out loud. But he answered hers in the same deep, passionless voice as always. "Those fires are lit by men with grudges against one place or another. I don't condone or condemn the practice. I am only their unofficial Laird. I am not their King. I am not their God. I do not tell them how many steps to take in a day, which hand to fuck themselves with and how guilty to feel about it. I do not tell them what to eat or how to pray. I only give them a code. It is the Berserker code. The only one I know and they chose to follow it if they chose to follow me."

Kamdyn vigorously thought about their conversation for a very long and silent moment until struck by inspiration. "You know what your men need that would fix this whole bloody mess?"

He raised an eyebrow, but the hard lines around his eyes softened a bit. "What would that be?"

"Women," she declared.

He shook his head. "My men are allowed whores when they want them, they just can't bring them to the camp as it creates too many problems with—"

Kamdyn placed a finger over his mouth to shush him, ignoring his look that said no one had ever dared to do that before. "Not whores, *women* of their *own*. Wives, family, community. Everything they were previously unfairly denied."

Soren looked at her in a way that stabbed at her heart. He was too barbaric for tenderness, but the resemblance was there. "You would fix the world with kindness, would you not, little Banshee?"

"If it would let me," she groused.

"You have an eternity for that." He nibbled at her fingertip, eliciting thrills of desire she'd thought too well sated to wake again so soon. "We only have tonight."

"This proves my point exactly!"   She forced a false brightness into her voice to balance out the hollow note that had crept into his.   "I'm here, and you're not out pillaging and plundering the countryside because you have something better to do."   Kamdyn frowned.   If only she'd shown up earlier, before his fate had been sealed.

He gave a grunt that might have been a chuckle to another man.   "I've been pillaging and plundering *you* for the better part of an evening."

Was that all they'd known each other?   Seemed longer. Kamdyn morphed her wistful frown into a sultry pout and moved her hips.   "You're not done, are you?"

His expression darkened as his cock thickened between them.   "I'd *never* be finished with you," he said savagely, surging up to take her mouth with his.

She resisted when he went to roll her beneath him.   "Nay, Let me."

Rising above him, she marveled as she lowered herself on and around him.   Taking him slowly, as they'd not yet done. This time, it felt as though she'd been shaped for him, by him, he fit so snugly and so well.

She sat atop him a moment, admiring the masculine beauty of his prone form.   She flexed herself with him inside of her, enjoying the steely warmth of his sex.

"Woman," he growled.

"Mmmmm?" she stretched over him like a cat, indolent and slow.

"If you don't start moving, I'm going to—"

She cut off his threat with a slow circle of her hips.   "You're going to what, Laird of Shadows?"

"I'm going to make you."   He gripped her thighs with his punishing strength.

"You are going to lie there and let me have my way with you," she smiled victoriously. "According to your code, *you* are in my possession."

His eyes snagged on her smile. Muscles bunched and strained.

"You knew I'd never been fucked by a man," she teased, lifting away from him until he could see every inch of his own sex, slick and glistening with her desire. His eyes latched right where she wanted them to. "And *I* have it on good authority you've never been *beneath* a woman." She let herself sink again, her breath catching at the pleasure.

His harsh groan pleased her beyond measure. He began to pant, nostrils flaring and chest heaving.

She rode him in long, slow, sometimes circular strokes. Each time she filled herself with him, tiny erotic pulses of pleasure stabbed into her abdomen.

She could tell she'd thrown Soren out of his element. He looked as though he didn't know where to rest his eyes. For a moment he'd watch her breasts bouncing and swaying with her movements, then lower, to where they were joined, to her lips, her hair, and every place in between.

Astonishment and awe lay like strangers on his face and they mingled with tight, mounting pleasure. His hands quivered on her thighs, kneaded them, but didn't control her movements.

He uttered her name like dying men plead with the gods. He said things to her in his guttural language that she was glad she didn't understand, because she couldn't hear them and still do what she had to do.

She just focused on the heat of him inside of her, and the movements that brought them both closer to bliss. She went slowly because she didn't want it to end. All she wanted was to melt around him, to become a part of his indescribable strength. To be tied to it and call upon it when hers failed.

Pressure mounted.   Different than before.   An aching, roiling pleasure that sizzled and snapped along the currents between them until she couldn't be sure which of their orgasms began first.   They simultaneously spun off into the night sky. Her pulsating sex throbbed around the warm spurts of his release.   They made little noise this time, both of them lost in the straining breaths of an incredible, excruciating paroxysm.

When it released her, Kamdyn collapsed atop his chest.

Soren still quivered and jerked a few times beneath her, and even when his great body stilled, the muscles of his thighs and chest twitched every few moments in little unbidden aftershocks.

His big arms came around her and clasped her to his body, even though he seemed to struggle for breath. *"Du är min. Och jag är evigt din."* So filled with veracity was his low murmur, that Kamdyn had to lift her head.

"What?" she queried.

"I said: You may kill me now." He slanted a sated look of humor in her direction that wasn't exactly a smile.

Her jaw cracked on a monstrous yawn. "Must I? I'm too tired to do anything just now. Can it wait until morning?" Her eyes flew open. "Oh, is that too cruel?"

He nuzzled his nose into her hair. "You would sleep with me? What if I try and kill you first?"

Thoroughly unconcerned about that, Kamdyn burrowed her face against his warm chest, the chill of the evening finally seeping through her skin. "Please don't."

In a swift, graceful move, he was standing and carrying her back toward the camp.

"All right, my little Banshee, you can kill me in the morning."

My little Banshee. Kamdyn chewed on the inside of her cheek even as she snuggled into the warmth of his arms. He'd not said it like *that* before.

Chapter Nine

Soren lounged on his furs and cursed the sun as he felt dawn approaching. He'd woken inside her, halfway to release, and she'd ridden him to yet another soul-shattering end.

This time, she'd allowed him to help.

"It kept flexing at my back while you slept," she offered by way of explanation when she rolled off of him with a contented sigh.

Only an idiot would explain a morning erection to someone willing to put it to good use, most especially when it might be his last.

Besides, she hadn't stopped talking since.

Soren didn't mind. He enjoyed the sound of her voice, its brogue and cadence a pleasant melody in the darkness. In fact, he'd asked her the question that had catalyzed her, but had since forgotten what it was. At first, he'd listened to every word. He'd learned of her older sisters. About the honorable men they'd married. The Druid seemed to be the most prolific, spawning what sounded to him like a tribe of MacKay babes. The Laird and her eldest sister had only daughters and Kamdyn was pleased that her brother-in-law didn't seem to mind.

He'd chuckled at her stories of the Laird's overprotective antics while chasing suitors away from his girls. He'd snarled fiercely when she'd told him of her violent end in a fire. Then she'd shocked him further by revealing that the very Berserkers who'd contracted after his death also had avenged hers.

Soren wanted to thank them for that. He wanted to hate them for it, too. What would he ever be able to do to protect her? To show her what it was to be mated to a fierce Berserker. He could not feed her from his hunts or warm her with his fires. He could not give her sons. Kill her enemies. She didn't need his long life as she had an endless one of her own.

Without him.

She'd moved on quickly from the subject of her death to that of her immortality. She expressed her fear of her sisters and their mates aging and dying, leaving her behind. She'd bonded with their children, but her sisters were her immediate family and she loved them dearly.

It seemed her duties as a Faerie were important to her, though she mourned the last twenty years spent as one.

"Everything is perfect in Faerie," she'd complained. "How I hate it."

She'd flitted to a tangent some time ago and had lost him when one story or another had caused her to sit up and cross her legs. Though her lower half was covered by the furs at her waist, her breasts, only the size of ripe apples, bobbed and swayed with her animated gestures.

A few errant words reached him, but it had been quite a while since he'd known just what the hell she was saying. Fortunately, she didn't seem to require any kind of affirmation from him, just his eyes on her. He was happy to oblige. In fact, there was no chance of him looking away, not while she moved like that.

He could worship those breasts. Build shrines to them. His greatest regret about his life ending was that he hadn't spent a sufficient amount of time with them.

With *her*. Because he— "I love you," he interrupted her stream of chatter the moment the truth occurred to him.

She paused, blinked, and opened her mouth. "I—I'm sorry... What?"

"I fucking love you." It felt better to say it again. He wanted to say it a million times, in all the languages he'd ever learned.

"I think you meant to say that you love fucking me... to which I return the sentiment, of course." She offered him a blush and an odd sort of solicitous smile.

"I do not say one thing when I mean another thing." Soren shook his head, still mesmerized by her breasts, but caught her dubious expression in his periphery.

"Saying that... won't save you," she said haltingly.

"I know." He reached for her, but she deftly dodged his lazy grasp, rolling away to stand over him with her hands planted firmly on her hips.

"Besides," she continued, a note of frenzy creeping into her voice. "You *don't* love me. You don't even know me all that well. We don't even agree on anything."

He rolled his eyes. Sometimes his woman made things too complicated. "I do not think love and agreement have much to do with each other."

"What does someone like *you* know about love?" Her face crumpled, which was not the reaction he'd anticipated, but it rarely was with her.

The question insulted him and he sat up to glare at her in a way that had brought sages and seasoned warriors to their knees in fear. "I know more about it than you do, and I *know* that I love you."

"How *could* you?" She flung herself from the furs, whirling to accuse him with gigantic, watery green eyes. "It's not as simple as all that!"

"It *is* that simple to me." Everything was. Something existed or it didn't. A truth was or it wasn't. Soren didn't live in the in-betweens as some did. He didn't bend truths to suit his pretenses or manipulate the cast of a word so it shone brighter in someone's eyes and darker in others. There was no time for that. No need.

"How could you even *know* what that word means?" she asked in a dramatic whisper. "You don't just throw it around a tent in a war camp like—like—some kind of—"

He stood, not appreciating the challenge in her voice. "I think the better question would be, do *you* even know what the word means?"

Her eyes flared with that spark of green fire and her little nostrils flared with the first hint of anger he imagined she'd shown in decades.

"*Excuse me*?" Her voice had lost all husky notes of pleasure and sex, infused with a shrillness that was not Banshee, but purely female.

He continued, unfazed. "What do you know about hatred? What do you know about being so consumed with an emotion that you're willing to give your life for it? Have you ever experienced darkness so cavernous, that you could throw yourself into it and take an eternity to reach its depths?"

She just stared at him.

"Have you ever explored the capacity of your own brutality? Have you forced yourself to accept the ugliness that lives in your own soul?"

Kamdyn shook her head with such vehemence, her curls bounced over her shoulders. Denial shone in her stance, in the clench of her tiny fists, in the intensity of her delicate features. "I don't have the capacity for brutality."

His sound was so devoid of mirth it didn't qualify as a laugh. "No? How do you describe a woman who will accept a man's cock, but deny his love?"

She shrieked, and reached for him. For a brief moment, Soren thought that he'd goaded her enough to finally jolt him with her magic, but she merely pushed at his chest in utter frustration.

He took a step back, just so she'd feel like she'd gained some ground. Now if that wasn't love, he'd cut out his own tongue.

"I do not deny your love!" she insisted. "Because you do not *feel* love. Lust, yes. Possession, perhaps. But because you are capable of feeling hatred, doesn't mean you can just as easily fall in love. And not in one night."

It's exactly why I can," he insisted. "I've seen the most vile ugliness man or God is capable of producing. I've been consumed with hatred, vengeance, and emptiness for more decades than you've been alive. And I know what I feel for you is love because it is the opposite of all that, but equally as powerful, perhaps more so."

When she began to chew on the inside of her cheek, Soren knew he'd gotten to her, at least a little.

"You live in a perfect world full of perfect immortals and you hate it," he pressed. "Everything in your soul rejects it, and do you know why?"

"Nay," she whispered.

"*Because* in a place devoid of ugliness, a land without flaws, how can you appreciate the beauty of perfection? How can it hold any meaning?" Soren suddenly knew he could not convince her. Not with words. Frustration warred with the more tender, foreign emotions she nurtured inside him. His little Banshee was afraid and love and hope couldn't pierce such fear unless she reached beyond it. And maybe there wasn't time for that.

"Because of the ugliness I've seen, I find your sweet, innocent beauty more tempting than all the other women in this world."

She crossed her arms over her breasts, a gesture he didn't appreciate. "You haven't seen that many women."

"I've seen enough." He waved her words away. "I know that I enjoy no sound above your voice. Not the wind in the trees, the roll of the sea, or the dying screams of my enemies."

Her brows drew together at that last one, but she said, "Go on," in a mulish voice.

"I know that after having you, I will never lust after another."

"Of course you won't," she argued. "I'm going to kill you in a couple of minutes."

That dragged a harsh laugh from him, which seemed to startle her. He liked that she was stubborn. She'd have needed it were they to share a life together. "I could live a couple of centuries and still never find the pleasure you've given me in one night. I've experienced enough pain to know that, beyond a shadow of a doubt. But if I still belonged in this world, it would be to live beside you. Inside you." He stalked her like the predator he was. She backed away from him, but there was only so far she could go. "I know that every Berserker searches the decades for his mate, and I know that I've found you, that my beast has claimed you with that kiss that bound my soul to yours."

"Wha—what are you talking about?" she whispered.

"The only thing about death that I find distasteful is that it will be an existence without you. That I will never know what it is like to win your love and acceptance. I find I had no true desire until you came to my tent. I took whatever I thought I wanted, and still remained empty. And now, my only need is the fulfillment of yours. All my possessions I would give to you. I would kill whomever you asked me to kill. I will die, whenever you tell me to die. For a man such as me, this is love. This is all. And I *know* what it is when I've found it." Soren scowled at his mate because she, again, shocked him with her reaction. "Why are you crying?" he demanded.

Why was she crying? *Why* was she crying? Because the words he'd just said were so absolutely and damnably... perfect. Actually, they were sort of—excessively violent, but beautiful in their own way.

Kamdyn had known many warriors in her short life and not one of them would have dared to say such things to a woman. They tripped over their egos to find a compliment. They would compete with one another for the greatest prize of the most beautiful women's favor. For all she knew, they might even feel something close to what Soren had just described. But she'd never heard such a pure and honest confession. He'd given it without shame. Without fear of emasculation or rejection. He'd stated the truth as he saw it, as he accepted it, and now he stood looking at her with no expectation or condemnation for what she would... what she *must* do.

Kamdyn backed into the table and caught herself with both her hands. Her eyes squeezed shut as the memories of what had transpired on that very table the night before overwhelmed her and hot tears fell like an eternal stream down her cheeks.

Silk slid over her body, draping over one shoulder and knotting about her in a soft covering. Kamdyn knew what color it would be when she opened her eyes. The color of sapphires. Because it smelled like him.

"It is time, little Banshee," he breathed into her ear. His rough cheek rasped against hers and came away wet with her tears.

"Don't tell me when to kill you," she wailed. "I'll do it when I'm ready." She'd never be ready. Not ever. And yet, what could she do? She never should have let him touch her. She should have finished the job after he'd kissed her the night before, when he was flat on his back, already half-dead from her first jolt. But she couldn't then, either. She'd just looked down at his strong, angular face, at his hair that was too dark to be red and too red to be black, at the lonely frown on his hard mouth. And she'd willed him to live. Because some broken, lonely part of her yearned to fill one of the dark corners of his black heart, if only for a moment.

She hadn't expected to take all of it, to have him so freely give it to her. Now that she possessed it, she didn't want to give it back. She wanted to keep it, like the selfish little girl she'd always been. And that's what he thought of her, wasn't it? That she was a little girl, incapable of the depths of emotion he'd just described.

The rough pad of his thumb wiped at her cheek. "Remember I'm a bad man, who does terrible things." He softly gave her words back to her. "I've killed many, and would likely continue to do so if you didn't stop me."

Her eyes flew open and she pushed him away from her. "Don't try to make this easier!" she sobbed. "It only makes it more difficult!"

"It's the truth. Killing is all I know. It's all I'm good at." That clear blue gaze speared her, as did the reality of his words. "You may have opened my eyes to many things, but I still remain what I am."

"Which makes me wonder why you are not yet dead." The arctic voice stunned them both.

Kamdyn looked up in horror. She'd been found out, and her queen had come to punish them both.

Chapter Ten

"You're dressed like a Roman." Tah Liah dispassionately observed, taking in Kamdyn's blue silk wrap. Apparently Soren was better at dressing her than she was him.

Instantly dropping to a knee, Kamdyn prayed to the gods for mercy.

Soren remained standing and unabashedly nude. *He'd* likely never knelt to anyone.

"Forgive me, my queen, I take full responsibility for my actions. I was carried away by—" She paused. By what? Primal, all-consuming lust? Did one say such a thing to a royal?

"This is not unprecedented." Tah Liah's silver gaze snagged on Soren with faint appreciation, and Kamdyn felt equal amounts relief and possession. "As long as the relations were consensual on the part of the human, and you kill him when you are finished with him."

Kamdyn winced. She *wasn't* finished with him. Couldn't imagine ever wanting to be.

The queen addressed the Berserker. "She didn't force you, or misuse you in any way?"

His laughter was rich and rusty, as though stored in a dark place, unused for decades.

The look she shot him could have contained all the ice in the north. Though, after consideration, Kamdyn had to admit the idea was ludicrous.

"She *did* hold me down a good deal of the time," he chuckled.

"*Soren!*" Of all the times for him to develop a damned sense of humor.

"In truth, it is thus far the most pleasant assassination attempt I've ever experienced." He addressed the queen, but his eyes glimmered at Kamdyn. "I believe I will give you something, Banshee Queen." He strode to his trunk, unaffected by the stares of the two women following him. Reaching in, he pulled out a palm-sized chunk of black rock that glistened like volcanic glass. "I was told this is required of you by the terms of your pact."

Kamdyn gasped. The *Scáth bhfolach*, she'd almost completely forgotten about it.

Tah Liah regarded him with an air of skepticism, the flakes of frost in her aura danced a little faster. "You would give it to me freely?"

Soren held it out to her, and she took it. "The little Banshee asked it of me."

The queen turned to Kamdyn. "If I do not mistake what I sense, what I *see*, then this man loves you."

Kamdyn gulped around a lump of terrible emotion in her throat. "He said as much."

"Interesting." The queen took an extended moment to study Soren. "I can also see why you are reticent to slay him."

Soren cast her a look of smug amusement, standing proudly with his legs splayed.

Insolent man, Kamdyn thought fondly.

"I actually sought you out as a courtesy," Tah Liah continued. "The MacKay are in the midst of a terrible battle with the Sutherlands at *Druin na Coub*. Your family still lives, but the outcome of the battle is unsure."

Kamdyn's heart plummeted at this worst possible news. "Even with Laird MacKay's four thousand men?"

"The Sutherlands have commissioned the help of the Murrays and other mercenaries, I believe. Your Clan is outnumbered. There will be many MacKay widows."

"Nay," Kamdyn seized the hand of her queen. "May I go to them? I *must* help. I have to protect my sisters. They've already been through so much. And their children!"

"You may use your scream, but aside from that you may not kill humans." The queen was very firm on this point. Banshees were already under intense scrutiny of the Fae Council of queens due to the last sovereign's behavior.

"Allow me to march with you." Soren stepped forward, his fists clenching and his eyes flashing with anticipation. "I will bring my men."

Tah Liah seemed to consider. "It would have no bearing on the outcome of the pact. You are still marked for death."

"Consider the relic I gave you a gesture of good faith." Soren shrugged. "If I do not fall in battle, kill me once the Sutherlands are defeated."

Once the Sutherlands were defeated? So arrogant. Kamdyn's eyes burned. Despite herself, she loved his superior audacity. "You would fight for my Clan?"

He gave her a haughty, impatient look and then reached for his armor.

Dressed in the colors of earth and leather that set the russet undertones of his dark hair ablaze, he looked exactly like what he was. A ruthless, violent Berserker who'd fought and won battles that would have crushed a lesser man.

Plucking his gigantic axe from its perch, he swung it to a jaunty angle on his shoulder with one hand and held the other out to her. "Come on, little Banshee." He gave her a brilliant smile, the first she'd seen grace his grim mouth. Kamdyn came to understand that Soren's smile was the most terrifying thing about him. If the Devil, that Prince of Darkness, ever smiled, it would be exactly like the one the Laird of Shadows was giving her now. Full of teeth, eagerness, and the promise of blood. "Let us go and slaughter your enemies."

Chapter Eleven

"Absolutely not!" Rory thundered. "What in the name of the Gods possessed ye to bring these—these land pirates to Strathnaver!"

"Watch your tone with her, Highlander." Soren said in a low, quiet growl.

"I doona care if ye're the bloody Laird of Shadows, I'll still take yer head and mount it on my battlements."

"Not if your battlements belong to the Sutherlands." The Berserker's caustic, unperturbed smirk was doing little to help things.

"Um, actually…" Kamdyn stepped between the men and put a staying hand on Soren's chest piece. "They were already camped at the Naver Forest, not a half-day's march from here. It wasn't anything at all to bring them here to *help*."

The MacKay had been driven up against Ben Loyal and the Sutherlands were loath to break upon the mountain, so they stood at an impasse, hurling insults and arrows at each other, each Laird frantically strategizing. Soren had brought his men around the north side of the mountain, and they stood at the ready. The Berserker and his trusted general of sorts, a rangy Monroe named Murdock, had boldly marched across the line to meet with the Laird.

"Ye mean to say they were hiding on MacKay lands?" the Laird roared, then turned on Kamdyn and jabbed a finger at her. "I thought ye were supposed to kill this man. Katriona would have jolted him to the moon by now. We canna afford to make enemies of the MacLauchlan's, as well."

Soren grabbed the burly Laird by the neck and all the surrounding MacKay men drew their swords. Murdock did the same, falling back to shoulder with Soren. "She will keep her word, after I keep mine to defeat her enemies. But point that finger at her again, and you'll lose the hand before I go," the Berserker promised in a lethally quiet voice.

Daroch, who brandished his sword at the Berserker but watched the exchange with sharp and mighty interest, gave a few shocked curses in his ancient language. The tattoo crawling toward his left eye crinkled as he narrowed a discerning gaze leveled mostly at Kamdyn. "There's something between the two of ye."

Kamdyn could feel a guilty flush crawl up her neck. "Now's not really the time," she evaded. "Not when we have a battle to fight. Soren, put him down."

The Laird's feet touched the earth and everyone seemed to breathe again.

"My men will have no one to lead them when I am gone," Soren spoke to the Laird conversationally, as though he hadn't just threatened dismemberment. "The Banshee thought you might have need of them, so I give them to you with their word to be loyal."

"What need have I for blackguards and criminals?" Rory snarled.

Kamdyn seized the arm of her brother-in-law and pointed him toward the band of two hundred and fifty men wearing an air of restless bloodlust rather than Clan colors. "Look at them, Rory. They're *here*, prepared to fight for you, to swear fealty to you as their Laird if you'll have them." Her desperation on their behalf surprised even her. But defeat wasn't an option. Kamdyn was first and foremost a MacKay, and she'd do what she could to protect her Clan. If that meant by these unorthodox means, then so be it.

Rory rolled his sinewy shoulders and ran a hand through hair bronzed lighter by years in the sun. "Ye doona ken the position ye put me in, wee one," he said more gently. "These men, they willna be welcome in my Clan after the wrongs they've done. Not only because of me, but because of the people they've sinned against."

"I don't think that's true," Kamdyn argued. "If they fight next to MacKay today, I believe that will be a start. They'll bleed for you, Rory, some of them will die only for the *promise* of a Clan and a name. Imagine their loyalty once you've given them one."

The Laird MacKay was known and respected for his practicality and fair-mindedness and Daroch for his faultless logic. They looked out over the men assembled at the base of the mountain, backlit by a grey autumn sky. Some of their faces were hopeful. Young. Others older and more cynical. Their sins shone like defiance in their eyes and were carried as different weights on each shoulder. But they awaited their fates out of earshot, next to a force many times greater than them, their weapons down.

"They'd have to return what they've taken," Daroch said, ignoring the quelling look from Rory.

"Done," Soren agreed with a nod of finality.

The two MacKay men, who'd become as close as brothers over the years, held silent court with their eyes. Daroch threw his head toward the Sutherland horde. They were advancing again, splitting their forces around the mountain, making a move to flank and divide the MacKays.

"And make public amends for their crimes," Rory gritted out.

Murdock stepped forward. "All those who followed us here have already agreed to that per the Laird of Shadows's wee

Banshee's request." He dropped to his knee before the Laird. "We've given our word."

"We'll see if that means anything." Rory pinched the bridge of his nose. "Gods save me from battlefield promises."

"Only time can prove us true," Murdock said wisely.

With a short nod, Daroch turned to Kamdyn with a brow raised. "The Laird of Shadows's wee Banshee?"

"Let's kill some Sutherlands, shall we?" Kamdyn said with forced brightness. "The day's light is wasting." She marched toward the approaching army, towing a gigantic, ambling Berserker in her wake.

Chapter Twelve

Soren was glad Kamdyn did not fight. Though the magic in her hands was as deadly as his entire army, the pacts between Faerie and human could not be usurped, even by Clan loyalty. Besides, his little Banshee's hands were not made for killing. They were gentle. They were kind. Her scream, however, *that* could do plenty. Sutherlands melted before it, clutching their heads as though to keep the blood inside. And still, she'd killed no one. Not directly.

He would be her sword. *He* would be her wrath. He was the shadow of death awaiting the sentence from her soft lips, and once she gave it, his execution was swift and merciless.

The Sutherlands would remember their defeat at *Druin na Coub* for a thousand years at least. And though his name would morph over the centuries, it would be the Laird of Shadows who'd defeated them.

Splitting their forces had been the Sutherlands' gravest mistake, for they found an extra two hundred and fifty fresh and bloodthirsty warriors at the head of the MacKay army to the north. To the south, they fell beneath the Laird MacKay's smaller faction due to some ingenious explosive accelerant crafted by a brilliant Druid, paired with a Banshee's keen, and the axe of one Berserker who thoroughly enjoyed his blood-soaked vocation.

Soren's final gift to his mate was the safety of her Clan. The word would spread that the mighty Laird MacKay not only had four thousand men left, even after the battle was over, but a Berserker protecting them, as well.

When the last of the Sutherland forces fell or fled, Soren saw that Kamdyn's predictions proved wise. A number of his men hadn't survived the day, but those that did joined the post-battle frenzy with the air of brotherhood only shared by those who'd bled next to each other.

Soren was satisfied by this, surprised to discover the depth of his anxiety for the future of his men only after that future had been somewhat secured. The fates worked in strange ways, he supposed, and pointed his boots toward his own short-lived destiny.

His blood was high, pounding through his veins with all the feral intensity of his past Berserker rage, but with a new abject clarity.

He found his mate surveying the battlefield with the surprising satisfaction of a warrior. Her hair caught fire as the clouds gave way to afternoon sunlight.

"One last time," he murmured in her ear when he came up behind her.

Her response was instant and ecstatic.

They escaped to the Kyle with their preternatural speed. Their hurried and frigid bath was made too long by their inability to separate their ravenous mouths for more than a handful of moments.

Soren didn't lose his frenzied sense of heart-pounding, gut-wrenching, almost fear-inducing need until he had her splayed naked in the grass beneath him. He was very glad she was an immortal, for he'd be afraid to break her with the strength of his passion otherwise.

This time, it wasn't just her legs he wanted wrapped around him, but her arms, her lips, her very soul. Soren had given her everything. Would still give more. But he wanted something from her before she put him in the ground. He wanted to take a piece of her heart with him to the afterlife.

He couldn't bring himself to ask for it. He didn't know the words, in her language or in his. Instead, he busied his tongue in other ways that kept either of them from talking. He claimed her mouth, worshiped her breasts, and nipped a trail of alternating kisses and nibbles down to the womanly flesh he most craved.

Splaying his fingers on each of her slim thighs, he spread them wide, settling his shoulders between them. She was so delicate. So small and soft. As Soren dipped his head to kiss her intimately, he gloried in her gasps of delight. In the demanding little fingers she threaded in his hair. She tasted of salt and musk and insatiable desire. Her pliant flesh parted for his tongue, the bud of her pleasure nestled and waiting for him to pay it heed.

To be cruel, he danced around it. Using his lips and tongue to torture her to the zenith of yearning need, only to deny her when her body tensed in the anticipation of her release.

"Soren." His name became a demand. Her fingers gripping and pulling at his hair with insistent pressure. His smile curled against her glistening sex as he looked up over her mound, the quivering muscles of her belly, and through the narrow valley of her breasts. The look in her eyes would follow him into the eternities. The sweetness had vanished. The charming naiveté gave way to a new creature. This one as primitive and selfish as he.

He wanted to meet this creature. Wanted to mate with her, as well.

"Do not make me beg," she warned in a voice that was too husky with sex to be stern.

His chuckle vibrated against her, causing her to dig her heels into the soft ground as her entire body tensed and trembled. Before his mouth drove her to a long and loud final release, she'd not only begged for it, she'd pled, entreated, and beseeched.

Finally able to breathe, Kamdyn adjusted her exhausted legs as her Berserker beast crawled up her body with predatory grace. He left slick kisses on her belly, on her ribs, her breasts, and in the hollow of her throat.

In such a short time, he'd become her world. She was aware of the fragrant Scottish earth beneath her and the rare blue autumn sky above. In between existed only him, only them, pressed so close together that she'd thought they'd melded into one form of pleasure and flesh even before he sank inside her welcoming body.

Though a storm of frenzy raged within her, she was grateful that his movements within her were torturously slow. The same storm turned his eyes from the color of ice to the color of an angry sea as they locked onto hers. She felt every slick, heavy inch of his length as he pressed it in and retracted. His hips were the only part of them that moved, the rest clutched in an embrace that each feared to break.

When she could no longer stand the open, naked emotion in his eyes, Kamdyn buried her face in his neck and buried her fingers in the flesh of his back and shoulders. She undulated beneath him, not only opening her body to him, but her heart, her soul.

Neither of them said a word. They communicated in thrusts and moans and the short, curious noises exclusive to love-making. When she felt the web of nerves threading through her moist flesh begin to sizzle and pulse, she fought her release. She willed it to die, needing him for longer.

Forever.

But her traitorous body pulled taut and a ragged warning cry accompanied the first clenching, unparalleled sensation.

His large, strong hand clamped over her mouth before she realized that her screams of pleasure had become a Banshee keen. Her muscles locked as the storm broke upon her in wave after wave of dizzying, crippling ecstasy.

He followed her into that place, his movements becoming shorter, stronger. The pulses wracking the whole length of him until he curled over her, uncovering her mouth to replace his hand with his lips.

She tasted herself on him but didn't care. His kiss was the sweetest, most lovely thing she could readily imagine. Even after the storm passed, they stayed like that for an eternal moment. Their hands caressed and explored the other's face as though to commit it to memory, only punctuated by languorous kisses.

Eventually, Soren rolled to his back and pulled her to rest against his chest. His other arm bent behind to support his neck. He yawned like a big cat and blinked down at her upturned face.

"You're still not...afraid?" she asked once more, placing her hand on his chest.

"Of course not, little Banshee," he said, pulling her closer. "I already told you that." And proved his point by promptly falling asleep.

Kamdyn lie in the warmth of his arms for a long time, her hand pressed to where she could feel the strong, sure beat of his heart beneath her palm. Any moment, a quick and lethal bolt could leave her skin and enter his, stopping that heart forever. Gasping, Kamdyn pulled her hand back as though his flesh had burned her. His muscles twitched, but he remained relaxed, his eyes closed and breaths even. It was her fault he was so exhausted. She'd kept him awake most of the night. He'd Berserked at least three times in the past day, once to fight and win an entire Clan battle. Despite his unparalleled strength, he was still for all intents and purposes a human.

Kamdyn smiled a little. He was so unapologetically *alive*. How could he not fear death? She was terrified of it. Not her own, of course, but of his.

He couldn't leave her. Not now. Not when she'd begun to— to what? Love him? Logic still insisted that such a thing was impossible in so short a time. But he'd professed the emotion for her in such a way that made complete and unfathomable sense. She had a feeling that lifetimes wouldn't contain the experiences she wanted to share with him. Even though he was a marauding criminal, at his core he was an incredibly decent man. If only she could be given the time to nurture that part of him. But their time had run out, and if she didn't kill him now, the consequences would be intense and far-reaching, and not just for her. For her family and Clan.

"I can't," she whispered, curling her deadly hands into fists. "I *have* fallen for you, and now I'm at a loss for what to do. If it's not me, it'll be some other Banshee she sends... But I can't bring myself to—" Gods, she couldn't even bring herself to say the words anymore. She just knew she couldn't kill him.

"Even though you're a massive, arrogant, and violent brute. You're *my* massive, arrogant, and violent brute and I plan to keep you. Even after everything you've done. I accept it. I accept you, all of you, for all that you are. And I'm going to do what I can to get you out of this so you can right your wrongs. So you can make it better, and leave a legacy that is separate from the Laird of Shadows." Her fist clutched tighter. "I swear it."

Chapter Thirteen

Soren had wanted her heart, and she'd given it to him while he fought through the fog of sleep, and then she'd promptly disappeared. It was enough. She'd accepted him, without being told what it meant. Without fanfare or ceremony, she'd accepted him and it was all he had needed for the Berserker mating to be complete.

He wanted to do all the things that would make him great in her eyes. He wanted to build a legacy she would respect.

Now he was doing the only thing he could to prove to her that he'd changed. He could die without her. Soren didn't struggle as Finn MacLauchlan and his brother Connor led him into their courtyard in chains. This was the one final thing he could give to Kamdyn. She didn't have the heart to slay any man, let alone the one she loved. But Soren comprehended the dangerous consequences for her if the terms of the pact were not kept. So he did the one thing he could think of that would release her from all danger and distasteful responsibilities.

"I'm trying to decide if it was courage or recklessness that drove ye to show yer face at Castle Lachlan," Laird Connor growled. "This is where we keep our mates, where we raise our wee ones."

Soren didn't correct the Laird. It was neither courage nor recklessness.

It was love.

He smiled to himself, admiring the sturdy castle with its lovely fountain and strong battlements. "It was pride," he told them. "So best take my head and be done with it, then."

Standing side by side as they were, Finn and Connor resembled a golden-hued angel and a dark satyr, but they intently studied Soren with identical green eyes.

"We heard about the battle at *Druin na Coub*," Finn said. "What we can't figure out is why you would fight for Clan MacKay against the Sutherlands when one of their own is contracted to slay you."

Soren knew that news traveled with startling speed in the Highlands. Though he hadn't expected it to travel faster than a Berserker. He'd just left *Druin na Coub*. "You sent a tiny girl to kill me because you couldn't find me." He shrugged, doing his best to keep his features blank and unaffected. "So here I stand, ready to give you a chance to regain your honor as men by doing the deed yourselves."

Connor had a pole axe in his hand poised beneath Soren's chin in the space of a breath, his eyes swirling black with barely leashed anger. Oh, to be a fully accepted, mated Berserker. The powers were, indeed, mighty and impressive. Soren only regretted he wouldn't get the chance to fully explore them. His beast called for him to fight, and he nearly trembled with the control it took to allow the Laird's contempt to go unanswered.

Finn put a staying hand on his half-brother's arm, scrutinizing Soren through narrowed eyes.

"Ye are the only one here without honor," the Laird snarled, then glanced at Finn. "He lies. I can sense it. I say we put him down."

Finn shook his head, a curious frown drawing his flaxen brows together. "We sent the Banshee after him some time ago, and it's still unclear *why* he's alive."

"What does it matter?" Connor asked.

"The *why* of it is simple," Soren explained. "I didn't want it to be known I was defeated by a tiny woman. Not an appropriate legacy for the Laird of Shadows."

Finn leaned forward, his eyes boring into Soren's with leashed meaning. "We *both* know it isn't that simple."

Soren bared his teeth. He was finished with this conversation. Every moment alive without his mate was like an eternity of torture. Every beat of his heart created new anxiety about her survival if she broke the terms of the pact. He had to goad them into finishing him. His death was the only way to ensure her safety.

"The years have made you soft, Finn the Bastard." Soren arranged his features into the most mocking, condescending expression he could. He remembered the ferocity of Finn's defiant eyes back at the temple, more than two decades ago. His lack of bloodline had made him a pariah among his own kind. He'd been fed with the dogs. Beaten regularly by the temple Elders. Shunned and mistreated by his own kind. He'd become one of the strongest, most fearsome Berserkers in their history. And they'd still sent him to kill his own Celtic half-brothers, or die.

Soren was younger than Finn. But he remembered the Gael's disgrace, and wasn't above using it to goad him to violence. "'Tis no matter. I imagine even you Highlanders can find the strength between the two of you to kill a man with his hands chained behind him who refuses to defend himself."

Finn's eyes flared with a shadow of his former rage, but he made no move against him.

"I could still kill ye if *ye* were armed and *my* hands were bound behind me, boy," Connor threatened. "Or don't ye remember the battle we fought all those years ago? The slaughter we wrought upon countless other Berserkers? Our only mistake was letting ye survive."

Soren lunged toward the pole axe, and was astounded when Connor pulled it safely away from his flesh. "Here's your chance to correct that mistake," he urged. "End me here and keep your precious Highlands safe from me."

Finn shook his head, folding stubborn, massive arms over MacLauchlan colors. "First, I want to know *why* you showed up here, asking for death but not a fight. You are not the Soren Neilson I remember."

"You look good in a Highland tartan," Soren sneered again at the handsome, golden-haired Berserker who shared his native tongue and half his heritage. "You're lucky your brothers let you wear their colors even though your mother was just one of their father's discarded whores."

The moment Finn's temper overwhelmed his curiosity and his eyes swirled with onyx and wrath, a very small figure dashed from the doorway.

"Soren!" To his complete and unfailing shock, Kamdyn stood in front of him, her curly head barely reaching his chest and her arms flung wide in a protective stance. Soren would have laughed at the preposterousness of it all had he not been so astounded to see her there. "How could you *say* something so hateful?" She glared over her slim shoulder at him with unreserved censure.

"What are you *doing* here?" he demanded. He'd thought to protect her from his death, not have his executioners step around her wee body to cleave him in half. Blood would stain her new pretty Fae robes.

Again.

"He's *very* sorry he said that," she addressed the two irate Berserkers, all the while standing in front of him.

"I am *not* sorry," he argued.

Her heel stomped down on his foot with such force he suppressed a wince.

A third dark-haired MacLauchlan brother appeared in the doorway and they blinked from her to him in unison, their shock only somewhat less apparent than his own.

"Ye were just telling us, wee Banshee, that he'd reformed his ways and deserved for the pact to be rescinded." The newcomer, Roderick, lifted an unconvinced eyebrow.

"Aye..." Kamdyn cast another scathing look over her shoulder, but kept a solicitous smile fixed on her mouth for the sake of the scowling brothers. "Um... you see..."

"I *see* that he's the devious, criminal despot his reputation charges him to be, and he deserves to die screaming," Connor's gaze lit with a blood-thirsty gleam.

It all made sense to Soren now. His little Banshee had come to plead his case to the men who'd ordered his death. Finn's reluctance to end his life stemmed from the fact his very own assassin hadn't wanted to kill him. If such a sweet and decent lady could find forgiveness for his sins, perhaps he deserved to be heard. She'd been trying to save his life. And he'd gone and cocked it up by trying to save her.

"But he was all *alone*." Kamdyn had found her voice and employed it still on his behalf. "He organized others who were alone and abandoned, because it was what he knew how to do. My lords, I know they were misguided, but given a chance—"

"Misguided?" Connor said slowly, as though he couldn't believe the word. "Is that what I tell the children who are cold because of the villages he burned? Or the Highland widows of those who dared stand against his marauders? Do pardon that ye have to waste the time to rebuild ye're homes, ye're lives, but forgive this Berserker, he was alone and *misguided*."

"I understand, Laird." Though he couldn't see her face, Soren could hear the tears and desperation building in Kamdyn's voice. "I also thought thus when I was dispatched to take his life. But I feel that he can find a place among us. Reparations will be made on his behalf and... he's given back all the property he took and pledged his men in defense of the Highlands. They've already saved more innocent lives than they've taken and they promise to evermore."

"It's not enough." Finn's eyes were hard now, unforgiving.

Mouth twisting in an ironic smile, Soren nudged her. Just when he'd thought he couldn't love her any more than he already did. He should have expected she would attempt the impossible. "They're right, my little Banshee," he murmured. "How could I find forgiveness if someone had so wronged you? There would be none. So have I done to their people and they are right to claim their justice."

"Bloody Christ on the cross." A horrified, awe-stricken look seized the features of the MacLauchlan laird. "Ye've *mated* with yer Banshee assassin."

Kamdyn's body tensed and she could feel heat crawling up her neck. "I don't see how what we did last night has anything to do with this discussion."

"Have ye accepted him, lass?" Connor asked, eyeing her like her answer may mean the difference between life and death.

"Of course I did—I *do*." She took a protective step back toward Soren and bumped up against his unerringly solid chest. "Else why would I be here, trying to save his life?"

Two of the three Berserkers seemed to be wracked with indecision. Roderick and Finn both wore inscrutable expressions, but Kamdyn could read the turmoil in their emotional signatures. Their Laird remained provoked and angry. She could feel the love of his people mixing with the pressure to protect and avenge them. He was a good man with a bad temper, and that combination might prove to be the death of hope for her.

"Mated? That certainly changes things, doesn't it?" A husky, feminine brogue preceded a lovely ebony-haired woman into the courtyard. She wore the circlet of a chieftain's woman though she looked rather young to be mated to a Berserker who'd nearly met the century mark.

"Lindsay, I told ye to remain inside until this was dealt with," Connor barked at the woman.

Lindsay waved an elegant, dismissive hand at her surly husband and regarded Soren and Kamdyn with keen amethyst eyes. "Since when have I ever done what you tell me to?"

"Woman, this wee lass could decimate our entire household with her little finger if she had a mind, and I doona like that fact combined with yer sharp tongue." Connor's words were delivered with more concern than severity, and his wife's smile only widened.

"Oh! No. No. No. I would *never*!" Kamdyn put out a hand and belatedly realized that might not have been the best gesture, but the lady didn't so much as flinch.

Lindsay also strategically placed herself in between the MacLauchlan Berserkers and Soren and Kamdyn, smoothing the front of her fine dress and smiling as though receiving important guests.

"Didna our wedding vows have something to say about honoring and obeying yer Laird and husband?" Connor grumbled, grasping her shoulder and pulling her out of the middle of the courtyard.

"I do honor you, my love." She cupped his cheek and wriggled out of his grip. "But we both know I lied about the second part." Turning back to Soren she said, "I believe Finn brought up an excellent question. Why would this powerful, mated Berserker give himself over to you when he'd already cheated death by winning the heart of his Banshee?"

Why, indeed? Kamdyn turned to Soren, who'd remained his usual quiet, unperturbed self. He was looking down at her with the oddest expression, a mix of maybe exasperation and sheer, encompassing devotion.

"She is bound by a contract," Soren stated simply. "The contract calls for my death and if the terms are not met, she will be severely punished. When my mate could not bring herself to kill me..." he paused and let his shrug explain the rest.

An overwhelming rush of emotion drove Kamdyn's arms around him, despite their audience. "I realized what you meant this morning. Not because I felt hatred, but because I felt fear. I realized my greatest fear, which was living an eternity without you." All this was said against his chest, as she couldn't bring herself to let him go. "I love you, too. I'm sorry I didn't tell you before."

He flexed and broke the chains that held him, not surprising the gathered Berserkers now that they'd learned of his mated status, which came with an exponential growth in strength. His arms gathered Kamdyn impossibly closer.

"You didn't have to say it, I would have known when I saw you here," he said against her hair in a husky voice.

"*You* didn't have to sacrifice yourself for me." She pulled back and looked up into blue eyes that were more solemn than she'd ever seen them.

"Yes, I did."

Lindsay's teary voice permeated the tender moment. "You simply *can't* kill him now. There *has* to be another way. You've all sold your swords for battle, all of you have killed many who would be considered innocent."

"War is one thing, Lindsay," Connor said gruffly. "What he's done... it's unforgiveable."

Kamdyn released her mate and turned toward the emotions she could feel the strongest. "Master Finn, I sense a change in you." She put all her hope into her eyes, and the fair-haired MacLauchlan cast his gaze away from her, studying the stones of the courtyard arch with a clenched jaw.

"What say ye, brother?" Roderick asked from the doorway.

Finn hesitated, then locked eyes with Soren. "It is true that in the north, where we come from, possession and death are regarded much differently than here." He turned to his brothers. "Life *is* war. Anything you wish to possess, you must take from those who are weaker than you. You must kill to defend it. It is how we were raised."

Connor squeezed at his temples and heaved a deep breath before looking at Finn. "What is it that ye're saying, exactly?" he asked wearily.

"I am saying that my mate and the baby I found abandoned in the snow each had to teach me what the word *innocent* meant. I was sent here to assassinate the two of you, my own brothers, and I would have likewise killed any who stood in my way... Man. Woman." He looked back at the stones. "Or child."

Kamdyn's eyes widened as she could feel the shift of emotion occur in each of the darker MacLauchlan brothers. Astonishment. Uncertainty. Perhaps, understanding? She dared not hope.

"I am saying, that perhaps in similar circumstances, I could easily have become the Laird of Shadows."

Kamdyn gasped. "I don't understand. It is you who first called upon my queen for the contract. You were the most adamant that Soren should die."

Her mate growled from behind her and she elbowed him sharply.

Finn's eyes fixed above her head once again, holding some kind of silent court with his fellow Northman. "Perhaps, I was somehow trying to put that part of *me* to death, as well... because it still haunts me at times," he admitted.

Kamdyn looked up and noted that the two Norse Berserkers did have something in common besides their immense, rough-hewn bodies and stunning gem-colored eyes. The more inscrutable, expressionless features they adopted, the more intense the emotions they experienced. It was as though they were incapable of emoting complexity or uncertainty, so they simply hid it until it was all sorted out.

Fascinating.

"Is there not room for forgiveness?" Lindsay stroked her husband's cheek and his eyes gentled when they touched upon her. "It's obvious they love each other, and his self-sacrifice has to count for something. Say he promises not to pillage and such, could he not be given some sort of atonement rather than death?"

Connor eyed Soren with absolute skepticism. "Let me discuss it with my brothers."

"Of course," Lindsay agreed. "Discuss it amongst yourselves and when you've all decided that I'm right, we'll let these lovers have a second chance at life together. Won't we?"

Kamdyn nudged her mate, hoping he'd say something to buoy their faith.

Soren grunted then took a deep breath. "I—promise not to pillage."

Kamdyn elbowed him a second time.

"And such," he amended.

The Laird looked at his wife, then Roderick, and finally Finn, who held his gaze the longest. After a breathless moment, he turned and addressed Kamdyn rather than the other Berkserker.

"He and his men would have to rebuild what they destroyed. Stronger and better than it was before." He rubbed a hand over his shorn scalp and finally looked up at Soren. "We Berserkers are protectors of the Highlands. I'd like ye to take a pact that would replace the one against yer life, that anytime ye're called upon to fight for the Highland people, ye'll answer that call, no matter the circumstances."

Soren nodded without taking any time to think about it. "I would do this. My mate's people would become my people and

I would lay down my life for them." He and Finn exchanged meaningful nods.

"You would become a MacKay?" Kamdyn breathed.

Soren tucked a curl behind her ear. "I would link your name to mine," he conceded.

"But what about your queen?" Finn asked. "Where would you live?"

Kamdyn offered him her most brilliant smile. "I went to her before I came here," she admitted. "She told me that if I could convince you to rescind the pact and allow us our future together, we could reside with my Clan as an emissary of the Fae. You see, my brother Daroch found a way to poison Faeries, and they've been reticent to much bother with humans since then. So they've been in need of someone willing to conduct their affairs here. Also, apparently, I'm a pretty good hand-maiden, but I'm a terrible Banshee."

The Berserkers seemed to find that plenty amusing.

"Come, my love, let's go share the good news with my sisters." Kamdyn pulled him toward the gates, then paused to bow to the MacLauchlans. "Thank you, my lords, for this chance."

"We'll be in contact," Finn promised.

Soren followed her with an odd sort of dazed smile on his lips. "I don't think your sisters' husbands will find this news to their liking.

"Nonsense." Kamdyn eagerly towed him toward the castle gate. She lied, of course, they would hate it at first. "They'll have their own Berserker brother-in-law. Soren Neilson-MacKay." She loved the name instantly.

"MacKay-Neilson," Soren corrected.

Kamdyn patted his arm. "We'll discuss it later." She knew exactly when he was most agreeable.

Soren grabbed her and claimed her mouth, pouring all the honesty and hope for their future into his kiss.

Kamdyn clung to him and returned his kiss with all the love she'd discovered, feeling a giddy sense of liberation.

He broke the contact too early, his eyes twinkling down at her with that all-too-familiar arrogance. "I'll take a mighty long time to be influenced, but I know how persuasive your lips can be."

The MacLauchlan's hearty laughter tangled with the Highland winds and followed them home over the moors.

About the Author

Kerrigan Byrne's stories span the spectrum of romantic fiction from historical, to paranormal, to romantic suspense. She can always promise her reader one thing: memorable and sexy Celtic heroes who are guaranteed to heat your blood before they steal your heart.

Kerrigan lives at the base of the Rocky Mountains with her husband and his three lovely daughters. She's worked in Law Enforcement for the better part of a decade.

*Kerrigan donates a percentage of all book sales to www.womenforwomen.org to help the innocent survivors of global war and oppression.

To find other books by Kerrigan, visit her website at: www.kerriganbyrne.com